Also by Julia Brannan

HISTORICAL FICTION

The Jacobite Chronicles:

Book One: Mask of Duplicity

Book Two: The Mask Revealed

Book Three: The Gathering Storm

Book Four: The Storm Breaks

Book Five: Pursuit of Princes (Summer 2017)

CONTEMPORARY FICTION

The Bigger Picture (Autumn 2017)

a SEVENTY-FIVE percent SOLUTION

Julia Brannan

DISCLAIMER

Formatting by Polgarus Studio

Cover Design by najlaqamberdesigns.com

ACKNOWLEDGEMENTS

First of all, I'd like, as ever, to thank Jason Gardiner and Alyson Cairns, my soulmates and best friends, who put up with my incessant chatter on the days that I see them, but who understand my deep need for solitude and the freedom to travel when the wanderlust takes me. And who still love me, in spite of all! You are wonderful, and I'm grateful for every moment I have with you.

I also have to thank Mary Brady, who reads every chapter I write, as I write it, gives me an honest opinion as to what she thinks of it, and makes very useful suggestions for revisions. She has encouraged me in my endeavours to be a writer from day one, and I am more appreciative of her friendship and help than she'll ever know.

To Mandy Condon and Kym Grosso, who have both encouraged me in their own ways, and who have given me helpful and practical advice, as well as allowing me to vent at times!

Thanks to Jason and Marina at Polgarus Studio, for the excellent and speedy formatting, and to Najla Qamber for the wonderful book covers she produces from my vague ideas.

And lastly to all my wonderful readers, who keep me going when I'm tired and uninspired and would rather do anything (even ironing!) than write. I hope you enjoy my first contemporary book as much as you've enjoyed my historical ones. Please be gentle with me!

September 2008

After it was all over, Joanne politely declined the police's offer to run her home, although she did take their advice about leaving from the back door to avoid the reporters lying in wait at the front of the building. Kate had supported Joanne steadfastly and unwaveringly throughout the past twenty years of hell; it seemed fitting somehow that she alone should accompany Joanne on the first faltering steps of her new life.

After the initial expressions of relief, Kate took her cue from Joanne, and they drove home in the companionable silence that only intimates can enjoy. Joanne looked out of the window, barely registering the vista of grey streets and redbrick buildings as they flashed by. She desperately needed some time alone to reflect, to make sense of what had happened, and her sister, sensing that, did not protest when Joanne asked her to drop her off at the park some two miles from her house, only telling her to phone if she wanted company later.

It was a crisp sunny autumn afternoon, and Joanne walked along the paths for a time, kicking idly at the leaves which crunched under her feet. She knew she should feel happy; but instead melancholy overwhelmed her, and the green of the newly mowed grass blurred as she fought back the tears that threatened, angry with herself for giving in, showing weakness. She had spent much of her life crying pointless tears, allowing others to control her when she should have been taking charge of her life instead. Now, finally, she had, and had faced the consequences and survived. She would not cry again. She blew her nose and swallowed determinedly, and her vision cleared.

As a child she had loved the autumn, she remembered; had delighted in gathering the leaves into piles then diving headlong into them, emerging giggling, with gold and copper leaves entwined in her hair. As soon as her sister had learned to walk, Joanne had taught her to kick her way through the crunchy leaves on the family's rare outings to the park, holding tightly to Kate's hand so she wouldn't fall as she wobbled along on unsteady legs. Joanne had gathered armfuls of leaves and poured them over her tiny sister, who had crowed with delight as she was showered in a deluge of bronze, copper and gold. Memories like that were precious, Joanne realised, smiling to herself; precious because they were happy, and she had only too few of them for over forty years of life. Where had she gone wrong? She sat down on a bench, pulled her coat tighter around her, and let her mind drift back.

She couldn't remember her first mistake, which was in being conceived. Whilst she had been growing in her mother's womb, her unwilling teenage parents had argued and fought, and finally, giving in to parental pressure, had married, and Joanne had emerged into the world to be greeted by a resentful father and mother who blamed her for their misfortune. It hadn't helped that she had not inherited her mother's delicate elfin features. Although she had taken after her mother in her slight build, her hair and eyes were brown like her father's, and from the first time she had become aware of her appearance she had known that she was ugly, because she did not have green eyes and blonde hair. Later she had found out that she was stupid too, in spite of her teachers' praise for her academic achievements.

She knew that she was stupid and ugly because her father told her she was, and her mother never disagreed with him. Her father ruled the household and her mother did as she was told. Men dictated and women obeyed; that was a fact of life, and as a child Joanne had never questioned it. She had gone to a Roman Catholic school, not because her family was religious, but because it was just at the end of the street they lived on, which meant her mother didn't have to go to the trouble of taking her in the morning and collecting her at the end of the day. All the other children were accompanied to school, but Joanne had assumed that was because they lived a long way away and had to cross busy roads to get there. Besides, her mother was too busy. What she was busy doing Joanne had no idea; she didn't have a job like her father did. But she said she was, so it must have been true.

When she had learned of the existence of God from her teachers, Joanne had prayed to Him fervently every night to turn her into a boy, believing that in spite of her other failings, her greatest sin was in her gender. Her father often reproached her mother for not even managing to give him a son. Every morning Joanne would wake up to be disappointed that God hadn't answered her prayer.

Eventually she gave up, realising that God must also, like her mother, be too busy to bother about her. She had wondered if there was any other way to turn herself into a boy. Maybe the doctor could give her some tablets or something. She remembered tentatively asking her teacher, who had laughed and ruffled her hair, and said there was nothing wrong with being a girl. But there was. Joanne had been convinced that if she could only become a male, her father at least would then love her.

Until Kate was born. Joanne was six when her sister came along, and the moment she had seen the screwed-up face and tiny waving arms of her sibling, Joanne was entranced. She had loved her baby sister from day one with a ferocious intensity. It was a shame that Kate was not the longed-for boy; but at least now there would be someone else for Joanne to share the hurt of her parents' disappointment with.

Except that her parents had not been disappointed that Kate was a girl. Instead they had doted on her, although she was a demanding, fractious infant who didn't sleep through the night until she was nearly a year old. By the time she was two, it was clear that she had inherited her mother's best features; Kate's hair was beautiful, a thick wheat-gold mane, which combined with her large green eyes, drew gasps of admiration and praise from everyone. Kate had accepted her parents' indulgent adoration as her due, while Joanne looked on in puzzlement.

Slowly she had come to realise that her father's dislike and her mother's indifference toward her had nothing to do with her gender, or her looks; they disliked her because she was Joanne. There was something intrinsically unlovable about her as an individual, something so overwhelming that no amount of excellent school reports and helping with housework could overcome it. Having no idea what this terrible flaw was, she had done the only thing she could, which was to avoid, as far as possible, drawing her father's attention to her. She had concentrated on her studies and withdrawn into herself, both at home and school, mistrusting the friendly overtures of her classmates, sure that when they got to know her better they would also see this terrible flaw, and would then hate her. It was better to be ignored than hated, Joanne had decided.

As a result she had had no enemies, but neither had she had any real friends. Her peers neither hated nor liked her; they didn't understand her. Some of them thought her a snob; others thought her shy. Mainly they ignored her.

Only with her sister did Joanne let her defences down. It was impossible not to; Kate was completely and utterly loveable. Everyone said so. Beside the happy, light-hearted blonde angel, Joanne seemed serious, sullen, even. But she was always there for her sister; she dried Kate's tears when she lost her favourite doll, and understood why the identical replacement her father bought for her just wasn't the same; she listened to her babyish confidences with a seriousness which adults never achieved; and never betrayed her trust, even when Kate sheepishly admitted to doing things that Joanne had been blamed for. Joanne was loyal to her sister, and as Kate grew older, she had repaid that loyalty in kind.

Secure in the love of her parents, Kate had breezed her way through school, confident and charming. Her circle of admirers was enormous. The teachers loved her in spite of her chattiness and mediocre academic results. The children adored her because she was funny and daring, and always came up with the best games. She was also easily bored, and carelessly flitted from one group to the next, refusing to have a single 'best friend', preferring freedom to intimacy.

The two sisters were as different as chalk and cheese, both in looks and personality, people remarked when they saw them together. Yet they were devoted to each other, sharing a common bond that no one else knew about. It was to Joanne's bed that a trembling Kate crept for comfort in the middle of the night when their parents were fighting downstairs. Kate knew that Joanne's reserve disguised a desperate craving to be loved, just as Joanne knew Kate's gregariousness masked a fear of intimacy which in her experience brought arguments and discord.

Both of them had learnt about relationships between men and women from their parents, and had responded in their own ways. Kate had decided she would never fall in love; Joanne had decided no one would ever fall in love with her.

Joanne pulled herself back to the present, stretched her arms and looked around. The park was almost deserted, which suited her solitary mood; she had been surrounded by people for weeks, it seemed, and in the rare moments when she had been alone, her predicament had understandably absorbed all her attention. Now it was over at last, she could afford to indulge in thoughts of the past.

She knew now, forty years too late, that she could not have done anything to win her parents' love. They had not hated her because she was ugly, stupid, or female. It had been easier to blame her for the mistake that had led to their disastrous marriage, than to face up to the fact that it was their own fault. They had taken their frustrations out on her and on each other, instead of admitting their mistake and separating. Her mother Angela had been too weak to make the break. It had been simpler to give in to her husband's bullying in exchange for a roof over her head. She had never taken responsibility for anything; even now, ten years after Jim's death, Angela still didn't know how to pay a bill on time. In despair, Kate had finally set up all the direct debits on her mother's behalf, but Angela still bombarded her youngest daughter with complaints and problems. Kate threatened on a regular basis to change her phone number and go ex-directory, and Joanne had wondered whether Angela would turn to her if Kate ever carried out her threat.

Maybe she would have done in the past, Joanne thought, but not now, after all that had happened. Most people would probably keep their distance, apart from the ghouls, and she wanted nothing to do with them. It didn't bother Joanne to be lonely; she had had plenty of practice. She had been lonely, really, for most of her life. Apart from Kate, of course. Kate would always be there. Joanne knew how lucky she was to have such a wonderful sister.

And, possibly, there was another person who cared. He hadn't been there today, which had surprised her a little. She would phone him tonight, maybe, when she got home. And who knew, perhaps when everything had died down… but no. It was too soon to think about that. Better to concentrate on picking up the threads and trying to achieve some semblance of normality. Even so, Joanne couldn't help the tingle of anticipation she felt at the thought of having someone who would really care for her.

It was good to actually feel emotions again, to have hope for the future. For so many years, she realised now, she had felt nothing but a dull misery, a leaden numbness that had sapped her will to live. She had seen no way out except for suicide, and had spent many hours over the years contemplating the various ways of ending her life. But in the end she had lacked the courage to go through with it.

No, that wasn't true, Joanne thought, chastising herself. Courage she did have; she'd proved that at various times throughout her life, and especially in the last months. It was the *energy* to kill herself that she'd lacked for so long, and when her circumstances had changed so dramatically just over three years ago, the energy she'd gained had opened her eyes to both the beauties and the horrors of the world, and she'd realised that she didn't want to die; she just couldn't continue the life she'd been enduring for so many years.

How could she have been so blind, for so long?

Any guilt she felt now was not over the things she had done, but over all the things she had *not* done. So much damage that could have been avoided, if only…

Joanne shook her head abruptly, as though by doing so she could shake off the past. She would have to put it behind her, and turn her mind to the future.

She leaned back on the bench and closed her eyes. The sun was surprisingly warm for the time of year. This time last week she had thought she would never be free to sit like this again, alone in a park, enjoying the warmth of the sun on her face and listening to the distant excited laughter and shouts of children playing on the swings.

In spite of her resolution to only look forward from now on, she found her mind slipping back again, remembering her first meeting with the only person who had ever succeeded in smashing all her carefully erected defences to pieces, and who, in doing so, had changed her life forever.

CHAPTER ONE

April 1980

The small group of fifth-form girls huddled together in the corner of the playground to gossip. They had commandeered this choice spot, sheltered from the wind by the mobile classroom erected at the edge of the playing field, and gathered each playtime to discuss the events of the day, which, at their age, mainly revolved around makeup, fashion, and, most importantly, boys. It was generally agreed by the group, which was the cream of the year in looks if not in intellect, that this year's crop of sixth-formers were not worth even thinking about. Even so, they generally spent a good deal of their time discussing this worthless bunch of males, even if it was only to declare in voices louder than was strictly necessary that the thought of letting spotty Brian or fat Mike even *touch* them was just too awful to contemplate.

Today however, the girls were discussing a far more interesting male, namely the one who'd been contracted to repaint the school two weeks ago. It was a shame that he was so old, they all agreed; he must be at least twenty-five, but even so, he was to die for.

"He looks like a film star," Sheila Bradley commented, dreamily observing him as he painted the window frames. Although she was prone to exaggeration, in this case she was speaking no less than the truth. Tall and muscular, with golden-blond hair and blue eyes, he had the classic good looks so prized by Hollywood.

Personally Joanne thought he was a bit too aware of himself, but she didn't share this opinion with her companions. She knew that her admittance to the group was based not on her looks, but on the fact that she was always willing to help the others with their homework, and on occasion even to actually do it for them. Her membership was tenuous, and she was not about to jeopardise it by contradicting anyone. Particularly Sheila, who could be a real bitch at times.

"It's a hot day," Christine Jones observed hopefully. "With a bit of luck he might take his T-shirt off."

"No, he won't," Hazel Theaker replied. "Mrs Johnson told him he had to be decently clothed at all times while on school premises. I heard her telling him yesterday when I was coming back from hockey practice."

"Miserable old cow," Sheila said venomously. "I bet she's just jealous because he isn't interested in her, dried-up old witch."

He was painting the classrooms in the evenings, to the girls' disappointment, but the corridors and exterior of the building were being done in school hours, and he had driven nearly two hundred pubescent girls wild since his arrival. His presence had led to many a detention when various pupils, absorbed in watching his tanned athletic half-naked body through the window as he painted the outside walls, had failed to answer, or even to hear the teacher's question. Even the way he stroked the paintbrush up and down the walls seemed erotic, and he'd had a friendly smile and a word for all the girls. Or at least for all the pretty girls, Joanne noticed. Not that many of them actually had the courage to talk to him. He seemed like a god somehow, a part of the glamorous adult world to which they were not yet allowed admittance.

Even so, they had found out some basic information about him. His name was Steve Harris, he had his own business, lived out in Hale in Cheshire and, most importantly, he was single.

"He must be loaded if he lives in Hale," Christine said.

The object of their attention finished the frame, turned, and seeing them all gazing at him, waved and smiled. As one the girls all turned away, red-faced.

"Oh God," murmured Cheryl, as though he could hear them from across the playground, "now he'll think we all fancy him."

"Well, you do," Joanne pointed out logically.

"I know, but we don't want *him* to know that," Sheila said, exasperated.

He knows anyway, Joanne thought. They were all making it obvious enough. They took every opportunity to walk past him, giggling self-consciously and tossing their hair, and at least half of them had been told off by the head for wearing mascara and lipstick to school. He must find them pathetic, a man of his age. He was just being kind, talking to them. No doubt he already had a girlfriend, a sophisticated and beautiful woman of the world with a great career and a rich family.

Joanne tried her best to behave normally, not that he'd even notice her, with the long-legged Christine and large-breasted Hazel around, but she didn't want him to think she fancied him and feel sorry for her. When he was painting the ground floor corridor she made sure to go to the toilets on the first floor, and when he was working at the front gate she took to entering the school from the side entrance. He was so handsome, it was hard *not* to look at him; it was easier to avoid him, whenever possible.

However, she hadn't been able to avoid him when she'd gone into the school library one day to find one corner covered with dust sheets and Steve busily preparing the paintwork. He straightened up as she came in and bestowed his most charming smile on her.

"Hello," he said cheerily.

"Hello," she muttered back, blushing. She couldn't just turn and walk out now; that would look silly. He was obviously busy; if she appeared occupied too, he wouldn't feel obliged to speak to her. She went to the shelves and started looking for the book she'd come in for.

"I can pull the sheets back off these shelves, if you want," Steve offered.

"No, it's all right," she managed.

"So what's your name, then?" he asked. Joanne looked up, amazed. Why was he talking to her? He never spoke to the ugly girls. He must be feeling awkward because she was the only other person in the room. He didn't appear awkward, though. He seemed relaxed and at ease in her presence. In direct contradiction to how she felt.

"Joanne," she said. She decided to leave; she could come back for the book at lunchtime. By then she might be able to remember the title, which had fled her mind on seeing him.

"Joanne," he repeated, as though to commit it to memory. "Well, Joanne, which book are you looking for? Maybe I can help you find it."

"No, it's all right," she said. She could hardly admit she'd forgotten the title; he'd think she was just making an excuse to be near him, something the other girls did whenever they got the opportunity. She didn't want him to think she was infatuated with him. "I'll come back later," she said.

"It's OK," he said, grinning. "I don't bite."

Joanne was mortified. He actually thought she was frightened of him! She tried to think of a retort, something sophisticated that would show him she wasn't affected by him at all, but her mind had gone completely blank. Instead she hurried out, his amused laughter ringing in her ears as she closed the door behind her. Her whole face burned with humiliation. *No wonder he laughed,* she thought. She was plain enough as it was; she must look hideous with her face as red as a tomato. And to add to that she'd behaved like an idiot; now he'd be convinced she was dying of love for him. It was just too embarrassing.

After that she stepped up her efforts to avoid him altogether, preferring to walk all the way round the perimeter of the school rather than go down the corridor he was painting. He'd been there for two weeks; surely he must have nearly finished by now? She prayed for him to leave, even as she determined not to think about him at all.

Steve Harris showed no preference for any of the girls he spoke to, so it came as something of a surprise a week later when Hazel broke the unbelievable news that he'd been going out with Carol Hughes for two weeks. Instead of retiring to their favoured corner the next playtime, the elite group converged on Carol instead, demanding to know why she hadn't told them.

"Why should I have?" Carol responded. "I don't need your permission, do I?" Carol was different. She was very intelligent as well as being pretty, so automatically qualified for admission to the elite group, but showed no interest in being part of any clique. She was pleasant and good-natured, and very popular, yet private at the same time. She reminded Joanne very much of Kate, and because of that, Joanne liked her.

"Well, no," blustered Sheila. "But you might at least have told us. What's he like, then? Is it true he lives in a big house in Hale? Have you been there yet?"

"That's one reason why I didn't tell you," Carol replied scornfully. "Because I knew you'd ask me all sorts of stupid questions about him, which I'm not going to answer."

The other reason, Joanne thought later, after the group, rebuffed, repaired to their usual corner to tear Carol to pieces, was because she was only fifteen, and Joanne doubted that Carol's father would be happy about her going out with a man of Steve's age.

Joanne had met the Hughes family when, out of the blue, Carol had invited her round after school a few months before. Joanne had automatically assumed she wanted help with some homework; it was the only reason anyone ever invited her to their houses, but to her surprise, instead of writing an essay or explaining the mysteries of algebra, Joanne had spent a wonderful two hours in the bosom of

Carol's riotous and loving family. Her mother had welcomed Joanne with open arms, and when Carol took Joanne up to the gloriously untidy room she shared with her two sisters, no one had complained when they'd played The Boomtown Rats and Madness at eardrum-bursting volume. Her mother had even come up with sandwiches and biscuits for them, and had actually knocked on the door before coming in.

As Joanne had been leaving, Mr Hughes had come home from work, greeting all his children with a kiss, swinging the youngest ones up in the air and shaking Joanne's hand, with a warm smile that reached his eyes. He had, predictably, asked her how she was doing at school, but had seemed genuinely interested in her replies. Carol had confided in Joanne that she wanted to be a doctor, and Joanne was sure Mr Hughes would encourage her all the way. Unlike her own father, who only seemed to show an interest in her when the opportunity arose to spoil her life.

Two years previously Joanne, buoyed by her excellent third-year results in maths, English and science, had announced to her father over dinner her intention to stay on at school and take A levels in the hope of pursuing a degree in psychology. Instead of being proud of her academic aspirations as she had hoped, he had told her in no uncertain terms that she could think again, and quickly.

"Psychology?" he'd said with disgust. "What sort of stupid subject is that to study? If you think I'm paying for you to spend years at university getting pissed and smoking pot, you can think again."

"It's not stupid," Joanne had replied, for once ignoring her mother's frantic eye signals not to contradict her father. This was important to her. Important enough to risk his wrath. "I've been looking into it. There are all sorts of jobs around for people with degrees in psychology. Well-paid jobs," she'd added, in the hope that the thought of his daughter earning stacks of money would influence him.

"They don't do psychology as part of your O level

options, do they?" Angela had put in nervously. "Wouldn't you be better to think of..."

"Like what?" Jim had put in as though his wife hadn't spoken. He'd bestowed his most contemptuous scowl on Joanne, but for once she hadn't backed down.

"I'd like to be a counsellor," Joanne had replied, keeping her voice deliberately calm. "The NHS employ a lot of psychologists, but I could also go into private practice. There's a lot of money in that. The police use psychologists too, or I could be a social worker. There are lots of things I could do."

"Right. So you want to be a do-gooder, prancing about with your bloody degree, looking down your nose at people and telling them how to live their lives." Jim had stood up, but Joanne had denied him the psychological advantage of being able to loom over her by standing as well. She had been researching non-verbal communication in her spare time, and had impressed the careers' advisor with her knowledge. He had told her he thought her choice of career to be an excellent one, which she tried to remember now. She would not let her father destroy her with scorn and contempt this time. They'd faced each other across the table, and Joanne had forced her legs not to tremble.

"No," she'd replied, her voice shaking a little, but still resolute. "I want to help people, to make a difference. I don't have to do O level psychology to take the A level. And they're offering it at the college. If I go there instead of staying on to sixth form I can..."

"Oh, you've got it all worked out, haven't you?" Jim had interrupted. "Did it occur to you to ask me whether I was willing to feed and clothe you while you went swanning off to college?"

"I've made a rice pudding," Angela had announced. "Would anyone like some?"

"Shut up," said Jim without breaking eye contact with his daughter. Angela had subsided immediately, and Joanne had felt her mother trying to make herself invisible. She would be no help.

"Now you listen to me," Jim continued, raising his arm and wagging his finger in his daughter's face. "*You* will be leaving school as soon as the law says you can. And then you can go out and get yourself a job and start paying me back for all the money I've wasted bringing you up. Which is a bloody lot, I can tell you. When do you have to decide on your options?"

"By the end of term," Joanne said. "But…"

"Don't you but me," her father interrupted. "You can take shorthand and typing, and get a job in an office when you leave school like any normal girl. Make yourself useful for a change."

His colour had risen along with his voice, and Joanne had known she should give in at that point. But this wasn't a small thing, like what time she had to be in the house of an evening or whether she could wear tights instead of socks to school, as all the other girls were doing. They had seemed important at the time, but this really *was* important. She could not allow him to shout her down or destroy her with belittling comments as he usually did. Her whole future depended on it. She'd tried to think of the words that would bring him round to her way of thinking, and, taking the silence for capitulation, Jim had turned away from the table.

"I'm going out for a bit," he said. He would go down the pub, and by the time he came home Joanne would be in bed, and she'd known that she would never find the courage to broach the subject again. In desperation she ran past him to the door, blocking his exit.

"Dad, please," she'd said, her eyes shimmering with tears, "I can get a part-time job and pay for my food and stuff. It won't cost you anything, I promise. And when I go to university I'll get a grant, so…"

She had managed to get this much out because Jim had been stunned, unable to believe that this thirteen-year-old kid had the nerve to stand up to him. Suddenly he'd reacted, grabbing her by the throat and slamming her against the door, watching with satisfaction as her eyes widened in terror.

"Don't you argue with me," he said through gritted teeth. "Don't you ever argue with me, my girl, or you'll be sorry. Do you understand?"

Unable to speak due to a combination of sheer terror and his tight grip on her throat, she had instead managed to nod, after which he'd pushed her to one side and gone out.

Her mother had waited until she heard the front door slam before she became visible again and went over to Joanne, who had now collapsed back onto the chair and was sobbing helplessly.

"Oh Jo," Angela had said, fluttering helplessly around her daughter without actually touching her. "Why did you have to argue with him? You know what he's like."

Because it matters, she'd wanted to scream. *Because I want to do something with my life.* But she hadn't. There had been no point. Her mother would find excuses for him. She always found excuses for him. In Jim's world, the men laid down the law and the women did as they were told, and Angela was someone who always took the line of least resistance. It was easier to agree with him than not.

Because of this, Joanne was now committed to leaving school in a couple of months and looking for work. She had continued to borrow books about human behaviour from the library, but her reading was half-hearted. What was the point, when she'd never get a chance to make use of it?

If only she'd had Carol's understanding father, she'd now be looking forward to sixth form, instead of reluctantly scouring the Situations Vacant columns of the Manchester Evening News every night for an office job she didn't want. Even so, Joanne doubted Carol had told her parents about Steve, and so when she found her crying in the girls' toilets one day a few weeks later, her first thought was that Mr Hughes had found out and had put an end to the relationship. Tentatively, not wanting to be thought nosy, Joanne asked Carol if she was all right.

"I'm fine," Carol said, blowing her nose. "It's just getting to me a bit, that's all."

"You mean exams?" Joanne said, giving Carol an excuse, should she want it.

"Yes, that's it." Carol grabbed at the excuse with such obvious relief that Joanne knew exam nerves weren't causing the tears. She went over to the sink and splashed cold water on her blotchy face.

"You don't need to worry about your O levels," Joanne said reassuringly. "You'll pass them easily."

Carol smiled weakly.

"So will you," she said. "Are you staying on to sixth form?"

"No," Joanne replied. "I'm going to look for a job."

"Are you?" Carol looked up from the sink, surprised. "You're really bright. I thought you'd have wanted to go on to uni."

Joanne looked away, embarrassed. She didn't want to lie straight out and pretend that she actually *wanted* to leave school.

"Yes, well, my family need the money," she said instead, to the floor.

"Right." There was a moment of uncomfortable silence. "Do I look all right?" Carol asked.

Joanne looked up, relieved that Carol hadn't pushed her into telling the truth.

"Yes," she said. "You can hardly tell you've been crying at all. You can always say it's a bit of hay fever, if anyone notices."

Carol dried her face and moved towards the door, then turned back.

"You won't say anything will you? You know, to…"

"No," Joanne said. "Of course I won't."

"Thanks," Carol replied. She bit her lip, and sniffed. "I'm OK now," she said quietly, as though trying to convince herself. "He's a bastard, that Steve is," she added vehemently, "don't you have anything to do with him." Then she opened the door and was gone before Joanne could answer.

Joanne never asked what Steve had done that was so

awful, or why Carol should think Joanne was in any danger from him. It was pretty obvious that he'd just used her, then dumped her. Men as good-looking as him were bound to be fickle; after all, they could have any woman they wanted.

After coming to that conclusion she endeavoured to put the whole incident to the back of her mind. It was better if you could do that, then you weren't likely to blurt anything out without thinking. Joanne was good at keeping secrets; she'd had plenty of practice at it. No one, apart from Kate, knew what her home life was like. It was better that way. And she couldn't confide too much in Kate, not because she wasn't trustworthy, but because of her age. Kate was mature for her years; but she was only ten. She had no conception of the emotional turmoil puberty brought, for one thing. Also, Kate seemed indifferent to her parents' love for her. Joanne wished she could feel the same way about the hostility she suffered. But every time they rejected her, it cut to the bone, in spite of her resolution not to let it affect her. Kate was still at the age where she could only see things from her own viewpoint, and as much as she would have tried to understand Joanne's feelings, she had no personal experience to compare them with.

There was little doubt that if Joanne had stayed on at school, she and Carol would have become friends. But it was never to be, because Joanne, in spite of her excellent O level results, had to leave and find a job.

Which she did, but not without many tears, which were shed secretly under her bedclothes at night, partly so that Kate wouldn't worry about her and partly because she could not bear to see the looks of indifference or triumph on her parents' faces if they'd known how desperate she still was to continue her education.

She would get a job in an office, as her father demanded. And she would work hard and gain promotion, she decided. And then, finally, her father would say he was proud of her because she had done what he wanted, and been successful.

Then he would let her study A levels at night school. It would all work out fine, she told herself, when the tears finally stopped coming.

She told herself this every night for weeks, until she was successful in her fifth interview and, having completed her first stunningly tedious week as a filing clerk, had been praised by her supervisor for her efficiency. But when she turned over all her first wages to her father, keeping only enough for bus fares and lunches, he neither smiled nor looked proud, but only mumbled that it was about time she started making herself useful.

It would not all work out fine after all. Nothing she could do would ever make her parents forgive her for ruining their lives. It was pointless.

When she got a pay rise at the end of her six-month probation period she didn't tell anyone, but kept the money for herself, opening a post office account to save it. Her initial idea of opening an account at the bank was abandoned when she discovered they would send quarterly statements to her house, which her father would probably open. She hid the savings book in the bottom of her underwear drawer, and watched with mingled satisfaction and guilt as the balance slowly increased.

Joanne's seventeenth birthday promised to be a sunny, warm day. Kate, who normally stayed in bed until five minutes before she had to leave for school, set her alarm to go off early so she could get up and sleepily give Joanne her card and present while she was dressing for work. The present was a silver heart-shaped pendant, which Joanne thanked Kate for with a hug and clasped round her neck immediately.

During breakfast her parents made no comment on the fact that it was her birthday, from which Joanne deduced that they'd either forgotten the date or thought it not worth mentioning. Their indifference still stung her, even though she told herself regularly that it didn't matter, that she was beyond being hurt by them any more.

So when her colleagues at work told her they were going for a pub meal and a few drinks that evening, and invited her along, she abandoned all caution and agreed to go with them. Her father had no right to dictate where she went and who she went with, if he couldn't even be bothered to remember the date of her birth, she thought. Buoyed by her rebellion, she even confided to her workmates that it was her birthday, after which they insisted that they'd pay for her meal.

The meal turned out to be a standard pub affair; indifferent meat, slightly overcooked vegetables, and brightly coloured elaborately decorated desserts which looked appetising but were relatively tasteless. Joanne hardly noticed; she basked in the fact that she was part of a group. Not hovering on the outskirts, as she had at school, but, for tonight at least, a central member, the focus even. They all sang 'Happy Birthday' to her, and insisted she have an alcoholic drink rather than the lemonade she asked for. They teased her unmercifully when she admitted she had never ordered a drink in a pub before and was worried the landlord would realise she was underage, but the teasing was good-natured, rather than malicious as Sheila Bradley's had been, and she opened up like a flower under their attention, finally accepting a dare to go to the bar herself and order the next round.

"If you get thrown out," Phil, one of the filing clerks assured her, "we'll take our custom elsewhere."

Joanne grinned, then repeated the round of drinks once to be sure she had them all right, and made her way through the early evening groups of drinkers to the bar. After two glasses of wine she felt a little tipsy; she would stay on soft drinks from now on, she told herself. She didn't want to spoil this perfect evening by getting drunk and making a fool of herself.

* * *

From the vantage point of his seat in the corner, the man watched her. He had initially gone in for a quick pint after work to drown his sorrows at having lost a contract he'd worked hard for, but failed to get. He'd intended to have just the one, then head for home, but then he'd heard the rowdy group at the back of the pub singing happy birthday and raising their glasses to their blushing, smiling colleague, and something about her had caught his interest. Instead of leaving, he'd ordered another pint and had settled himself at a table where he could observe the group surreptitiously.

The birthday girl was pretty; very pretty, in fact, with her clear skin, sparkling brown eyes and long, glossy hair the colour of dark chocolate. But he'd seen hundreds of pretty girls, and had been out with more than a few. He was tall and broad-shouldered, with a perfect physique that he took some pains to maintain. He had a way with women too; they flocked round him, not just because he was good-looking, which he was, or reasonably wealthy, which he also was, or at least his father was, but because there was an air of danger about him that hooked women in like fish gasping on a hook.

He only went out with beautiful girls, especially girls who knew they were beautiful and were used to winding men round their little finger. He got a great kick out of playing them at their own game, seeing how far he could go and what they'd let him get away with. It was fun, treating them like goddesses, standing them up on the third or fourth date, then buying them flowers and hooking them back in again with apologies and promises of undying love, only to dump them once he'd got fed up of screwing them.

They were all the same, pretty women. They thought they were something special, but when it came down to it they were all whores, virtually dragging him into bed after the second or third date. It got boring after a while. He was twenty-six now, and had started to vaguely think about settling down at some point, if he could meet the right girl. Up to now, he'd come nowhere near.

He ignored the flirtatious smile of the barmaid who came to collect his empty glass, and watched the birthday girl thoughtfully. She was laughing and joking with the others, but there was something different about her. She didn't seem part of the group, somehow. There was a nervousness, a sense of insecurity about her. There, just then, when that lanky guy had thrown his arm round her shoulder; she had flinched away a little, then forced herself to endure it. She wasn't used to being touched, then. Now he came to think of it, although she was the centre of attention and was obviously enjoying it, at the same time she seemed embarrassed by it all. She was all contradiction. It was fascinating.

He liked watching people when they didn't know they were being watched, especially women he was thinking of hitting on. It gave him a chance to plan his strategy. He was good at it, he knew that. No girl he'd asked out had ever refused him. This one definitely wouldn't, if he played his cards right. He'd have to be gentle though; if he wasn't, he'd scare her away.

She was standing up now, holding her fingers up to count. Christ, what a figure! She was wearing a short summery sleeveless dress which showed off her willowy figure and long shapely legs beautifully. And she seemed to be completely unaware of how lovely she was. He watched for the signs as she made her way to the bar; the tossing of the head to show off her hair, the surreptitious glances round the room to make sure she was getting her due attention.

Nothing. She just made a beeline for the bar, her whole focus on remembering the round of drinks, completely oblivious to the admiring looks she was getting from the group of builders near the fruit machine. She had no idea how to go about ordering a drink either, that was obvious. She stood near the bar, politely waiting for her turn without trying to catch the barmaid's eye or waving her money in the air to show she was awaiting service. She was unbelievable; innocent, naïve. Irresistible. He had to talk to her.

He stood up, picked up his empty glass and walked over to stand behind her at the bar. He waited a minute, watched as she was overlooked twice by the barmaid; then he made his move. He raised his hand and smiled, and the barmaid, seeing the gesture, asked him what he wanted.

"This young lady was before me," he said.

He waited while the birthday girl reeled off the list of drinks she wanted. Then she turned to him, as he'd known she would.

"Thank you," she said, smiling politely, then her expression changed, not to appreciation of his looks, as might be expected, but to confusion. What was it? Did he have paint on his face or a bogey hanging from his nose or something? He felt slightly unnerved, but continued his planned pitch anyway.

"You'd never have got served standing quietly like that, you have to virtually jump on top of the bar to get noticed in here," he quipped.

She smiled, but there was no warmth in it.

"Happy birthday, by the way," he continued. "I heard your friends singing to you earlier."

She actually blushed, to his delight. God, she was lovely. Tiny, delicate, and just had to be a virgin. She was too natural, too obviously pure not to be.

"Thank you," she said again, then started to turn back to the bar. Damn. He thrust out his hand to her.

"Pleased to meet you," he said formally. "I'm Steve." Now she would introduce herself and he would start a conversation. She was obviously with work colleagues. He'd ask her about that, and what she was doing later, see if he could edge his way into the company. She placed her hand in his and he shook it once then released it immediately, so as not to frighten her. She seemed very edgy.

"Yes, I know," she said. "We've met before, last year. You're Steve Harris."

Her reply threw him completely. How could he have met this woman before, enough for her to know his name, without him remembering her? It wasn't possible. His brow creased in puzzlement. Christ, had he been drunk the last time? Had he tried to stick his hand up her skirt or something? Is that why she was so nervous?

"I'm sorry," he admitted reluctantly. "I really don't remember..."

"You painted my school last summer. You were Carol's boyfriend," she supplied helpfully, her tone cool.

It was obvious that she expected him to remember this Carol, whoever she was. He cast his mind back, running through the list of girls he'd been out with, and came up with a blank. Shit. *I'm making a right mess of this*, he thought, irritated that she'd managed to throw him off track. Obviously from her tone this Carol was her friend, and he'd done something she didn't approve of. It'd help if he could remember what the hell it was.

"I didn't mean to upset her," he said, groping in the dark.

"No, it was probably for the best in the end," the girl said. "It was just a bad time, that's all, in the middle of her O level revision. But it didn't matter. She got good results anyway."

She was obviously trying to reassure him, and he smiled in a relieved way as though he'd been worried sick about this Carol's exam results. Still, at least she didn't remember him because he'd tried to screw her in a club. But how could he chat her up now? She obviously didn't think much of him for upsetting her friend so much. Having said that, she'd said it was last year. Ancient history.

He pulled his thoughts away from the past, and tried again.

"You haven't told me your name," he said.

"Joanne," she supplied. "Joanne Maddock."

"Well, Joanne Maddock, let me help you carry the drinks back," he offered.

"Oh, no, it's all right," she began, then noticed the glasses piling up in front of her, and looked back at him. "Thanks," she amended, seemingly reluctantly.

Expertly balancing four glasses in his hands, he followed her back to the group and placed them on the table. The lanky guy moved up to let Joanne sit next to him. There was a moment's silence while the women eyed Steve with appreciation and the men with hostility. There was nowhere he could sit. He waited for someone, hopefully Joanne, to invite him to join them.

"Er, this is Steve," Joanne said. "We know each other from…"

"School," Steve interrupted quickly before Joanne could finish her sentence.

"Bit old to have been at school with her, aren't you, mate?" said Phil with barely disguised enmity. *Little tosser*, Steve thought.

"Yeah, I painted Joanne's school," he said, smiling. "I've got my own business, specialist decorating, gilding, scagliola, trompe l'oeil, that sort of thing." He doubted any of this lot would know what trompe l'oeil was, but he knew it sounded impressive. One or two of the women leaned forward, and he smiled at them, his blue eyes warm. The blonde one ran her tongue over her lips and smiled suggestively back at him. He could probably have her right now on the table if he wanted, the slut.

"A lot of call for fancy marbling and gold leaf in the local schools, is there?" said Phil contemptuously. Steve fought down the urge to smack the little shit one right there and then. He might impress the blonde tart if he did, but Joanne would probably be horrified. *You wouldn't be so brave if you weren't with your mates,* he thought.

"No, you're right," he replied jovially. "The school was just emulsion and glosswork. Bread and butter stuff. But that was over a year ago. I'm up for the contract to restore the stately home out at Dunham Massey at the moment." That was the contract he'd just lost today, but what the hell. It should have been his.

"I've been there," put in the blonde enthusiastically. "It's great. They've got this big deer park and everything, and they have these huge garden parties every year, where everyone dresses up in Edwardian costume."

Well, she was clearly impressed, anyway. Joanne, however, didn't seem to be. She'd picked up on Phil's hostility and was obviously very ill at ease. He wasn't going to get anywhere like this, by spoiling her little party; he'd have to get her on her own, somehow, where he could work his charm to relax her without this lanky bastard putting the kibosh on everything.

Joanne stood up again and asked where the Ladies' was, and as soon as she'd gone, Steve made his excuses and left the group. The toilets were on the other side of the pub, down a little corridor. He stationed himself there, trying to look as though he wasn't stalking her. When she came out and saw him, she hesitated slightly.

"I've got to go in a minute," Steve said, to reassure her. "I just wanted to say goodbye, and ask if I could buy you a birthday drink before I go."

Joanne smiled, a natural smile this time. Good. He was getting somewhere.

"I've already had two," she said. "I'm not used to drinking. I don't think I'd better have any more."

"I could buy you a soft drink," Steve suggested. "Or better still, I could take you out for a meal one night instead. We could go to a proper restaurant, where they serve decent food. Food you can actually eat."

"The food's OK here," she said.

"Is it? Really?" he replied, raising his eyebrows in surprise. He looked at her and she met his gaze, recognising his interest in her.

"Well, no, it's not that nice," she admitted. "But I'm having a good time anyway."

"And so you should, on your special birthday. Eighteen, is it?"

To his surprise, she flushed bright red.

"Seventeen," she admitted, darting a furtive glance down the corridor as though expecting the landlord to swoop on her and throw her out. She was like something out of Victorian times, sweet and old-fashioned. All his chivalric male instincts were aroused. He wanted to sweep her off, shield her from the brutalities of the world. She was too delicate to survive in the modern world. She needed a protector. She needed him.

"I won't tell anyone you're underage, on one condition," he said. She looked up at him, alarmed for a moment, until she saw the warmth in his eyes and realised he was teasing her. She smiled and relaxed a little.

"What's that?" she asked.

"That you agree to go out for a meal with me. Or to the theatre. Whatever you like."

"Why?" she asked, throwing him again. *Why?* Wasn't it obvious? She was bloody gorgeous. Didn't men ask her out all the time?

"Well, because you're beautiful and I'd like to get to know you better," Steve said.

She looked at him in disbelief. She thought he was mocking her. She really had no idea how attractive she was.

This is not a girl I'm going to fuck a few times, then forget, Steve thought. *This is the girl I'm going to marry*. She wasn't like the others. She was pure, clean, perfect. He would take her out, no, he would court her. Court, that was the right word for a girl like this. He would ask her father for permission to court her, and later, for her hand in marriage.

"I'm sorry, no," she said.

Shocked by the unaccustomed sensations she aroused in him of romance, protectiveness, he didn't register her words of refusal at first, and stared at her blankly when he did. She was looking at him nervously, biting her lip, and he realised he was inadvertently blocking her exit. He moved quickly to one side to let her know that he was harmless.

"Look, if it's because of what happened with me and Carol, I'm sorry, but…"

"No, it's not that," she said. "I just can't, that's all."

"Why not?" he asked. "Don't you like me?"

"I don't know. I don't know you," she replied with disarming honesty.

"Well then, where's the harm in going out for a meal? At least then you can find out whether you like me or not, and if you don't, then I promise I'll never bother you again."

She bit her lip again. It made her look vulnerable and very young. He wanted to put her in his pocket and take her home with him, keep her all for himself, forever.

"I'm sorry, really I am, but I can't," she repeated. Her eyes as she looked into his were truly distressed and pleading, and because of that he let her walk past him without stopping her and demanding to know why, as he wanted to.

He went in the same pub every evening after work for the next six weeks, but she never came back in. He saw some of the others, and toyed briefly with the idea of waiting outside for Mr Lanky Shit and giving him a good kicking, and with the other idea of screwing the blonde slut a few times, while finding out more about Joanne. He knew nothing about her except her name and that she'd attended the school he'd painted last summer.

But if he did either of those things, word would no doubt get back to her, and then he wouldn't have a snowball's chance in hell of going out with her. And he *would* get her to go out with him, somehow. He always got what he wanted, one way or another. She had found him attractive, he was sure of that. So why had she turned him down? Was she seeing someone else? The thought of another man kissing her lips, touching her body, made his blood run cold. It wasn't possible.

No, he would have her. And he would be her first lover, and her last. She must work nearby. He would find her and persuade her to go out with him. He would do whatever it took. She was worth it. And in the meantime he could amuse himself with the redhead he'd met the week before. Ruth. She was OK; very inventive in the sex department. Cracking blow jobs. She would do, for now.

* * *

In the August following her seventeenth birthday Joanne withdrew the bulk of her meagre savings and enrolled for A level psychology at the local college. In order to conceal this from her father she took up ballroom dancing classes, which were held in a draughty hall above a shop five minutes' walk from the college. She went twice a week, on Tuesday and Thursday evenings, from August until the end of September. Kate did not clamour to go with her; she considered ballroom dancing to be old-fashioned and stuffy, as Joanne had expected her to. When Jim Maddock rang her dance teacher, as Joanne had known he would, to check that she was actually attending the classes rather than sneaking off to the pub with some local delinquent youth, Miss Stapleton had enthused about Joanne's enthusiasm and speedy mastery of the steps, and had informed Jim that it was delightful to see a young face in the hall, as all the other members were retired gentlemen and ladies. Jim didn't tell Joanne he'd phoned, of course, but Miss Stapleton did, telling Joanne it must be wonderful to have such a caring father, when so many parents couldn't care less what their children were up to.

At the end of September Joanne dropped the Thursday class with some regret; the elderly members were kind to her, and to her surprise she actually enjoyed learning the complex sequences of steps. She discovered that she had a natural sense of rhythm, and resolved to keep on with the Tuesday class, which she did for a few more weeks, until the pressure of coursework forced her to abandon it in order to spend time in the library writing essays she dare not attempt at home in case her mother came into her room without warning, as she often did. She spent all her lunch hours studying, and kept her books at work. Only her colleagues knew what she was doing; and Sheila Bradley, who she had run into one Saturday in the supermarket, and who had talked incessantly about the joys of sixth form and how it was *so* different from normal school, no uniform, their own common room, and the teachers couldn't care less what you got up to in your free time.

"What a shame that you had to leave," Sheila had

concluded with feigned sympathy. "You wanted to stay on, didn't you?"

In a fit of pique, Joanne had informed Sheila that she actually had the best of both worlds; she had plenty of money from her job *and* was studying for her A levels as well, at Fernwood College. That had wiped the smug smile off Sheila's face, to Joanne's satisfaction.

No one else knew, not even Kate; it was the only way Joanne could be sure her father would not find out.

* * *

She was sitting in the corner of her favourite café, a half-eaten sandwich and cooling cup of coffee pushed to one side to make room for her reference book and an A4 notepad, on which she was scribbling furiously. She glanced occasionally at her watch, noting how many minutes she had before she had to return to work.

"'Emotional factors can enhance recall in some circumstances, but make memories less likely to be retrieved in other circumstances.' Sounds interesting." The male voice repeating the title of her essay was close enough to make Joanne jump violently and render the word she was writing unintelligible. She looked up into a pair of beautiful, azure-blue eyes.

"I'm sorry," the owner of the eyes continued. "I didn't mean to frighten you. I recognised you, and thought I'd say hello. Can I get you a coffee?"

How long had Steve Harris been sitting directly opposite her, without her noticing? Joanne tore her attention reluctantly from her work and glanced at her watch.

"I've got one already, thanks," she replied politely, wishing he would go away. This essay had to be in tomorrow night, and it was only half-finished.

"It's cold," he said, raising his hand for the waitress. Of course one came straight away, smiling and blushing, and he ordered two coffees. Joanne resigned herself to having to study through her tea break as well as lunch the next day.

"So," he continued, "are you going to accept my offer of a drink this time or are you going to spurn me again?"

She looked at him, searching for signs of mockery; but she saw only a handsome young man dressed in a tight-fitting blue T-shirt and jeans, with a warm smile on his face and in his eyes, all directed at her.

"No, I'll accept a coffee," she replied. "Thank you."

"My pleasure, Miss Maddock," he said formally, stretching his hand across the table and enfolding hers in a strong grip that was almost, but not quite, painful. He seemed even more attractive and compelling now that his charisma was directed wholly at her instead of being diluted by her colleagues. She felt her colour rising at this contact with the handsomest man she had ever seen, and prayed that he wouldn't notice her blush. "Steve," he reminded her, as though she could have forgotten his name. She had thought about him intermittently for weeks. He was the first man who had ever asked her out.

"I remember," she said.

There was a pause while the waitress brought the coffee.

"Did you get the contract at Dunham?" Joanne asked.

Steve smiled, and she realised that he was flattered that she remembered so much about him, and was encouraged by it. Silently she cursed herself. She didn't want to encourage him into asking her out again.

"No," he replied.

"I'm sorry."

"That's OK. I'm a small fish in a big sea at the moment. But I'm growing all the time. You can tell your friend at the office that I've been painting another school recently. That'll please him."

Joanne looked away, embarrassed.

"Phil's just a colleague," she said. "I don't know what got into him that night. He's not normally like that."

"Forget him," Steve responded dismissively. "Can I confess something to you?"

Joanne was taken aback.

"Yes, if you want," she said uncertainly, not sure she wanted him to. He was unnerving, this man. Mature, and confident, and compelling. The warmth of his handshake glowed on her hand, tingling through her fingertips.

"I lied to you, that night in the pub, when I said I didn't remember you from before," he said.

This unexpected confession rendered Joanne momentarily mute. Why would he have lied to her? He hadn't remembered her, she'd been sure of it. He'd been thrown off balance by the fact that she'd known who he was.

"Why?" she asked.

Steve sipped his coffee, and looked her straight in the eye, which he would never have done had he been lying. Maybe she was wrong after all. Maybe her knowledge of body language wasn't as comprehensive as she thought. His eyelashes were long, light brown and gold-tipped.

"I felt uncomfortable, I guess. I didn't want to bring it up, when Carol had obviously told you such horrible things about me," he finished.

"Why?" Joanne repeated, genuinely curious. She glanced at her watch. Five minutes.

"Because I fancied you the first time I saw you, and I knew I shouldn't be having thoughts like that when I was going out with your friend."

The tingling spread up her arm, tearing through her body like wildfire, and the suppressed blush blazed on her cheeks. He watched her, his mouth turning up slightly at the corners.

"I've embarrassed you," he said. "I embarrassed you in the pub as well. I'm sorry. I'm always getting into trouble for speaking my mind. But it's true. I've thought about you often since then. I couldn't believe it when I saw you sitting here. I just had to come in and explain it to you."

"I work near here," Joanne managed. "I eat here most days."

"I don't, though. I'm only here for a couple of days, decorating the foyer of the hotel round the corner. My next job's out in Sandbach. Listen," he said earnestly, leaning forward over the table. "I don't know what Carol told you, and I know she's your friend and all, but I didn't finish with her, it was the other way round. She saw me out with my cousin and assumed I was two-timing her. She threw a fit and dumped me. I tried to explain the truth to her, but she wouldn't see me."

"I have to go," Joanne said suddenly, scraping her chair back and standing up. She wanted to get away from this disturbing man. She had no experience of talking to men apart from her father and casual talk with her male colleagues, and had no idea what to say. Steve stood up as well and accompanied her to the door, gently placing his hand on her waist to guide her, as though they were a couple. Then they were standing outside in the early spring sunshine, and he took his hand away, smiling down at her.

"Well, goodbye," said Joanne, wondering whether she should extend her hand for him to shake again, and deciding against it. She was unnerved enough already.

"I won't ask you out for a meal again, in case you say no." He smiled. "But would you like to go out for a drink tonight? We could have a chat, get to know each other a bit better. Just one drink, after work?"

"I go to night school tonight," she lied.

"Ah. Well, tomorrow night, then? Or at the weekend, maybe?" he suggested.

"I…no, I'm sorry, I can't," she said, mortified. "I'm doing A levels. I have to do a lot of studying."

"Right. OK. I understand," he said, in a tone which made it clear he didn't. He smiled sadly and looked away for a moment, and then back at her. "Good luck with your studies," he added.

She couldn't do it to him. Unbelievable as it was it seemed that this gorgeous man actually fancied her, and she had just rejected him, for the second time, and had hurt him unbearably. It was evident in every forlorn line of his body as he turned away. In a moment he would be gone, and she would never see him again, or if she did, he would nod politely at her and pass on. He would never ask her out again and risk a third humiliation. Suddenly she knew she could not bear that. Even telling him the truth would be better than having to bear him treating her as a stranger.

"It's not that I don't want to," she blurted out. "I do, a lot. But I can't, really."

He turned back.

"Why not?" he asked, hope flaring in his eyes.

"It's just that, well…" Joanne hesitated. It would sound ridiculous. But better he thought her pathetic than that he feel rejected. "My dad has told me I can't go out with boys until I'm eighteen," she said.

"What? *Eighteen?*"

"Yes, I know it sounds stupid, but…"

"It sounds a bit Victorian, but it's sweet as well, in a way," Steve interrupted.

She looked up, puzzled.

"I mean, he's obviously really protective of you. Either that, or he's just living in the Dark Ages."

"He's living in the Dark Ages," Joanne replied with conviction, buoyed by the fact that Steve hadn't laughed at her. "He'll kill me if I go out with you and he finds out. He had a fit when I got home from the pub after my birthday, because I hadn't told him I was going out after work. I'm sorry." She looked at her watch again. "Oh God, I'm late," she said. "I really have to go." She turned and started to walk away, and he ran to catch up with her.

"Do you really mean that? Is that the only reason you turned me down? That night in the pub as well?" he asked.

"Yes," she replied. "Well, no, you did upset Carol, but I can see now how it might have been a misunderstanding. And it was a long time ago. No, I thought you'd think I was pathetic."

"I don't think you're pathetic," he said, walking beside her as she hurried back to the office. "When will you be eighteen?"

"July," she replied. "July the eighth."

He stopped her at the entrance to the office block and took her hand, raising it to his lips in an old-fashioned gesture.

"Well, then," he said, his eyes bright with affection, his lips warm as he pressed a kiss on to the palm of her hand, then curled her fingers over it. "See you on July the eighth, then."

He released her hand and walked away, and Joanne spent the afternoon in a haze of incompetence which it took her the rest of the week to sort out.

He would forget, she thought that evening, counting the days until her birthday. Over three months. An eternity. He could have any girl he wanted; why would he want her? She looked at herself in the mirror, noting the dark brown eyes, the long straight boring brown hair, the facial features which separately were acceptable, but when put together just didn't fit properly. Her eyebrows were too thick, her eyes too big for her nose, which was too small for the generous mouth beneath it. No, he had just been bored, had noticed her in the café, remembered her from the pub for some reason and had decided to brighten up the dull little mouse's day. He had probably forgotten about her before he'd reached the end of the street.

She put him firmly to one side and forced herself to concentrate on her psychology A level. After this she would take English A level, and then she would try for university. Some of them would take students with two good passes. She would be twenty by then, but she would also have savings. And the independence to do what she wanted.

Her future did not lie with Steve Harris, or any other man she could imagine. Her future lay in her career as a top psychologist.

CHAPTER TWO

July 1982

Joanne's eighteenth birthday fell on a Thursday and she arrived at work to find several cards and small, gaily wrapped parcels on her desk. The gifts they contained were inexpensive; bath salts, chocolates, perfumed soap, but Joanne was overwhelmed by the thought that had gone into them. She hadn't told anyone it was her birthday, and she realised they must have found out from her personnel file. She spent the morning wrapped in the warm atmosphere of popularity.

She hadn't realised before today how much the others liked her. They had always been friendly, asking her if she would like to accompany them for a drink after work on Fridays. But they hadn't persisted when she declined, and she had often wondered if they thought she was standoffish, as she could hardly explain the true reason why she didn't accept their invitations. What would they think of her if they knew that at seventeen she was still not allowed to stay out after eight without being cross-questioned by her father? They would feel contempt for her, or even worse, would pity her.

Now it was clear that they hadn't taken offence after all, and Joanne resolved that the next time they asked her to go for a drink, she would accept. She was eighteen now, a woman, although she didn't feel any different than she had yesterday.

In the afternoon she was summoned to the manager's office. In spite of the fact that she knew she hadn't done anything to be disciplined for, she still felt a moment's trepidation as she entered the well-appointed room where Mr MacDonald reigned. She had only seen him a handful of times since her appointment, and as she accepted his offer of a seat she glanced round the room and thought how lonely it must be to spend every day ensconced alone, no matter how plush the accommodation.

"Now Miss Maddock, I expect you're wondering why I asked to see you," Mr MacDonald began. Joanne waited, recognising that he was not expecting an answer.

"First of all, of course I wanted to wish you a happy birthday," he continued.

Joanne smiled.

"Thank you, Mr MacDonald," she said. Everyone was really so very kind.

"How are you going to celebrate becoming an adult?" he asked.

He sounded genuinely interested, although it couldn't possibly be of any consequence to him how one of his junior employees chose to spend her birthday.

"Some of my relatives are coming round for a meal," Joanne replied, trying to sound as though an evening with assorted uncles, aunts and cousins who she saw rarely was exactly how she wanted to celebrate becoming an adult.

"That sounds nice," Mr MacDonald replied, his tone mirroring her lack of enthusiasm precisely. They looked at each other for a moment, then he grinned, she smiled back and for a few moments they were equals. "The second reason I asked to see you," he continued, "is because there's a vacancy for an accounts clerk coming up soon, and I wondered if you'd be interested. You'll have six weeks' initial training, and if you do well you'd have the opportunity to take external accounting courses if you want."

He looked at her while she digested this information.

"It's very kind of you to consider me," she said. Whilst

she didn't want a career in accounting, the extra money would come in very useful until she went to university. "Would I have to attend another interview?" she asked.

"No, the job's yours if you want it," he said. "I prefer, when I can, to choose my employees based on their true abilities rather than how good they are at acting in interviews. You seem a little uncertain, though."

"No, I'd love the job. I like working with figures, but…" She hesitated. Mr MacDonald was a nice man. He deserved honesty. "I'm studying for A levels in my spare time," she continued. "Eventually I'd like to go to university and study psychology. I want to be a counsellor. It doesn't seem right for you to spend a lot of money training me, when I intend to leave in a few years."

There, she'd just done herself out of a better job. Her parents would think she was mad if she told them. Mr MacDonald seemed to share the view. He was looking at her as though she'd just grown another head or something.

"How long do you expect it to take for you to get enough qualifications to go to university?" he asked after a few moments.

"At least another three years, maybe as long as five, depending on whether I need two or three A levels," she replied.

"Then my offer stands. Are you interested?"

"Yes," she said, vastly relieved. "But…"

He interrupted her with a wave of his hand.

"I'm sure that one day you will make a great counsellor," he said. "And in the meantime, I am sure you will make an equally good accounts clerk. Your integrity is refreshing. If you continue in this way, you may even restore my faith in the younger generation."

"Thank you," she said, relaxing visibly.

He opened his desk drawer and rummaged around in it for a moment, and then stood up, signalling the end of the interview. Joanne got to her feet. He held his hand out to her. In it was an envelope.

"When you have endured this evening," he said, "I would like you to take this, and have the sort of party every young adult who comes of age should have. One that involves a lot of friends of your own age, considerable amounts of alcohol, and ends in you dancing on the table, or some such activity. Just make sure you get home safely at the end of it."

Once outside the door Joanne opened the envelope. Inside it was a twenty pound note. She floated back to her desk on a cloud. What a fabulous birthday it was turning out to be. A promotion and a bonus, so to speak. What a wonderful surprise.

The surprises were not over. Lying on her desk when she got back was the biggest bouquet of long-stemmed pink roses she had ever seen. Joanne picked the bouquet up in disbelief. Surely these couldn't be for her? She looked behind the huge white bow which encircled the flowers.

"There's no card," Cathy, sitting at the next desk, supplied helpfully. "You didn't tell us you had a boyfriend."

"I haven't," Joanne said, her brow furrowing in puzzlement. "Are you sure they're for me?"

"Yes, the delivery boy said they were for Miss Joanne Maddock," Jennifer, one of the more gossipy girls replied. "Surely you must have *some* idea who they're from?"

"I don't, honestly," Joanne said, placing the bouquet carefully back on the table. Who could have sent them? Certainly not her parents. Kate, although only twelve, would be thoughtful enough to do that sort of thing, but she didn't have enough money for flowers like these. They were perfect blooms and there were at least thirty of them. They must have cost a fortune.

"You must have a secret admirer," Cathy said, bending down to sniff at the roses. "A rich one, too."

Joanne spent the rest of the afternoon wondering who could have sent the flowers. At five o'clock she made her way out of the office into the summer sunshine, two carrier bags full of presents in one hand, and the roses balanced carefully in the crook of her arm. It was going to be difficult on the bus with this lot.

Parked on a double yellow line outside the office building was a car. Leaning nonchalantly against it was a tall, blond, devastatingly handsome young man, who smiled warmly at Joanne as she approached.

"Happy birthday," he said.

Joanne stopped. She felt her face flush instantly scarlet. For a moment she couldn't believe what she was seeing. Then she realised her mouth was open in shock and that she must look a complete fool. She closed her mouth and tried to will the blush to disappear, unsuccessfully.

"Thank you," she said. Light suddenly dawned. She looked at the roses, then back at him.

"Do you like them?" Steve asked. "I didn't know what else you might want." At the far corner of her vision she saw Cathy and Jennifer appear at the office door and stop to watch, wide-eyed. She felt like Cinderella, confronted by Prince Charming whilst still in her rags.

"Yes," she replied shyly. "They're beautiful. I had no idea they were from you. There was no card."

To her astonishment, he actually looked a little hurt.

"You didn't think I'd forget your birthday, did you?" he said. "I've been counting the days since we last met." He stood away from the car, and opening the door, he beckoned her to get in. "Here you go." He smiled.

Joanne looked up the street, suddenly panicked. This couldn't be happening, not to her. It wasn't real. She looked at the car. It was a Porsche. A *Porsche!*

"Is that yours?" she asked idiotically.

"Of course it is. Did you think I'd stolen it?" He grinned, and Joanne became aware that he was enjoying her discomfiture. "Here," he continued, reaching across to relieve her of her bags. "Let me help you with those."

She had a sudden, inexplicable urge to flee for her life. He was too handsome, too confident, too worldly for the likes of her. What would she say to him if she let him drive her home?

He'd think she was gauche and stupid, and he'd no doubt be polite as he dropped her off at her front door, then he'd drive away as fast as possible, never to be seen again.

While she was thinking all this, he had placed her bags in the car and was now waiting for her to follow them.

"Come on," he said gently. "I just want to talk to you, that's all."

And then before she realised it she was sitting in the car, inhaling the wonderful smell of expensive leather mingling with the scent of the beautiful roses he had bought for her, and she knew she had to be dreaming. He started the engine up and drove smoothly away, ignoring the crowd of girls now openly admiring him from the office building. She would have some explaining to do tomorrow.

He drove for a few minutes in silence, letting her become accustomed to her situation, and she was grateful to him for being so considerate. He wore blue jeans and a sleeveless T-shirt, and he was gorgeous. She tried to concentrate on the road, but his presence in the car was overwhelming. She forced herself not to look at him, to calm down.

"What are you doing this evening?" Steve asked.

"My mum's having a sort of a party for me," she answered, taking his question literally rather than as an invitation.

"What 'sort of a party'?"

"She's invited some of the relatives round. Aunts and uncles, cousins, that sort of thing," she said.

"That sounds really interesting," Steve replied. He sounded so much like Mr MacDonald in that moment that Joanne laughed, and in laughing, relaxed a little.

"What did I say that was so funny?" Steve asked, smiling across at her. His teeth were perfect, straight and white.

"Nothing. You just sounded exactly like my boss when I told him the same thing. I don't sound very enthusiastic, do I?" She would have to make more of an effort when she got home, or her dad would be down on her like a ton of bricks.

"Why don't you come out with me tonight instead?" Steve suggested.

"Oh, no, I couldn't! I mean, it's not that I don't want to or anything, but I just…I can't. Mum's been planning it for weeks." Joanne felt mortified. She'd rejected him. Again. He'd be cool and polite now. At least she was nearly home.

"That's all right. How about tomorrow night, then? We could go out for a meal, get to know each other a bit better. What do you think?"

A million thoughts ran through her head all at once, rendering her dumb. What would she wear? What could she say that would impress him? Was he serious?

He pulled up outside the house and smiled, taking her silence for assent.

"Here we are," he said, then actually got out of the car and went round to open the door for her. She climbed out, and he reached back in to get her parcels, handing her the roses. She held out her free hand for the bags, but he was already opening the gate.

"It's all right, I can manage," she started to say, but he was already walking ahead of her, and before she could catch up with him he had knocked on the door. Joanne closed her eyes. Her dad would be home from work. There would be hell to pay if he knew that she'd allowed a strange man to drive her home. *I'm eighteen,* she thought. *I can do what I want.* Maybe her mother would open the door. Maybe they'd argued and her dad was already in the pub.

Her father opened the door.

"Hello Mr Maddock," Steve said, thrusting out his hand immediately, so that Jim Maddock instinctively took it. They shook hands, then Steve turned back to where Joanne had stopped on the path. "My name is Steve. Steve Harris," he continued. "I know Joanne from work, and I offered her a lift home because she had a lot of presents to carry." His car keys were dangling from his fingers, the Porsche key ring clearly visible. Jim looked at them, then past Steve to where the car was parked right outside the front gate.

"That yours, is it?" Jim said, trying not to look impressed.

Steve glanced back briefly, winking surreptitiously at Joanne in the process.

"Yes," he said nonchalantly. "My business has been doing well lately. Mr Maddock, I know it might seem old-fashioned and strange to you, but I would like to take your daughter out tomorrow night and I'd feel a lot happier if I had your permission to do so."

Jim was flabbergasted. He spent half his life complaining that the younger generation had no respect for anyone or anything any more, yet here was a member of that very group asking permission to court his daughter. Jim prided himself on being a good judge of character; he could spot mockery a mile away. There was no hint of mockery in this young man's honest blue eyes.

"What's your line of business, Mr Harris?" he asked.

"I'm a specialist decorator," Steve said. "I do a lot of work out in Cheshire. That's why I've got the car. It gives a good impression, if you know what I mean, lets me bump the prices up a bit."

In three sentences he'd managed to tell Joanne's dad that he was a successful businessman, but that he didn't consider himself better than the Maddock family, and had even admitted himself into the working class club of getting one over on the wealthy when possible, a club of which Jim was a fully paid-up member.

"Where were you thinking of taking Joanne?" Jim asked, clearly warming to this very presentable young man.

"There's a lovely little restaurant in Wilmslow," Steve said. "I thought we could go there for our first date. Get to know each other a little better over some good food. What time would you like me to bring her home?"

It wasn't until much later that Joanne realised she had never actually said yes to Steve. Her father and him had arranged it all between them, and she was so overwhelmed by the fact that this incredibly handsome man with impeccable manners actually wanted to spend time with her, that it never occurred to her to think that she had been treated as though she had no will of her own.

Over the next six weeks she was swept up and carried away on a wave of wild, romantic, old-fashioned courtship. Steve brought flowers for her mother and chocolates for Kate. He showered Joanne in flowers, expensive perfume and compliments. He took her to exclusive restaurants where they ate oysters, caviar and lobster, accompanied by the finest wines. He took her to art galleries, museums and the theatre, and insisted on buying her some new dresses which flattered her slender figure. She spent some of her precious savings for university on having her hair cut and styled, and he noticed immediately and was full of admiration for her sleek, shoulder-length bob. He sent a single red rose to the office every day for two weeks, and rang her every day to tell her he couldn't wait to see her again.

It was unbelievably, wonderfully romantic. The girls at the office were green with envy, and demanded blow-by-blow accounts of every night out. Buoyed by Steve's constant attention and her colleagues' envy, Joanne bloomed. She temporarily abandoned her studies, telling herself she would catch up in September, when she had to enrol for the second year. She lived in a constant dream of Steve. Her whole life was taken over by him. She had thought he would be bored by her naivety, but he found it refreshing. And in truth, he did most of the talking on their dates and she was happy to let him. He was so interesting, so full of plans for the future.

"What I want to do is to get into the really specialist decorating," he confided to her one evening. They were sitting in the garden of a country pub, plastic glasses of wine in front of them. It was one of those wonderful summer evenings when the British, soothed by days of endless blue skies and sunshine, start to feel continental and shed their inhibitions to some extent. The garden was full of couples and families in brightly coloured clothes, the children running dizzily between the tables, the adults laughing and joking. Directly ahead of Joanne, over Steve's shoulder, there was a table full of young couples. Two of the girls were sitting on their boyfriends' knees, their arms intertwined. Joanne looked away and forced herself to concentrate on what Steve was saying.

"There's a lot of money to be made in trompe l'oeil, scagliola, that sort of thing. I just need to get one good contract and I'll be able to establish my reputation. It'd be good to prove to my dad that art isn't a subject for poofs, too."

Joanne looked at him, shocked.

"Your dad thinks you're gay?" she said.

"No, of course he doesn't!" Steve replied. "He just wanted me to go into the law, end up a police inspector like him. When I said I wanted to do art and set up my own business, he nearly had a heart attack."

"He helped to set you up in business though, didn't he?" Joanne pointed out.

"Yes," Steve admitted. "And now he's waiting for it to fail, so he can gloat over me." He was irritated, Joanne could see that. He was always edgy when he spoke about his father. Her eyes flickered over to the group at the next table again, then back to him.

"What's the matter with you, anyway?" he said. "You've been miles away all evening."

How could she broach the subject that was on her mind, without making herself sound cheap? She hadn't thought anything about it until the girls at work had brought it up, and now she could think of nothing else.

"So, what's he like in bed, then?" Jennifer had asked a few days ago. Joanne and Steve had been going out for six weeks now, and it was assumed they must be sleeping together. Joanne had blushed. "Come on," Jennifer coaxed. "You can tell us. He's got a fabulous body. Is he just as gorgeous in the nude?"

After a great deal of teasing Joanne had finally admitted that they had not made love yet. In fact, he had not tried to coerce her into having sex with him at all. He was very affectionate. He had kissed her with increasing passion as the weeks had gone by, until she was weak with desire for him. But he had never suggested she spend the night with him. She had thought it was because he was a gentleman. The other girls had a completely different view.

"Come off it," said Cathy. "That's all men think about. I don't care how gentlemanly he is, he's bound to have tried to get in your knickers by now."

"Unless he's gay," Jennifer offered. She ignored Joanne's protests. "One of my mates went out with a gay guy once. She didn't know until she got fed up of waiting for him to make a move on her and asked him straight out."

"What did he say?" Joanne asked.

"He denied it at first, of course, but later he admitted it. He wanted to marry her and have a couple of kids to please his parents."

"What did she do?" Cathy asked, aghast.

"What do you think? She dumped him, that's what she did. Disgusting. You want to watch your Steve isn't the same way. I thought he was too good to be true."

Joanne had not been concerned about his lack of sexual interest towards her before. Now she looked at him, torn. He wasn't. He couldn't be. Could he? He leaned across the table and took her hand in his.

"What is it?" he asked, his eyes full of concern. "There's something bothering you. Tell me."

"You'll be angry," she said.

"No I won't," he reassured her. "I could never be angry with you. What is it?"

There was only one way to be sure of finding out the truth; she knew from her studies. If she asked him straight out, his face would betray the truth before his brain could catch up and formulate the right response, which might be a lie.

"Are you gay?" she asked.

He looked at her in complete disbelief for a long frozen

moment, in which she realised for certain that he was, most definitely, not a homosexual. Then he dropped her hand and sat back, giving her a look of such contempt that her soul shrivelled up inside her.

"What makes you think that?" he asked coldly.

"I…I don't, it's just…the girls at work. They wanted to know if we'd…and when I said no, one of them said she'd been out with someone who was gay, and she only found out because he never tried to….you know. And…"

"Do you know," he interrupted icily, "I actually thought you were different from those slags you work with. I thought you had more respect for yourself than to let a man fuck you the first time you went out with him."

"I have!" Joanne protested. "I haven't…I've never…"

He lunged across the table suddenly and, plunging his hand down her blouse he grabbed her breast, squeezing it painfully.

"Is this what you want?" he said. "Do you want me to fuck you right now on the grass? Is that what you want?"

"No!" she cried, mortified. She had had no idea he would react in this extreme manner. The people at the next table were staring at them. She tried to pull back, but he grabbed a handful of her blouse and pulled her towards him.

"I thought you were different from the others," he spat at her. "And all the time you were thinking I was queer, just because I respected you. You make me sick."

For one terrible moment she actually thought he was going to carry out his threat and pull her down onto the grass. He seemed oblivious of the people around them, who were now openly watching them. Then he let go of her so suddenly that she almost fell backwards off the stool, and standing up, he walked away.

She sat there for a moment in shock, trying to swallow down the huge lump that had risen to her throat. Tears trickled down her cheeks. She straightened her blouse as best she could; he had torn two of the buttons off. Then she picked up her bag, stood up and walked out of the beer garden, looking straight ahead of her so that she would not see all the other customers staring at her.

She thought he'd driven away and left her stranded. She would have to phone a taxi. But his car was still there. He was standing next to it, much as he had on her birthday outside the office. Only his expression was different. Joanne didn't know whether to walk past him or confront him. She was really distressed that she had upset him so much. But she was also angry. She had asked him her question quietly, and he had responded by humiliating her publicly. And he had hurt her as well. Her breast was throbbing.

"I'm sorry," he said as soon as she came within earshot. He was looking down at the tarmac, unable to meet her eyes. She stopped, keeping enough distance between them that he couldn't lunge for her again. "I don't know what came over me."

"I'm sorry if I upset you, Steve," she said. "But you had no right to grab me like that. You hurt me."

He looked up at her then, and she saw that his eyes were full of tears.

"Please," he said simply, "don't leave me."

Her anger melted away instantly. She crossed the space between them and his arms came round her, folding her to him.

"I'm sorry," she said into his chest. "I don't think you're gay. I never did. I should never have listened to the girls at work."

"I love you," he said. "I want you, you know that, don't you? I just wanted to wait until the time was right."

She lifted her face up to his, and then he was kissing her, desperately, passionately, and she responded to him instinctively, wrapping her arms around him and opening her mouth to him. She felt him swell against her and she realised how humiliating and insulting he must have found her question. How could she ever have thought he was gay, even for a minute?

Eventually he broke the kiss, pulling back from her. He

was breathing heavily, his pupils dilated so wide that his eyes looked black in the twilight.

"You can't believe what it's doing to me, holding back like this," he said. "I want you all the time. I can't sleep, I can't concentrate at work. All I can think about is you. I've never felt like this before. When I make love to you for the first time, I don't want it to be squashed in the car, or down a back alley. I want it to be special, because you're beautiful and perfect, and I love you." He took her face between his hands and kissed her on the tip of her nose. "I want to spend the rest of my life with you," he said.

They were lying companionably together in bed, covered only with a sheet. The bedroom window was open and the night breeze played gently with the curtain.

"He's asked me to marry him," Joanne said into the darkness.

"What!" cried Kate, sitting up.

"Sshh!" Joanne replied frantically. "You'll wake Dad up."

"Sorry." Kate lay down again, and mulled this news over for a minute. "What did you say to him?" she asked finally.

"I said I needed to think about it. What do you think?" Joanne didn't find anything odd in asking her twelve-year-old sister's opinion. In some ways she felt Kate was more mature than she was. And down inside Joanne knew that her reason was being swept away by Steve's constant attention. She had never been adored before, and it was wonderful beyond belief. Kate was sensible and honest, and Joanne needed someone who would give a candid opinion, someone who cared about her. With a slight jolt of loneliness, Joanne realised that no one else she knew fitted the bill.

"It's too soon," Kate said. "You've only been going out with him for a few weeks."

"I know. But he's wonderful, Kate. He takes me to the most amazing places. He really cares about me. And when I told him I wanted to go to university, he started working out straight away how he could afford to support me while I took my degree. I have to be really careful when I'm out with him because if I say I like something in a shop window he'll insist on buying it for me straight away. I feel as though I'm living in a fairy tale."

She hadn't told her sister about Steve's outburst in the pub garden. It would give her the wrong impression about him. And now she'd had time to think about it, she didn't blame Steve for reacting as he had. After all, she had insulted him in the worst possible way. She was lucky he hadn't dumped her on the spot, instead of begging her forgiveness as he had.

"Do you love him?" Kate asked.

That was the fundamental question. Did she?

"I think so," Joanne said. "He loves me, he tells me he does, every day."

"But you're not sure if you feel the same way?"

Joanne hesitated for a moment.

"I don't really know what love is, Kate." Kate was the only person in the world who would accept this, without argument, without pity, with full knowledge of what life was like at home. "I love being with him. He makes me feel special, beautiful even. I don't know if that's love, feeling like that."

"Did you tell Steve that?"

"No."

"Why not?"

"I don't know, really. I just didn't want him to feel sorry for me, I suppose. Why, do you think I should tell him?"

"It's up to you," Kate said. "But if I was in love with someone, I'd want to feel able to tell them anything at all and know they'd understand. Why don't you tell him you want to wait for a bit, see how things go?"

Joanne tried to work out how to tell Kate that being with Steve was like being with a tornado. She couldn't think straight when she was with him.

"I don't know how long he'll wait around if I keep saying no," she admitted. "I'm frightened he'll get fed up and find someone else." Even the thought of that happening made her feel sick. She wasn't really much of a catch, in spite of what Steve seemed to think. She didn't want to spend the rest of her life a spinster, regretting having thrown away her only chance of true love.

"If he does that, then he can't have loved you very much, can he?" Kate said with all the assurance of someone who had never been infatuated. "Look at Mum and Dad. They got married six months after they met. They must have thought they were in love, and look at them now."

"That's different," Joanne replied. "They got married because Mum was pregnant. You had to get married in those days. I'm not pregnant."

"No, but Mum must have thought she loved Dad to let him get her pregnant in the first place, mustn't she? If she'd waited until she'd got to know him better she'd have found out what he was really like, and I bet she wouldn't have married him then."

There was no arguing against the logic of this. As loved as Kate was by her parents, her father made no secret of the fact that he disliked both his wife and his eldest daughter equally.

"Don't you like Steve?" Joanne asked. Everyone else liked him. All the girls at work would have given their right arm for a date with him. Her mum and dad thought he was wonderful. Kate, now she thought of it, had never offered an opinion one way or the other.

"I don't know," Kate said. "He's very good-looking, but he knows he is. And he certainly seems to love you, and…no, I don't know what it is. He just seems too good to be true, somehow, as though he's acting a part. Just make sure you really love him before you agree to marry him, that's all. Don't let him rush you into anything."

Kate was right, Joanne thought later when she was alone again. I mustn't let him rush me. If he loves me, he'll understand.

The next evening she told him that she thought it was a

bit soon to be talking of marriage, that she wanted to wait for a while. To her immense relief he was absolutely fine about it, saying that while he was sure she was the only girl for him, he wanted her to be as sure about him.

He was just wonderful.

The following Friday, at the end of a lovely meal in an expensive candlelit restaurant, the waiter came over with a bottle of champagne, two crystal glasses and an ice bucket. Steve waited until the waiter had opened the bottle and poured for them, and then he lifted his glass and looked at Joanne, his eyes alight with love and anticipation.

"Cheers," he said.

Joanne raised her glass and touched it to his.

"Cheers," she responded. "What are we celebrating?" She took a sip of the fizzy contents. She had never drunk champagne before; it tasted sweet and sharp at the same time and the bubbles went up her nose, making her cough. When she looked back at Steve he was smiling at her. In front of her on the table was a small square velvet-covered box.

"What is it?" she asked.

"Open it and see," he said.

She opened it. Sitting inside on a white satin cushion was a solitaire diamond ring. The diamond seemed huge to her; it flashed and sparkled in the candlelight.

Incredibly, her first reaction was one of horror. This was an engagement ring. Engagement meant a promise to marry, and she had told him she wanted to wait for a while before making any decision. She looked up at him, saw the disappointment flicker across his face at her lack of pleasure, and felt guilty.

"Don't you like it?" he asked.

"Oh, Steve," she replied, "of course I do. It's beautiful. I just wasn't expecting it, that's all. I mean, I haven't even met your parents yet."

"Oh, don't worry about that. They'll love you. How

could they not?" Steve said, his eyes shining. "I know you said you needed to think about it, but I just wanted to be sure that you were mine. We don't have to get married until you're ready. I won't pressure you or anything."

Joanne looked back at the ring and took it out of the box.

"God, Steve," she said. "It must have cost a fortune."

He waved his hand dismissively.

"You deserve the best," he said. "Try it on."

She placed it carefully on her ring finger. It was just a little too big. She looked across at him and smiled, the joy at receiving such a fantastic present from a man who so clearly worshipped her overwhelming any traces of unease.

"We can get it altered to fit. That's no problem," Steve said. "Say you'll wear it, for me."

"Of course I will," she replied. "I don't know what to say." She raised her hand, and tiny rainbows sparked from her finger. He reached across for her hand, enfolding it tenderly in his.

"I love you," Steve said softly, "so much."

"I love you too," she replied.

It was the first time she had said the words to him, and right then she meant them with all her heart.

CHAPTER THREE

After the unexpected presentation of the engagement ring, Steve waited a whole month before he started tentatively suggesting they might want to set a date for the wedding. Joanne put her foot down and insisted that she was too young; she wanted to finish her A levels before she even thought about marriage. She was very happy as she was, she said. There was no need to rush things. Steve used every tactic he could think of to try to persuade her into setting a date, but Joanne, with Kate's secret moral support, stood firm against all his declarations of undying love and emotional blackmail, and was proud of herself for doing so. As much as she loved Steve, when she was with him she felt as though she was on a runaway train; she had to put the brakes on, give herself time to think things through and be sure that she was doing the right thing.

Then her father found out that she was secretly studying for her A levels, and everything changed.

He had met Sheila Bradley in the supermarket, and Sheila had innocently asked Jim to pass on her best wishes to Joanne, and her hopes that the exams would go well. Jim had gone ballistic when he got home and had told Joanne in no uncertain terms that she could either give up her studies or find herself somewhere else to live.

Joanne, distraught, ran to Steve in floods of tears. She couldn't afford to rent a flat on her wages, she said; she'd have to give up her studies, and she was doing so well, her tutor had given her an A in her last assignment. All her hopes for a fulfilling career were crumbling to dust.

Steve listened patiently to her, letting her sit on his knee and soak his shirt with tears, while he gently stroked her hair until her sobs gave way to muffled sniffles and she began to feel embarrassed that she had collapsed so completely.

"There is one solution," he said, after he'd dried her eyes and made her a cup of hot chocolate heavily laced with brandy. "You could marry me. I'm earning enough to support you through your A levels and university too, if that's what you want."

"I couldn't ask you to do that," she sniffed. "It wouldn't be fair."

"I love you," he said simply. "I want you to be happy. Marry me. Then you can do whatever you want."

She agreed. It seemed to her that she had no other option. And she had no reason not to marry Steve, apart from a deep-rooted nagging feeling that he was too good for her. He was gorgeous, intelligent, dynamic and confident. He couldn't possibly love her as much as he said he did. She wasn't worthy of this much devotion.

There was something wrong, but she couldn't put her finger on it. Maybe it was just that she didn't recognise a good thing when she saw it. Any other girl would be ecstatic to be asked to marry such a wonderful man. She was living in a fairy tale; she should just go along with it, get married and live happily ever after.

The wedding was a quiet one, attended only by close family on both sides. Steve was unhappy about this; he had wanted a huge wedding, with a Rolls Royce bringing his expensively dressed bride to the flower-bedecked church thronged with hundreds of well-wishers. This would be followed by a four-course banquet for three hundred, an overnight stay in a four-star hotel for him and his bride, and a honeymoon abroad.

But Jim Maddock had made it very clear that he had no intention of funding such a ridiculously extravagant waste of money, and Steve, overriding Joanne's tentatively worded desire for a small affair, had gone straight from her parents to his, livid with rage at Jim's attitude, only to be told by them that they too thought a modest wedding would be more appropriate. It was nothing to do with cost, they insisted; they just didn't want to financially embarrass the Maddocks, and anyway, neither family was religious, so what was the point of an expensive and vulgar church wedding? Small weddings were so much the vogue nowadays in any case, Susan Harris told her son.

Joanne had no idea what the latest fashion in weddings was, but she agreed with her mother-in-law to be. She didn't want Edward and Susan Harris to pay out a great deal of money for their youngest son to marry a working-class girl from a council estate, when it was clear they thought he could have done much better for himself. They didn't voice their feelings aloud, of course; but every time Susan Harris addressed Joanne, she spoke condescendingly, using overly simple vocabulary; and Edward Harris didn't think her worthy of attention at all, ignoring her as much as possible.

She disliked Steve's mother and father; she suspected Edward Harris of being a bully. He was a police inspector, and no doubt used to intimidating suspects at work, he continued the practice at home. He resembled a verbal bulldozer, using his commanding voice to good effect, taking over conversations and stating his opinions as though they were law.

His wife Susan was a snob, peppering her conversation with prices. When Joanne had politely expressed admiration for their beautiful detached house on her first visit, she had been inundated; the wallpaper was £20 a roll, the lounge carpet had cost over £2000, and as for the suite, well, their Mercedes had cost less! Joanne reminded herself daily that she was marrying Steve, not his family, and that in doing so she would escape from her own far-from-perfect parents.

Although the wedding was finally held in the register office in Manchester, and the meal, though excellent, had been for fifty guests rather than three hundred, Steve insisted on paying for them to stay in a four-star hotel on their wedding night, and they did have a honeymoon abroad.

They went to Tenerife for two weeks, and it was wonderful. Joanne had never been abroad before and found everything fascinating, to Steve's amusement. She was apprehensive about flying, and had gripped his hand tightly as the plane roared down the runway, but once they were airborne she forget her fear in the excitement of watching the patchwork of fields and tiny houses as the plane ascended until the landscape was swallowed up by white and silver-grey clouds that looked solid enough to walk on.

The hotel was large and welcoming, and their second-floor room had a balcony which looked out on to the swimming pool below. In the distance the sea sparkled, an impossible shade of turquoise blue. Joanne ran straight to the French windows and flung them open, raising her face to the afternoon sunlight.

"It's wonderful!" she cried, thrilled. "Come and look!"

Steve dropped the suitcases on the tiled floor and sat on the king-size bed, bouncing up and down a little.

"I'd rather test this out," he suggested, but Joanne didn't hear; she was leaning over the balcony to watch the people splashing in the pool below. A waiter carrying a tray of glasses looked up and smiled at her, and she waved to him, exhilarated. The water looked cool and inviting, and Joanne wondered if she would ever have the courage to wear the micro bikini Steve had bought for her, in front of all these people.

She felt his arms slide round her waist as he came up behind her, and he rested his chin on the top of her head as he looked at the view.

"Do you fancy a swim before dinner?" she asked, leaning back into him.

"I fancy something else more," he murmured, his hands

moving up to cup her breasts. Her nipples hardened immediately in response, and she felt a delicious languor flood through her body.

Their wedding night had been perfect. Joanne had been exhausted after the emotional turmoil of the day. All she had really wanted to do when she got into bed was sleep. She didn't feel she could face the further ordeal of losing her virginity.

But Steve had other plans, and had expertly kissed and caressed her until she forgot all about her fatigue and apprehensions and had just wanted to feel him inside her, to be part of him and know that he was part of her, forever. He had been tender and gentle, and had held back until he was sure she was ready before entering her slowly, a little at a time.

He had never had a virgin before and was almost as nervous as she was, although he didn't show it. Her orgasm, when it came, took her by surprise. She had never known it was possible to feel such incredible, mind-blowing pleasure. Afterwards they had lain together, wrapped in each others arms, and he had talked about the day, re-working it through his perspective until she realised it had, in fact, been wonderful after all.

"I don't know if I can," she said now as he led her from the balcony towards the bed, feathering tiny kisses up her neck and making her shiver with delicious anticipation. "I'm still a bit sore from last night," she admitted, blushing.

She felt his lips curve into a smile against her hair.

"That's all right," he said. "There are lots of other ways to have fun."

Joanne didn't get any dinner that evening. Nor did she go for a swim. But she was initiated into the dark and delightful mysteries of oral sex.

The first week of their holiday flew by. They spent their time strolling along the beach, lazing by the pool, enjoying romantic candlelit dinners, and dancing the night away in the hotel club. Steve's skin turned a lovely golden-brown in the sun, which emphasised his sculpted physique, and his hair developed streaks of pale blond. He was the most handsome man in the world, and Joanne knew she was not the only person who thought that. She saw the way the other women watched him as he swam lazily across the pool, and still found it difficult to believe that he had chosen her.

She couldn't believe that she could have been so stupid as to be unsure about marrying him. He bent over backwards to satisfy her every whim, and showered her with so many compliments, he made her feel that she really was pretty after all.

In the second week they hired a car for a few days and went off to explore the island. They went to Playa de las Americas, a town teeming with tourists, where Joanne, encouraged by Steve, bought a skimpy dress that she was sure she'd never have the courage to wear. They drove to Santiago del Teide and took a boat ride beneath the incredible eight-hundred-metre cliffs, aptly named Los Gigantes, which plunged straight into the glorious azure-blue sea. And they ascended the volcanic Mount Teide, gasping a little in the thin air as they speculated on what they would do if it erupted at that moment.

"It hasn't erupted properly since 1909," Steve said, his nose buried in the guidebook they'd picked up in Las Americas, "but it could go again at any time."

Joanne shivered, not just because of the temperature. It would be terrible to die now, just when she'd begun to truly enjoy life. A little film of a perfect future played in her mind. Steve would become a specialist decorator as he wished, and she would be a counsellor to the stars. They would move to London, or even America, and would live in a gilded baroque mansion, all the interiors designed by Steve, where she would see her famous clients in a spacious office overlooking acres of gardens. A peacock would strut majestically around the lawns, crying mournfully for its mate, and…

"So what do you think?" Steve said, breaking into her thoughts. He had thrown the guidebook down on the ground and moved closer to her. He laid his hand on her knee, and walked his fingers slowly up her leg.

"What do I think about what?" she asked, dragging herself back to the present. His hand moved higher, disappearing under her skirt. He grinned, his blue eyes sparkling.

"I don't think we'll qualify officially for the mile-high club," he said. "You have to do it in a plane for that. But technically speaking, we're well over a mile above sea level." His free arm curled round her body and his hand slid under her blouse, cupping one breast. Joanne blushed scarlet as she realised his intentions.

"We can't do it here!" she protested, placing her hand over the one on her leg and arresting its progress momentarily.

"Why not? There's no one around," he said. This was true. They had seen no one for at least five minutes. Even so, they were on the main track to the crater and someone could come around the bend at any moment. His hand continued its progress, brushing aside her lacy panties. Joanne felt a thrill of arousal, which was immediately quenched by the realisation that he was deadly serious in his intentions.

"No," she said, gripping hold of his wrist to pull his hand away from her crotch. "Steve, we can't! Someone might see us!"

"So what?" he replied laughingly. "It'll add a bit of spice."

Her tugging on his wrist was having no effect at all. He slid one finger up inside her, and she tried to squirm away from him. His other hand played with her nipple, which hardened automatically. Any moment now, she was sure, he would move over on top of her, and if someone came along the path…

"No!" she cried, standing up abruptly and dislodging his hand in the process.

"Why not?" he asked. "You want to, I can tell you do."

"No, I don't," she replied. "Not here, in public. It's not right. Children come up here too. Can you imagine if they came round the corner and saw us....like that! We might be arrested."

"Oh, for fuck's sake," he said angrily. She flinched at his casual use of a word she hated. "Where's your spirit of adventure? I thought I'd married a proper woman, not some bloody Victorian prude. We're not going to be arrested for screwing. Everyone does it."

"Not on top of a mountain in broad daylight, with tourists all over the place, they don't!" she retorted hotly.

"Well, if you think I'm going to be satisfied only ever doing it in bed with the lights out," he said, "you've got another think coming. Christ, I'll be bored shitless in a month."

He got up and stalked off down the track without a backward glance. Joanne rearranged her clothing, picked up the guidebook, and walked slowly after him. The beauty of the day was gone. The air was cold, the volcanic landscape suddenly grey and barren. He was being unfair, she thought as she picked her way carefully down the rocky path. She didn't just want to do it in bed with the lights out. In fact, they hadn't. They'd only been married for ten days, and already they'd made love in the bath twice, and once on the floor of the room when they'd been too aroused even to make it the few feet to the bed.

She looked at him as he marched down the path without a backward glance, petulance written in every line of his body. Could he have fallen out of love with her that quickly? Had he already tired of her? Was that possible? Even the thought of him not loving her was too unbearable to contemplate. Her life would be empty without him.

"Steve!" she cried, suddenly panicked. He hesitated momentarily, then carried on. She tore down the track after him, heedless of the treacherous surface. She had to catch up with him, had to make him understand that she hadn't been rejecting him when she refused him. As she reached him her feet skidded from under her and she would have fallen if he hadn't instinctively reached out and grabbed her arm. As soon as she'd regained her footing, he released her. She felt bereft.

"I'm sorry," she said breathlessly. "I didn't mean to upset you. I just… I just couldn't…"

"That's all right," he interrupted in a tone which clearly implied the opposite. "It doesn't matter."

They drove back to the hotel in silence, Steve focussing doggedly ahead at the road, Joanne staring unseeingly out of the window and wishing she was dead. A lump of misery churned heavily in her stomach.

When they got to the room he went straight into the bathroom for a shower, leaving Joanne sitting on the bed in a haze of despair. Her wonderful future had vanished. They would spend the next four days in Tenerife like strangers. Then they would fly home, and he would leave her. He could easily find someone else, someone more adventurous, a real woman who would be delighted to have sex anywhere he wanted her to. They had met no one else all the way down the path. If she'd let him have his way on Mount Teide nobody would have seen them after all, and everything would be all right. She had to put aside her inhibitions and try harder if she wanted to keep him.

He came out of the bathroom, a towel wrapped round his waist. He was like a golden Greek statue, beautiful beyond belief. She sat on the bed looking at him, and then the tears welled up and he shimmered out of focus.

"We'll be late for dinner if you don't get a move on," he said coldly. She stared at him for another moment, then threw herself at him in despair, nearly knocking him off balance.

"I'm sorry," she wept. "I'm so, so, sorry. I wouldn't hurt you for the world."

He listened to her half-hysterical apologies for a short time, and then his arm came up and wrapped itself around her.

"Hey, hey, calm down," he said gently. "It's all right. I was a bit angry, that's all. I thought you'd think it was fun too. It's OK."

He cradled her in his arms and murmured soothing nonsense until she calmed down enough to get changed. Then they went down to dinner.

She wanted to talk about it, to clear the air. That was what she had always done with Kate when they'd had a disagreement. But Steve wouldn't let her.

"It's over now," he said firmly when she tried to broach the subject. "There's no need to talk about it. Forget it."

But later that evening when he went to order drinks at the bar, he spent a long time chatting to the attractive barmaid. And when they danced a slow dance together later, instead of smiling into her eyes as he usually did, he looked speculatively around the room and his hand on her waist was cool and impersonal.

It was after one when they got back to the room. Joanne was tired, and the air in the room was sultry and hot. She went to the French windows and opening them, walked out on to the balcony. A group of teenagers were enjoying a late night swim, and their shouts of tipsy laughter drifted up to her. A thin partition separated their balcony from the one next door, and Joanne listened carefully for a moment. Nothing. The elderly couple in the next room had probably been in bed for hours. She steeled herself.

"Come here," she called casually back into the room. Steve had started to undress for bed, and padded over in bare feet to join her. He looked over the railing.

"They look as though they're having fun," he said. "Do you want to go down for a swim?" His voice had an edge of contempt, she thought, as though he felt she wouldn't even have the guts to swim in a hotel pool after dark.

"No," she said, hooking her fingers into the waistband of his jeans and pulling him towards her. "I was thinking of something a little more private."

It had been horrible, Joanne thought later in bed. Steve was asleep, his arm flung over her waist. She could feel the heat emanating from him and she felt sweaty and uncomfortable.

The marble tiles on the balcony had been hard and bruising as he'd thrust excitedly into her, and her head had banged painfully against the railings at one point. She had nearly died when the couple next door, far from being asleep, had decided to share a bottle of wine on their balcony. She could hear their every word, and was sure they would hear Steve sucking greedily at her nipples.

She had to force herself not to freeze. He would notice if she did, and would know that she was not adventurous at all, that she was only doing this to humour him. Then he would be *really* angry, and would probably never speak to her again.

He had grinned when he heard the voices coming from inches away, and she had smiled up at him as he'd thrust even harder into her, aroused by the presence of strangers. She had not been aroused at all.

She wanted their lovemaking to be private and intimate, not a public show. It made her feel cheap, and she had remained unmoved as he grunted his way to his climax, although she tightened her legs around him as he came, and arched her neck backwards so he would think she had also reached orgasm.

But it had been worth it. For the rest of the honeymoon he was as attentive and affectionate towards her as ever.

She had learned something important. If she wanted to keep Steve, she must not deny him sex. That was the quickest way to lose a man, and her future depended on keeping him now.

Once the honeymoon was over they returned home, and life started to take on a routine. Steve's parents had put down a deposit on a house for them, and Joanne was ecstatic. She'd visualised them having to live in a rented flat, or even worse, with his parents until they could find somewhere. To have her own three-bedroomed semi in the suburbs with a garden front and back, was a dream come true. Every week when she got paid she would go off to the market and buy some small item to make the place more homely; a lamp, a couple of cushions, a colourful rug to put in front of the fire. Steve was less satisfied.

"It'll take us years to furnish it properly," he said moodily as he sat on the lumpy secondhand sofa and frowned at the hideous 1970s flowered wallpaper in the lounge. "Dad could at least have bought us some decent furniture. God knows, he earns enough."

"We're OK," Joanne said. "We've got all the basics, and we can get the other things gradually. It'll be fun building a home together."

"Fun?" he answered disparagingly. "Is that what you call fun, scrimping and scraping for years to buy bloody curtains and bedspreads?"

All of a sudden it didn't seem like fun at all. She sighed.

"It's all right for you," he continued. "You're used to having nothing. *You* probably think this is luxury. But I want something better."

"So do I!" she said, stung by this unfair accusation. "But we've only been married a few weeks. It takes time to build a home. And at least we've got each other. That's the most important thing."

"Yes," he said unenthusiastically.

Was he already regretting marrying her? It seemed so, but there was nothing she could do about it. She couldn't suddenly produce a houseful of lovely furniture. He would just have to be patient.

But Steve had other ideas. On the following Friday Joanne came home from work to find her husband already home and waiting for her with an excited expression on his face. He swept her up in a crushing embrace and swung her round the hall.

"Don't take your coat off," he said happily. "We're going window shopping."

Their first stop was a furniture store, where he insisted they try out the various three-piece suites and beds, just to see which ones they'd buy if they could. This was followed by a visit to a carpet shop and a decorating store, where, caught up in his fantasy, she chose one of the most expensive wallpapers in the shop, a silky cream brocade-effect paper. She couldn't understand why he was so euphoric about looking at things they'd never be able to afford in a million years, but if he was happy then she was too.

A week later she came home to a house shrouded in dust sheets and a trio of paint-spattered men drinking mugs of coffee in the kitchen. The sunflower-patterned paper in the lounge was gone, replaced by beautiful cream brocade. While she was staring at it, Steve came barrelling down the stairs.

"What do you think?" he said. His face was alight with happiness.

"It's beautiful," she said uncertainly. "But we can't afford this."

He waved a hand dismissively.

"Don't worry about it," he said. "I've got a big contract coming up. Can you take Wednesday off?"

"Wednesday?" she said, her brow still furrowed. "It's a bit short notice, but I might be able to. Why?"

"They want to deliver the furniture in the morning, and I've got too much on to take any time off," he explained.

"Oh God, Steve, you've not ordered all that furniture we looked at as well, have you?" she said, aghast. "How are we going to pay for it?"

"I've got a credit card," he said. "I'll put it on that. I'll be able to pay it off easily in a couple of months."

"But the suite alone was over a thousand pounds!" she cried. "It'll take us years to pay for it!"

"Will you stop worrying about the bloody money?" he said. "I told you I'd sort it out. Trust me. I did it for you. I know you want a lovely house. I thought you'd be pleased."

There was no point in arguing with him, in telling him that she didn't care about how the house looked as long as she had him, that it was he who'd wanted all this stuff they couldn't afford. It was too late. So she made the best of it and tried not to think about the credit card bill and the interest that began to accrue when the hoped-for contract fell through and he couldn't pay it all off.

She stopped buying little things on the market and started to put all her wages aside to try to stem the ever-increasing tide of debt as he added a dining table, chairs, a huge television and stereo system and various other items he considered essential, to the card. He seemed to have no restraint where money was concerned. If he wanted it, he bought it.

Joanne had been brought up to believe that if you wanted it, you saved for it or did without, and while she recognised that that idea was perhaps a bit archaic, Steve's apparent disregard for debt frightened her. But he was so happy surrounded by beautiful things that she didn't have the heart to voice her concerns. Once the house was completely furnished he would stop impulse-buying. They would pay for everything somehow.

In August Joanne found out that she had passed her Psychology A level with flying colours. Steve took her out to an expensive restaurant to celebrate. She was bubbling with happiness, her eyes shining in the candlelight as she outlined her plans for the future.

"I thought I'd enrol to do English in September," she said. "If I can get an A grade in that as well, I might be able to get into Manchester University with just the two A levels."

"You still want to go to uni, do you?" Steve said, leaning over to fill her wine glass.

"You know I do," Joanne said, surprised. "You've always known that."

"Well, yes," Steve admitted. "But you don't need a degree now we're married. It's not as though you need to escape from home any more, is it?"

"No," she replied. "But I didn't want to go to uni just to get away from home. I want to do something worthwhile with my life."

"And you think being my wife isn't worthwhile?" The question was put lightly, but Joanne sensed the tension underneath and realised she would have to choose her words carefully if the evening was not to be ruined.

"Of course it is!" she said, reaching across the table to capture his hand. "Marrying you was the best decision I've ever made! But I want…."

More.

"…to make you proud of me," she continued. "I don't want to be an accounts clerk all my life. I want to have a fulfilling job, one that pays well. Then, with both of us earning well, we'll be able to move to a bigger house, one with a swimming pool. And a sauna!" She couldn't care less about having a pool or a sauna, but she knew Edward and Susan Harris wanted one, and if Steve could get there first he'd be ecstatic. "Please, Steve, it means a lot to me," she finished.

To her relief, he squeezed her hand and smiled.

"If it's what you want, of course you can go to university," he said. "How could I deny you anything?"

Joanne was shattered by the time she got home on the evening of her first English class. She had worked all day, rushed off to buy a notebook and some pens, and had just managed to grab a quick coffee before dashing off to the college. When she came out at eight thirty, it was to see her bus disappearing up the road into the distance. She had to wait over half an hour for the next one and it was nearly ten o'clock when she finally arrived home.

"Hi!" she called brightly as she hung up her coat in the hall and went through to the lounge, where Steve was sitting in front of the television. "Have you eaten? I'm just going to make myself a sandwich."

"No, I haven't eaten," he replied tightly, flicking the television off. He turned round in his chair to face her. "Where the hell have you been?"

"At night school. I told you I'd be late tonight."

"No you didn't," he said. "You go to night school on a Thursday, not Monday. Where have you really been?"

"Nowhere. The psychology class was on Thursday, but the English class is on Monday, six thirty till eight thirty," she explained, puzzled. He knew this; she'd talked it through with him. She'd told him only this morning that she'd be late. He'd wished her good luck before he'd gone out.

"I've been worried sick," he said. "How do you think I felt when I came home and you weren't here? The house was cold, no meal ready for me. I expect better than that when I've been out at work all day!" His voice started to rise, and Joanne felt the familiar churning start in her stomach. "I rang work and they told me you'd already left."

"I *did* tell you, Steve, honestly I did," she insisted.

"No you bloody didn't! I thought you'd had an accident or something! And now you waltz in at ten o'clock and start calling me a liar." He stood up. "Eight thirty, you just said the class ended. It doesn't take an hour and a half to get home from Manchester. What were you up to?" His face was livid with anger.

"I wasn't up to anything! I missed the bus, that's all," she said. "I'll leave a couple of minutes earlier next week. And I'll put something for you to heat up in the oven. I'm sorry," she added. "Do you want me to cook you something now?" She started to turn towards the kitchen, but he reached out and grabbed her hard by the arm, pulling her towards him. She squealed with shock.

"I'll tell you what I want!" he spat at her, shaking her. "I want what any man wants after a hard day's work. I want my wife at home and food on the table. That's what I want. It's not much to ask when I've given you all this." He swept his free arm around the room.

It was you who wanted all this, she thought, *not me. And I'm paying for it, too.* But she didn't dare voice the thought. His grip on her arm was like a vice, and she was uncomfortably aware of how enormous he was. She had always felt protected by his size before. Now, for the first time, she felt threatened by it.

"Steve, you're hurting me," she said. "I'll be home earlier next week, I promise."

"You just make sure you are," he said, "or you can forget this night class of yours altogether." He released her arm suddenly, pushing her backwards in the process so that she fell onto the sofa. Then he walked from the room and she heard his feet banging up the stairs and the bedroom door slam.

What was wrong with him? She *had* told him she was going to be late that morning. She was sure she had. Or had she imagined it? She must have done. He wouldn't have been so angry if he'd known where she was. He was concerned for her safety, because he loved her. She rubbed her throbbing arm. He didn't know his own strength. He must have been *really* worried.

The next evening he brought her a bunch of flowers and said he was sorry he'd got mad at her, but she'd made him so worried because of her thoughtlessness in not telling him she was going to be late. Was she all right?

She was all right, of course she was. Next week she would leave him a note. Next week she would have a meal bubbling in the pressure cooker for him to come home to. Next week she would not miss the bus.

After that, everything went well. The debts mounted up, which didn't seem to bother Steve at all, and Joanne, not wishing to provoke him into another outburst, said nothing. Then he landed a contract to redecorate a small stately home, and he was over the moon.

"I'll have to work longer hours for a while," he said. "But there are pillars in the hall that need that marble effect, scagliola, remember I told you about that? And there's gilding to be done as well. This could make my name, if I do a good job. The client's got a lot of influence."

In his wild enthusiasm he reminded her of an excited little boy. She was really pleased for him and tried to find meals to cook that could be successfully reheated, as she never knew what time he would come home, and he always got a bit grumpy if his meal wasn't waiting for him. She listened for hours as he talked about the technical details of special finishes, and tried not to mind that he hadn't asked her anything about the books she had to read for her A level.

At least she got more time to study while Steve was working late, and she enjoyed the peace of not having the television mumbling away all the time. When he came in, the first thing he always did was flick it on, after which it would stay on all night, even if they were not watching it. Joanne got a lot more work done without its distracting presence.

All in all, she was happy. Much happier than she'd been living with her parents, although she missed Kate creeping into her room for a late-night chat. But Kate did come round to visit more often now that Steve was working late. They chatted about their parents, about schoolwork and exams. When Steve came home he often brought her a little present, flowers, chocolates. Work was going well. Their sex life was wonderful. Life was good.

* * *

Joanne stood waiting for the bus in the pouring rain. It had rained non-stop for three days and the drains had overflowed so that every passing car sent a spray of cold dirty water across the pavement, soaking her legs. Preoccupied with her thoughts, and with her coat collar pulled up around her face, she didn't realise that the person in the silver Mercedes that had stopped by the kerbside was trying to attract her attention until the occupant actually got out of the car.

"Would you like a lift home?" he called.

She looked up, startled, to see her employer's kindly face smiling at her.

"It's out of your way, isn't it?" she said.

"Not much. Come on, get in, it's horrible out here."

She hurried gratefully across and opened the passenger door, then hesitated.

"I'll get your lovely car wet," she said worriedly.

"That's OK, I'll put the blowers on and you and the car'll be dry by the time you get home," he replied.

She got in and shut the door, and the car moved smoothly off into the traffic. It was lovely and warm. Water trickled from her hair down her face, and she brushed it away with her hand.

"It's very kind of you," she said, smiling. She saw a lot more of Mr MacDonald since she had become an accounts clerk, and they got on well together.

"Not at all," he replied.

They drove in silence for a short time and Joanne was sinking back into her thoughts, which were far from pleasant, when Mr MacDonald suddenly spoke again.

"Are you enjoying your work as an accounts clerk?" he asked.

"Yes, it's more interesting than I thought it would be, to be honest," she answered. She tried to think of something more to say, but was too preoccupied to engage in small talk.

"How are your studies going?" he asked.

"Very well," she said. She had to make an effort. "I found the language of Shakespeare really difficult to understand at first, but now I love it. I got a B-plus for my last essay."

"Good. Well done," Mr MacDonald said. There was another short silence, while she frantically tried to think of a topic of conversation. Everything seemed such an effort today.

"Only you seem to have been a bit down the last few days," he ventured before she could speak. "I wondered if it was a work-related problem."

"No," she said worriedly. She thought she'd hidden her

mood well. Obviously not. "No, it's nothing to do with work," she continued. "I didn't realise I'd seemed depressed."

"Not depressed exactly, but not your usual cheerful self." Her boss smiled. "Don't worry, no one else has mentioned it. I make a point of keeping an eye on my workforce. If they have a problem, I like to know. Especially if there's something I can do about it."

He waited a moment.

"Is there anything I can do?" he prompted gently. "Even if it's only to listen, in confidence?"

She glanced up at him. His eyes were full of genuine concern for her. For a moment she was tempted to tell him what was wrong. Just sharing the burden with someone else would help her get it into proportion. And he was a kind man, like a father figure, or a priest. She was sure he'd be understanding. But she couldn't do it. Not when she hadn't told Steve yet. He should be the first to know. She smiled, but her eyes were sad.

"Thank you," she said. "It's just…it's private, that's all. It's not that I don't trust you, or anything, it's just…"

He took her hand and squeezed it briefly, then let go.

"That's all right, I understand," he said. "But the offer stands, if you want to talk at any time."

She was so lucky to have an employer like him, she thought as she got out of the car a few minutes later. She was sure he'd be supportive when she did tell him, which was a consolation. She waved as he drove off, then turned, surprised to see Steve standing in the doorway waiting for her. She would make the dinner, she resolved; then she would tell him.

"Hello!" she said. "I didn't expect you to be home this early." She stood on tiptoe to kiss him and he moved aside to let her pass into the hall.

"Obviously," he said, closing the front door and standing with his back against it. "Who was the man in the car?"

"Mr MacDonald," Joanne replied, taking her coat off and hanging it up. "He saw me standing in the rain, so he offered me a lift home. I wish they'd put a proper shelter up at the bus stop."

"How long have you been seeing him, then?" Steve asked.

"I see him nearly every day," she said, puzzled. "He's my boss."

"OK, let me put it another way, then. How long have you been screwing him?"

Joanne had been turning towards the kitchen to get the evening meal ready, but now she turned back. He was serious. How could he be serious?

"Steve," she said. "He's old enough to be my grandfather. He's married, with four children and ten grandchildren."

"Tell you all this in bed, did he?" said Steve, moving away from the door. "Isn't he the bloke who gave you money on your birthday?"

"What the hell are you talking about?" Joanne said. She could feel her temper rising at his ridiculous accusation. She had enough on her plate right now without this.

"He's been trying to get in your knickers ever since you started work, hasn't he? Giving you money, promoting you…"

"He promoted me because I'm good at my job," she interrupted. "And he gave me money for my eighteenth birthday because he's a considerate man." She went into the lounge, and he followed her.

"I'm sure he's very considerate," he sneered. "What else has he bought you?"

"He hasn't bought me anything. What's wrong with you?" she asked.

"What's wrong with me?" he shouted suddenly, making her jump. "Nothing. I've just found out my wife is screwing her boss while I'm out working hard to buy her all the things she wants, that's all. Got more money than me, has he?"

"Probably, yes," she answered. His eyes widened; he hadn't expected that response. "But even if he was the richest man in England, I wouldn't screw him. I don't fancy him, for one thing. I'm married, for another. And I have more respect for myself than to sell my body for money!"

"I don't know, you sold it to me so you could carry on doing your A levels," he said. "Sold yourself pretty cheap there, didn't you?"

She stared at him.

"I married you because I loved you," she said, "and I thought you loved me. If you were lying to me, you tell me now, and I'll go."

"Go? Where? Your dad threw you out, remember? Who else would have you if you left?"

His voice was mocking, scornful, and something in her snapped. She hadn't lost her temper since she married him. She'd walked on eggshells for months, bent over backwards to please him. She deserved better than this, to be falsely accused of prostituting herself for money. She made to walk past him but he moved to the side, blocking her exit.

"Where do you think you're going?" he said. "I haven't finished yet."

"You haven't?" she answered hotly. "Well, I have. I'm sick of it. You don't work hard all day to buy things for me. I never wanted a huge TV and fancy furniture. You bought this stuff for yourself. I work all day as well, remember? And when I come home I have to carry on, cleaning and cooking for you while you sit on your backside and watch TV all night. Then you accuse me of selling myself to my boss for twenty pounds and a lift home! And you expect me to be grateful?"

His hand shot out like lightning, his palm cracking hard across her face. She staggered backwards a couple of steps, then her knees buckled under her. Stars danced across her vision and she tried to shake her head to clear it, but he had hold of her hair and was twisting her head back so that she had to look up at him.

"I could have had anyone, anyone I'd wanted. There are loads of beautiful women out there, just gagging for it. You think anyone else would fancy you? Christ! Look at yourself, for God's sake! That old fart only wants you because he feels sorry for you!" he said, his voice laced with contempt.

The pain was excruciating. Joanne lifted her hand toward her head, trying to ease the pressure on her scalp, but he grabbed her wrist with his free hand. "You listen to me, you bitch," he said viciously. "You're married to *me*. You ever fuck anyone else and I'll kill you." He released her and stood over her for a moment, breathing heavily, his fists clenched. He was waiting for her to say something, to give any sign of defiance, to give him an excuse to hit her again. She stayed silent, her head bowed, the left side of her face burning. After what seemed an eternity, he turned and left the room.

Joanne stayed where she was. She couldn't think properly. Her face was throbbing, but she didn't dare go to the bathroom to examine the damage. She had no idea where Steve was. She levered herself up on to the chair, her legs shaking with shock and disbelief. He couldn't possibly believe that she was having an affair with her boss! Could he? Surely he wasn't that insecure?

It was true that he'd married her to get her away from her parents. No, it wasn't; he'd wanted to marry her anyway, before that. Why, if he could have anyone he wanted? What was she going to do now? He was right, she didn't have anywhere to go, and she couldn't leave anyway, not now. She sat hunched up on the chair, shivering with misery and apprehension.

If he could get so angry because she'd accepted a lift home from her boss, what would he say when she told him she was pregnant, when they'd agreed not to start a family for at least two years?

CHAPTER FOUR

Amy was born in February 1985 after a prolonged and painful labour. Joanne had never known anything like it, and vowed at the time that this baby would be an only child. Finally, completely exhausted, her hair hanging in lank sweaty ribbons round her face, Joanne slumped back onto the pillows, her body aching unbearably from the effort of giving birth. Then she heard the thin wail of her daughter protesting feebly at being torn from her safe, dark sanctuary, and the cry cut through the pain and tiredness, and she found herself trying to sit up, to get a sight of this miracle that she and Steve had wrought.

When Amy, hastily washed and wrapped in a towel, was laid in Joanne's arms, she knew that this was the most perfect moment of her life, and that whatever happened to her throughout the years to come, she would never, never be as happy as she was right now. The baby mewled slightly, her eyes tightly closed, and Joanne felt tears of pure joy roll down her cheeks.

Then she remembered, and looked up at Steve apprehensively. He had stayed with his wife through her labour, stroking her hand and muttering endearments, telling her how beautiful she was, although she knew that she must never have looked so hideous in her life. He had been wonderful, and all the nurses had commented on how lucky she was to have such an attentive husband, when so many couldn't bear to be in the delivery room at all. He gazed down at his first child impassively, and Joanne couldn't ascertain from his expression what he was thinking.

"I'm sorry," she said. "You wanted a boy."

"It doesn't matter," he answered. "She's beautiful." He looked up at her and smiled, but she saw the flicker of disappointment in his eyes and her surge of joy trickled away.

When Joanne had finally summoned up the courage to tell Steve that she was pregnant, far from being disappointed, he had astonished her by expressing absolute delight at the idea that he was soon to be a father. He had talked endlessly about all the things he was going to do with the child.

"I'll have to get the sign on the van changed," he said happily. "Stephen Harris & Son. Has a ring to it, don't you think?"

In vain Joanne had tried to point out that the baby was as likely to be a daughter as a son. He was convinced; and when his brothers had laughingly pointed out that both of them had sons, so it was his turn for the girl, he had made a considerable bet with them as to the outcome of the event.

"Boys run in the family," he said. "I'm one of three boys, my dad had five brothers. The odds are stacked in our favour."

For her own part, Joanne couldn't care less about the sex of the baby. She just wanted it out of there. In the final months of her pregnancy she had been tired and listless all the time, and had dragged herself leadenly to work each day.

"Why don't you give up work?" Steve suggested one morning when she was drooping over her breakfast, having hardly slept a wink. The baby was pressing on a nerve and she hadn't been able to find a comfortable position all night.

"I'll be all right when I get there," she said. "I like the company. It takes my mind off the aches. And we need the money." They did need the money. Steve had insisted on buying everything new for the baby, rejecting his sisters-in-laws' offers to donate the cots, prams and baby clothes that their own infants had outgrown.

"I'm not accepting handouts from them," he'd said scathingly when Joanne tentatively pointed out that it would save them a lot of money. "I'll never hear the end of it if I do."

He had spent a fortune on furniture for the spare bedroom and had decorated it in blue, as though by doing this the male gender of the baby would be ensured.

"You'll have to give up work when the baby's born, anyway. A couple of months won't make much difference," Steve pointed out as he shrugged on his jacket.

"I know," Joanne said. She didn't want to give up work. She enjoyed the feeling of independence having her own money gave her, and she had a good rapport with her colleagues, although she no longer went for a drink with them on Fridays, after Steve had repeatedly complained that she preferred her friends to him, and had started making more insinuations about her and Mr MacDonald. It had been easier to give up the Friday trip to the pub than to put up with Steve's sulkiness and jibes, which could go on for days at a time.

In the end she worked until her eighth month, and when she left was presented with a deluge of presents for the baby. Mr MacDonald had called her into his office and told her that if she wanted to return to work once the baby was a little older, she must contact him. He had presented her with a Mothercare voucher for £100, and when she protested, told her that all the management team had contributed, although she personally doubted it, as they hardly knew her.

Over the next few days in hospital Joanne had a lot of time to think. Sometimes when she woke up the birth of her perfect daughter seemed to her like a dream, and she would lean over to the little cot at the side of the bed, panicked that she would find it empty, then would sit for a while, memorising the beautiful miniature features, the tiny pursed mouth, the button nose, the hazy fuzz of blonde down covering her scalp. She was so amazing that Joanne's heart contracted with a love so powerful it was painful. *This child will be the first person in my life who truly loves me*, she thought.

No, that wasn't right. Steve loved her, she knew that. He had gone back to work straight after the birth, but swirled into the hospital for half an hour or so a day like a whirlwind, still in his work clothes, bringing flowers or fruit and regaling her with stories of how well the work on the mansion was going. Then he would disappear again, and it would only be after he was gone that Joanne would realise he'd given the baby no more than a cursory glance.

Her mother came to the hospital once, fluttering ineffectually over her granddaughter, and her in-laws visited for an uncomfortable half hour of pleasantries, during which Susan commented with satisfaction that the baby bore a remarkable resemblance to Steve. Joanne was not sure whether Susan had doubted the paternity of the child, or was just relieved that it wouldn't take after its plain working-class mother, but either way she was pleased when they left and even more pleased when they didn't return.

Kate visited every day, over the moon at being an auntie. She was fourteen and studying for her O levels, and the first time she visited she chatted merrily about her school friends whilst casting surreptitious glances at the crib.

"Do you want to hold her?" Joanne asked, amused.

Kate looked up at her sister, alarmed.

"No!" she said. "Well, yes. But she's so tiny. I don't want to hurt her."

"You won't hurt her," Joanne said. "Just make sure you support her head, that's all. Her neck isn't strong enough to take the weight."

The sight of her sister carefully lifting her tiny niece out of the cradle and holding her awkwardly in her arms, her eyes wide with wonder as she gazed rapturously at the sleeping bundle, would stay with Joanne for the rest of her life.

"Oh God," Kate whispered reverently, her eyes full of tears. "She's gorgeous."

She sat down carefully in the chair, never taking her eyes off the baby.

"You're going to call her Amy," Kate said. "It's a lovely name."

"Amy Kathryn," Joanne replied on the spur of the moment. No one else except herself had looked at the baby with such unadulterated love. Kate deserved to have her niece named after her. She would argue it out with Steve afterwards.

Joanne didn't have to argue it out with Steve. He agreed without hesitation to the baby's second name and to Kate being godmother to Amy. Joanne would have been relieved, if she hadn't realised that the reason he couldn't care less what the baby was called was because it was not the precious son he had craved.

He spent more and more time at work, and the care of their baby devolved completely onto Joanne. When she suggested that he might want to feed or bath Amy, or just hold her, he complained that he was too tired. It was Joanne's fault that he was tired, he implied. If she hadn't got pregnant and had to give up work, he wouldn't have to work such long hours now. And there were three mouths to feed.

Joanne wanted to argue that as far as she knew there had only been one virgin birth in history, and that he had urged her to give up work, had wanted her to leave before she actually needed to. But it was not worth the effort. It wouldn't make any difference anyway, and she needed all her energy to look after Amy. Joanne had never been so tired in her life.

She loved Amy desperately but she had not realised one tiny baby could cause so much work. The work she could have handled, it was the lack of sleep that sapped her spirit. Steve had complained several times that the baby had woken him up in the night, although it was always Joanne who got up to see to her, who fed her, changed her nappy and walked round and round the lounge with her until she went back to sleep.

"It's all right for you," he said grumpily. "You can sleep all day if you want. I've got to go to work."

She found herself staying awake at nights, on edge, listening for the slightest sound that indicated Amy was awake, so that she could go and attend to her before she started crying and disturbed Steve. But she couldn't sleep all day, because Steve expected the house to be immaculate at all times, his meal to be ready on the table at whatever time he walked through the door, and, once the statutory six weeks were up, he expected his conjugal rights too. He was still tender in bed, an expert lover, but Joanne was too exhausted at the end of the day to be turned on. Besides, Steve rarely touched her any more unless he wanted sex and she felt the loss of the physical affection very keenly.

Was it like this for every couple after they'd had their first child? Joanne had no way of knowing. She didn't know any other couples with small children, apart from Steve's brothers, and her pride wouldn't let her ask them. She had no friends, and realised now that she had managed somehow to become completely alienated from the world. The only time she saw people was when she went to the shops, or when she took Amy for a walk in the park in her pram. But those people were strangers; she couldn't ask them. They'd think she was mad. Maybe she was. How could she tell anyone that she, who had a handsome, hard-working husband, a beautiful baby and a lovely home, was desperately lonely?

She couldn't talk to Steve. He never asked her about her day, and when she volunteered information about Amy he listened politely for a few minutes before changing the subject. She couldn't blame him for that. He was working all day, meeting other people, having interesting experiences. It was perfectly understandable that he wouldn't want to know when Amy smiled for the first time, or when she followed Joanne's finger with her eyes. They were tiny things to him, but huge to her. Her daughter was an endless source of fascination. Everything she did seemed remarkable to Joanne.

And to Kate. If it wasn't for Kate, Joanne often thought she'd have gone mad in those first few months after Amy was born. She called round every time she got the chance, often popping in for a few minutes on her way home from school, listening attentively as Joanne related the small events that comprised her day. Changing Amy's nappy suddenly became amusing when Kate, all fingers and thumbs, insisted on learning how to do it.

"It's all right," Joanne said, highly amused by her sister's expression as she tried not to retch at the disgusting smell that arose from Amy when her nappy was removed. The baby, completely oblivious, waved her tiny arms and legs about happily. "I'll do it if it's making you feel sick."

"No, no," said Kate, determination written all over her face. "I want to do it. I'll get used to the smell, I suppose, after a while."

She carefully followed Joanne's instructions, gingerly cleaning Amy's bottom with baby wipes while Joanne disposed of the offensive nappy, then putting the clean nappy on, and she sighed with relief when the process was complete and Amy was clean and sweet-smelling again.

"That's better," she said, rubbing her nose against the top of Amy's head. "You smell of baby now. It's a lovely smell, isn't it? All sort of milky and sweet." She sat down, cradling the baby in one arm and accepting a cup of tea with the other. "How you manage to do that six or seven times a day is beyond me. Doesn't it make you throw up?"

"No, not at all," said Joanne. "Changing a nappy's nothing compared to projectile vomiting."

"Not now, please." Kate laughed. "I don't think my stomach could take it! Thank God for disposable nappies! At least you can just throw all the mess away. Can you imagine having to wash all that yucky stuff off? It must have been horrible for Mum when we were babies."

"It's different when it's your own baby," Joanne said. "You'll find out when you have one."

Kate looked up in surprise.

"Me?" she said. "No thanks. I don't ever want children. They're too much of a tie. And as for a husband…yeuk. No, I'm going to stay single, thank you all the same."

Joanne was sure she'd change her mind when the right boy came along, but didn't want to sound condescending by saying so.

"You're very good with Amy," she suggested.

"Yeah, well, that's different. She's my niece. And I can go home and leave her with you and have a life of my own. Don't you get bored, sitting here on your own all day?"

"Yes, a bit," Joanne admitted. "But I don't have much choice really. I take Amy out for a walk in her pram nearly every day now the weather's picking up."

Kate observed her sister as she moved about the room, fluffing up cushions and straightening the rug. She took in the carelessly combed hair, the dark circles under the eyes, the inability to sit and relax for more than a minute at a time. Was that a bruise on her neck, or a trick of the light?

"There's a group for single mothers every week down at the community centre," she said. "Why don't you join? It'd be company for you."

"I can't do that!" protested Joanne. "I'm not a single mother!"

"You might as well be," Kate pointed out. "I mean, he's never here, is he?"

"It's not his fault," Joanne said defensively. "He has to work longer hours now we've not got my money coming in. And when he gets home he's tired."

"Yeah, right," replied Kate. "Anyway, I don't think you *have* to be a single mother."

After Kate had gone, Joanne pondered her suggestion. It would be nice to meet other women in the same situation as herself. It was difficult being a mum for the first time. There was so much to learn and it was so important to get things right. It would be great to share stories and get tips off other mums who had more experience. Maybe they would know some exercises she could do to get back in shape, too.

The previous night Steve had cuddled up to her in bed and had gently squeezed her breasts with one hand while he stroked her thigh with the other. Joanne was deathly tired, but she told herself that it was good that he desired her, and had responded to his caresses, becoming more aroused as his fingers worked expertly inside her.

"You want to do something about your stomach," he said suddenly. "It looks like a floppy blancmange."

Her arousal drained away instantly, and it was all she could do not to push him away as he positioned himself to enter her. She felt a tear trickle down her face and gulped as she swallowed the huge lump of misery down, which he presumably had taken for her orgasm, as he came almost immediately afterwards.

In the morning she had examined herself in the mirror, eyeing the stretch marks with dismay. He was right, she thought miserably. She had thought that she was regaining her figure quite quickly, all things considered, but now she could see that she looked disgusting. She would have to make more of an effort.

But she couldn't join a single mothers' group. She might meet someone who recognised her. What would they think if they found out she had a husband? They'd assume she was unhappy in her marriage, which she wasn't. She was just tired. They both were, and it was making her weepy and him irritable. The way he'd gripped her by the neck to pull her out of his way when she was cleaning her teeth this morning, for instance, because he wanted to use the sink; he hadn't intended to bruise her, she knew. He didn't know his own strength sometimes. Everything would be better when Amy slept the nights through and he had finished this big job that meant so much to him.

Instead of going to the single mothers' club, Joanne went to the public library and borrowed some books about baby care and gentle exercise.

* * *

On the first Monday after the Easter holidays, Kate turned up at Joanne's straight from school with a large bag full of books.

"Hi, it's only me," she called cheerily as she walked straight through to the kitchen, plonking her bag in the hall on the way. "What time do you have to leave?"

"Leave?" Joanne said, bewildered. She looked up from the potatoes she'd been peeling. Kate leaned against the doorframe, tall, blonde and elegant in spite of the unflattering maroon and gold school uniform.

"It's your night class tonight, isn't it? I thought you'd want to get back to it as quick as possible. I'm here to look after Amy until Steve gets in. What time's he due home?"

"I don't know," said Joanne. "Listen, Kate, it's nice of you to offer but I'm not going back this year."

"Why not? You've already paid for the year, haven't you?"

"Yes, but…"

"Be a shame to waste the money then, wouldn't it? You've only missed a few weeks, you'll soon catch up. Here," Kate continued briskly, taking the vegetable knife out of Joanne's hand, "I'll finish those, while you have a shower."

"I can't," Joanne protested. "I'm not ready, and Amy'll need feeding, and…"

"You can feed Amy just before you go," Kate interrupted. "She'll be safe with me."

Joanne hovered in the kitchen uncertainly. Kate picked up a potato, then glared at her sister.

"You do trust me with her, don't you?" she said.

"Of course I do!" Joanne replied immediately. "It's just that…"

Steve won't like it. Even as the thought entered her head she realised how pathetic an excuse it would sound to the super-confident, independent-minded Kate.

"You'll be doing me a favour, to be honest," Kate inserted into the pause. "Mum and Dad have been at it hammer and tongs all week. It'll be great to do my homework in peace for a change."

In the end, it was wonderful. Everyone in the class seemed genuinely pleased to have her back and John the tutor said he'd photocopy all the coursework she'd missed. The feeling of being a part of the world again after two largely solitary months was fantastic. Her depression lifted, and as she got off the bus she felt a new sense of purpose. She couldn't just spend all her time with the baby; she had to get out occasionally and use her mind. Nevertheless, as she walked up her road and saw the Porsche parked in the drive, she felt a twinge of anxiety.

Kate was still there, tidying away her books. Steve was in the dining area at the back of the lounge, eating his dinner.

"Hi," Kate said brightly. "How did it go?"

Joanne glanced at Steve, but he was concentrating on cutting his steak, and she couldn't ascertain his mood.

"Fine," she said. "Great, in fact. How was Amy?"

"Brilliant. No trouble at all. Here, I'll get your dinner out of the oven. Steve's only been in a couple of minutes. He said it's fine if I come round every Monday and revise while you're out. Isn't that right?"

Steve looked up from his plate and smiled at Joanne.

"Course it is," he said. "It'll do you good to get out too, darling. You look a bit tired. Sit down."

Joanne couldn't believe it. She had no idea what Kate had said, but this was the first time he'd called her darling since Amy's birth. She wondered if he was waiting until Kate had gone before he started complaining, but he only made one comment.

"I didn't think you wanted to carry on with the A level, seeing as you won't be able to go to uni now," he said while she was clearing the table.

"I might be able to do a degree at the Open University," she replied.

"Yeah, sure, whatever you want," he said, flicking on the television. Not quite the response she'd have liked, but much better than she'd expected.

It was great to be back in the world again.

* * *

Kate was sitting on the couch, books scattered all around her, when she heard the front door open. A moment later Steve popped his head into the lounge.

"Hi," he said. "Everything OK?"

She glanced up at him, then put her book down.

"Your dinner's in the oven," she said. "I'll heat it up for you." She started to get up, but he shook his head.

"It's OK," he said, "I can see you're busy. I'll do it."

Kate returned to her reading, scribbling notes from time to time in an exercise book.

"What heat should I set the oven to?" he called after a moment.

Kate rolled her eyes heavenward.

"Low," she shouted back. "About mark two." She'd recently agreed with Joanne to stay until she got back from her class, presumably so Steve wouldn't be inconvenienced by the terrible burden of having to look after his own daughter for an hour or so. Initially he'd arrived home only a few minutes before Joanne, but over the last few weeks he'd been getting home earlier, and insisted on making small talk, showing a great interest in the subjects she was studying.

He seemed genuine enough, but Kate just couldn't take to him. She tried to though, for Joanne's sake.

He came back in with two cups of tea, and Kate started to pack her books away. Hell, it was only eight o'clock! Joanne wouldn't be home for at least an hour.

"Actually, do you mind if I just go through these notes again?" she said, re-opening her book. "I've got an exam in the morning."

Steve sat down on the sofa next to her.

"What subject?" he asked.

"Maths," she said. "I'm trying to get some of the formulas in my head. I should be OK then. Was that Amy?" She waited a moment, and when Steve showed no sign of reacting, she got up and went to the bottom of the stairs. At sixteen months Amy usually slept straight through the night with no problem, but if she did wake up she might try to climb out of bed. Kate ran lightly up the stairs. False alarm. Amy was sleeping soundly, flat on her back, arms flung out across the pillow.

Kate tucked her quilt around her, planted a gentle kiss on her forehead and went back downstairs. When she sat down she put a bigger space between herself and her brother-in-law. She picked up her book again, hoping he would get the hint and leave her alone.

"What do you want to do when you leave school?" he asked. "Are you carrying on to do A levels?"

"No," she replied. "Joanne's the academic one of the family. I've already got a job lined up as a clerical assistant. As soon as I can, I'm going to get my own place."

Steve looked surprised.

"I thought you got on well with your mum and dad," he said.

"Did you?" She looked back at her book.

"Have you thought of modelling?" he asked. She glanced up at him to see if he was taking the mickey, but he looked serious.

"No," she said. "Not my sort of thing. Models strike me as being too self-obsessed and insincere. I'm not tall enough, anyway. Or thin enough."

"You could do glamour modelling," he suggested, running his eyes the length of her body. "You could make a fortune doing that. You're very pretty. And you've got a great figure."

She didn't respond to his compliment, because she knew he was expecting her to.

"How about yourself?" she said instead. "Didn't you ever think of it? I mean, you've got the superficial good looks modelling agencies are looking for. And the right personality."

"Are you joking?" he replied, smiling. "My dad would have disowned me if I'd become a model. He thinks they're all poofs."

"There *are* a lot of gays in the fashion world," she said.

"One of the boys at school models part-time, and he's just admitted he's gay. I admire him. He's got a lot of courage to do that."

"Are you trying to tell me you think I'm a poof, but won't admit it?" He laughed.

"No, not at all," she responded. She didn't like this conversation. "Look, I think I'd better go home," she said. "I could do with an early night."

She went to stand up, but he put a hand on her knee to restrain her. She froze.

"No, it's all right," he said, oblivious to her reaction. "You carry on revising. My dinner'll be ready in a minute."

His hand stayed on her knee. *It's innocent,* she thought. *Don't overreact.*

"Is that why you didn't like me?" he said softly, "because you thought I was queer?" His fingers played delicately along her leg, and she looked him straight in the eye, placing her hand firmly on top of his to arrest his motion.

"No, that's not why I don't like you," she said sweetly, returning his smile. "Let me remind you of something. I'm fifteen. If you don't take your hand away right now, I'll have you done for child abuse." His smile vanished, and he pulled his hand from under hers. "And if you think you can try it on again in a few weeks when I'm sixteen, then I'll have you done for indecent assault." She stood up and picked up her bag.

"You've got the wrong idea," he said. "I didn't mean…"

"Don't give me that crap," she said coldly. "I know exactly what you meant." She shoved her books haphazardly into her bag and swung it onto her shoulder. "And I'll tell you something else," she added, walking to the door. "You even hint to Joanne that *I* came on to *you*, or try to stop me looking after Amy while she goes to night school, and I'll go to the police anyway. See you next Monday."

Without waiting for a response she turned and walked towards the front door, straight into Joanne, who was just entering.

"Hello!" Kate said brightly. "You're early! I was just on my way home. I wanted an early night, I've got an exam first thing tomorrow. Steve said he didn't mind, didn't you, Steve?"

He appeared at the door, and smiled tightly.

"That's right," he said.

Joanne looked from one to the other uncertainly.

"The teacher had to leave at eight," she said. "I just managed to catch the early bus."

"Great!" said her sister. "I looked in on Amy a few minutes ago, and she was fast asleep. Your dinner'll be warm enough by now, Steve," she added, turning to her brother-in-law and smiling. "Goodnight, then."

Steve was surly all week. Everything Joanne did was wrong. The vegetables were overcooked. The house wasn't clean enough. Where was dessert? She knew he liked something sweet after his meal. She was looking haggard, and ugly, and fat. Why didn't she pay more attention to her appearance? She had plenty of time, sitting at home all day, for God's sake.

Joanne waited for him to tell her what had happened between him and Kate, for him to forbid her to come to the house again. But he didn't, and when Joanne approached Kate, she said there was nothing wrong, she just wasn't that keen on him and he must have sensed it.

The following Monday, Steve did not come in until ten o'clock, by which time Kate had already gone home.

* * *

When Amy was two and a half, Joanne had a miscarriage. When she was four, Joanne had another. The first miscarriage happened three months into the pregnancy. Afterwards Steve had been very supportive of her, consoling her when she cried, buying her new clothes, and listening to her whenever she needed to talk.

He had suggested a weekend away, but Joanne was

unwilling to put the responsibility of Amy on to Kate, and wouldn't countenance the grandparents on either side of the family looking after her. After all, Amy hardly knew them, Joanne pointed out. Instead Steve took her out for a meal and afterwards to the theatre.

Joanne enjoyed the evening out, but even more than that she enjoyed the fact that the Steve she had fallen in love with had returned to her. For a while everything went well, and if he still didn't take any more than a vague interest in Amy, at least he wasn't ignoring her completely.

The second miscarriage took place in hospital, twenty weeks into the pregnancy. When she'd found out she was pregnant again, Joanne had waited for the twelve-week milestone apprehensively. After that she had relaxed. The chance of miscarrying after three months was much slimmer. She hoped it would be a boy, for Steve's sake.

This miscarriage was much worse than the last, because the baby had been inside her long enough to become part of her, to become a real living person in her mind. The emptiness that was left when the baby was gone was a constant ache that expanded to fill her whole consciousness, rendering the world grey and leaving her weary and hopeless. If she hadn't had to put on a bright face for Amy, she would have spent most of her day in bed.

The doctors told her there was nothing obviously wrong with the foetus and there was no reason why she shouldn't carry the next baby to full term, but the thought of facing that ordeal again was more than she could bear.

She needed desperately to share her grief with Steve when she got out of hospital. But instead they talked about his business, about how his team was doing in the pool league, and whether or not she was going to apply for the Open University course, now Amy was nearly old enough for school.

They didn't talk about the baby, because it would have been a boy. And because three days before Joanne miscarried, Steve had lost his temper with her. She had washed the towels and forgot to put clean ones up in the bathroom, so that when he'd had a shower he'd had to go dripping through to the bedroom to get something to dry himself with.

They had met on the landing as she was rushing up the stairs, having belatedly remembered her error, and he had elbowed her out of the way. If she hadn't managed to grab the stair rail as she fell, she would have gone all the way to the bottom. As it was, she wrenched her shoulder badly and twisted awkwardly, banging her stomach and chest on the stairs as she sprawled down the first few, her toes finding purchase on the fifth stair down. She had lain there winded for a few minutes to get her breath back, before returning to the kitchen to finish the meal.

When she was taken into hospital she told them she had tripped over one of Amy's toys and had caught herself on the wall as she fell. If they had pressed her for more details, she probably would have told them the truth, in the vulnerable state she was in.

But nobody did, because nobody was really interested. As long as you appeared to be happy no one ever tried to scratch the surface, because they didn't want to know what lay beneath. Steve was handsome and a good worker. She had a lovely home and a beautiful daughter. She was very lucky, she knew that. Everybody told her so. And she *should* have remembered to replace the towels.

* * *

When Amy started school, Joanne was bereft. She missed their daily walks and her daughter's endless curiosity about everything, from why ladybirds had spots to what made the leaves fall off the trees in the autumn. What did the wind really look like? Why did the man in the butchers have lots of pictures all over his arms? Could she have some?

When Amy was three Joanne started teaching her to read. By the time she was five and had to go to school, she knew the alphabet, could write simple sentences, count to a hundred, and had read all the picture books Joanne had bought for her.

The little girl was ecstatic about going to school. She looked really grown up in her uniform, Joanne told her proudly, a lump in her throat. At the end of her first day she came running to the school gate clutching a picture she had painted of her mummy and daddy, and complained that she hadn't done any proper reading and writing like she'd thought she would, although her teacher Miss Moore was very nice.

Joanne proudly sellotaped the picture to the fridge door, and when Steve came home Amy took his hand and dragged him into the kitchen to see it.

"Very nice," he said indifferently, glancing at the series of coloured blobs and lines. In the corner was a big yellow circle, which represented the sun.

"It's you and Mummy in the park," Amy said excitedly.

"Which one's me?" he asked.

Amy stared up at her father.

"That one, of course," she said indignantly, pointing to the orange blob with two little lopsided blue dots in the middle and a yellow stripe on the top. "Mummy's got brown hair, but I did yours yellow, like mine."

Steve had already walked away and was lifting the lid of one of the pans bubbling on the stove to see what was for dinner. Amy looked at him for a moment, then bit her lip.

"Why aren't you on it?" Joanne asked quickly.

"Daddy doesn't go to the park when I'm there," she explained.

Joanne had no answer to that.

***

The hoped-for business from the stately home restoration did not materialise, and Steve was back to wallpapering and painting again. Joanne had no idea how much he was earning, and as all the bills were addressed to him she never got to see them, but she knew by the envelopes that some of them were red. Sometimes when he came home late she could smell smoke in his hair and beer on his breath, and knew he'd been in the pub rather than working as he claimed. It was better not to question him, and she preferred it when he came in late.

Amy was always more subdued when her father was at home, even though Joanne tried her utmost not to provoke Steve when her daughter was around. She didn't want Amy to grow up in the sort of atmosphere she had known. She had secretly started taking the pill, hiding the packet in her underwear drawer. She didn't think she could bear to suffer another miscarriage.

And on balance, she now thought it better that Amy remain an only child. The little girl took her father's casual indifference for granted. Joanne was certain that had the baby boy survived, Steve would have doted on him, and Amy was too bright not to notice that and wonder about it.

After a few months of sitting at home during the day missing her daughter, Joanne suggested to Steve that she might get a part-time job.

"It'd get me out of the house a bit," she said, "and we could do with the extra money."

Steve protested that she didn't need to go out to work, and said he'd thought she wanted to do a degree.

"I do," she said. "But it's expensive. If I can earn a bit of money I might be able to pay for it myself. Mr MacDonald told me to have a word with him if I wanted to come back."

"No," Steve said.

"Why not?" Joanne asked, bewildered.

"I don't want you anywhere near that bastard again."

"But…"

"I said no. Don't argue with me on this."

She didn't argue with him on this. Not when he used that tone of voice. She knew what would happen if she did, and she was still aching from the last time.

She didn't phone Mr MacDonald. Instead she went to the job centre and made an appointment to see an adviser.

* * *

On the day she was due to attend her first interview the school rang to say Amy was ill, and after phoning the company to cancel her appointment she hurried round to collect her wan-faced daughter, who was sitting on a chair in the secretary's office, a plastic bucket near her feet.

"There's a bug going round the school," the secretary reassured Joanne. "She'll be fine in a day or two."

Amy was sick once in some bushes as they walked home, and once in the house. Joanne settled her on the couch in her nightdress, with lots of cushions. She looked like a little doll snuggled under the pink blanket, with her porcelain pale skin, huge blue eyes and mass of wavy blonde hair. She was a beautiful child, everyone said so. Everyone except the father she resembled so closely.

They played Ludo and Snakes and Ladders for a while, then Amy managed to eat half a bowl of soup. After that Joanne showed her how to fold and cut paper to make a string of dolls, and Amy was busy colouring her third string of dolls in when Steve came home from work. He threw his coat casually over the back of the couch and sat down on the chair.

"What's wrong with you then?" he asked his daughter.

"I'm poorly," she said. "Look!" She held up the dolls, shaking the paper to make them dance.

"You don't look very poorly to me," her dad commented.

"She's got a tummy bug," Joanne explained, coming in from the kitchen with two cups of tea. "She was white as a sheet earlier. She's got a bit of colour back since she managed to eat something. They're beautiful!" she exclaimed to her daughter. "Shall we see if we can do a string of dogs after dinner?"

"Cats," replied Amy, who had desperately wanted a kitten ever since one of her schoolmates had brought hers in to show the class.

"OK, cats, then. Are you any good at drawing cats?" Joanne asked Steve.

"You've made a mess there," he answered, eyeing the bits of paper which littered the carpet near the couch. He flicked the TV on, and Joanne sighed before going back into the kitchen to put the meal out. She would try Amy with just one potato and a little meat.

She was just stirring the gravy ready to pour on the meal when she heard the angry cry from the lounge and went running in to see Amy cowering back against the cushions. Steve was standing over her, his face red with anger, his hand raised.

"You stupid little bitch!" he roared.

Joanne cannoned into him, knocking him sideways so he nearly lost his balance. She put herself between him and Amy and glared at him, her chest heaving with emotion, her fists clenched.

"Don't you dare hit her!" she shouted.

"Look what she's done!" he said.

Joanne glanced back over her shoulder. His expensive grey suede jacket was covered in vomit.

"It cost a fortune, that did!" he cried, still incensed. "It's ruined."

"I didn't mean to," Amy said in a small voice, then burst into tears.

"She's ill," Joanne said, "she couldn't help it."

"Do you know how much it cost?" he said.

"I don't give a damn how much it cost!" Joanne shouted, losing her temper. "You should have hung it up in the cloakroom where it belongs! Don't you ever hit her."

"I didn't hit her!" he protested.

Joanne sat down on the couch and lifted her sobbing daughter on to her knee.

"It's all right, sweetheart," she said in a soft voice. "It was an accident. It doesn't matter."

"It does bloody matter!" Steve said. "I can't afford to…"

"Your dinner's in the kitchen," Joanne interrupted without looking at him. "Hush, hush now, it's OK," she crooned, rocking the child backwards and forwards to soothe her. Then she scooped her up and took her off upstairs to bed.

When she came down a few minutes later, Steve was

sitting at the dining table eating his dinner and watching the television. Joanne walked up to it and switched it off.

"What are you doing?" he asked.

"You ever hurt Amy," Joanne said quietly, "and I'll kill you."

Steve looked her up and down and smiled.

"I'd like to see that," he said.

"You've never paid her any attention," Joanne continued as though he hadn't spoken. "But you ever hit her, and you'll regret it."

"I didn't bloody hit her!" he said, pushing his plate to one side.

"You were going to," Joanne said.

"That coat cost over a hundred…" he began.

"I told you, I don't give a damn what your coat cost!" she shouted. "She's your daughter and she's ill! And all you can do is whinge about your bloody coat. I'm sorry she's not a boy, OK? But I won't have you take it out on her! I'll leave before I let you treat her like you treat me."

"What do you mean?" he said. "I let you do your stupid A levels, didn't I? I married you to get you away from your dad, and I gave you all this…"

"I never wanted all this!" she raged. "I'll tell you what I wanted. I wanted you to love me and treat me like a wife, not a servant. I'm sick of running round after you, terrified of saying the wrong thing in case you get angry! And don't give me all that crap about rescuing me. It's rubbish, and we both know it. You begged me to marry you for months before Dad threatened to throw me out."

Steve stood up. He expected her to back off, like she always did when he loomed over her. Part of her knew she should, that she'd gone too far. But she'd wanted to say this to him for so long, and now she couldn't stop.

"I wish I'd had the guts to get my own flat, like Kate has," she said. "If I'd known what marriage was going to be like, I'd never have said yes."

The first blow sent her flying backwards into the wall.

She braced herself against it, willing her legs to keep her upright. She wiped her hand across her nose, and it came away smeared with blood. She looked at it, and then back at him.

"I should have left you the first time you hit me," she said.

He stepped forward, grabbing her by the throat. It was a favourite move of his. She owned several scarves in different colours, bought to cover the evidence. He shook her hard, her head bouncing back against the wall, and his mouth was moving, his face twisted. She felt his spittle on her face but couldn't hear the words properly because of the roaring in her ears. Then he released her, and this time her legs did buckle under her and she slid down the wall.

She kept her head down for a while until the dizziness passed, then she pulled herself up the wall, breathing slowly and carefully. She walked into the lounge, picked up the ruined jacket, and put it in the bin. Then she pinched her nose hard to stop the blood flowing and cleaned herself up before she went to check on her daughter, who was not asleep as she'd hoped, but was sitting up in bed, wide-eyed.

Joanne sat down on the edge of the bed.

"It's all right now," she said. "Daddy's gone out."

"Daddy hates me," Amy said.

"No he doesn't, sweetie, he's just a bit annoyed about his coat, that's all."

"He hates you, too," Amy persisted.

"No he doesn't," Joanne said. It hurt to speak, but she tried to make her voice sound normal.

"He shouts at you a lot," Amy said.

Joanne sighed.

"He works very hard," she explained. "And he's tired when he comes home from work. You get grumpy when you're tired, don't you?"

"Sometimes," Amy admitted.

"Well, then, Daddy does too. And sometimes he shouts. But he doesn't mean it."

"But even when I'm grumpy, I don't hit you," Amy reasoned.

Joanne wanted to burst into tears.

"Would you like to go and see Auntie Kate?" she asked.

Amy's face lit up immediately.

"Now?" she said.

"Yes, if you feel well enough. Shall I ring her and see if she's in?"

The little girl nodded.

"I feel better now I've been sick," she said.

***

Kate put a camp bed down in her bedroom for Amy, making it sound like a great adventure.

"This is a special bed," she explained to her niece. "It's magic, that's why it has to be folded away most of the time, to keep the magic in."

"Why is it magic?" Amy asked, wide-eyed.

"Because when you go to sleep in it, the fairies come and visit you in your dreams, and you can go to Fairyland with them. And when it's time to wake up, the fairies'll bring you back here again."

"Really?" Amy said doubtfully.

"It's true." Kate billowed a sheet over the bed and then tucked it in carefully. "Sometimes when I feel a bit fed up, I sleep in it myself, and I always have lovely dreams. Last time I met Cinderella in Fairyland."

Cinderella was Amy's favourite story at the moment.

"Do you think I might meet Cinderella too?"

"You might, if she's still there. You have to go to sleep first, though."

"What are you going to do?" Kate asked her sister half an hour later. They were sitting in the tiny living room of Kate's flat. A curtained-off alcove served as a kitchen, and the bathroom and toilet was across the landing, shared by the other first-floor tenant.

"I don't know," Joanne said. "He was going to hit her, Kate, I'm sure he was. He had the same look on his face as he has just before…" Her words trailed away, and she looked embarrassed. She had never talked about Steve's violence to anyone.

"Just before he hits you," Kate finished.

"Yes," Joanne whispered. A tear trickled slowly down her cheek.

"You can stay here," Kate offered, "for as long as you like."

Joanne looked round the room.

"There isn't enough room," she observed. "You don't want us here."

"Yes I do. I wouldn't offer if I didn't want you to stay."

"Won't the landlord object?"

Kate snorted disdainfully.

"How's he going to know? He doesn't come round if he can avoid it in case we remind him about all the repairs that need doing. He wouldn't dare complain about you. I'll wipe the floor with him if he does. It'll be fun," she continued, eyeing her sister's bruised face. "It'll be like old times. Except I won't have to creep in your room at night anymore."

"No, because me and Amy will have stolen yours."

Kate waved her hand dismissively.

"I slept on the couch for weeks when I first moved in, until I could afford a bed," she said. "It's lovely and comfy. Don't worry about it. It'll be great."

Joanne was profoundly grateful to her sister over the next week. She was wonderful. She treated the whole thing like a game. Every night Kate would come home from work with some small token. One night she brought home a bright yellow plastic flower with a smiley face, in a little pot. She put it on top of the portable television.

"Watch this," she said. She switched the TV on. It was the six o'clock news, and the newscaster, his face suitably solemn, was reporting a tragic pile-up on the motorway.

Kate flicked a little switch on the plant pot and sat down. Every time the reporter spoke, the little flower danced, wiggling merrily about in its little pot. When the voice stopped, the flower ceased gyrating immediately, and seemed to be waiting for the reporter to start again so it could perform once more.

"Isn't it brilliant?" Kate said, eyes shining.

Amy was nearly hysterical with laughter at the little flower's antics. After a while they switched the TV off and took turns to shout at the flower. Then they switched the radio on and watched it dance in time to the music, Amy attempting to copy its swaying motion. This was just the sort of silly thing they should have been sharing with Steve, Joanne thought sadly later in bed. She was surprised that he hadn't tried to contact her, but then realised that he didn't know where Kate lived. He never showed any interest in Joanne's family, so she had long ago stopped telling him about them. When Kate left, she didn't give her address to her parents.

"If I do," she'd said, "I'll have Mum round all the time, crying and telling me it's not the same without me there. I put up with eighteen years of them arguing with each other. I want some peace."

"They'll both miss you," Joanne had pointed out. "They love you."

"I know they do," her sister answered. "But I'm fed up with it. I never know when the argument's going to start. I'm sick of Dad laying down the law all the time. And Mum's so pathetic. She just puts up with it, then comes moaning to me when he's gone out. Why doesn't she leave him? Sometimes I think she likes him bossing her around. It means she doesn't have to think for herself."

Is that what Amy will think of me if I stay with Steve? Joanne wondered. It wasn't the same, though. Neither Angela nor Jim had ever shown their eldest daughter any affection. Whereas she tried her utmost to make up to her daughter for Steve's indifference. And Steve wasn't normally nasty to

Amy, like Joanne's dad had been to her. She'd hoped he'd come to love Amy in time. This wasn't how it was supposed to be. Where had it all gone wrong?

* * *

The following week Amy returned to school. She found it exciting, going on the bus, and insisted they sit upstairs at the front so she could see more.

At home time Joanne arrived fifteen minutes early. Steve was waiting at the gate. As she approached, he shifted from one foot to the other uncomfortably. He looked dishevelled. His T-shirt was crumpled and he looked as though he hadn't shaved for a couple of days.

"What do you want?" she asked.

"I wanted to see you. I didn't know where you were. I've been really worried."

"I'm fine," she replied. "We both are."

He looked at the fading bruises on her neck and cheek. She had made no effort to cover them up.

"I'm sorry," he said. "I can't believe I did that. I don't know what came over me."

"The same thing that comes over you every time you hurt me, I assume," Joanne replied levelly. He blushed and looked away.

"I just couldn't bear that you thought I'd actually have hit her," he said. "I've never hit her. I never would, you know that, surely?"

"I don't know anything any more, Steve," she said. "I never know when you're going to get angry. There's no pattern to it. Amy thinks you hate her."

The shock on his face was genuine.

"I don't hate her!" he said. "She's my daughter! I love her!"

"You don't show her you do, Steve. We never go out as a family. You don't do anything with her at all."

He digested this for a moment in silence.

"You're right," he said. "I've neglected her. I've neglected both of you. I've been a bit preoccupied. The business isn't going as well as I'd hoped. I've had to lay Jack off. I've put the Porsche up for sale, too."

"How long has this been going on?" Joanne asked, shocked.

"A few months now. I didn't want to worry you. I should have talked about it with you. I'm sorry. I miss you. Both of you. Please come back. I'll never touch you again, I swear it. I'm so lonely on my own."

His eyes filled with tears, and Joanne was glad that Amy chose that moment to come running out of school. Her apprehension as she saw that her daddy was there reminded Joanne why she had left him, and instead of moving into his arms as she'd been about to do, she took her daughter's hand and walked away.

* * *

"Don't do it," Kate said two weeks later.

"We can't stay here forever," Joanne replied. "It's much too small for three people."

"I know, but when you get a job of your own, we can move somewhere a bit bigger."

"That could take months, Kate. It's not just that. Amy needs her father as well as her mother."

"She hasn't got a father," Kate pointed out. "He doesn't give a shit about her. Or you."

"He does. I think me leaving has shaken him up a lot. He's started bringing little presents to school for Amy. And she actually smiled at him when she saw him tonight. He's really miserable, Kate."

"Let me ask you something," Kate said. "How many times has he apologised to you before, after he's hit you?"

"A few times," Joanne admitted. "But I've never left him before. He was really upset that I could believe him capable of hitting Amy."

"Why shouldn't you think that? He's capable of hitting *you*, and you're tiny next to him. It's bullshit. I don't think he's sorry at all. He's just trying to get you to go back to him."

"He's promised me he won't do it any more. Tonight he begged me for another chance. He's had a lot of money problems lately, and he's been trying to keep it to himself because he didn't want to worry me. He's talked to me about them now. He's spent years building up that business. It means so much to him, and now he's on the point of bankruptcy, Kate. I can't let him go through that on his own. He's learned his lesson, I'm sure of it. I've got to give him a chance to prove he means it."

"You still love him, don't you?" Kate said incredulously.

"Yes. Yes, I do," Joanne admitted. "He's wonderful most of the time. He's just got worked up about the business, that's all. It'll be better when everything's wound up. He'll have no trouble getting another job, with his skills. He won't be so edgy once he isn't a boss any more."

To say Kate looked sceptical would be an understatement.

"Well, it's up to you. Personally I think you're wrong, but I've never been in love, thank God, so what would I know? It's your life. I just hope you're right."

* * *

She *had* been right, Joanne thought, months later. Steve had managed to wind up the business without having to declare himself bankrupt, and due to his many contacts in the trade, had found another job almost immediately. It made things easier for Joanne, knowing he'd be home at the same time every night.

He bought Amy little presents, and asked her about school. On Saturdays they went out together, like other families, to the park, the zoo, the cinema. Amy, naturally affectionate and loving, started to open up to him, little by little. She didn't know that Dad had to be gently prompted by Mum to go up and read her a story before bed, and that it was always Joanne who suggested their weekend outings.

It was understandable. He was the youngest of his family and had no experience of children. He was learning how to be a father, and if he was still a little sharp with his wife from time to time, he hadn't raised his hand to her once, even when he came home drunk from the pub on Friday after his weekly pool match and she complained that he was making too much noise. He hadn't spoken to her for three days, but he hadn't hit her. It wasn't perfect, but he was trying, and that was enough.

CHAPTER FIVE

1997

"You might as well take that off," Kate said, nodding towards the blue silk scarf encircling Joanne's throat.

"What do you mean?" Joanne asked, her hand automatically reaching up towards it.

"It's August. We're having a heatwave. There are only two reasons why a woman would wear a scarf in this weather, and thirty-three is too young to be hiding a sagging neck. You don't need to hide from me. I'm your sister, I know what's going on."

Reluctantly Joanne unwound the gauzy material, revealing a series of purple finger-sized marks around her neck. Kate's mouth tightened.

"It's not as bad as it looks," Joanne put in hurriedly before her sister could comment.

"I thought you said things were going well," Kate said.

"They are. Well, until last night. But it was only a little argu…" She changed tack, seeing the expression on Kate's face. "He's got a lot of problems at the moment, he's upset. I just wound him up the wrong way, that's all. I should have known better."

"What terrible thing did you do to make him try to strangle you?" Kate asked, her voice heavy with sarcasm.

"He didn't try to strangle me," Joanne protested. She was glad that the lump on the back of her head where he'd banged it repeatedly against the kitchen door was hidden by her hair. "He…just…it doesn't matter. He was sorry as soon as he did it."

"I bet."

"No, really. Things have been great for ages. It's just a hiccup, that's all. He's got a lot on his mind. It'll be OK when he finds another job."

Kate leaned over and refilled Joanne's cup from the cafetiere sitting on the table.

"It's not right, you know," she said. Joanne poured cream into her cup, avoiding Kate's gaze.

"I know, but…"

"I don't mean that," Kate said. "I mean it's not right to judge your marriage as being fine just because your husband's not beaten you up for a while. We're living in the twentieth century, not the thirteenth. He's not supposed to hit you at all."

"He didn't hit me," Joanne said.

"You're splitting hairs," Kate replied. "Tell me this. When was the last time you went out together, somewhere *you* wanted to go? When did he last make you feel like a woman? How long is it since you felt relaxed in his company?"

"He often buys me flowers and chocolates," Joanne pointed out. "And he tells me he loves me."

"Yeah, course he does, when he's apologising for treating you like shit," Kate said. "Anyone can say the words, Jo. It's their actions that tell the truth. Let me put it another way, then. How many arguments have you had where you've backed down, even though you were right, because you're afraid of him?"

An uncomfortable silence descended on the room, which told Kate more than any words her sister could have uttered.

"You've done really well for yourself here," Joanne said when it became clear that her sister wasn't going to break the silence. She looked around the spacious, luxuriously furnished city-centre apartment, with its polished hardwood floors, cream leather suite, expensive stereo system and tasteful paintings. "Do you remember that crappy little bedsit you had when you first left home?"

Kate knew what Joanne was up to and was tempted to give in. But this was too important.

"Yes, I remember it," she said. "I also remember how great it was when you and Amy came to stay."

"It was too crowded," Joanne replied.

"Even so, I prayed every night that you'd stay away from him."

"You, praying?" Joanne teased. "You don't even believe in God!"

"I went to church with Aunt Lorraine every Sunday for months when I was little," Kate countered indignantly.

"That was nothing to do with God. You did that to get away from the horrible Sunday breakfasts when we had to sit silently for an hour while Dad read the paper."

Kate smiled.

"True," she admitted. "I remember you wouldn't come with me, because you were frightened God would strike you dead for being a hypocrite. But you know what I mean, Jo. You might not believe me, but I can actually understand why you went back to him, that one time. You still loved him, and he was very plausible. You thought he was worth another chance. But I can't understand why you've stayed with him for all these years."

"He changed for a long time after that," Joanne said. "It really shook him, me walking out on him."

"Six months," Kate said. "It didn't shake him enough, did it? You should have pressed charges and divorced him then."

They sat for a couple of minutes in silence, remembering the night when the argument had been so loud that the neighbours had phoned the police. Steve had walked out just before they arrived, and Kate, woken from a deep sleep by her six-year-old niece's frantic phone call, had turned up in a taxi at one in the morning to find her sister covered in blood and trying to console Amy, whilst two police officers stood about, looking bored.

"The police weren't interested, Kate. All they did was ask me what I'd done to make him lose his temper. They made me feel as though I was just making a big fuss about nothing. It looked worse than it was, anyway. All he did was throw a plate at me."

"You needed stitches, Jo," Kate reminded her.

Joanne reached up automatically to touch the faint silver scar just above her left eyebrow.

"I would have done it, you know, if they hadn't made me feel as though it was my fault," Joanne said quietly.

"Done what?" Kate asked.

"Left him. Took him to court, I don't know. I'd had enough, then. But the police were so…indifferent. They just wanted to get out, I could tell. They made me feel stupid and worthless. They didn't say that, but that's what they were thinking. I knew after that, that whatever happened, there was no point in going to the police."

"That was over six years ago. Things have changed. Domestic violence is taken more seriously now. You could still have left him for good though, anyway," Kate said. "Why didn't you?"

"Amy didn't want me to," Joanne replied.

"What?" Kate's face was a picture of disbelief.

"The next day I sat down with her and asked her what she wanted to do. I told her that if she wanted we could come and stay with you for a while, until we found a place of our own. She told me she didn't want us to leave Dad, but that she wanted him to stop fighting with me all the time."

"I don't believe it!" Kate said.

"It's true. He'd been a lot better with her, you see, buying her sweets and comics, asking her about her day when he came home, even playing the odd game with her now and again, that sort of thing, you know."

Kate did know. Her brother-in-law could be very charming

when he wanted to impress someone. He could switch it on and off at will. People who didn't know him well found him likeable, a real gentleman. She found him false and unctuous. He encouraged people to show their weaknesses, then exploited them. He was hot-tempered and unpredictable.

Kate was not afraid of him. She was cold-tempered and hard; the opposite to him. She had no vulnerabilities that he knew of, and gave him nothing to attack her with. He hated her, and the feeling was mutual. He was ruining her sister's life and she could never forgive him for that.

No, Joanne had a part in it. She was ruining her own life too, by staying with him.

"You should have left him anyway," she said. "Amy would have been OK."

Joanne shook her head.

"No, I wanted her to have two parents, not one. And he was learning how to love her, in his own way. So when he came home the next day I sat him down and I told him that if he ever hit me again in front of Amy I'd leave him, and I wouldn't come back this time. I lied to him, told him that the police had encouraged me to prosecute him but I'd decided to give him one more chance, and that was it. I said it really quietly, because I meant it."

"What did he say?" Kate asked. Her sister had never told her this before.

"He told me that if I ever left him again, he'd find me and kill me. He said if I took him to court I'd be sorry. And a lot of other things. But he never hit me again in front of Amy, and he's got more and more affectionate towards her over the years. She loves him, Kate. It'd destroy her if I left, and I won't do that to her."

"Jo, you can't ruin your own life because of Amy!" Kate protested.

"Of course I can!" Joanne replied hotly. "She's my daughter! The only worthwhile thing I've done in my life is to have her. I'd kill for her if I had to, and die for her without hesitation. She's everything to me."

"But…"

"No," Joanne interrupted. "You haven't got children, Kate. You don't know what it's like. You love Amy, I know that, but you don't know what it's like to feel that life growing inside you, to know it's a part of you, and that when it's born it will be completely dependent on you, that it's entirely up to you whether your child grows up healthy and happy, or a mess."

"Amy's a wonderful girl, Jo," Kate said. "You should be proud of yourself for the way you've brought her up."

"I know, and I am," Joanne replied, relaxing back into the sofa a little. "I'm sorry, I sounded very melodramatic then. But I meant it. I won't do anything to hurt her. And leaving Steve would hurt her, a lot. Anyway, my life isn't being ruined. Most of the time it's fine. And he really is great with Amy. He always drops her off and picks her up from her friend's houses. And when her friends come over he never complains, even if they play music very loud in her bedroom. In fact he often goes up for a chat, and he'll play games with them, too. And he runs them home afterwards. He even goes swimming with them every Sunday."

"Does he?" Kate said, surprised. "Do they like that?"

"Of course they do!" Joanne replied. "Steve enjoys it too, he says the exercise is good for him, helps to stop the middle-age spread."

"Right," Kate said in a neutral tone. Joanne looked at her.

"What's wrong?" she asked.

"Nothing. I just thought the girls would prefer to go swimming on their own, that's all. After all, they're not babies any more. Amy's nearly thirteen."

"No, it's part of their special time together. God, I'd have been ecstatic if Dad had let me bring friends home or had taken me swimming," Joanne said wistfully.

"And I'd have died of embarrassment if Dad had insisted on coming with me when I was going out with my friends," Kate said. "When I was thirteen the last thing I wanted was for anyone to even know I *had* parents, let alone have them trailing round after me, especially when I was with my mates."

"Amy's never said anything to me about feeling embarrassed," Joanne said. "She loves her dad. It's great to see them together. They look so alike, especially now she's growing up. I'm glad she inherited his eyes and hair."

"She's got your build, though, and your shape of face and mouth," Kate added.

Joanne smiled.

"I can't believe how quickly she's growing up," she said.

"She told me last week that Steve won't let her grow up," Kate said.

"Did she? What did she say?"

"Something about him going off on one because she wanted to wear eyeshadow. She changed the subject when I told her that I thought she was a bit young for makeup, too."

Joanne laughed.

"It wasn't just eyeshadow. It was lipstick and blusher too. Steve told her she looked like a clown and made her wash it all off before she went out. She was fuming."

"Poor kid," said Kate.

"He could have been more tactful about it, but he was right. She did look like a clown. He is strict with her now she's getting older. He won't discuss the idea of boyfriends until she's sixteen, he said. He won't even let her wear tights to school, although a lot of her friends do. If it was up to me, I'd let her do that at least, but…." Joanne stopped. "He loves her and he's trying to protect her. He knows what boys are like. He just comes on a bit too strong at times. And Amy inherited his temper, which doesn't help. God, some of the things she says to him…Dad would have killed me if I'd spoken to him like that."

"But he's never hit her?" Kate said.

"No, never. Not once. If he had I'd have left him, he knows that. They just have these slanging matches, then Amy usually storms off to her bedroom for a while to cool down. Then she comes down and apologises, and everything's great again. They don't argue that often, but when they do…"

"It shows he can keep his fists to himself when he wants to, though, doesn't it?" Kate commented.

Joanne reddened.

"At least Amy's got a father who cares for her," she countered.

"Unlike you, you mean," Kate said.

"Well, yes," Joanne muttered. She had lowered her head so that her hair fell over her face. They rarely spoke about their childhood. It was over, and by mutual consent was not discussed. There were plenty of other things to talk about; they only met once a fortnight, and Kate knew that Joanne had to fight even for that. Steve would have loved to stop his wife seeing her sister altogether.

Kate sat forward on the chair.

"Jo," she said. "Just because Steve's better with Amy than Dad was with you doesn't make him a perfect father. Dad was a complete shit."

Joanne's head shot up.

"Kate!" she protested. "Dad's only been gone six months!"

"So what?" Kate replied. "Being dead doesn't automatically qualify you for canonisation, you know."

"I know, but even so…he was always great with you."

"You're right, he was. And in a way that made the way he was with you worse. At least if he'd treated us both the same it would have been fair. But it wasn't your fault Mum and Dad had to get married. And just because he loved me doesn't mean I didn't see what he was like with Mum as well as you. I don't want you to end up like her."

After Jim's death Angela had gone to pieces. It had been left to Joanne and Kate to notify everyone and arrange the funeral. Angela had roused herself only to go to the service, and then had fallen apart again. Jim had never let her take responsibility for anything, and she had no idea how to start. Bills were left unopened, the dishes were left unwashed, the house became untidy, then dirty.

Initially Joanne spent a lot of time at her mother's,

cleaning and opening the mail. She persuaded Angela to have a bath and comb her hair, and cooked proper meals for her. In the evenings Kate would come round and sort out the financial things; she found Jim's will, applied for probate, and in the meantime paid the urgent bills herself. Both sisters assumed their mother would emerge from her grief at some point and start to take responsibility for herself.

But after three months of this it became clear that Angela was not going to do anything for herself if she could avoid it. Jim had controlled every aspect of her life; what she should wear, what she should do, even her opinions. Angela felt helpless, incapable of starting again at her age, and Joanne began to resign herself to caring for her invalid mother for the rest of her life.

Steve had different ideas. Although Joanne always got home before Amy came in from school, and Steve's meal was on the table when he got in from work, the housework was neglected and Joanne was permanently tired. On top of that, Angela would phone at least three times most evenings, to ask where her red skirt was, or was it two or three paracetamol you were supposed to take for a headache?

Joanne knew these questions were just an excuse to talk to someone; Angela was lonely. She was bound to be; she'd been married for over thirty years. Joanne had toyed with the idea of asking Steve to let her mother come and live with them, but he was growing increasingly annoyed about the small intrusions the phone calls made into their evenings. Joanne decided it would be better to wait for a while before broaching the subject.

"No, Mum, it's in the third drawer down in your bedroom," Joanne said one evening, after the third call in as many hours. Her dinner was growing cold, and she could hear Steve tapping his knife on the side of his plate, irritated. Amy was over at one of her friends. Joanne turned to him and mouthed the word 'sorry'.

"Right, have you found it? Good. No, Kate's sorting the electric bill out. I think she's going to set up a direct debit for it. A direct debit? That's when you write to the company with your bank details, and then they take the money straight out of…"

The phone was wrenched from her hand, ripped out of the wall and thrown across the room. Joanne squealed with shock as Steve grabbed her by the arm.

"That's it," he said. "I've had enough of your fucking mother ringing morning noon and night. It's about time she got her act together."

"She just needs a bit of time, that's all," Joanne said. His fingers were biting into the soft flesh of her upper arm and she tried not to wince.

"She's had a bit of time. A lot of time. It stops, now. I don't want you going round there any more. And if she rings up again. I'll tell her to piss off myself."

"I can't just stop going to see her, she's my mum!" Joanne protested.

"And I'm your husband. And I'm telling you now, I've had enough. Come and eat your food." He pushed her in the direction of the table, and she sat down. He retook his seat opposite her and picked up his knife and fork.

"I mean it, Jo. If I find out you're still going round there every day after this, you'll regret it. Let your bloody sister look after her. She's single. You're married. It's your job to look after me and Amy."

"But Kate *is* looking after her, as well!" Joanne said. "She's paying all…"

Steve looked at her.

"Are you arguing with me?" he said quietly.

Joanne swallowed and looked down at her plate.

"No," she said.

And that had been it. The whole burden of caring for Angela had been dumped on Kate. She had brushed aside Joanne's apologies and excuses, saying it was probably for the best anyway, because Joanne was too soft. Kate had then told her mother in no uncertain terms that she would sort out the finances but she had no intention of cleaning and cooking for a perfectly healthy woman of fifty-two. And Angela had managed, in a fashion, although Joanne knew she still phoned Kate several times a week, crying and complaining that no one cared about her.

"I won't end up like Mum," Joanne said firmly.

Kate sat back into the soft cream leather of the chair, and eyed her sister speculatively.

"Why don't you get a job?" she asked.

"What?" Where had this come from?

"I'm trying to get Mum to think about it."

"Mum?" Joanne said, astounded. "She's never worked in her life!"

"Well, she should have done, then maybe she wouldn't be so pathetic now. I thought she might do a bit of voluntary work, you know, in a charity shop, something like that. It'd do her good to get out and about a bit, meet people. It'd do you good, too. And you *have* worked before."

"Well, yes, but that was before Amy came along. I haven't worked for years."

"You'd soon get back into the swing of it. Amy's growing up now. She doesn't need you to be at home twenty-four-seven. There's a lot of part-time work about. And you could certainly do with the money, with Steve out of work. I don't know how much you could earn without his benefit being affected but you could find out easy enough."

"He isn't claiming benefit," Joanne said, then cursed inwardly. She hadn't meant to tell Kate that, but had been distracted, thinking about what Steve would say if she told him she was going to be the breadwinner of the family. He'd go nuts.

"Why not? If he was made redundant, he's entitled to claim…" Kate began, then saw the expression on her sister's face. "He wasn't made redundant at all, was he? He got the sack, again. Who did he punch this time, Jo?"

"It wasn't like that," Joanne protested.

"What was it like then?"

"It….he…it's difficult for him, having to take orders off kids. He's forgotten more about decorating than his boss'll ever know. And he's frustrated because his talents aren't being used. If he could just find someone who appreciated him, he'd be fine."

"Right. Of course he would."

"I have to go," Joanne said, standing up. She really did have to go. It was after three and she wanted to get home before Amy got in from school. But she wanted to go, too, before Kate said anything else about Steve. She found it difficult to defend his actions to her sister. She didn't know why, but when Kate was belligerent like this, Joanne always felt as though *she* was the younger sibling. It made her feel uncomfortable.

Kate followed her to the door.

"You forgot your scarf," she said, holding it out.

Joanne wrapped it round her neck, biting her lip as Kate's eyes rested on the bruising.

"You know, Steve should look to a change in career," Kate remarked as Joanne waited for the lift to come.

"He's always worked as a decorator," Joanne said.

Kate shrugged.

"Even so," she said. "The clubs and pubs round here are crying out for bouncers, and he'd certainly get to use his great talent for kicking the shit out of people who can't fight back. He's a damn sight better at that than he is at painting."

The bell pinged, the door opened and Joanne walked in. Kate dashed across the hall and pressed the button to stop the doors closing.

"I'm sorry," she said. "I shouldn't have said that. But he's a bastard, Jo. For God's sake, leave him while you're still young enough to start again. You know I'll help you in any way I can."

"Yes, I know that, and I appreciate it. But I can't, Kate."

"Why not? Amy's not a little kid any more. She's old enough to know what's going on. She'd understand. I know you don't want to hurt her, but…"

"That's a big part of it, but it's not just that," Joanne interrupted.

Kate's brow creased in puzzlement.

"What is it, then?" she asked.

"I still love him," Joanne admitted.

Kate took her finger off the button and stepped back, and the lift door closed

CHAPTER SIX

September 2008

A pigeon fluttered down, landing at Joanne's feet and startling her from her reverie. She looked up and saw to her surprise that the sun had moved a considerable distance across the sky. How long had she been sitting here? She automatically glanced at her wrist, then remembered that she was not wearing her watch. Over the last months time had seemed to go excruciatingly slowly if she could keep track of it, and she had no need to wear a watch any more. She wasn't working, and there was no one waiting at home to complain if she was five minutes late.

Just as well, Joanne thought, stretching her limbs out. She must have been here for hours. Even so, she was not ready to go home yet. She wanted time to think through all that had happened, and if she was at home she would find other tasks to distract her; housework, gardening, the phone ringing, possibly even journalists lying in wait outside the door.

There was a burger van parked just outside the park gates and Joanne went over to it and bought herself a cup of coffee, responding politely to the man's predictable comments about the weather being good for the time of year, but rain being apparently forecast for tomorrow. Why were the British so obsessed with the weather? Joanne supposed it was a way to converse with strangers in a friendly way, whilst keeping a distance.

The burger man had started his conversation with the standard 'how are you?' and Joanne walked back into the park, wondering what his reaction would have been had she answered his question honestly, instead of uttering the expected, automatic response that she was fine, thank you.

Although in a way she was. At least she had closure now, and could, at last, start to pick up the pieces and move on. And she had to move on, put the past, which could not be changed, behind her, and think about the future, with all its endless possibilities. She strolled aimlessly along the tarmac path, sipping her coffee. The trees were almost bare now and although the skies were blue and the sun bright, she knew it would be cold tonight. Winter was coming. She would have to tidy the garden, which was badly overgrown; it had been neglected since…she forced herself to concentrate on her surroundings; the daisy-spattered grass, the shiny leaves of the rhododendron bushes, anything but the one event from the past she would not let her mind dwell on, which threatened now to overwhelm her, to drive her back into the darkness from which she was struggling to emerge.

Having walked a whole circuit of the park, Joanne found herself back at the bench, and sat down again, gently cradling the styrofoam cup between her palms.

Things would have been so different if she'd taken Kate's advice and left Steve when Amy was six, or even twelve. But if she had left him then, would she have had the courage to stay away? She'd told Kate she still loved him, that day in the lift, but she'd been wrong, she realised that now.

She'd had no idea what love was, or at least what love between a man and a woman should be like. She'd mistaken possessiveness and tyranny for love, had believed, in the way of many neglected children, that any attention was better than none at all, that her husband wouldn't have gone to the trouble of controlling every aspect of her life if he hadn't cared for her. He hit her because he was jealous, because he loved her. He had told her that and she'd believed him.

And he'd tried to control Amy too, as soon as she started to grow up and show signs of wanting her independence. At the time Joanne had thought he was being protective of his daughter because he loved her. She laughed to herself, a harsh, derisive sound. How could she have been so naïve, so stupid? Steve had loved one person, and one person only, and that was himself.

She remembered the arguments between father and daughter, which had increased in frequency and intensity as Amy had reached puberty and started to blossom into a very attractive young woman. Gradually her friends had come round less and less and then not at all, and Amy had spent more and more time incarcerated in her room, moody and sullen.

If Joanne knocked on the door to ask if she was OK, Amy would say she was studying and didn't want to be disturbed. Angela would have just walked in anyway; Joanne had left her daughter alone, respecting the need for privacy that her mother had denied her as a teenager.

Sometimes Amy would be like her old self, cheerful and affectionate, and would offer to help Joanne with the dusting or the washing. Now and again they would have a precious evening together watching a video, usually when Steve was out playing pool or working late. But these occasions grew more and more infrequent as Amy turned sixteen.

In spite of her respect for her daughter's privacy, Joanne had started to worry; in the evenings Amy played with her food instead of eating it, and began to lose weight. Joanne had probed gently, trying to find the underlying cause for her daughter's state; was she being bullied? Was that why her friends had stopped coming round? Amy had mumbled something incoherent then subsided into silence, before making an excuse to go to her room.

Steve had dismissed Joanne's concern as that of an hysterical mother.

"She's just being a teenager," he'd said. "All girls of her age are obsessed with dieting and boys. She's probably got a crush on some spotty kid. She'll grow out of it."

Then Joanne had been tidying Amy's room one day whilst she was at school and had seen the little arrowed hearts doodled on her daughter's exercise books, with the initials BF and AH entwined inside. Ben Farrar, it must be. Amy had mentioned him once or twice, casually. He was in the sixth form, Joanne remembered, and had once helped Amy to learn some complicated algebraic formulas. So Steve was right. She had a crush on this Ben.

Joanne had said nothing about it to Amy. Her daughter would talk to her if anything serious developed, she knew that. She was a sensible girl, and had self-respect; she wouldn't let any boy take advantage of her. All teenagers had moods and secrets; it was part of the hormonal nightmare of growing up. That, coupled with exam nerves, was enough to make anyone moody.

Joanne had gently reminded Amy that her mum and dad were there for her, and that she could tell them anything at all if she wanted to, and then had backed off, keeping an eye on her from a distance.

Amy had finished her exams, and then had said she wanted to wait for the results before deciding whether to stay on for sixth form. She had taken a part-time job at the local supermarket for the summer holidays, and occasionally went to the cinema with her friends, who she met up with in town. Often she would stay overnight at her friend Alice's house, and Steve would always phone Alice's parents to make sure she really was there. Alice's mother had commented more than once on how lucky Amy was to have such a caring father. Joanne knew that Steve would have preferred Amy to come home every night, but if she said she was staying at Alice's, that was where she stayed. And otherwise she always kept the 10.30 p.m. curfew Steve had set. She never smelt of alcohol or cigarettes and never complained about having to pay the keep he demanded from her now she was working. She gave him no excuse to ground her; but she remained quiet and withdrawn for much of the time at home.

And then had come the night that Joanne would never forget. Tuesday the seventh of August 2001. When she got home from the supermarket Amy had already gone out. She was going to the pictures, Steve had announced from his chair in the lounge, but she was coming home afterwards. Joanne had cooked the dinner and sat with him to watch a film on TV. He had been edgy, and when he was like that he usually managed to pick a fight with her. She couldn't remember anything about the film; she had been too nervous, waiting for the argument to start. Amy was out, and that meant that he would feel free to hit her if she angered him.

But he hadn't hit her, or picked a fight. Instead he had gone to bed at ten, saying he had an early start in the morning. It had been a lie; he had got up the next morning at his usual time of seven-thirty. Joanne knew that because she was awake. She had been awake all night, because for the first time in her life Amy had not come home at ten-thirty. She had not come home at all.

At midnight, after much deliberation, Joanne had nervously woken Steve up. He had grumpily mumbled that maybe he was wrong and Amy had stayed over at Alice's after all, and then had gone back to sleep. Joanne had gone to bed, and had lain awake staring at the ceiling until it was light enough for her to see the swirls of the artex clearly, and then had got up.

Steve was quiet and irritable at breakfast so she waited until he'd gone to work before phoning Alice's mother, who told her the devastating news that Amy had not stayed overnight at her house, had not, in fact, gone out with Alice at all.

Joanne had panicked and phoned everyone she knew with whom Amy had even the slightest connection; the supermarket, every number of every schoolfriend that Amy had ever stayed with since she was ten. Nothing. She had her hand on the receiver, about to phone Steve, although she knew he would be angry about her contacting him at work, when it rang, making her heart leap into her throat.

It had been Kate, with the shattering news that Joanne had been unable to comprehend. Amy had phoned her aunt to say she was all right, that she was in Birmingham, had found a place to stay, and was not coming home.

Kate left work early and came round to console her sister, assuming that Amy had left because Steve had assaulted Joanne, but after she'd been disabused of that notion, the two of them had gone up to Amy's room. They worked out by a process of elimination that Amy had taken one change of clothes and an overnight bag, and then the sisters had sat down for the afternoon to try to work out what could have made Amy leave home so suddenly without any warning at all.

Remembering now, Joanne crushed her hands together, and the styrofoam cup cracked, drenching her hands with tepid coffee. She threw the cup in the litter bin next to the bench and distractedly wiped her hands on her beige jacket, oblivious to the marks she was leaving on the woollen fabric.

She should have known. Why hadn't she known? She should have seen the signs, somehow. She was Amy's mother. Mothers were supposed to instinctively know when their children needed them, when they were miserable and suffering, rather than just hormonal and moody.

She had been so blind to everything, so stupid. It had been her fault as much as anyone else's that Amy had left. Amy would never forgive what her mother had done, Joanne knew that, but at least she had tried to atone for her fault, had tried to redress the balance, as far as she could.

She had put Steve's apparent indifference to the news of his daughter's leaving down to the fact that Kate was present when he came home that evening. He had listened as she explained to him that Amy had left home, and had merely nodded and gone upstairs for his shower without comment. He would rather die than show any emotion in front of his despised sister-in-law, Joanne had thought.

His continued indifference she had put down to his macho instincts; she had thought his reluctance to discuss the possible reasons for his daughter leaving home was because it upset him too much. Even so, she had tentatively brought the subject up again and again in the following weeks, until he had lost his temper and threatened to smash her face if she mentioned Amy again.

"She's gone and that's it," he'd shouted. "She's old enough to look after herself now. Forget her."

How could you forget your own daughter? Joanne had sat at home, going over and over the last few days before Amy left, searching for clues to her disappearance until she thought she would go mad. Amy rang Kate three times in the six months after her departure, to say she had moved again, to London, had a job, and was sharing a flat with three other girls. She did not contact her mother or leave a forwarding address.

Joanne cleaned the house, prepared the meals, watched the TV, accepted Steve's insults about her increasingly dishevelled appearance with indifference, and looked forward to the evenings when he went out and she could lie in bed in the dark, her mind like a broken record, running over and over the days leading up to Amy's disappearance, searching for the elusive clue that would not reveal itself.

Then one day she had woken up and had suddenly realised that she could not carry on like this. Sooner or later Amy would contact her. She was convinced of it, and the conviction galvanised her into action. She had to be ready for when her daughter got in touch. She had given in to her grief; she was weak and pathetic, and would be no use to Amy like this.

She got up and went to the bathroom and scrutinised her image in the mirror. There were yellowing bruises on her shoulder and a fresher, darker one on her upper arm. In the last weeks Steve had become more violent. It was understandable; he was worried about her state of mind, and when he was upset he often lashed out.

He was right in his criticism too; she had let herself go. Her hair was lank and tangled on her shoulders, her complexion was pallid and lifeless. How had she let herself go so badly? No wonder Steve was disgusted with her. She wasn't even forty yet, but she was growing old; her breasts were drooping and her stomach was flabby, the skin on her bottom and thighs was dimpled, and she had a fine web of lines round her eyes; whilst her husband's body was still as firm and well-muscled as the day she had married him. No one looking at them would guess that she was nine years younger than him. If she didn't do something, he would find another woman, and then he would leave her, or more likely, would make her leave.

She could not let that happen. She had to keep everything perfect, everything just as it had been, so that when Amy came home she would find both her parents waiting for her, ready to accept her back as though she had never left.

She had had a bath, washed her hair, and had cleaned the house with new-found enthusiasm. When Steve came home that night, she told him she had to get out of the house, and that she was going to get a part-time job. To her surprise he had said it was a good idea, although he had insisted on vetting the list of clients the cleaning agency she enrolled with had given her, to ensure it contained no men. And he had bought her the mobile phone which had become the bane of her life, so he could keep tabs on her, although he had said it was to ensure her safety. It was also to ensure her safety that he turned up outside clients' houses every so often.

Joanne had accepted this as normal. Although Steve never mentioned Amy, he was distressed at losing his daughter, Joanne had reasoned. He was being possessive because he was afraid of losing his wife, too. Because he loved her.

Looking back now, Joanne realised that she had had something of a breakdown at that time. Common sense should have told her that she couldn't turn back the clock, that Amy would never be her innocent little girl again, would probably never come home, and that her marriage was, and always had been, a violent farce.

But at least she had got something out of it. She had got a job, and with it, in spite of Steve's constant interference, she had gained a tiny measure of independence. She couldn't have sustained the energy she had felt on that day if she had continued to stay at home all the time; she would have sunk back into her depression. Her job had pulled her out of her lethargy enough to function, to stop her going under completely.

But, ironically, it had been a death that had started the chain of events that brought her fully back to life, and had brought her, ultimately, the freedom to sit on a park bench for hours as she was now doing, contemplating the past for, she determined, the very last time.

Then she would move on, and throw herself into the future she had created for herself.

CHAPTER SEVEN

November 2003

Joanne impatiently turned the key in the lock and, pushing open the swollen door, stepped into the hall, relieved to be out of the squalling rain.

Before she made her way up the stairs to the second floor, she paused for a moment to admire the dusty plaster cornice, exuberant vines with their bunches of fat grapes which trailed around the edges of the hall ceiling, a reminder of the long-ago days when this crumbling slum house had been home to a family made wealthy by the industrial revolution.

Joanne tried to imagine the rooms as they would have been a hundred and fifty years ago, stuffed with dark mahogany furniture, thick-piled burgundy rugs underfoot, heavy velvet curtains at the windows, oil lamps casting a warm yellow glow around the room. A cosy fire would have burnt merrily in every hearth. There would no doubt have been an aspidistra in the hall, a ponderously ticking grandfather clock, and an umbrella stand made from an elephant's foot which some eccentric uncle had brought home from his travels in exotic India.

Joanne pressed the yellowing ceramic light switch on the landing, which illuminated a bare hundred watt bulb dangling from the ceiling on a worn flex. The image of Victorian opulence was dissipated by the harsh electric glare, and Joanne was left alone at the scuffed door of flat 2c, one of the larger flats in this converted house in a run-down suburb of the town. The house smelt of damp and vermin, overlaid by the cooking smells of whatever the various tenants were having for their evening meals. This was her last job of the evening.

She opened the door and went in. There were no appetising smells of roasting meat coming from this flat. Joanne doubted that the occupant had ever cooked a meal in her life. What food Suzy did eat seemed to be ordered in from the local Indian, Chinese, or Pizza Parlour. The poky lounge, as usual, was cold and damp. Joanne walked over to the hearth and switched on the gas fire. She held her hand in front of the bars for a moment until she felt the heat start to penetrate, then straightened up, rotating her shoulders to loosen them ready for her hour of frenetic cleaning.

Joanne believed in giving value for money. The cleaning agency paid her five pounds an hour, but she knew they charged the clients far more than that. She had got this job privately through one of her other clients, and she charged Suzy six pounds, which was still a lot less than the agency asked. For that she gave sixty minutes of pure efficiency. She didn't stop to make herself a cup of tea, as many other cleaners no doubt did, and she often worked on for a few unpaid minutes in order to finish some task she had started.

She glanced at her watch. Four forty-five. A full fifteen minutes before she was due to arrive. Some clients would complain if she was five minutes early or late, but Suzy didn't seem to mind what time she came. In fact, Suzy hardly seemed aware of the time of day at all. Joanne cleaned for her twice a week, two o'clock on Mondays and five o'clock on Thursdays. Very often when she arrived Suzy was in bed or sitting in the sagging armchair in front of the TV, still in her dressing-gown, sniffling and picking half-heartedly at the remains of a takeaway.

No doubt she was in bed now. Joanne did not clean the bedroom. Suzy had told her not to bother. Just the living room, tiny kitchen, no more than an alcove, and the bathroom. At least when the tenant finally surfaced, the living-room would be warm and welcoming.

Before she started work, Joanne looked under the porcelain shepherdess sitting on the mantelshelf, where Suzy left her wages if she was not in. Under it, folded in half, was a twenty-pound note and a scrap of buff-coloured paper torn from an envelope with the single word 'SORRY' scrawled across it in felt pen. Joanne stuffed the money in her coat pocket. Suzy had obviously had no change, hence the note, although she had never left one before.

She would nip down to the corner shop after she'd finished. Mr Patel was a nice man, always chatty, and would change the twenty-pound note for her without insisting she buy anything first. She should have time to nip back up and put the eight pounds change under the ornament before the bus came.

Joanne took off her coat, pushed up the sleeves of her jumper and set to work, picking up the half-empty foil containers from the floor and sweeping the crumbs from the scratched pine coffee table into her hand before making her way to the kitchen. She crushed the cartons into a ball and put them in the bin bag hanging from the knob of the door.

The kitchen, as usual, was relatively clean. There were a couple of dirty plates in the sink, and a few dribbles of tea across the yellow formica worksurface. Joanne pulled out the bottle of kitchen cleaner, spray polish and cloths from under the sink, and set to work. It always cheered her to see an untidy or dirty room become clean, neat and welcoming, surfaces clear and gleaming, cushions plumped up, carpets vacuumed and ornaments dusted.

Forty-five minutes later she looked around the lounge and allowed herself a nod and a smile of satisfaction. Just the bathroom now, and after that she could spent the extra few minutes she had on account of being early in sorting through Suzy's laundry basket. She would put a load of washing in the communal basement washing machine for her and leave a little note to explain what she'd done. She needed to be home in time to cook Steve his tea, but she should manage to catch the ten past five bus, if she was quick.

Armed with cream cleaner and a sponge she opened the door to the bathroom. The room was, unusually, quite clean, and Suzy's pink towelling dressing gown was neatly folded at the side of the bath.

Lying in the bath was Suzy. Her head lolled back against the edge of the chipped white bath, her eyes open and staring sightlessly at Joanne, who stood frozen on the threshold. Suzy's mouth hung open, and she was white, not white as someone looks when they are about to faint, but a greyish-white that Joanne had never seen before. The ends of her long dark hair floated in the water around her body. She had filled the bath almost to overflowing, Joanne noted absently, and the water was red. Blood red.

The thought jerked Joanne out of her shocked stupor; she saw the bare, bloody razor-blade placed neatly on the side of the bath, and dropping her cleaning materials she rushed to the woman, pausing as she leaned over her, trying to remember what she had been taught at the first aid class she had attended years ago, not long after her daughter had been born. God, nearly twenty years.

Breathing. Check for breathing. How did you do that? And a pulse. She could remember that bit. It was better to check the pulse in the neck than the wrist, because it was easier to find. Don't use your thumb, or you'd feel your own pulse instead of the casualty's. Tentatively she put her hand on Suzy's neck feeling for the artery, then recoiled instinctively. The flesh was cold and rubbery, and she knew in that moment that it was too late, that the woman was dead.

"Oh God, oh God, oh God," she repeated over and over to herself as she backed away out of the room. A cold sweat broke out all over her body and she leaned against the doorpost with her eyes closed, breathing heavily through her nose until the nausea and faintness had passed. Then she straightened, and tried to think what to do. 999. That was it, she must phone for an ambulance, the paramedics would know what to do, that was their job.

She spent a few pointless minutes hunting round the room before she remembered that Suzy didn't have a phone. She would have to go out to the call box on the corner and call from there, if it hadn't been vandalised.

It was only as she delved into her coat pocket for change that she felt the solid, despised rectangle of her mobile phone, and she pulled it out, cursing herself for her stupidity. She pushed the button to switch it on, and as she waited for the little welcome tune she was suddenly filled with a sense of urgency. She had read somewhere that a person could be dead for twenty minutes before their brain suffered irreparable damage.

The phone played its tune and she punched in the number, waiting an interminable time for the answering voice to ask her which service she wanted, and then for even longer, it seemed, for the ambulance operator. She gave the address and was going to put the phone down, thinking that was all that was needed, but then the woman told her the ambulance was on its way, and started asking questions about what had happened.

"I don't know," Joanne said. "I just went in the bathroom, and she was lying there in the bath, and the water is all red, and…" She felt her voice start to spiral upwards in panic, and stopped, swallowing hard. The woman was asking her what relation she was to the lady in the bath.

"I'm her cleaner," Joanne said, wondering why it mattered what her relationship to Suzy was. "I think she's cut her wrists. There's a razor blade on the side of the bath, and lots of blood."

The operator's voice continued, calm and steadying, asking Joanne to check to see if the woman was breathing, and explaining exactly how to check for a pulse, and that Joanne should hold her finger on the spot she described for some time, because if Suzy was still alive her pulse might be very slow by now.

Then suddenly the ambulancemen were ringing the bell and Joanne was so overwhelmed with relief that her legs turned to jelly as she answered the door. She was helped into a chair by one of the men, while the other one disappeared into the bathroom.

The paramedic was very kind and made her a cup of tea, while asking her what time she'd arrived at the house and what she'd done when she'd seen the lady in the bath. After a few minutes of gentle questions and professional concern, Joanne calmed down and began to feel herself again, for the first time since she'd walked into the bathroom nearly half an hour before. She heard the man in the bathroom talking softly, and for a moment her heart leapt, and she thought Suzy must be alive, but the other man told her that his colleague was not talking to Suzy, but was contacting the station.

After a short time the police arrived, a man and a woman, and after spending a few minutes in the bathroom the woman came back out and sat down on the coffee table, facing Joanne.

"How are you feeling?" she asked. She was very young, quite pretty, with short blonde hair. Joanne remembered the old saying that it's a sure sign you're growing old when the police seem like children to you, and she almost smiled, but then remembered why she was there, and the smile died before it appeared on her lips.

"I don't know," Joanne said truthfully. "Sort of numb, I suppose." And a bit apprehensive too, although she didn't say this. Just being in the presence of the law imbued her with a vague sense of guilt, a feeling that she was about to be accused of something, and that when she was she would be unable to prove she hadn't done it.

"Do you feel well enough to come down to the station and tell us what happened?" the policewoman asked.

Joanne looked up in alarm.

"I wasn't here when she did it!" she said. "I'd have stopped her if I had been."

"Yes, I'm sure you would," said the policewoman gently. "It's just routine. You were the first person to find her. We just want to talk to you, that's all. We have to make a report and you might be able to help us. If you don't feel up to it, we can take you home instead and you can come down to the station tomorrow. But we'd rather do it now, while it's all fresh in your mind."

Joanne thought about what the neighbours would think and say if she turned up at the house in a police car. What Steve would say.

"No," she said. "I'm all right. I'd rather get it over with now."

At the police station she was shown into a small room furnished with a desk and two chairs, and was offered another cup of tea. She sat for a few moments with her fingers wrapped round the mug, trying to dispel the cold, clammy feel of Suzy's neck when she had felt in vain for the throb of a pulse.

She looked around the room. It was almost exactly as she would expect a police interview room to look; institutional. The unplastered brick walls were thickly gloss-painted in two shades of drab green, there was a barred window high on one wall, and a heavy atmosphere of defeat and gloom pervaded every inch, as though every person ever interviewed there had left a piece of their desperation and misery behind when they left.

Joanne tried not to feel oppressed by her surroundings; after all, she reasoned, she had done nothing wrong. Nevertheless the depressive atmosphere was making her feel claustrophobic, and she was relieved when the two men who were to interview her entered the room.

She had expected the same police officers who'd come to the flat to interview her, but the man who introduced himself as DI Gibb before sitting down opposite her was middle-aged, with receding dark hair and the beginnings of a paunch bulging over the top of his grey trousers. His companion was younger and looked more lean and athletic, but as he just sat in the corner and didn't speak, Joanne soon forgot he was there.

DI Gibb fiddled around with a tape recorder for a moment, then asked her just to describe in detail exactly what had happened, from the moment she entered the flat. Joanne did, taking great pains to try to remember everything, and when she finished with the arrival of the police, she thought she'd divulged every detail.

"Is she dead, then?" she ventured tentatively in the short pause that followed.

"Yes," said DI Gibb. "I'm sorry." He was soft-spoken, and sounded genuine in his regret at the young woman's death, although Joanne supposed he must see this sort of thing, and worse, often.

Joanne looked at her fingers, which she'd laced together on top of the table to stop herself from biting her nails. Steve would go mad if she bit them now, after five weeks of growth. She glanced up at the detective. She had to ask the question, but was dreading the answer she might receive.

"Did I…if I'd gone straight into the bathroom when I arrived, do you think I could have saved her?" she asked in a very small voice.

John Gibb leaned his elbows on the table.

"No," he said. "She'd been dead for some time before you arrived, a few hours, probably. There's nothing you could have done."

Joanne let out her breath in a great sigh, and her eyes suddenly filled with tears.

"I'd never have forgiven myself if…" she began in a choked voice.

He leaned across and took her hand, an uncharacteristic gesture that caused his colleague to raise his eyebrows, though he made no comment. He was there to observe, to look for the tell-tale signs of guilt, of a lie being told.

"Don't blame yourself," Gibb said. "You did the right

thing, calling the ambulance. That's all you could do."

There was something about this woman which called up his protective instinct. There was an innocent and almost childlike vulnerability about her, something he rarely saw in the people he dealt with. He judged her to be in her late thirties at least, hardly a child.

She could be pretty if she made an effort, he thought, but she seemed to take little heed of her appearance. She was dowdily dressed in a cheap brown woollen skirt and acrylic jumper, her hair scraped back into a ponytail. She wore no makeup. And she seemed nervous, not in the way he would expect her to be, a law-abiding, normal person suddenly thrown into exceptional circumstances, but as though it were a part of her character to be so.

"What sort of woman would you say Miss Devine was?" he asked, removing his hand gently and sitting back. This cleaner, Mrs Harris, had nothing to do with the death, he decided. She was just in the wrong place at the wrong time, poor bugger.

Joanne was thinking, her forehead screwed up a little.

"I didn't speak to her a lot," she said. "She isn't the talkative kind. I don't think she was very well though, hadn't been for a while."

"What made you think that?" Gibb asked.

"She seems to have a cold all the time," Joanne said. "She's always sniffing. She's very pale, and very often she was still in bed when I called round, even at five o'clock sometimes. And I don't think she's had a proper nutritious meal in years. She lives on pizzas and stuff like that. I suggested she went to the doctor once, get her cold seen to at least."

"What did she say?"

"She just laughed and said it wasn't a cold, that she was just saving all her energy for the evening. I think she works nights, although she wouldn't talk about her job. She must have some money though, or else she wouldn't be able to afford a cleaner. She doesn't need one, really, with such a small place. Oh!" Joanne finished on a shocked note.

"Have you remembered something else?" asked the detective.

"Yes," Joanne replied, feeling in her pocket. "You asked me if I'd found a letter or anything, and I said no." She drew the twenty-pound note out and laid it on the table, then handed the scrap of paper it had been wrapped in over to him. "She left this with my wages. I thought she was just saying sorry because she didn't have the right money and knew I'd have to go down to the shop to change it, although she'd done that before and had never left a note. But I suppose she might have been saying sorry because she knew I'd find her when I came to clean." She bit her lip and looked at the money guiltily. She hoped they didn't think she'd been trying to steal it. "Could you change it for me?" she asked.

The detective looked up from his perusal of the single scrawled word.

"No," he said, smiling gently. "You keep the money, Mrs Harris. I think she intended you to, and I certainly think you deserve it."

All the way home Joanne was rehearsing what she would say when she walked in the door. Steve would go berserk. Nine o'clock, and she'd been due home at six. He'd have had to get his own tea and everything. She should have phoned to tell him she was going to be late and why, but she'd left her mobile in the flat, and hadn't thought to ask if she could call him from the police station.

She chewed on her lip and thought frantically. It was no good starting by saying she was sorry, because he probably wouldn't give her time to say anything else, so she had to explain what had happened straight away in her first sentence, enough to calm him down so that he'd listen to the rest of her explanation. How could she do that?

She felt the salt of the blood in her mouth and sucked at it. She must try to stop biting her lips. They were permanently raw, and it was a bad habit, almost as bad as biting her nails.

Perhaps if she just blurted out that her client had killed herself as soon as she walked in the door, that would surprise him enough to let her apologise properly, and then she would cook him a steak, his favourite, making sure it was well-done but not burnt, just the way he liked it. And maybe then…

"Are you alright, Mrs Harris?" Detective Gibb asked her. Joanne jumped. She had been so preoccupied with her thoughts that she had forgotten all about him.

"Yes, I'm sorry," she said automatically. "It's very kind of you to run me home. It's a long way."

"No, it's not that far," he said. "I live in Stretford, so it's only a couple of miles." In a hurried conversation outside the room his colleague, Barry Jones, had agreed that Mrs Harris seemed to be telling the truth. Suicide. Open and shut case. Still a pile of paperwork though, and a post mortem and inquest.

He repressed a sigh and turned off the main road, down to the mini roundabout, then left into her drive. He still didn't know why he'd offered to drive her home. Normally he'd have called a taxi.

"Here we are," he said. "Number fourteen, you said. Looks like someone's in, anyway."

She looked out of the car window at the low wall and neat garden of her home. The light was on in the living room and through the gap in the curtains she could see the flicker of the television. A lump of panic rose in her throat and she swallowed it down with difficulty. At least she wasn't in a marked police car, so it was unlikely that the neighbours would comment. She unclasped her seatbelt and turned to the policeman. He was looking at her strangely, and she felt heat flood her cheeks.

"Thank you," she said. She turned to open the door.

"Would you like me to come and explain to your husband why you're so late?" Gibb asked impulsively.

A sudden flare of gratitude and relief lit up her face momentarily, and he suddenly knew why his instincts had told him to take her home.

"I couldn't put you to all that trouble," Joanne said uncertainly, glancing at the house. "You've done enough already."

"It's no trouble at all," he said, switching off the engine and undoing his seatbelt. "It'll only take a minute."

He walked ahead, politely opening the gate to allow her to go first, then waiting while she opened the door, fumbling the key nervously in the lock. Coming down the hallway as the door swung open was a large, heavily built man with blond hair and a belligerent expression on his face.

"Where the f..?" he began, then saw the detective come into view behind his wife and stopped, confused, although his right fist remained clenched.

"Good evening, Mr Harris," Gibb said, smiling and holding out his hand, forcing the other man to unclench his fist in order to shake it. "Detective Inspector Gibb. Your wife's had a nasty shock, I'm afraid. Can I come in for a moment and explain? You must have been worried about her."

He watched Harris's facial muscles re-form and settle into an expression of the deepest concern in response to his words. He was dressed casually but expensively, Gibb noticed, in Armani jeans and a Ralph Lauren T-shirt.

"Yes," Harris said, sounding genuinely upset. "I've been worried sick. What's happened? Why didn't you phone?"

Joanne was taking off her coat.

"I left my phone at the flat…" she began.

"One of the ladies your wife cleans for has died. Your wife found her and called an ambulance, and then had to come down to the station to be interviewed. A cup of tea would be lovely, thank you, milk and two sugars, please," Gibb said, as though Joanne had offered him one. He followed Harris into the living room, and sat down in the proffered seat.

By the time Joanne came back with the tea a few minutes later, Steve's face was relaxed, and she knew with a great surge of relief that there would be no argument that night.

She had no idea what the detective had said, but at that moment she almost loved him.

Of course, Joanne told herself later, he was just doing his job. He must be very good at it, she reflected. After he had gone, assuring her that her phone would be returned to her the next day, Steve had grumpily turned down her offer to cook him a meal, saying that he'd made himself a sandwich and was off to bed as he had an early start in the morning.

When she said that she wasn't tired yet, and would make herself a cup of chocolate and watch a bit of TV before she came up, he just nodded and went upstairs. No recriminations, no accusations, nothing. He hadn't even asked her for all the gory details regarding Suzy's death, as Joanne had expected him to. It was wonderful. She felt almost happy as she boiled the milk for her drink, and then she remembered what had happened that day and the sadness welled up, and she allowed herself the luxury of tears, now that she was alone.

She sat in the living room, curled up in the chair with her chocolate and a box of tissues on the glass coffee table, and stared mindlessly at the TV for a while, before reaching over for the remote and switching it off.

She sat and blew her nose, and wondered what would cause someone to take their own life. Suzy had been young, no more than twenty-eight, twenty-nine, perhaps. She seemed to have no commitments, no one telling her what to do and not do. Surely things couldn't have been *that* bad? Suzy was far too young to have a daughter old enough to walk out without a word of explanation. Over two years without any direct contact.

For the thousandth time Joanne wondered what she could have done to make her daughter hate her enough to not even feel able to speak to her on the phone. All contact, infrequent though it was, was through Kate. The latest call had been over six months ago. Anything could have happened to her in that time.

A sense of helplessness washed through her. It was killing her, waiting for Amy to make contact. Sometimes it was almost unbearably difficult to get out of bed in the morning and drag herself through another grey and meaningless day.

Maybe that was how Suzy had felt, just for different reasons. Maybe the only difference between her and the girl lying in the mortuary was the fact that she had had the guts to do what Joanne could not. She would never have the courage to slice into her own flesh as Suzy had. But there were other ways, more peaceful ways. Tablets, if you took enough of the right kind. It would be nice to drift away in a drug-induced haze, just let go…

No. She had to stop thinking like that. She would hurt too many people if she killed herself. Kate, for one. Her mother. Amy, who would re-establish contact one day, she had to believe that. And Steve. She had almost forgotten him. Of course he would be upset. Devastated, even.

She finished her chocolate, washed and dried the cup, and then made her way wearily to bed.

CHAPTER EIGHT

Joanne was mildly surprised over the next two days that Steve expressed no desire whatsoever to talk about what had happened at her client's flat. She had thought he would at least want to know the gruesome details about Suzy's appearance when Joanne had found her.

She could have told him, in minute detail; the image of the naked woman lying in the bloodied bath, her sightless eyes gazing expressionlessly over Joanne's shoulder as she'd stood in the doorway, was permanently etched on her memory. But she would not volunteer the information. She had no interest in talking about it with anyone, and just wanted her life to get back to normal as quickly as possible.

To that end she took no time off work as the kind detective Mr Gibb had suggested she should, and the next afternoon found her carefully dusting the expensive Royal Doulton figurines in the overly fussy lace-bedecked living room of Mrs Jenkins, who had once met the Queen, in 1958, and of which meeting Joanne knew every moment as though she had been there herself.

This morning she found it difficult to give the lonely old lady the required attention as she described for the hundredth time the outfit the monarch had worn to the opening of the library at which Mrs Jenkins had then worked. Joanne smiled and muttered encouragingly in what she hoped were the right places, while her mind ran over the likelihood of the police needing to interview her further.

She had given them her mobile number, which she now realised to have been a mistake; the phone lurked like a time bomb in her pocket, and she anxiously awaited its explosion at any moment.

She had grown used to awaiting explosions in the last twenty years, but had always considered herself safe during her working hours. They had become a sort of respite for her, and in the simple act of telling the police her phone number she had relinquished that respite, for a few days or weeks, at least.

"Are you all right, my dear?"

The quavery voice cut through Joanne's musings and she looked up from her kneeling position by the fireside into the anxious face of her client, cursing herself for not responding to the woman's monologue more attentively. *Get a grip,* she told herself fiercely, and forced a bright smile.

"I'm sorry," she said, "I didn't sleep very well last night, that's all." She sought around in her mind for a plausible reason as to why she hadn't slept, expecting the old lady to ask.

"You do look tired," Mrs Jenkins said. "And here's me going on about stuff you've already heard. Here, leave those and sit down for a minute. I'll make us a cup of tea." She reached for her walking stick and began the cumbersome process of levering herself out of her armchair.

"No, no, don't trouble yourself," Joanne said, leaping up at once. "I'll make us both a cup, how's that?" She shot off into the kitchen before the old lady could see the tears that had sprung into her eyes at this unexpected kindly gesture.

Maybe the detective had been right, Joanne thought as she mopped her eyes with kitchen roll and waited for the kettle to boil. She had thought work would take her mind off things, but the mindless job she had only occupied her hands, leaving her thoughts free to wander where they would. But if she stayed at home it would be no better, and she would have the added tension of knowing that Steve could come in at any moment. His working hours had become very erratic lately, and Joanne had known better than to ask the reason why.

She abandoned her cleaning and instead sat with Mrs Jenkins for half an hour, gently manoeuvring her away from the subject of the Queen and on to her wartime romance with an American airman, who had taken her dancing during the blitz and had given her nylon stockings and chocolate.

Staring out of the bus window on the way home, Joanne tried to imagine what Manchester would have looked like during the war. She re-clothed the other passengers in military uniforms, in seamed stockings and pencil skirts, and temporarily forgot about Suzy altogether.

Her hazy sense of pleasure evaporated the moment she entered the house and saw Steve sitting in the living room, although it was only four o'clock. He looked up at her with excited anticipation on his face and she instinctively knew that whatever he was about to say, she did not want to hear it.

"I'm making a drink," she called, walking straight through to the kitchen. "Do you want one?"

Her delaying tactic didn't work. Steve followed her into the kitchen and leaned against the work surface. In his hand he held a copy of the morning's tabloid paper, which he now waved at her.

"Have you seen this?" he said excitedly, flicking through the pages until he found the article he was looking for. He laid the paper on the worktop, and Joanne glanced at the headline, guessing that it was about the suicide, then, surprised, she put the tea caddy down and read the whole article. When she'd finished she glanced up at her husband, who was watching her intently.

"You didn't tell me she was a pop star," he said, his tone mildly accusing.

"I didn't know, that's why," Joanne replied, picking the tea caddy up again and putting two spoons of tea into the teapot. She would have preferred to use teabags, which were less messy, but Steve wouldn't have them in the house, saying they made the tea taste like dishwater.

"Surely she must have talked to you about it?" he persisted, picking the paper up again and scrutinising the smiling, pretty face of a Suzy that bore little resemblance to the woman Joanne had known. "Didn't she have her gold discs framed on the wall? You cleaned the house for God's sake, she must have had photos or posters of her concerts or something."

"Well, if she did, I never saw them," Joanne replied. "She was usually in bed when I was there, and when she was up she wasn't the chatty sort. She didn't look anything like that picture. It must have been taken years ago." She added boiling water to the pot and put the lid on, before reaching into the cupboard for two cups.

"1995," Steve said. "Not *that* long ago. What did she look like, then?"

Joanne looked up at him. His face was alight with interest, and she knew he wouldn't give up until she'd told him something to satisfy his curiosity. The only thing she could think of that he might find interesting was the circumstances in which Joanne had found her, and she didn't want to talk about that. She glanced down at the photograph again.

"She was thinner," she said, running a finger lightly over the image. "And very pale. I don't think she was very well. What do you want for dinner?"

Steve waved his hand dismissively.

"In what way?" he asked.

"In what way what?"

"In what way was she not well?" His voice was slightly impatient. Joanne stopped prevaricating.

"She seemed listless all the time. She had dark shadows under her eyes. She lived on takeaways, from what I gathered. I think she was depressed. And she was always sniffing, as though she had a cold."

Steve laughed suddenly, and Joanne looked up in surprise.

"Did you tell the police that?" he said, grinning.

"Yes. I thought it might be important, you know. If she'd just found out she had cancer or something, it might have…"

"You really don't know anything, do you?" he interrupted. "She wasn't ill, you stupid cow. She must have been a drug addict. That explains it," he continued, half to himself. "I wondered why she was living in a dump in Longsight. The band sold millions of records. She must have been loaded. That sniffing'll be cocaine. That's what it does to you. I wonder what else she was on? Did you find any needles and stuff while you were cleaning?"

"No," Joanne replied, pouring the tea. She wiped her hand across her face. "I really don't want to talk about it, Steve. It upsets me. I told the police everything I knew, and they can't think there was anything suspicious or else they wouldn't have let the paper say she committed suicide."

"She was famous," he said. "People love to read about stars. That's what sells papers. I bet if you ring the editor and tell him who you are, they'd pay us a packet for you to spill the beans about her."

She looked up at him, shocked.

"I can't do that," she said. "It wouldn't be right."

"Why not? She's dead. She won't care, will she?" he said brutally.

"I don't know anything that the papers would be interested in," she said, wishing he'd drop the subject. "They wouldn't pay me unless I had something important to say."

"Tell them about how you found her. Tell them what you've told me," he said. "That she was a drug addict. Tell them you found a stash of coke or some needles or something."

"But I didn't!"

"It doesn't matter, does it? Who's going to know? We could use the money, that's for certain."

"Steve, don't ask me to do this," she said desperately. "I don't know anything. What would people think if they found out that I'd lied about the poor woman just to make some money?"

"Who gives a shit what people think?" Steve said hotly. "What about us? This is the first chance you've ever had to make some decent money and you're going to throw it away because of what the neighbours might say?"

She saw his right hand bunch instinctively into a fist and felt the butterflies start in her stomach.

"Please," she said, her voice trembling in spite of herself, "I can't. I can't. Please don't make me do this." She looked at him pleadingly.

He moved away from the work surface, straightening up so that he could look down at her. In her bare feet she was nearly a foot shorter than him. He stared at her until she looked away, down at the floor, and even then she could feel his eyes burning into her. His fist was still loosely clenched. He moved forward suddenly and she flinched backward, raising her hand defensively. The corners of his mouth lifted slightly at her reaction, and he picked up his cup of tea.

"Think about it while you make the dinner," he said. "We'll talk about it later."

She couldn't eat. A lump of apprehension had formed in her throat and she couldn't swallow it down, no matter how hard she tried. She couldn't talk to the papers, tell lies about someone who'd shown enough consideration to leave her wages and an apology before killing herself. It was wrong. Joanne knew that she would not phone the paper, and she knew that Steve would not let it rest until she did. Steve ate his meal with relish, the plate balanced on his knee as he watched TV, while Joanne picked at hers and tried to think of a way out.

Could she tell him that she'd called the paper, but that they weren't willing to pay for her story? That might work. But then if he phoned up to check and found out she'd lied, he'd go mad. No. She should have told him that the police had warned her not to speak to anyone without their say-so. Why hadn't she thought of that? But she never could think straight when he was looming over her.

Maybe if she phoned Detective Gibb up tomorrow, she could get him to agree to say that he'd told her not to divulge anything to the media. He had been really kind and had treated her with respect. But what would he think of her if she did that? He'd think she was pathetic and worthless because she couldn't stand up to her husband. She *was* pathetic and worthless, but she didn't want the detective to know that.

In the end, having completely ruined her evening, Steve went to bed without broaching the subject again. In the morning Joanne feigned sleep, ignoring the overly loud noises he made while dressing. She waited a full half hour after he'd gone out before dressing and going downstairs.

It was her day off, and she made herself some toast and then sat in the living room trying to work out what to say when he brought the subject up again. She had no doubt he would; he would wait until she thought he'd forgotten, then catch her off guard. She had the whole day to think of a foolproof reason why she couldn't go to the papers. Or at least the whole morning. Steve never came home before lunchtime.

She discarded several plans over the next hour, and was on her third cup of coffee when the doorbell rang. She ignored it, sure it would only be a salesman or Jehovah's Witness, but when the bell rang a second, then a third time, it occurred to her that it might be the police, and she hurried to the door.

The young man standing on the step was pleasant-looking enough, but his smile was just a little too wide to be genuine and he thrust his hand out just a little too aggressively.

"Mrs Harris?" he asked. Although he pronounced her name as a question, Joanne was certain he knew exactly who she was, and this, combined with the falseness of his greeting, irritated her enough that she ignored the proffered hand, and instead of replying, looked at him questioningly.

"My name's John. John Wright, of the Recorder," he

said, reaching into the breast pocket of his jacket and pulling out a card. He flashed it in front of her face too quickly for her to see more than a glimpse of it, then replaced it in his pocket. "I wondered if I might have a word with you." He glanced over her shoulder into the hall, clearly expecting to be invited in.

"About what?" Joanne asked.

"About Suzy Devine. You were her cleaner, weren't you? You're the one who found her last week?"

For a moment Joanne was tempted to tell this over-confident youth that he'd got the wrong house, but she realised she would only make herself look foolish if she did.

"I told the police everything I knew," she said instead. "I'm sure if you call them, they'll be able to tell you more than I can."

"I've already spoken to the police, Mrs Harris," the young man said. "I wanted to talk to someone who knew Suzy, who could give us a picture of what sort of person she was, what might have driven her to do such a desperate act." The smile vanished, to be replaced by an equally false expression of concern. "Could I come in for a minute?"

"No," Joanne said, more forcefully than she'd intended. "I can't help you. I didn't know her very well. I just cleaned for her, that's all."

"I know, but you worked for her for quite a long time, didn't you?"

"Two years," Joanne said, then immediately regretted volunteering even this much information.

"So you must have known quite a bit about her. I'm sure if you think about it you'll remember all sorts of little things."

"Mr Wright," Joanne began.

"John."

"John, then. I'm sorry, but I don't have anything to say to you."

John's brow puckered in what appeared to be his first genuine expression; puzzlement.

"Oh," he said. "But when your husband rang us this morning he said that you and Miss Devine had known each other well, and that you would be quite happy to talk to us. We would be willing to remunerate you, of course, if we use the information."

The surge of rage took Joanne completely by surprise. She glared at the reporter through a red haze, and imagined her fist landing squarely on his nose. No, it was Steve she should be mad with. How could he have done this, without even telling her?

"I mean, we would be able to pay you, if…." the reporter explained, clearly misreading her silence.

"I know what remunerate means, Mr Wright," she said coldly. "My husband was wrong. I have nothing at all to say to you. Goodbye."

She shut the door rudely in his face, something she had never done before, not even to the most persistent salesman, and walked back into the living room, the adrenaline surging through her body.

"You bastard!" she shouted, smashing her fist into the chair cushion.

We'll talk about it later, he had said. He had let her stew all evening, knowing that he had no intention of discussing it with her. He never discussed anything with her. He told her what to do, and she did it. But she hadn't this time. The anger drained away as quickly as it had risen, and she sank down on the settee. Oh God, what would he say when he came in?

She cleaned the house from top to bottom, so that he could find no cause for complaint. The towels were arranged perfectly on the rail ready for his shower, his clothes were warming over the radiator, and his favourite lamb casserole was bubbling gently in the oven, ready for the moment he sat down at the table. Joanne closed her eyes briefly in silent prayer to a God she did not believe in as she heard his key in the door, and went into the hall to greet him. *It will all be alright,* she told herself desperately.

"How did it go?" Steve asked as soon as she appeared. He shrugged off his leather jacket and hung it up.

With a supreme effort, Joanne managed to keep her voice level when she answered him.

"How did what go?" she asked innocently. She moved back into the kitchen. He was not covered in paint as she'd thought he would be. He'd probably been pricing up jobs. He would want his dinner before he went for a shower. She turned the oven off and took the casserole out.

"The interview with the newspaper reporter. When I phoned this morning they said they'd send someone straight out."

She could say that no one had called. Then the evening would be OK. But she knew him; he would phone the Recorder tomorrow, and would be even more angry when he found out she'd lied to him. She couldn't spend another day on pins.

"I told him I didn't want to talk to him," she said. She had her back to him, but she could feel his sudden stillness, and took a deep breath to ready herself.

"You told him what?" Steve said, very quietly.

She couldn't turn round. If she turned round she would see the expression on his face. She felt the hairs on her arms and the back of her neck rise as her body prepared for fight or flight. She spooned the casserole out onto two plates to gain time, then turned round.

Flight was out of the question. He was between her and the door. His eyes were chips of ice and his jaw was clenched. He stood like a rock, barring the way to the dining room, and she knew that he wouldn't let her pass with the plates until she had pacified him. She put them down to free her hands.

"I couldn't do it, Steve, I'm sorry," she said. "They sent a young boy round, and he was horrible, really slimy. I couldn't…"

"You fucking bitch," Steve said, his voice slightly louder

now. "I told them you were willing to talk to them. How do you think that makes me look now?"

For one suicidal moment she thought of throwing his words of the previous evening back at him. *Who gives a shit what people think?* He did, she knew that, and the words died on her tongue.

"I'm sorry," she said instead. "I never thought of that."

"Of course you didn't," he spat scathingly. "You never think of anyone but yourself." He glanced at his watch. "They'll still be there," he said.

"Who will?"

"Who do you think? The reporters. You can phone them, right now, and tell them you made a mistake."

Her eyes widened in horror, and she took a step backwards away from him.

"Can't we eat first?" she said. "It'll get cold if…"

With one smooth movement Steve swept his hand under one of the plates and flung it across the room. It hit the wall to the side of her with a wet splat, meat, carrots and gravy cascading down the tiles and splashing across the pristine worksurface.

Joanne flinched and tried to back away further as he lunged for her, but there was nowhere to go, and then he had her by the hair and was dragging her out of the kitchen into the hall, where the phone sat on a little shelf by the stairs.

"Phone them," he said roughly. His fingers were digging into her scalp, and tears of pain prickled in her eyes.

"Please, Steve," she cried.

"*Please, Steve*," he repeated mockingly. "God, you're so bloody pathetic." He reached over with his free hand and picked the receiver up, thrusting it at her. "Phone them," he repeated.

She took hold of the phone.

"Eight-three-seven," he began, waiting for her to dial.

She replaced the receiver in the cradle.

"No," she said. She felt his grip on her hair tighten, and drew a sharp breath.

"What do you mean, no?" he said.

"I won't do it. I can't."

He twisted her head up to face him, and looked at her incredulously. She was breathing heavily now, and her face was white with pain and fear, but she met his gaze steadily.

"What about her parents?" she said.

"What the hell are you on about?" he asked. He let her go, pushing her backwards a little in the process, and she resisted the temptation to run away, knowing she would only inflame him again if she did.

"Can you imagine what Suzy's parents must be going through right now? What if it was Amy who'd done that, killed herself in a horrible little bedsit? We'd never forgive ourselves. And if we read a load of lies in the paper about her being a drug addict," Joanne said, knowing her words were coming out jumbled but unable to stop them. "They must be going through hell as it is. I'm not going to make it any worse for them."

"Don't be so stupid," Steve spat. "She probably hasn't got any parents. And if she did have, they must be a waste of space. They can't think much of her, if they'd let her live like that."

"Amy might be living like that," Joanne said softly. "We don't know how she's living, what she's going through. But we love her, Steve. I can't do it, it isn't right."

Surely he would understand now? He was a parent, he loved Amy as much as she did. He had been devastated when she left; it was why he couldn't bring himself to talk about her.

Steve looked at his watch again, and saw that it was after five.

"I know what you're up to," he said, snapping her out of her thoughts. "You thought you could keep me talking about all that ancient history until the office shut, and that I'll have forgotten by the morning, didn't you? You think I'm bloody stupid!"

"No!" she cried. "No, I don't, you know I don't."

"Yes you do!" he shouted. He was working himself up now, working up the courage to do what he wanted to do. Even before he lifted his hand, before it made contact with her face, splitting her lip and sending her sprawling on the stairs, she knew what was going to happen and knew that it was as inevitable as night following day.

Her mind calmed and she accepted the blow when it came, knowing that accepting it was the only thing that might stop him following through. If she pleaded with him at that stage, she would only excite his contempt. She had given up trying to fight back long ago. You couldn't fight someone twice your size, it was ridiculous to even try. She had learnt through experience that if she accepted it silently, without screaming, without recrimination, without reacting in any way at all, there would be nothing for his rage to feed on.

She didn't listen to the words he spat at her as she lay on the stairs, blood trickling down her chin. She only saw his eyes, which were averted from the damage he'd done, the guilt already dampening his temper. She waited until he'd finished his tirade, until he'd grabbed his jacket from the peg, gone out and slammed the door behind him.

Then she used the banister to pull herself upright and walked slowly into the kitchen, absently rubbing her elbow, which had made painful contact with the edge of the stair as she'd landed. She tore off a piece of kitchen towel and wet it under the tap, wiping the blood away, wincing a little as she did. Then she got some ice cubes from the freezer, and wrapping them in a tea towel, held them against her swelling mouth with her left hand, while with her right she started to clean up the pieces of broken crockery and congealing food from the floor, and wondered how she could have done things differently to avoid making him lose his temper.

* * *

Joanne scrutinised her face in the bathroom mirror, turning from side to side so that she could see her jaw from different angles. Then she sighed and replaced the tube of foundation cream in her cosmetic bag. It was pointless, she realised. She didn't normally wear makeup to work and to do so now would only draw attention to her face rather than divert it. Her bottom lip was still swollen after two days and the dark bruise that had formed along the side of her jaw was now turning a nasty greenish-yellow. Better to think of a plausible reason as to how she could have sustained such an injury; hiding it would only make her clients suspicious.

She tied her hair back in its customary ponytail and went downstairs. Steve had not spoken to her since their argument, and had not come home at all last night; he had probably had too much to drink down the pub and stayed over at one of his mates' houses, although it was unusual for him to do so. He usually came home at some point, even if at dawn, to have a shower and get fresh clothes for work; he was very fastidious in his appearance.

Maybe he'd stayed at his brother's and borrowed some of his things; they were of similar height and build, and had the same expensive taste in clothes, although apart from that Mike and Steve were like chalk and cheese.

Joanne glanced at her watch, and decided to catch the earlier bus to Mrs Jenkins. The old lady would no doubt be eager to continue the story of her wartime romance, and Joanne wanted to hear it. Better that than sit here for another half hour ruminating about what kind of mood Steve would be in when he came home this evening.

She was just locking the front door when the telephone started ringing. For a fleeting moment she thought of ignoring it. Kate always rang her on her mobile so as not to risk having to speak to Steve. Of course it could be her mother, in which case Joanne would regret answering it, but on balance it was more likely to be Steve. He knew her cleaning rota to the minute; if she didn't answer the phone he'd demand to know what she'd been doing and who she'd been doing it with.

She caught it on the sixth ring.

"Steve?" she said.

"No," the voice replied. "It's Amy. Are you disappointed?"

Joanne sat down heavily on the stairs, dropping her keys on the floor. She closed her eyes. Over two years without a word.

"Are you still there?" Amy asked.

"Yes," Joanne responded immediately, afraid her daughter might hang up if she got no response. "Are you all right?"

"Yes, I'm fine, Mum. I take it Dad's not there then?"

"No, he's at work. But he'll be in this evening. If you give me your number he can ring you back later. Where are you?"

"I'm in a payphone. I haven't got a phone at home."

That wasn't what Joanne had meant, but she didn't press Amy for her location; she didn't want to do anything that would result in her hanging up.

"How are you?" she said awkwardly. "What have you been doing for the last two years? I've been so worried."

"Didn't Auntie Kate tell you I'd phoned her?"

"Yes," Joanne said. "But that was over a year ago, Amy." She paused for a moment, realising that she was sounding a bit frantic. "Are you still in London?" she continued, trying to calm her voice.

"Yes. It's great here, Mum. I've got a good job, and I'm in a flat near Greenwich. I read about you in the paper."

"Me?" said Joanne, confused.

"Yes. There was an article in the paper about Suzy Devine committing suicide. Zac was a big fan of hers in the nineties, and he was really upset. He showed me the article. It mentioned that her cleaner, Mrs Harris found the body, and I knew you worked as a cleaner, so I thought it was probably you. Was it?"

"Yes," replied Joanne. "Yes, it was me. How did you know I was a cleaner?"

"Auntie Kate told me. Listen, Mum, I was hoping Dad wouldn't be there. I wanted to talk to you for a few minutes. Is it OK?"

"Yes, of course it is," said Joanne. If the house had been on fire she'd have ignored it to talk to Amy. She was trying to absorb the fact that her daughter had apparently kept in regular touch with Kate, and Kate hadn't told her. "Who's Zac?" she asked.

"What's wrong, Mum?" Amy asked unexpectedly.

"Nothing," said Joanne. "I'm just a bit shocked, that's all. And pleased. You can't imagine how wonderful it is to hear your voice."

"No, I don't mean that. You sound strange. Sort of mumbly."

"Ah, I've…er…just got a bit of a cold, that's all," Joanne lied. She had been speaking with her mouth almost closed, trying not to open the cut on her lip.

"He's hit you again, hasn't he?" Amy said. Her voice sounded different somehow, more mature. "Why don't you leave him, Mum? He's a shit. He's always been a shit."

"No, he's not, Amy. He just has a bad temper, that's all," Joanne said. "He was distraught when you left. He'll be so sorry to have missed your call."

"Yeah, I bet," her daughter replied. "He didn't even notice I was there for most of my life. I'm glad he's at work. It's you I wanted to talk to, not him. I didn't ring before because I didn't want you to tell him where I was, and I still don't. Will you promise me you won't tell him?"

"Yes, if you really don't want me to," Joanne said, puzzled. "But why not?"

The silence on the phone went on for so long that Joanne began to think her daughter had hung up after all.

"Amy?" she said fearfully.

"Yes, I'm still here. Look, I just don't, that's all. He wouldn't approve of my boyfriend, for one thing."

"Is that who Zac is?"

"Yes."

"What's wrong with him, then?"

"Nothing," Amy replied. "He's wonderful, Mum. He's gentle and caring and he really loves me. He works with computers. And I love him. We want to get married. We're saving as much as we can towards a deposit on a house."

"That's all that matters, then. Why wouldn't your dad approve of him?"

"Because he looks a bit different. And because he's everything Dad isn't."

Joanne had no idea what to make of this piece of information.

"I'd love to meet him," she said.

"I'd like that too, Mum. That's why I phoned you. I didn't want to get married without telling you. It didn't seem right. I'm sorry. I should have got in touch before. I never wanted to upset you. Are you mad with me?"

"No," said Joanne. "I was never mad with you. I was just worried sick, that's all. Why did you leave, Amy?"

"I…look, I'm sorry, Mum. I've got to go. I'm running out of money. I'll ring you again. Very soon, I promise. I love you. Bye."

"I love you too, darling," Joanne said, but the phone had already gone dead.

She put the receiver down and sat on the stairs for a few minutes, trying to come to terms with the fact that her little girl was getting married. Of course she wasn't a little girl any more; she was a woman now, nearly nineteen, as old as Joanne herself had been when she got married. It was unbelievable.

Was that why Amy had left? Had she met this Zac here in Manchester and known that her dad wouldn't approve? Was that why she'd left so suddenly, in the middle of the night?

That must be it, Joanne thought, deeply relieved. She had never mentioned anyone called Zac; as far as Joanne had known, at sixteen Amy had been infatuated with Ben Farrar.

Amy had promised to phone again soon, and she set great store by promises, had always done her utmost to keep them, even as a child. If she said she would phone again soon, she would, and this time Joanne would be prepared.

She had to get to know her daughter again. Two years was a long time to be apart from each other, especially in the teenage years, when children were developing their personalities so rapidly. What had she done to make Amy lose faith in her? She had to find that out if she was to regain her daughter's trust.

But to do that she had to keep the contact with Amy. And she had to meet this Zac. She would know if he really was kind and gentle, or if it was all an act. She knew only too well how easy it was to be swept off your feet, to become blind to someone's faults when you were in love. But providing her daughter loved him and he loved her, Joanne would approve of him, even if he had two heads or was thirty years older than Amy.

It didn't matter. None of it mattered. What was important was that the day she'd been waiting for, praying for for two years had finally arrived. Amy had made contact, and Joanne was determined that she would do whatever had to be done to bring her family together again.

She walked to the bus stop on a cloud, and finally arrived twenty minutes late for her first client.

CHAPTER NINE

It was nearly a week before Joanne saw Kate, because she was away on a business trip. Joanne had carefully rehearsed various ways of finding out what she wanted to know, but when Kate opened the door, she immediately dropped an exquisitely-wrapped present into Joanne's hands, throwing her off track.

"I bought it while I was getting something for Alex's wife," she explained, grinning. Joanne carefully untied the silver bow and unfolded the layers of tissue, while Kate hovered impatiently over her.

"Chanel!" she cried. "It must have cost you a fortune!" She opened the black box and sprayed a tiny amount on her wrist.

"It didn't cost me anything," Kate replied nonchalantly. "I put it on Alex's account."

"What? You can't do that!" Joanne exclaimed, aghast. "It's dishonest."

"About as dishonest as he'll be, then, when he tells Helen that he spent ages looking for just the right gift for her, when in actual fact he forgets she even exists the moment he arrives at work. If I didn't remind him of every anniversary and birthday, he'd be divorced by now. And that'd cost him a damn sight more than a bottle of perfume."

She walked into the lounge and Joanne followed, sniffing at her wrist. It was lovely. It smelt expensive, classy.

"*My* present to you's there," Kate said, waving a hand in the direction of the coffee table.

It was a beautiful cream-coloured shoulder bag, the leather so luxuriously soft and smooth that Joanne knew it had probably cost more than the rest of her wardrobe put together.

"You deserve it," Kate said before she could protest. "And I can easily afford it. There's nothing like good perfume and accessories to make a woman feel a million dollars."

"I don't know when I'm going to use them," Joanne said. She couldn't take a bag like this to Tesco, which was the only place she went, really, apart from work.

"Wear the Chanel when you go cleaning," Kate said, grinning. "Hopefully it'll give you the confidence you need to make sure you get your money off some of the skinflints you skivvy for. I made us hot chocolate, I'll just go and get it."

Joanne waited until Kate had poured the chocolate, sprinkled tiny pink and white marshmallows over the top of it and was settled on the couch, sipping ecstatically. "Thank God I inherited Mum's metabolism," she commented. "I'd be as fat as a pig otherwise."

"Amy rang on Tuesday," Joanne said suddenly.

Kate nodded, and wiped a blob of cream off her nose with her finger.

"She said she was going to. I'm glad she's done it at last."

She sat back and lifted her cup to her lips, eyeing Joanne over the rim. She could see her sister trying to build the courage to ask the question Kate had been dreading. She wouldn't anticipate her; Joanne needed to find her strength and this was a good place to start.

"Why didn't you tell me she'd kept in touch with you?" Joanne said finally.

"Because she asked me not to. She needed someone she could trust."

"She could trust me!" Joanne cried. "I'm her mother!"

"Yes, I know," Kate said.

"Well, why doesn't she, then? I've racked my brains

trying to think of what I did that could have made her leave like that. I can't think of anything, anything at all. Did she tell you?" Joanne was close to tears, and Kate felt her own eyes moisten in sympathy.

"You didn't do anything," she said. "Amy didn't want Steve to know where she'd gone, that's all. And she thought you'd tell him."

"I wouldn't, not if she hadn't wanted me to," Joanne said. "But why didn't she want him to know where she was?"

Kate leaned forward.

"Joanne, you can't keep anything from Steve, you know that. You always give in to him in the end. If you'd known where she was you'd have told him, eventually, wouldn't you?"

"No, I wouldn't, not if she really didn't want me to. Amy means more to me than anyone!"

"Even more than Steve?" Kate asked gently.

"Yes, of course," Joanne replied without hesitation, then flushed and stopped.

"Do you mean that? Really?"

Joanne thought for a moment.

"Yes," she said wonderingly, as though a revelation had come upon her. "Yes, I do mean it. She's my daughter. I love her."

"That's what I told her," Kate said. "I told her that you were changing, that you wouldn't tell him anything if she asked you not to."

"Kate," Joanne said. "Does she really think I love Steve more than her? That I'd break her confidence if she trusted me?" Her eyes were huge and imploring, and Kate felt, as she often did, that it was she who was the older sister, that Joanne had somehow stopped developing when she married Steve. Which was true in many ways. She was still an insecure teenager, searching for reassurances that she was worth loving. She just never knew when to give up.

"No," she replied. "Amy didn't think you loved Steve more than her. But she does know that you always find excuses for him, no matter what he's done. And she did think that you'd give in if he hit you, or didn't speak to you for weeks. She didn't want to put you through that, so she decided it was better not to tell you anything. She was trying to protect you, in her way."

"She shouldn't be protecting me," Joanne said in a small voice. "I'm her mother. It should be the other way round. She said she's got a boyfriend, but he looks a bit different. She said Steve wouldn't approve of him. Is that why she left?"

"He's black," Kate said evasively.

Joanne looked up, but there was no shock on her face, just concern.

"Have you met him? Is he nice?"

Kate hesitated for a moment, then seemed to come to a decision.

"No," she said. "But I spoke to him briefly on the phone. He sounds lovely. According to Amy he's respectable, intelligent, good-looking, and best of all, he loves her. He's encouraging her in her career, he doesn't mind that she's got male friends as well. As far as you can judge someone from a five minute phone conversation, I liked him, and I think you probably will too."

"But Steve won't." It was not a question.

"No, he won't. He'll see the colour of Zac's skin, and won't get any further than that. Does it matter?"

"No," Joanne said. "As long as Amy's really happy."

"She is," Kate affirmed. "God, I'm so glad she's phoned you. It's been horrible keeping all this from you. It put me in a really awkward position. But when she left she really needed someone, and I thought it was better to hide it from you and keep the contact, than lose her altogether."

"Yes, it was. You were right. It's just that…I don't know why she couldn't have told me about Zac instead of leaving like that," Joanne said. "We could have worked something out."

"Why did he hit you?" Kate asked suddenly, eyeing the

yellowing bruise on her sister's jaw.

Joanne raised her hand instinctively to her mouth. She'd forgotten about it in the excitement of Amy's call.

"He wants me to talk to the newspapers about Suzy Devine," she said. "He thinks they'll pay for a good story."

Kate considered this.

"They might, if you have got a good story."

"Yes, but I haven't. He wants me to lie and say I found drugs and stuff around the flat. I can't do that. The poor woman's dead. Imagine what her family would think if they read a load of lies in the paper. And the police would wonder why I hadn't mentioned the drugs before, as well."

"Right. So he hit you because you wouldn't talk to the papers?"

"He'd told them I would, you see," Joanne said. "They sent a reporter round, a horrible cocky little teenager, all false smiles and sympathy. I shut the door in his face. Steve said I'd made him look pathetic."

"Because you'd dared to disobey him?"

"Yes, I suppose so."

"How long ago was this?"

"A week. He hasn't spoken to me since. Well, until last night, when he told me he's being made redundant again after Christmas. He said I should change my mind about talking to the papers."

"What will he do if you still refuse?" Kate asked.

"The usual, I suppose," Joanne replied tiredly. "Find fault with everything I do, remind me of everything he's done for me…I don't know."

"You can always come here. You know that."

Over the years Joanne had lost count of the times Kate had offered her sanctuary. But she couldn't make her sister understand that leaving would be like admitting her whole life had been wasted, that it had all been for nothing. And there had been good times. Lots of good times. They'd been together for twenty years; she was bound to get on his nerves from time to time. He'd been used to getting his own way since he was a child, just as she'd always been used to giving in to the wishes of others.

She was at fault too. She'd always let him take the lead, take all the responsibility. He was so good at that, so confident. She could never be as confident as him. It seemed to be a male thing. Her dad had been the same, and her mother still hadn't completely recovered from his death, even though it was nearly eight years now.

She would be the same if she left Steve. She didn't have a bank account in her own name; it was a joint account, and Steve controlled the finances. Everything was done on the internet now and she knew nothing about it. It would look ridiculous, a forty-year-old woman having to ask how to go about doing things that everyone else took for granted. They would all laugh at her, think she was mental or something. It was too much effort. She just didn't have the energy to leave; it was hard enough getting through the days as it was, when everything was familiar.

She finished her chocolate, and realised that she hadn't spoken for a few minutes. A thought suddenly occurred to her.

"Why did you tell Amy I was changing?" she asked.

"You said Steve will keep up the pressure to get you to change your mind about selling your story?" Kate said.

Joanne's brow furrowed. They'd just discussed this.

"Probably, yes," she answered. "But why...?"

"Will you?" Kate interrupted.

"No," Joanne said. "I can't. Not on this. It's wrong. It's not just me who'll be affected. If my daughter had committed suicide and I had to try to cope with that, then I read a load of lies about her in the paper...I don't know what I'd do. I can't do that to someone else's parents."

Kate laughed, although Joanne couldn't think of anything she'd said that could even vaguely be considered funny.

"Like I said, you're changing," she replied. "If I ask you a question, will you give me an honest answer?"

"Depends on what it is," Joanne replied cagily.

"I was under the impression that you stayed with Steve because you thought Amy needed two parents. But Amy's been gone for two years now. Why are you still with him, Jo? You can't still love him, surely?"

Joanne looked away, uncomfortable. She looked round the room as though searching for an answer in its clean, pristine lines. Everything about Kate's life was well-organised, cool, controlled. She would never let any man take her over until she didn't even know who she was any more. Steve was the only person who had made her feel important, wanted, desirable. Without him Joanne felt she would fade away, become a nonentity, like she'd been before she met him. Kate was the opposite, completely self-sufficient. She didn't need anyone.

"I don't know how to explain it," Joanne said finally. "You wouldn't understand."

"Try me," Kate said earnestly.

"It's like....it's like being on a rollercoaster," Joanne ventured hesitantly. "When things are going well, it's wonderful. It's like the whole world revolves around me. I'm the most beautiful woman in the world. He makes me feel so special, so cherished.

"We'll go out for a meal, and I'll see all the other married couples sitting at tables, not really looking at each other any more because they've run out of things to say to each other, and Steve's holding my hand and telling me he loves me, and I can sense the other women looking at us full of envy and wishing their husbands were handsome and romantic like that. I used to wonder how they could live their grey little lives, day after day, year after year. I'm not beautiful, I know that. I'm nothing out of the ordinary, really. If I left Steve I'd never feel special like that again."

"But those other women's husbands don't take them home and knock them about afterwards," Kate interjected.

"No, well, Steve doesn't do that most of the time, either. And when he does...when he does go too far, he's always so sorry, and then it's wonderful, for months at a time."

"When was the last time it was wonderful, Jo?" Kate asked.

"I knew you wouldn't understand," Joanne said sadly.

"You're wrong, I do understand," Kate countered. "Mum never took any notice of you at all, and Dad only spoke to you to criticise you. Steve's an improvement on that, because even though he doesn't just criticise you, but beats you up as well, he also tells you he loves you and makes you feel special now and again. And because you've never known any different, you think that's how it should be. Well it's not.

"Has it occurred to you that maybe all those grey couples sitting in the restaurants hadn't run out of things to say? Maybe they just felt so comfortable with each other that they didn't need to talk all the time. Maybe their husbands don't need to shower them with champagne and roses and all that crap, because they show their wives every day in small ways that they love them. By respecting their opinions, considering their needs and wishes, treating them like equal partners. Tell me Jo, when was the last time you felt relaxed with him, that you could say anything to him and know he'd listen to you and respect your views?"

Joanne stood up.

"I think I should go now," she said.

"No, don't. I'm not having a go at you, I'm asking a serious question. I'm not going to pretend I like Steve. I don't. I hate his guts. But if he'd really loved you, I'd have at least tried to like him. But love isn't all big overblown gestures, it's the little things. You can't live on a roller coaster all your life. It's too exhausting. It's only like that in films. After a while the excitement wears off and you start to get comfortable together. That's how it's supposed to be."

"Was that how it was with you and Rob?" Joanne asked. She sat down again. Kate didn't talk much about her only serious relationship, which had ended five years ago.

"Yes, that's how it was with Rob," Kate agreed. "We could talk about anything. It was wonderful. We understood each other. We were best friends as well as lovers."

"Until he got his job in India."

"Yes. He offered to turn it down and stay here but I wouldn't let him, because he'd have been miserable. He'd always wanted to make a difference."

"You could have gone with him," Joanne said.

Kate laughed.

"Come on! Could you see me living in a shack in the middle of nowhere, treating lepers all day? No electricity or running water? No, I'm not cut out to be Mother Teresa, and Rob wasn't cut out to be a Harley Street specialist. If we'd stayed together one of us would have been miserable, and we'd have drifted apart anyway. As it is we've stayed friends, which is the important thing. He's invited me to go out there for a couple of weeks in the summer."

"Will you go?" Joanne asked.

"I don't know, yet."

They talked for a while about India, and what Rob was doing, and whether there was a Hilton in Calcutta that Kate could stay in, and by the time Joanne left, the slight awkwardness between them had vanished.

Joanne was glad that Kate hadn't pushed her for an answer to her question. She couldn't remember the last time she'd felt relaxed with Steve. She never felt completely at ease with him. Exhilarated, yes, at times. Nervous and afraid, sometimes.

But mostly now she just felt nothing. It was all right when she was at Kate's. She didn't have to consider every word she uttered, and could just chat freely, forget how pointless her life seemed to be. The initial surge of energy that had pulled her out of her depression after Amy left had slowly ebbed away again, leaving her feeling tired all the time. It was an effort to get up in the morning; she showered and dressed because she knew she should, not because she had any reason to look good.

If she were honest, she neither loved Steve nor hated him. It took all her energy to behave normally, to go to work, come home, cook a meal, watch TV, when nothing interested her. It was a relief to go to bed, because then she could sleep, until another grey morning arrived and the whole cycle started over again.

It occurred to Joanne that she might be a bit run down. But it was nothing specific, nothing worth going to the doctor about. She should get a tonic; she'd been meaning to for ages, but kept forgetting. She needed to start making an effort. Things were changing. Amy had promised to call again, and hopefully visit.

She went into the chemist on the way home, and bought some multivitamins and a bottle of tonic wine. And made a resolution to remember to take them every day.

* * *

April 2004

The annual Harris family gathering took place outside this year, due to the unusually hot spring weather. Tables were laid out on the lawns, and the family sat around them on uncomfortable garden chairs, trying to find things to say to each other whilst batting wasps away from their finger rolls and bowls of raspberry pavlova.

"Stephen told me that Amy telephoned a couple of weeks ago," Susan said, dabbing delicately at her mouth with her napkin. She regarded Joanne with a similar expression to that she'd bestowed on the bluebottle that had taken up residence on the edge of her plate a few seconds before.

"Yes, she did," said Joanne, somewhat surprised. She had finally got Amy's permission to tell Steve that she'd phoned to say she was thinking of getting married, and had been shocked by his complete indifference when she did pluck up the courage to tell him. He'd merely stated that if she expected him to pay for the wedding she had another think coming, and had gone to the pub almost immediately afterwards. He hadn't asked how Amy was, where she was, anything.

Any slight temptation Joanne might have felt to reveal that Amy had been in regular contact for four months and was hoping to visit at some point vanished, and she had spent the evening wondering how he could be so uncaring. He hadn't shown any joy at all; if anything he'd seemed uneasy by the news that his daughter had phoned.

Maybe he was upset that his little girl was grown up now, independent, and had found another man to look after her. Maybe he was jealous of Zac. Joanne had heard that fathers often found it difficult to accept that their daughters no longer needed them. That must be what it was.

She hadn't mentioned the subject of Amy since, and neither had Steve. Odd that he'd told his mother about the phone call, then.

"I suppose she's going to come crawling home with her tail between her legs, and expect you to forgive her, is she?" Susan refolded her napkin and replaced it on the table. The bluebottle flew away and Joanne watched wistfully as it disappeared into the clear blue sky.

"No, not at all," she replied. "She's got a good job, and a boyfriend."

"Yes," her mother-in-law said. "So I heard. She expects Stephen to pay for her wedding. Or is she just going to cohabitate with him? So many couples do these days." She sighed. "Disgusting, in my opinion. Living in sin it used to be called, quite rightly too."

"No, she told me she wants to get married. I shouldn't think they'd need us to pay for anything. Amy's boyfriend has an excellent job in computers," Joanne said casually. The trick with Susan was not to rise to anything she said, no matter how annoying. If you didn't rise to the bait she would get bored and move on to someone else.

"Oh, really?" Susan's voice brightened at the thought

that her future grandson-in-law might be well off.

He could be Jack the Ripper and you'd approve, if he was loaded, Joanne thought, *Not if you found out he was black, though. Couldn't ignore that, like you do your eldest son's dodgy financial practices.*

It would be wonderful in one way to drop the little bombshell of Zac's ethnicity onto the table and watch it explode and annihilate the party. Joanne sighed and awaited the barrage of questions about Zac's financial position.

"Just as well, isn't it?" Steve's eldest brother Dave commented. "Couldn't even afford the ring, now, could you? How much does the dole pay these days?"

Joanne, sitting next to Steve, saw his fist clench under the table. Dave was a buffoon, one of the most astoundingly tactless men she'd ever met. How he managed to get so many clients was beyond her. But then, of course he was good with figures and could fiddle his clients' tax as well as he did his own.

"I don't intend to find out. I'll have another job soon enough," Steve replied tightly.

"Don't know, not getting any younger, are you, old chap?" Dave laughed. "What are you, fifty? Fifty-one?"

"I'll never catch up to you though. Be retiring soon, won't you?"

"Me, retire?" Dave smiled. "Never. Work till I fall off the tree, I will. Got a good few years left in me yet."

Joanne looked at Dave's florid face and huge stomach and wondered how people could be so self-deceiving. He was a heart attack waiting to happen.

"Thank God for that," Dave's wife Evelyn commented. "I'll divorce him if he ever stops work. It'd be unbearable having him under my feet all day. Doesn't Steve get in your way, Jo?"

Yes, thought Joanne.

"No, not at all," she said. "It's only twelve weeks since he was made redundant."

"Only twelve weeks? I'd kill Dave in twelve weeks."

"No you wouldn't, darling," Dave mumbled through a mouthful of meringue. "Wouldn't inherit a penny if you bumped me off. Get fifteen years instead."

"Not if it looked like an accident," Evelyn said coolly. She almost sounded as though she meant it.

"Have you got anything in the pipeline, then?" Mike, the middle brother asked, without much interest. He had been gazing across the lawns at his two youngest sons, who were playing a game of spinning round and round until they became dizzy and fell over.

"I've had a couple of interviews," Steve said. "Haven't heard back yet. I met a man at the job centre last week, though. He flies model planes."

Susan sat up straighter in her chair, following Mike's gaze to the two human spinning tops.

"Really, Michael, can't you stop them? They'll make themselves sick if they carry on," she said disgustedly.

"They're all right," he replied. "They're just enjoying themselves, that's all." He looked at Joanne and winked.

He knows I'm not enjoying myself, she thought. *He isn't either.*

Of all the Harris family, Mike was the only one she liked. Married and divorced twice, he judged people by their achievements, not their wealth. And he'd fought for and won custody of his three sons from his second marriage.

"Model planes?" she said, trying to take more interest in the conversation. Steve would be annoyed if she made it obvious she'd rather not be here.

"Yes. He's invited me to go up on Saturday and have a look, see if I'm interested. I thought I'd told you."

No, he hadn't told her.

"*Model planes?*" Dave echoed scathingly. "Going to get a job painting them, are you?" He laughed, and Steve's mouth tightened.

"No, you bloody idiot," he replied. "He's got contacts. All sorts of people fly planes. Lawyers, doctors, businessmen. Harry got his latest job through one of the men at the club. I thought I'd give it a shot. Can't do any harm, can it? Better than sitting on my arse getting fat." He grinned at his brother's waistline, of which he was very sensitive. "Sorry, they don't call it fat, now, do they? That's not polite. Morbidly obese, that's the correct term isn't it, Mike?"

Mike the GP ignored him. Dave's face turned purple.

"Damn, I knew I shouldn't have worn yellow," Evelyn inserted into the uncomfortable silence, brushing at her dress. "Every bloody insect for miles around thinks I'm a giant flower."

"Shall we repair to the poolside?" Susan suggested, reaching for her stick. "Then Collins can clear the tables. Joanne, my dear, you might want to go and reapply your lipstick. You appear to have lost it all during the meal."

Joanne was just about to say what her mother-in-law already knew, that she hadn't been wearing any lipstick, when in the distance Jeremy, the smaller of the two boys, fell face first into the hydrangeas. There was a moment's silence, then a loud wail erupted from the foliage. Mike and Joanne stood up together, and Joanne started to sink back into her chair.

"Would you care to take a turn around the grounds with me, madam?" Mike said, affecting an aristocratic tone and offering his arm to her. "We can check on my errant offspring before repairing to the poolside with the others."

Joanne managed to restrain from laughing out loud at her brother-in-law's imitation of his mother's formal tones. Anything to get a respite from Steve and Dave. Now they'd started, they would spend at least twenty minutes hurling insults at each other before Dave left. It was always Dave who gave in first. You'd think after all these years he'd have realised that he couldn't better Steve in a slanging match. She threaded her arm through Mike's and they walked off briskly together in the direction of the wailing shrubbery.

"I'm thinking of emigrating," Mike said unexpectedly, after they'd ensured that Jeremy had not poked his eye out on a twig, but merely had a slight scratch on his face. The two boys had been packed off to the house to don their swimming trunks.

Joanne looked at him. She was never sure whether he was being serious or not.

"Really?" she said. "Where to?"

"Somewhere where my family can't find me. And where Jeremy, Rupert and Bartholomew sound like normal names. It's costing me a fortune to send the kids to private school. I daren't send them to the local primary with names like that. They'd get their heads kicked in. I should never have let Jenny name them."

"You could go to India, like Rob," Joanne suggested.

"Who's Rob?"

"My sister's ex-boyfriend. He's a doctor. He went to work with lepers in Calcutta."

"I'd almost forgotten you'd got a sister," Mike said. "I remember her now. Very pretty, blonde hair, green eyes. Forthright. You should bring her here. She'd liven things up a bit. Karen, is it?"

"Kate. She wouldn't come if I begged her. Her and Steve don't exactly see eye to eye on most things."

"Sensible woman," Mike commented.

"Steve wanted to call Amy Algernon if she'd been a boy," Joanne said, not wanting to pursue Kate's hatred for Steve.

"*Algernon?*" Mike exclaimed. "Christ, she probably changed sex in the womb when she heard that! You're having me on, right?"

"No," Joanne said. "He really did."

"How come Amy isn't called Arabella or Euphemia then?"

"He didn't have any names ready for a girl. He was convinced she would be a boy."

"Yes, I remember. Dave won fifty quid off him over that. Gloated over it for months. Steve was mad as hell."

They were walking in a very slow circle around the rose beds. They remained at all times within sight of the others. Mike knew his brother well and would give him no cause for jealousy. But they were out of earshot.

"What's wrong?" he asked.

Joanne had been bending to smell one of the early roses, a beautiful creamy-white bloom. She straightened up. Mike had an urge to pluck it for her, but resisted. That could be misconstrued.

"Nothing," she said. "Well, I'm a bit bothered about Steve not having a job. But it's great that Amy got in touch. I've been worried about her ever since she left."

"Did she say where she is?"

"No," said Joanne, reddening slightly. It didn't feel right lying to him. "I think I'm just a bit run down, that's all. I've been taking multivitamins. And I got some Metatone tonic, too."

"Symptoms?" Mike asked. Joanne laughed.

"Well, Dr. Harris," she said, adopting a formal tone, "I have been feeling a little fatigued of late, and…" She stopped and looked at him. His face was serious. "I'm OK," she amended, "really I am."

"No you're not," he said. "You've lost weight. You look listless and pale, and you've got shadows under your eyes. Have you been to your doctor?"

"No," she replied light-heartedly. "I thought I'd wait until I saw you at a social occasion so I could bore you rigid with a list of symptoms. Isn't that what most people do when they find out you're a doctor?"

He smiled.

"I don't tell people I'm a doctor. I tell them I'm in accounts. No one wants to talk about accountancy. Do you want my diagnosis?"

"I know there's nothing wrong with…"

"You're depressed, Joanne."

"No I'm not!" she protested. "There's nothing wrong with my mind."

"I didn't say you were mad, I said you were depressed. And before you say it, it doesn't mean you're weak or pathetic, either. It's an illness. Do you find it hard to get up in the morning, difficult to think of anything that you'd like to do, find that nothing gives you pleasure? Everything grey and pointless?"

She looked away, which told him he was right.

"Go to your doctor. He can prescribe you antidepressants if you want. They can ease the symptoms, make it easier to get through the day."

"But not cure it?" Joanne said.

"There are different schools of thought about that. If it's just a pure clinical depression with no external cause, then yes, tablets can cure it. But there's usually an underlying reason. The tablets can help to pick you up enough to find that. Counselling can help too, but there's a long waiting list for that unless you go private. I can recommend someone, if you want."

"And then what do you do?" Joanne asked. "When you've found the underlying cause?"

"You change things, get rid of it, depending on what it is. If it's something from your childhood you can learn strategies to deal with it. After a while things get better. Not straight away, mind. It takes time. The tablets can help there, too. I can write you a prescription if you don't want to go to your own doctor."

He was looking across the garden towards the swimming pool. Steve was lying down on a sunlounger. Dave was huffily putting his coat on. Jeremy and Rupert were just emerging from the house, dressed in trunks.

"All quiet on the Western Front, in a minute or two, anyway," he said. "Do you want some tablets? Or you can come and see me, if you want, and talk about it a bit more first. In confidence," he added.

"No, I'll be all right, I think," she said. "It's a big relief that Amy's called. I think she'll keep in touch now. Thanks, though."

Mike nodded. They started to head back towards the others. Tactfully, he changed the subject.

"I wish Mother would sell up and get something smaller. It's ridiculous, keeping this place on," he said. "It takes her half an hour to get up the stairs, with her arthritis. She doesn't need a six-bedroomed house. She never has that many guests."

"It's very beautiful," Joanne replied. "Maybe it reminds her of your father, of when you were all little."

"I don't see why she'd want to be reminded of that," Mike snorted. "She never wanted kids in the first place. She couldn't wait to get us all married off and out of the way."

"Oh come on, surely you don't mean that?" Joanne said. "She takes a lot of trouble over these parties."

"Once a year, to keep up appearances. I do mean it. You must see that. How much notice has she ever taken of her grandkids? None. She didn't hate us or anything, she just wasn't interested. I don't blame her, it wasn't her fault. Dad wanted sons to carry on the name, and what Dad wanted he got. She's keeping the house on out of snobbery, that's all. So she can hold weekly bridge parties and say superior things like 'shall we repair to the swimming pool?' or 'Collins can clear away'. God, I'm surprised we're not all playing croquet on the lawn, dressed in blazers and boaters."

"I'll have to suggest it," Joanne laughed.

"Well, it'd have its advantages," Mike said thoughtfully. "At least Steve and Dave could bypass the tedious slanging matches and just lay into each other with the mallets straight away."

"Have they always been like that?" she asked.

"Yes. Ever since Steve started toddling and everyone made such a fuss of him. He was always good-looking and Dave hated that, because he wasn't. Even as a child he was pig-ugly. No one ever said *he* looked like an angel. He used to batter Steve every chance he got, until Steve got old enough to realise how powerful angelic looks could be. Then he learnt that if he broke something or walked mud into the carpet, he could go straight to Nanny in floods of tears and say that Dave had done it but had threatened to hit him if he told. Then Dave would get in trouble twice, once for whatever it was Steve had blamed him for, and once for bullying his baby brother. Dave couldn't fight against slyness. He didn't have the brains for it. And by the time Steve was thirteen he was bigger than Dave, and stronger, even though he was four years younger, so then Dave couldn't even beat him up on the quiet any more. I don't suppose Steve would have told you about that."

"Steve doesn't talk about his childhood much at all," Joanne said. "I didn't even know you had a nanny."

"No, well, it wasn't much fun, overall. Not worth talking about, really."

"What about you? Where did you fit in?" Joanne asked.

Mike looked down at her and grinned.

"Ah, I was the typical middle child," he said. When she looked puzzled, he elaborated. "The eldest gets all the discipline, the youngest is spoiled rotten, and the middle one's ignored completely."

"That must have been horrible!" Joanne said.

"Not with my parents, it wasn't. Mother ignored us all anyway, really. And Dad was a bastard. Nothing Dave did was ever right, and Steve was a girly poof because he had blond ringlets and big blue eyes and all our female relatives thought he was adorable. Steve spent most of his childhood trying to get Dad to love him, Dave spent most of his childhood hating Dad, and I managed to slip through unobserved." He winked at her.

"Steve was distraught when Edward died," Joanne said. "I've never seen him so upset."

"Yes, well, he never did get to prove to Dad that he was worth anything, did he? His business had gone under. I don't think he was even working when Dad died, was he?"

"No," said Joanne. "He was only out of work for a couple of weeks, though."

"It's odd that Dad never liked him much. Steve's much more like him than me or Dave."

"I think you look a lot like your dad," Joanne said.

"I didn't mean in looks, I meant personality-wise. Dad was a bully. He destroyed people with sarcasm, and if that didn't work, well, he was a big bloke and used his size to intimidate. It worked wonders in the police force, getting criminals to confess. Doesn't work so well when you're running a decorating business though. People can't be bullied into having their houses decorated, can they?" He looked down at his diminutive sister-in-law and saw how uncomfortable the conversation was making her feel. He felt a sudden urge to hold her, a very unbrotherly urge, and swallowed it down quickly. "Let's talk about something else," he suggested. "We're almost within earshot. Aren't you going to run off to repair your makeup? You can borrow some of Mother's hideous blue eyeshadow, if you want. The Barbara Cartland look is all the rage at the moment, I believe."

Joanne laughed.

"I think sarcasm must be a hereditary trait," she said.

"It's a selective gene. Granddad had it, but used it to be hysterically funny. He was great, you'd have liked him. Dad had it. Steve got partial sarcasm, it passed Dave by completely, and I got a double dose. I also got the gene for knowing how to use it to destroy bullies rather than to be one. I'd best go and see where Bart's got to." He released her arm and bowed graciously.

"Joanne," he said, as she started to walk away. She turned back. "When you change your mind, about talking, come and see me. Any time."

"Stupid old fart," Steve raged on the way home. "Trying to make me feel small, just because I've had a bit of bad luck. Your family's supposed to support you through bad times, not grind you into the dirt. How old do you think I look?"

Joanne had been prepared for this ever since Dave had made his comment.

"Late thirties, maybe forty at best," she said.

"Really?" He brightened. "Why?"

"You've looked after yourself. You've got a really good body."

This was true. He still worked out regularly at the gym, and his shoulders, arms and chest were heavily muscled. Kate was right, though. He had put on a bit of weight around his midriff. Best not to mention that.

"I'm going a bit grey now though," he said.

"Yes, but you don't notice it, with you being blond. A bit of silver hair on a man makes him look distinguished, anyway," she said. "When I go grey, you'll see every hair." She had no grey at all at the moment. She'd taken after her dad for that. He'd died at sixty with a full head of dark brown hair.

"What time are you going to the flying club on Saturday?" she continued before he could start talking about Dave's lack of virility, and his surfeit of it. She had no wish to have to massage Steve's ego by having a lengthy session of sex. It was too hot, the day had been long and mainly boring, and she felt sweaty and tired.

"Harry said he'd pick me up about ten. If I like it, I might stay for the day."

"I'll make you a packed lunch up, shall I?" she said. She felt a sudden guilty surge of elation at the thought of having a whole afternoon to herself. He was getting increasingly restless as the weeks went on and the unsuccessful interviews built up. She had suggested that she might look for another cleaning job to help tide them over, but Steve had dismissed that idea. It was a husband's job to be the breadwinner, he said shortly. She had not pursued it. Strangely, he had not pestered her further about talking to the media, apart from a few muttered comments about how useful the money would have been.

That fact that he might have realised he wasn't going to win this one, and had given up, occurred to her briefly. Then she dismissed it. Steve never gave up when he really wanted something. Maybe he'd rung the reporter again and had been told the story wasn't worth much after all.

Or maybe he was mellowing a little bit, as he got older. He hadn't laid a hand on her at all for nearly six weeks, in spite of being in the doldrums about work. He hadn't even been particularly critical or picky. Maybe things were finally going to change. Amy would get in touch and visit. Steve would accept Zac, when he got to know him. They would all go to the wedding. Everyone would be reconciled.

Well, it was worth hoping for. You had to hope. Without that, there was nothing.

September 2004

It was a warm but wet evening, the rain coming down in blustery showers. Joanne stood at the doorway of the Conservative Club watching the wind blow the dying leaves around the deserted streets. She took a deep breath, enjoying the smell of the clean rain-washed air, a contrast from the stuff she'd been breathing a few moments ago in the function room, which was laced with cigarette smoke, beer and fifty different perfumes. She would have to go back in a minute; she'd gone to the ladies about ten minutes before and Steve would start to wonder where she was soon. She shivered slightly in her sleeveless dress, but was still reluctant to return to the social evening. She'd been out so seldom in the last few years that she'd forgotten how to be sociable with strangers, how to circulate and make small talk. Probably because of that she'd been buttonholed almost immediately by a stout elderly man who had introduced himself as Harry and who had monopolised her until she'd made her excuses and gone to the toilet.

She sighed and turned away from the door. With a bit of luck Harry would have found someone else to bore by now.

Luck was not on her side. She had only been back in the function room for a few seconds and was still looking around for Steve, when Harry noticed her and, smiling, made his way to her side again. The couple he'd been talking with wore identical expressions of relief at his departure, and Joanne braced herself.

"The buffet's open," he said. "Do you want something?" He escorted her across the room as though she was incapable of finding the long table in the corner by herself, and then helpfully enlightened her as to the contents of every plate. "There's sausage rolls," he said, pointing, "crisps, cheese sandwiches, quiche, and salad for those ladies watching their figure." He smiled at her. "Of course you don't need to worry about that," he remarked gallantly. "And then," pointing to a trifle and a black forest gateau, already cut into slices, "there's trifle and black forest gateau."

Did he think she was retarded? She forced herself to smile and loaded her plate without enthusiasm. As she moved away from the table she located Steve in one corner of the room. He had a pint of beer in one hand and was performing some aerobatic feat with the other to an enraptured pair of women. He would not welcome her presence now. She resigned herself to Harry's company and resolved to make the best of it.

"How long have you been flying model planes?" she asked, hoping he hadn't already told her. She should have listened more carefully.

"Over twenty years now." He smiled. He popped a tiny sausage roll into his mouth. "Things have changed a bit since I started. Technology's changed. And some things are actually cheaper now than they were in '82. Radio gear, stuff like that."

"Really?" said Joanne. Steve's trainer plane had cost him over £300, and she had thought that expensive. She had no idea how they were going to pay the credit card bill when it came in, with him on the dole.

"Oh, yes. It's like everything now. Computers, for instance. Used to cost a fortune, now you can get them free with a packet of cornflakes." He laughed. "Your husband's doing very well, though. Should be able to do his test soon."

"Test?" Joanne said. "He has to do a test?" God, how much would that cost?

"Yes, of course. Dangerous hobby, flying, you know. We have lots of safety rules. You can't fly on your own until you've taken the test. Before you can pass, you've got to show you can do all the necessary pre-flight checks. That means checking the servos and….."

Joanne nodded and smiled politely as Harry went into excruciating detail about every check that had ever been done on every model plane in the universe, or so it seemed. It was nearly ten o'clock, she thought. Last orders in an hour, and then they could go. Or was there an extension? God, if there was that would mean another two hours of this. She forced herself back to the conversation. He was just finishing something about needing a clothes peg with your name on, for some reason she'd obviously missed.

"…take-off, make the plane fly a circuit and figure of eight, two loops, and two approaches to land, sorry, *rectangular* approaches to land," Harry was saying when she tuned back in. He was still talking about the test then, she couldn't have missed much. "Then you go around again, keeping the plane under twenty feet, and land it. If you manage all that, then you have to take off again, make the plane climb to two hundred feet and close the throttle, then land it again. It's to make sure you can land the plane if the engine cuts out, because if it crashes, that can be very expensive, depending on your plane, of course. Once you've got your certificate, you can fly planes on your own." At last he paused for a breath and Joanne leapt in quickly, before he could start rambling on again.

"Do some planes crash more easily than others, then?" she asked, aware that by asking him questions she was encouraging him to treat her to another ten-minute monologue. But she wanted to know how likely it was that Steve would be spending another £300 they hadn't got in the near future.

"Well, it depends on how proficient you are, of course. The trainer planes, like the one Steve's flying at the moment are pretty slow, but they're stable too. Where you crash makes a difference as well. If you crash it into a tree you might get away with minor damage. But if you go straight into the ground it's usually goodnight Vienna." He laughed, and Joanne smiled weakly. "'Course, once Steve's passed his test, he'll be wanting something a bit more challenging than a trainer, a Spitfire, something like that."

"How much do they cost?" Joanne asked.

"Well, it depends on what he wants. Planes can cost anything from a couple of hundred quid to over £25,000 for a top model!"

Joanne smiled and nodded while Harry carried on talking about the technical specifications of planes, and wondered whether Steve would really be irresponsible enough to spend thousands of pounds on a plane. He always liked to have the best; clothes, aftershave, shoes. He spent £50 every month having his hair cut. How could she persuade him to stick to the cheaper models? With a bit of luck, knowing Steve, once he'd mastered the basics and flown a few more times, he'd get bored and give up. Could a first plane after a trainer cost £25,000? Harry had gone on to talk about CG, whatever that was, and Joanne forced herself to listen, waiting for him to pause so she could dive in with her question.

"Of course, the first step in calculating the CG is to find the mean chord. The simplest one is the area divided by the span, that's called the geometric mean chord. Then there's the root chord, that's usually taken as being on the centreline of the plane. So if the wing has, say, a ten-inch root and a seven-inch tip, you can find the gmc by adding the root to the tip and then halving it, so that'd be eight and a half inches." He smiled at her. "Are you good at maths?"

"No, not really," she said. "I wanted to ask you if a Spit…"

"Well, if you're not very mathematical, there's an easy way of finding the MAC," he interrupted happily. "You have to extend the root chord forward by the length of the tip chord, and extend the tip chord aft by the length of the root chord. Then you…."

She was going to die of boredom. She had to get away from him. She could ask someone else how much a Spitfire cost. She managed to catch Steve's eye and waved somewhat frantically at him. To her utter relief, he broke away from the group he was with and came over to her.

"Hi, Harry," he said, then dismissing him, turned to Joanne. "I'm off downstairs for a game of darts with the lads. Are you OK for a drink?"

"Yes," she said. "But…"

"Great. See you in a bit, then." He bestowed a careless kiss on her cheek and wandered off. She looked back up at Harry, who clearly had another hour of technical information to impart.

"Do you play darts?" she asked desperately. Why couldn't she learn to dismiss people she wasn't interested in like Steve did? She didn't dare just walk away from Harry. It would be too rude. He'd be hurt, and then she'd feel guilty.

"No, pool's my game," Harry said. "I play for the Bull, have done for about six months now. We're doing OK in the league this year. I'm not a bad player, but John and Dave, well, we're lucky to have them."

"Do any of the flying club members play?" Joanne asked casually.

"No, not as far as I know," Harry answered. "Not for the Bull, anyway. I suppose I should ask. We can always use more members. How about yourself? We have a ladies team."

"Me?" Joanne smiled. "No, I've never played. So, tell me, what sort of plane would you recommend for Steve, once he's passed his test?"

"Are you all right to drive?" Joanne said a couple of hours later, as Steve fumbled to fit the key in the ignition.

"Yeah, fine," he said. The car roared into life, and he eased his foot back off the accelerator. "Drive better after a couple of pints, anyway."

He drove out of the car park and onto the main road without looking left or right. Joanne tried not to grip the edge of her seat.

"I saw you talking to Harry most of the night. Think he likes you," Steve teased.

"God, I hope not," Joanne said. "He's got to be the most boring man I've ever met in my life. If you want to know how to find CG, whatever that is, I'm your woman, now."

"Centre of gravity," Steve supplied. "Harry's a boring old

fart, but he certainly knows his stuff." He smiled across at her. "You looked really nice tonight. I like your hair up like that, it suits you."

He was in a good mood. Joanne toyed briefly with the idea of asking him how it was Harry had said he'd met Steve for the first time at the flying club, when they both played pool for the same pub team.

"Harry said that once you've passed your test you'll be able to get a better plane," she said instead.

"Already got it," Steve said. "Spitfire. They were doing an offer on them on the net, I picked it up for £150."

That was a relief. Even so, it was £450 on the card. Better than £25,000, though.

"One of the lads said he can get me an interview for the firm he works for," Steve said as they turned into their avenue.

"That's great!" Joanne replied. "Would you be painting?"

"No, it's a driving job. But it'd be better than sitting around all day, and the pay's not bad. He said he'd let me know on Saturday when I go up to the club."

It wasn't worth it, she thought. He'd think of an excuse if she challenged him. He'd say it wasn't the Bull he played for, she'd got the name of the pub wrong, shows how much she listened to him, that sort of thing. Then his good mood would evaporate, and he'd been drinking, which would make him more unpredictable.

"I was thinking about what you said." Steve broke into her thoughts.

"What was that?" Joanne asked.

"About it being easier to get another job if you're already working. So I'll take this job, if Paul can get me the interview."

He slewed the car into the driveway and got out, weaving somewhat unsteadily to the door. Joanne waited until he was asleep before she went back out, took the keys out of the ignition, locked the car, and set the alarm. In the morning he'd realise how drunk he'd been and see what a mess he'd made of parking, but he wouldn't comment on it.

CHAPTER TEN

Joanne sat curled up in a chair in her dressing gown, enjoying her second cup of coffee, engrossed in a historical novel she'd picked up for twenty pence in the local charity shop. It was quite reassuring to know that in the past people worked sixteen hours a day, six days a week, and still had to live ten to a room in a damp cellar. It made her troubles seem minor. And she had the whole morning and probably the best part of the afternoon to herself. It would take Steve at least two hours to drive to Birmingham, and then say an hour for the interview, and even if he came straight back it'd be at least one before he got home. And tonight was his pool night, so she had the evening as well.

She put the book down for a moment and wondered what he was really doing on Wednesday evenings. It had to be another woman. She couldn't think of any other reason why he'd lie to her. He was an extremely attractive man, but very aware of the fact that he was middle-aged; over the last few years Joanne had found herself increasingly having to reassure him that he was still handsome, that he looked ten years younger than he was. It was perfectly understandable that he might seek extra reassurance in the arms of another woman, probably one a lot younger than him.

Joanne was aware that she should be angry about this. She had never so much as looked at another man in twenty years; if Steve did have a lover, he was showing contempt for his wife by doing so. But she really couldn't be bothered being angry; it was just too much effort.

She picked up her book again, and the phone rang. It would be Steve, checking to see if she was where he wanted her to be. She reached over and picked it up.

"Hi, Mum, is Dad there?" Amy asked.

"No," said Joanne, her spirits lifting instantly at the sound of her daughter's voice. "Did you ring yesterday?"

"Yes," said Amy. "But Dad answered, so I put the phone down."

Why doesn't she want to talk to her dad?

"He just wondered who it was, that's all."

"Are you all right? Did he give you grief about it?" Amy's voice sounded concerned.

When Steve told her that the caller had hung up, the fact that she thought it might be Amy must have shown on her face, because he'd instantly become suspicious.

"No," Joanne replied. "I thought it might be you, so I told him that I'd read that it was something burglars do sometimes, phone to see if anyone's in, then hang up if they get an answer."

Amy laughed down the phone.

"Good. So he doesn't know I'm thinking of visiting?"

"No, you asked me not to tell him," Joanne answered. "Do you know when you're coming up yet?"

"Yes," said Amy. "Tomorrow. I can stay over the weekend and go back on Sunday afternoon."

Tomorrow?

"Is that a problem?" Amy added.

"No," Joanne said instantly. For the last nine months every time the phone had rung, Joanne had prayed it would be Amy announcing her intention to visit. She'd started to think she'd never get round to it. "It's just…I expected more notice, that's all. I haven't got your room ready or anything. But it's OK, of course it is."

"Mum," Amy said gently, "I've already agreed to stay with Auntie Kate."

"Oh," Joanne replied, trying not to let her disappointment

show in her voice. "Right. Maybe that's best. I mean, Kate lives right in the centre of town. Near all the clubs."

"It's nothing to do with that, Mum. It's…look, I'll explain everything when we meet. Why I left, what I've been doing, everything. I just don't want to do it on the phone, that's all. When can I see you?"

Joanne thought. She didn't want to meet her daughter for the first time in three years with Kate there. With anyone there. She might be being selfish, but she wanted her all to herself, just for a while. Just the first time.

"You can come here if you want. Your dad's taken up flying model planes. He'll be out all day on Saturday."

"Model planes? Dad? Isn't that something old people do? Mind you, he *is* getting old now, I suppose."

Yes, it was definitely better that she didn't see Steve if she was going to come out with comments like that.

"Can you come round? On Saturday? Or shall we meet up somewhere?" Joanne asked.

"Are you sure he won't come home early?"

"He never has up to now, and he's been doing it for three months," Joanne said. "He goes out at ten and gets in around five or six in the evening."

"Right, I'll come about twelve then. We can have lunch together, how's that?"

That was wonderful. They talked on for a couple of minutes, during which Amy said that Zac couldn't come up this time because he had to work, but that he'd come up with her again, soon. Joanne's heart soared. Amy meant to keep in contact, then. Whatever reason she'd had for leaving, it couldn't be that bad. Joanne would do whatever she had to do to resolve the problem and make everything right again.

"Mum?" Amy said, after they'd said their goodbyes. "Are you still there?"

Joanne had been just about to replace the receiver, but put it hurriedly back to her ear.

"Yes."

"I'm really looking forward to seeing you again. I've

missed you so much, you wouldn't believe."

Joanne had to swallow a big lump of tears down before she could speak.

"I've missed you too, darling."

Then she put the phone down and cried like a baby.

Joanne looked at her watch for the fifteenth time in ten minutes, sat down on the edge of the chair, then stood up again almost immediately and went to the window. She couldn't ever remember feeling so nervous before, and tried to tell herself she was being ridiculous. Her daughter was coming to see her, that was all. It wasn't an interview for an all-important job.

No, it was worse than that. There were lots of jobs. If you failed one interview, there were always other possibilities. But she only had one daughter. If she failed in this meeting, she might lose her forever. Everything had to go right. It had to.

How she had kept her mounting excitement from Steve over the last two days, she had no idea. Spectacularly insensitive though he could be, he was remarkably adept at recognising when she was excited or nervous about something, after which he wouldn't rest until he'd found out the reason. Most of the time she just came straight out and told him so that she could face the music immediately and get it over with. But this wasn't a smashed ornament or a favourite shirt that had run in the wash. This was important, no, more than that, crucial. She had forced herself to resurrect the long-dormant powers of deception that had enabled her to complete nearly two years of A level study without her father finding out, and had casually bustled around the house, doing only the normal amount of cleaning, expressing an interest in how his interview had gone, consoling him when the company phoned on Friday to say he'd been unsuccessful.

This morning she'd waved him off at the door as usual, and waited a full fifteen minutes to make sure he wouldn't come back for something he'd forgotten, before flying off down the road to buy all the things Amy had loved to eat three years ago; Ritz crackers and brie, olives, expensive out-of-season raspberries, chocolate eclairs. Back home, she laid everything out on plates on the dining table. Then she waited.

When the doorbell rang, she jumped violently and ran to the door, heart thumping so hard she felt she could hear it. Then she stopped, took three slow deep breaths to calm herself and opened the door.

The person on the doorstep was undoubtedly her daughter Amy. The golden-blonde hair, cut shorter than the last time Joanne had seen her, the beautiful blue eyes that she'd inherited from her father, the small, slender frame she'd got from her mother. That much was the same. But the Amy Joanne had last seen had been a little girl still, struggling to become a woman; this Amy had won the struggle. She had an air of sophistication about her that reminded Joanne of Kate.

She opened the door wider and Amy walked into the hall. She was playing with her keys, and Joanne realised that she was nervous too.

"You've got a car?" she said. She'd rehearsed a million opening lines. This hadn't been one of them, and she sounded too formal, but Amy seemed relieved that her mother had spoken, and smiled.

"Yes," she said. "I passed my test last year. Zac bought me the car for my birthday so I could get out more."

She followed her mother into the lounge and looked around.

"Not much has changed," she observed. "You've got a new telly."

"Yes," said Joanne. "Your dad wanted one of those flat-screen things."

God, this was horrible. They were like polite strangers.

Amy carried on scrutinising the room. Then her gaze fell on the dining table.

"Are you having a party or something?" she asked, looking at the plates and plates of food.

"I..I didn't know what you'd want to eat," Joanne said nervously. "I got you all the things I knew you liked, but if you want I can cook something instead."

Amy walked over to the table and ran her finger lightly round the edge of a plate. Then she smiled, and when she looked back up at Joanne, tears were trembling in her eyes.

"Oh Mum, it's so good to see you!" she cried, and then they were holding each other as though they'd never let go, and both crying, and it was all going to be alright after all.

After they'd hugged and kissed each other for an eternity, and gone through half a dozen tissues, Joanne put the kettle on while Amy took her coat off and then followed her mum into the kitchen. She leaned against the worksurface and looked out of the window at the garden.

"It's weird," she said. "Everything looks the same, but sort of different, somehow."

"It's because you've been away," Joanne said. "Everything looks a bit strange after two weeks holiday; it must be really odd after three years. You've changed too. You look…sophisticated."

"That's living in London," Amy said. "I can't slouch around in jeans and an old T-shirt all day now. Everyone is really fashion-conscious there, and it rubs off after a while."

She was wearing grey trousers and a matching jumper shot through with silver thread. Well tailored, but not too expensive.

"Next?" Joanne asked.

Amy grinned.

"Still know your fashion, then?" she said.

"Not really. But your dad still dresses well."

"Armani, that sort of thing?"

Joanne nodded and poured water into the pot.

"Do you still buy your clothes from Oxfam?" Amy asked.

"Do you know, your Auntie Kate bought me a handbag

when she came back from Paris," Joanne said evasively. "I had it with me when I went to this flying club do the other week, and one of the women went all gooey over it. Turns out it's Gucci. Must have cost an absolute fortune!"

"Yes, well, you deserve it."

"That's what Auntie Kate said."

"Are you all right, Mum?" Amy asked. "You don't look too well. You're very thin."

"Isn't that supposed to be good nowadays?" Joanne joked.

"It depends on why you're thin," Amy answered. "If you're ill, then no, it's not good."

"I'm not ill. I needed to lose a bit of weight anyway," Joanne said uncomfortably. She poured the tea out and handed a mug to her daughter. Amy sipped it, still eyeing her mother intently.

"Dad tell you that, did he?" she asked.

Joanne pulled all her courage together, put her own cup down on the worktop in case she spilt it if her hands trembled, and met her daughter's gaze.

"Amy," she said. "Let's get this over with. Why did…?"

She never finished her question. At that moment they both heard the front door open, and both of them froze. Amy paled visibly.

"You told me he wouldn't come home early!" she whispered fiercely.

"He never has before!" Joanne said. Amy glared at her, doubt written all over her face. "I didn't tell him, Amy, I swear to God I didn't!" she just had time to say before Steve appeared in the kitchen doorway.

Steve stared open-mouthed at his daughter, and Joanne, who had turned to look at him to gauge his reaction, saw fear and uncertainty flash across his face, before he pulled himself together and moulded his features into an unreadable, neutral expression.

"Hello Amy," he said carefully. "This is a surprise."

Amy had also pulled herself together. She stood erect, every muscle tense, her mouth tight.

"I bet," she said.

"Did you know she was coming?" he asked Joanne casually. She felt a cold sweat break out all over her. If she said yes, he'd want to know why she hadn't told him. If she said no, he'd see all the food in the lounge and know she was lying. He'd go mad once Amy had left.

"Yes she did," Amy said before Joanne could make up her mind how to respond. "I made her promise not to tell you. I told her I'd never contact her again if she did."

He was trying to bring himself under control now, but he was hurt by his daughter's words. Joanne could see that.

"Why?" he asked, confused.

"You know why," his daughter said. "It was Mum I wanted to see, not you."

Steve looked at Joanne, as if trying to ascertain something. She tried not to squeeze herself back against the cupboard as she wanted to, to make herself smaller. Apparently satisfied with what he saw, he dismissed her and focussed all his attention back onto Amy, who was standing coiled like a spring.

"It's wonderful to see you," he said, smiling. He took a step into the kitchen, and Amy automatically started to move backwards, then stopped herself.

"Is it?" she said, her voice hard and cold.

"Of course it is," he replied, amazed. "You look fabulous!" He reached out and laid his hand on her shoulder, obviously intending to embrace her. Joanne breathed a sigh of relief. He would give her a hug, and they would be reconciled. Then they could discuss whatever the problem had been between them, and everything would be all right. Amy had always been very tactile. She loved hugs and kisses. As a child all their disagreements had been mended with a hug. If Steve's caresses had been somewhat casually bestowed, they had still had an effect.

This one certainly had an effect. Amy leapt back out of

reach as though he'd hit her, and backed up against the worksurface.

"Don't you touch me!" she cried. "Don't you ever touch me again!"

Joanne looked from her husband to her daughter and back to her husband, searching for a clue as to what was going on.

Steve's face was a picture of puzzlement and distress. He took another step forward.

"What's the matter with you?" he said. "Are you all right?"

Amy laughed, but there was no humour in it.

"Going to try that one, are you? If anyone's sick here, it's not me."

"Amy," he said, "I have no idea what you're talking about." His tone was one of infinite patience, such as would be used to pacify a lunatic. The air crackled between them. Joanne tried to think of something she could say to relieve the tension.

"I haven't talked about anything," Amy said, "yet."

"Why don't we go into the lounge?" Steve said carefully. "Your mum can make some lunch and we'll sit down and catch up on what you've been doing."

"No, I don't think so," Amy said. She moved away from the worktop. "I'm leaving. I'm sorry, Mum. I'll give you a ring, OK?"

In that moment Joanne knew that if her daughter left now, she would not come back. She couldn't lose her. Not again.

"No, Amy, please, don't go, not like this," she said, her voice trembling. "I've missed you so much. Please, can't we just talk about it, whatever it is, and sort it out?" She knew she sounded pathetic, pleading, but right then she didn't care. She had to keep her daughter there, no matter what.

Amy turned back to her father.

"What about you, Dad? Do you want me to talk about it? Did you miss me, too?" she said. She sounded as though it really mattered.

"Of course I did," he said, smiling. "You're my daughter."

"Remembered that finally, have you?" Amy said.

What the hell is she talking about? Joanne looked at Steve, saw the sudden panic register on his face. He took two steps towards Amy, and she reached behind her, her fingers scrabbling along the worktop. When she brought her hand forward again, she was holding the breadknife. Steve froze.

"You should have remembered that when you were trying to screw me, shouldn't you?" she said, her voice shaking. "You bastard. You're not my father, you never were. You ever touch me again and I'll kill you, I swear it."

She was clutching the knife so hard that her knuckles were white. Steve stared at her for a long moment in which Amy never took her eyes from his, didn't even blink. He made a jerky movement towards her, as though wondering whether he could disarm her, whether she really would try to stab him if he did. Then he turned around and walked out of the kitchen.

Amy stayed rigid, the knife held out in front of her while his footsteps retreated down the hall. Then the front door slammed, and she closed her eyes and let out the breath she'd held for nearly a minute. She swallowed hard, and put the knife down on the kitchen table. Then she turned and looked at her mother.

Joanne knew she must be as pale as her daughter. She felt as though all the blood had drained out of her body, all the life force had gone. In a moment she would collapse on the floor and her heart would stop, and that was what she wanted right then, more than anything else in the world.

"I'm sorry, Mum," Amy said in a small voice, completely different from the hard, cold tone she'd used a moment before. "God, I didn't want you to find out like that. I'm so sorry."

"It's OK," Joanne managed to say, somehow. The words sounded strange, as though someone else was saying them, and she realised she was going to be sick, or faint, or both. She turned towards the sink, just in time, and then Amy wrapped her arms round her, and Joanne knew she had to pull herself together, for her daughter's sake, at least. She reached across and pulled a piece of kitchen paper off the roll and wiped her mouth with it.

"I'm all right," she said. "I need to sit down."

They went into the lounge and sat down, Joanne in the armchair, Amy on the sofa.

"Shall I make us another cup of tea?" Amy said. She had always done that when she was little, when there'd been an argument. Put the kettle on, have a cup of tea, and everything will get better.

Nothing could make this better.

"No," Joanne said. She was feeling stronger now that she'd been sick. "Why didn't you tell me about this, three years ago?"

Amy bit her lip.

"I wanted to. I didn't know how to do it. I was afraid that…" Her voice trailed away.

"I wouldn't believe you," Joanne finished.

Amy nodded.

"Yes. Or that you'd make excuses for him."

"I believe you," Joanne said. In the long moment after Amy had accused him, before he'd walked out, she'd seen it. Seen the guilt on his face before he could hide it. "How could I make excuses for that?" She felt her gorge rise again at the very thought of what he must have done, even though her stomach was empty.

"I don't know," Amy said. "But you always did. He was tired, he'd had a bad day, he'd just lost his job, he was worried about money. I was thirteen before I found out that it wasn't normal for your dad to hit your mum. And then, I was a real cow at times as well when I was a teenager, I know that."

"You still are a teenager," Joanne said, forcing a weak smile.

"Only just. But you know what I mean. Me and Dad seemed to argue non-stop about everything. It must have driven you mad."

"He was…I thought he was worried about you, that he didn't want you to grow up too fast."

"Yeah, that's what I thought too," Amy said. "Trouble was, as far as I was concerned, I *was* grown up. Then afterwards, when things calmed down, he'd give me a hug and everything was all right." She hesitated for a moment. "And then I started to feel a bit uncomfortable."

"In what way?" Joanne asked. She didn't want this conversation. She wanted to run away and hide. But she had to know.

"Sometimes he'd pat me on the bottom, which was OK. But then he started to stroke me there sometimes, and it just felt…different. I can't explain it. Then now and again he'd come in the bathroom when I was in the middle of having a bath, and pretend he hadn't known I was in there. But he must have done, because I always had the radio on when I was in the bath. He told me I was growing up, getting proper breasts and everything. Little things. I used to catch him looking at me funny, when he thought I wasn't looking. Sort of weighing me up, you know like boys do when they're wondering if you'll say yes or no. God, it sounds stupid, even to me."

"No, it's not stupid." She'd never seen it. Why hadn't she seen it? What sort of mother was she?

"He never did it when you were around, Mum," Amy said, reading her mind. "I knew then that he didn't want you to know, and that if I told you he'd deny it and say I was over-imaginative, hormonal. I was, so I wouldn't have blamed you if you'd believed him."

There was a little gulf between them. Joanne reached across it and caught hold of her daughter's hand.

"Tell me what happened on the night you left, Amy," she said.

Amy was quiet for a minute, trying to find the right words.

"You were out at work, and when I got in Dad was already home. He was watching something on the telly, but when he heard me come in he switched it off really quick, which was a bit odd, because he didn't normally do that."

Joanne creased her brow in puzzlement.

"I think now that it might have been a dirty movie or something, although I didn't think that at the time. Anyway, he came into the hall as I was going up the stairs and asked me if I wanted something to eat, and I said I didn't have time, I had to have a shower and go straight out, because I was going to the cinema with my mates. After my shower I went in my bedroom to get ready, and then he just walked right in. It always really pissed me off the way he did that, without knocking or anything, so I asked him to leave because I wanted to get dressed, and he said go ahead. But instead of leaving he came in and sat on the bed. He asked me if Ben was going to the cinema as well. I said he wasn't, even though I knew he was, because I didn't want him to give me a lecture about boys, or tell me I couldn't go, and then I asked him to leave again, but he just ignored me. I didn't know what to do, because I couldn't *make* him leave and I had to get ready or else I'd be late."

Amy looked at her mum uncertainly, as if she was expecting her to call her a liar.

"Go on," Joanne said quietly.

"Shall I make that cup of tea?"

"No, "Joanne said. "Finish telling me what happened. Go on, I believe you."

Amy gently took her hand out of her mothers, and Joanne understood her need for space and sat back in the chair.

"Anyway, then it occurred to me that he was trying to make me late so I wouldn't be able to go," Amy continued. "So I thought sod that, he's only my dad, so I turned my back on him and started getting dressed. I managed to put my knickers on under the towel, but then while I was trying to sort my bra out the towel fell off. I looked over my shoulder to see if Dad had noticed, and he was staring at me and then he asked me if I was wearing those lacy things for

Ben. I didn't answer him, I just bent down to get the towel, and when I stood up again he was right behind me. He took the towel off me and threw it on the bed. I…" Her voice broke off and she swallowed convulsively.

"I'm sorry," Joanne said immediately. "Don't tell me any more if you don't want. It's all right." She stood up intending to comfort Amy, but she held her hand out defensively.

"No, I want to tell you," she said. "I've got to. I've never told anyone before, and it's hard, but I want you to know. You should know."

"OK, then," Joanne said, and sat back down. She waited, calmly, until Amy was ready to carry on.

"He turned me round so that I was facing the mirror, the full-length one on the wardrobe door, and then he put his hands under my breasts, so he was sort of cupping them, and he said that I didn't need to wear a bra because my breasts were lovely and stood up really nicely all by themselves. Then he started playing with my nipples and they…got really hard, and he smiled, I could see his face over my shoulder in the mirror, and he asked me if that turned me on. But it didn't, honestly!" Amy looked across at Joanne, imploring her to believe her.

"That happens automatically, Amy, if someone touches them. It doesn't necessarily mean you're aroused," Joanne said. She could feel a cold hard lump of ice forming in her stomach. It was so cold it burned.

"I…He was standing very close, and I could feel him getting sort of…hard. It was pressing into my leg. I didn't know what to do. I tried to move away from him, but he just held me tighter against him, and he was still smiling and looking into my eyes through the mirror. It was like he'd hypnotised me or something, because I just let him do it. I didn't know what to do. He asked me if Ben did that, and then he…he…"

She took a deep breath. Tears were trickling down her cheeks, but she brushed them away impatiently with her hand and carried on. "Then he stuck his hand down my knickers and put his finger in....you know, and started moving it about. He was breathing funny, and I tried to push his hand away, but he's so strong, he actually lifted me up off the floor with his fingers still inside me, and it really hurt. I panicked then, and started screaming and trying to hit him so he'd let me go, but he didn't. He just put his other hand over my mouth and pinched my nose so I couldn't breathe, and then he carried on pushing his fingers in and out and started rubbing himself up and down against me from behind, and I was trying to pull his hand away from my mouth then so I could breathe, and everything was going all sort of snowy. I remember thinking that I mustn't pass out, because if I did he'd be able to do anything he wanted and I wouldn't know what he'd done afterwards."

"Did you pass out, Amy?" Joanne asked. The ice was spreading out, from her stomach, down her legs, and along her arms.

Amy shook her head. She was trembling, but when Joanne made a move to hold her, she held her hands up to stop her.

"No, don't," she said, almost pleadingly. "I need to finish. Please. He...he suddenly made this sort of moaning sound and shuddered, and then he took his hand out of my knickers, and he sat down on the bed with me on his knee. He let my nose go so I could breathe, but he kept his hand over my mouth and he told me that this was our secret. He said that if I ever told anyone I'd be sorry, because no one would believe me anyway, that I was still a virgin because he hadn't done anything to me, so there wouldn't be any evidence, and it would be my word against his. He told me that he wouldn't have touched me at all if I hadn't encouraged him by parading myself naked like that to try to turn him on. And then he let me go and got up and went downstairs. I sat on the bed for a bit, looking at myself in the mirror. I knew I didn't look any different, I mean I didn't have any bruises or anything, and I knew what a good liar he was. No one would believe me, no one would believe a father would do that to his own daughter."

"I would have believed you," Joanne said quietly.

"Would you? Would you really, then?" Amy cried. "You always believed him, Mum. Every time he told you he was sorry for hitting you, you believed him. I didn't know what to do. I couldn't tell anyone, because if I did he'd say I was a liar and everyone would believe him, and then he'd know he'd got away with it and that he could do whatever he wanted to me, like he does what he wants to you. And I knew that if I didn't tell anyone, then he might actually think I really *did* like it, and do it again, or worse. I felt dirty. I felt as though he was right, I had encouraged him, even though I knew I hadn't, he was just saying that so he didn't have to blame himself. And that's when I knew I had to leave, right away, because if I waited until you came home I wouldn't be able to hide it from you. So I put a change of clothes in a bag, took all the money I'd saved for Christmas out of my jar and just went down the stairs and out the door, as though I was going to the pictures. He was watching telly as though nothing had happened. He even shouted 'have a good time' as I walked past the lounge. I went straight to the train station and got the first train. I didn't care where it was going. When I got to Birmingham I managed to get a cheap B & B on the Hagley Road, rang Auntie Kate to tell her I was OK, and the next morning I went to a temping agency. Then I went to the social and asked for a crisis loan until I got paid. I temped for a couple of months and then I got a permanent job. After six months I was offered a transfer to London."

"Does Kate know all this?" Joanne asked.

"No," Amy said. "You know what she's like. I think she knew that something bad had happened, but she just said that if I wanted to tell her, I could. But I never did."

"Did you want to tell her?" Joanne asked. It didn't matter; she was just asking questions to give herself time to let the information penetrate her brain. The ice must have got there first; she felt sort of outside herself, as though it was something she'd just heard on the news, that had happened to another family. She felt a distant pity for herself, for this person whose life had just disintegrated. She should be feeling pity for Amy, but Amy had picked the pieces up and carried on. Amy had had the courage to do what her mother hadn't done. She felt cold, almost indifferent, and part of her knew that it was a defence mechanism, because if she let all this information get to her she would fall apart, and she couldn't, not now. Amy needed her to be strong.

"No, I didn't want to tell her," Amy was saying. "I wanted to tell you. You were the only other person who needed to know. Well, apart from Zac, that is. I should tell him. But I couldn't do it. I didn't know how to tell you. And then time went by and I had a new life to think about. I managed to push everything into the background and pretend it hadn't happened at all. But then I saw your name in the paper, and I thought, this isn't right, Mum's got to know what Dad's really like. And I knew then that even if you didn't believe me, I had to tell you anyway, and give you the choice."

"Thank you," said Joanne, and meant it.

"And it wasn't just that," Amy said. "I missed you, and I really wanted to see you again. I couldn't see you and not tell you. I've had the runs for two days, dreading today. I thought I'd talk to you for a while first, sort of find a way to get it into the conversation."

"How do you get something like that into a conversation?" Joanne said.

"I don't know," Amy admitted. "I probably wouldn't have told you at all, if Dad hadn't come in like that."

"I'm glad he did, then," Joanne said. "Are you going to tell Zac?"

"Yes, I should do. But I wanted to tell you first. And Dad was right in one way. He didn't do anything permanent, if you know what I mean."

Oh yes he did, Joanne thought.

"Will he understand? Zac, I mean?" she asked.

Amy smiled, and her eyes softened.

"Yes," she said. "I'm sure he will. The hardest thing'll be stopping him coming up here to confront Dad. I can't let him do that. Dad'd kill him. Zac's not the fighting sort."

"I think I might like Zac," Joanne said. "I must meet him." If anyone else had told her this about Steve, she would never have believed them, never. "It's strange," she said to herself, and only realised she'd spoken aloud when Amy asked her what was strange. "I've been thinking about you constantly since yesterday, trying to work out what made you leave, and how I could make it all right between us, and I was thinking about how great your dad was with you and your friends, taking you swimming and everything. Auntie Kate said at the time that she thought that was odd, but I never thought anything of it. God, I can't believe I was so stupid." Her voice faltered, and Amy leaned across and squeezed her hand.

"It wasn't your fault, Mum," she said. "It was never your fault, you mustn't think that. I never blamed you, not even for a minute."

Joanne looked at her daughter, and took a deep breath. She had to know it all.

"Amy," she said. "Your friends from school. They all stopped coming round all of a sudden, didn't they? I thought it was a teenage phase, you know, you trying to be independent of us. Do you think...could it..." she didn't know how to say it. She couldn't.

"You mean do you think he was touching them up, too?" Amy asked with a bluntness Joanne could never have achieved.

"Yes," she said.

Amy sat and thought for a minute in silence.

"Not Sarah and Michelle, no," she said finally, her eyes still far away. "We had an argument because I wouldn't do their maths homework for them. That's why they stopped coming. And if Dad had gone anywhere near them they'd have screamed blue murder. But Gemma…I don't know. Now I think of it, yes, because Dad really liked her. He was always teasing her, ruffling her hair, stuff like that. And she was a bit shy too, which he said was sweet. I remember that. And then she just said she couldn't come round any more, we didn't have a row or anything, and when I asked her why, she just said she couldn't, that was all, and got upset. I thought her mum and dad had grounded her or something. But now you've said it…it would explain how she was, yes."

Joanne closed her eyes. She'd been married to a paedophile for twenty years, and had never suspected a thing. They'd even discussed people like Ian Huntly, and Steve had said anyone who messed around with kids should be strung up by their balls. Her whole life had been a farce. He was a monster. How could she not have seen it? The way he'd acted around her schoolfriends the first time she'd met him, when he was painting their school. He'd gone out with Carol Hughes when she was only fifteen, and it had only taken her a few weeks to find out he was a bastard. Why had she never seen it, in over twenty years of marriage?

She had, she realised. She knew he was moody and violent, and that it wasn't right for a man to treat his wife like he treated her. She'd just been in denial. He *was* a bastard. But a paedophile? No, she would never have guessed that. Paedophiles were pathetic, ugly little perverts with no social skills, who spent their days hunched over pornographic websites in seedy bedsits. Not handsome outgoing men with jobs and families.

"Are you all right, Mum?" Amy asked nervously. Her eyes were red. Joanne looked at her, and realised that she must have been quiet for a long time, conflicting emotions passing across her face. She sat up, made an effort, smiled.

"Do you want to go to the police?" she asked. "Because if you do, I'll support you all the way, you know that."

Amy shook her head.

"No," she said. "I just want to forget it. It's over now. I'm glad I told you, I really am. I needed to do that. And I'm so relieved that you believe me. I was so frightened...But now I have, I just want to forget it ever happened and get on with my life. What are you going to do?" She looked up at Joanne apprehensively, her beautiful blue eyes swimming with tears. Steve's eyes. How could he do that to anyone, let alone his own daughter, his flesh and blood? It was unbelievable.

"What am I going to do?" Joanne said. "Well, first of all I'm going to give my daughter a hug, and tell her she's the bravest person in the world, and I'm more proud of her than she'll ever know. After that," she said, looking towards the dining table, "I'm going to have some of that food, because I'm starving, and hopefully you'll join me. And after *that*, I'm going to do what I should have done twenty years ago."

"What's that?" Amy asked.

"I'm going to leave my husband."

Joanne was halfway through packing when she heard Steve come back in. Into the bottom of her suitcase she had placed her family photograph album and some of her treasured souvenirs; Amy's christening shoes, the Easter card she'd made for her mum when she was four, a brightly-coloured certificate she'd got for swimming her first length. Joanne had thrown all the wedding cards and the sugary anniversary cards she'd received from Steve in the bin, and she felt a sense of relief, of closure, as though she'd thrown out all the wasted years with the cards. She was folding her clothes neatly on top of the album when she heard him coming up the stairs. He stopped in the doorway, leaning against the doorpost.

"What are you doing?" he asked.

Joanne placed the jumper in the suitcase carefully.

"I'm leaving," she replied, without looking at him. She returned to the wardrobe, took a blouse off its hanger.

"Why?" he asked.

"You know why," she replied calmly. She folded the blouse, put it in the case.

"What, because of…you didn't actually *believe* her, did you?" he said. "Come on, Jo, you know what she's like."

"Yes, I do," Joanne said. "And I know what you're like, too. I've been fooling myself that things would get better, for twenty years. I've just woken up at last, that's all."

"I'm her father!" he exclaimed. "How could you even think I'd molest her? You can't leave over that!"

"I could, and I am," she said calmly. "But it's not just that. What you did to Amy took the blinkers off, that's all. I should have had the courage to leave years ago. It would have been better for both of us. Neither of us are happy."

"I'm happy!" he said.

She considered for a moment.

"Yes, maybe you are," she acknowledged. "I'm sorry then, but I'm not." She opened a drawer and started putting her underwear into the case.

"Look, I'll tell you what," he said, unnerved by her calmness. "Why don't I open a bottle of wine and we'll talk about it."

"There's nothing to talk about, Steve," she said. "It's over. I'm leaving." That was all her clothes packed. Now she just needed her toiletries from the bathroom and she could go. She looked at her hand, and slipped her wedding and engagement rings off. They were loose. *Amy was right,* she thought, *I have lost weight.* "Do you want these back?" she said, holding them out to him on the palm of her hand. "You might get enough to buy another plane, if you sell them."

He reached out suddenly and smacked her hand away. The rings shot across the room and disappeared on the other side of the bed. She looked at him for the first time then, assessing him coolly, noting that he'd been drinking and that he would therefore be more unpredictable. Perhaps it would be better to leave the toiletries, just close her case and go.

"You're not leaving," he stated. He moved forward into the room, standing over her as he did when he wished to intimidate her.

She was not intimidated or afraid, even though a part of

her knew she should be. She felt calm, cold, even. She could not afford emotions right now. If she allowed them access they would overwhelm her, and she would be defeated by them. Later, maybe, but not now. She reached for the lid of the case, but he pushed her out of the way and threw the suitcase across the room. Clothes cascaded everywhere, draping the bed, the lamp, the dressing table mirror. Well then, she would have to leave without her belongings. She could always come back for them later. It didn't really matter.

She made to move past him, but he barred her way, standing between her and the door.

"I didn't do anything to Amy, you know I didn't," he said desperately.

"It doesn't matter, Steve," she said. "Excuse me." She went to move past him, but he grabbed her arm and threw her backwards, so she landed sprawled across the bed.

This is just an excuse, isn't it?" he said, his voice rising. "You've found someone else. Who is it?"

She knew what he was doing now. He was building up his courage, finding a reason to justify hitting her. She sat up on the bed, feeling almost relieved. It was nearly over. He would hit her for the very last time, and then he would feel guilty and go out. Then she could leave.

"There isn't anyone else, you know that," she said. He couldn't cope with her fearlessness, she could see that. He expected her to plead with him, cringe away from him. Maybe she would be able to get out uninjured after all, while he was off-balance. She stood up, walked past him, and for a moment she thought she'd succeeded.

Then he reached out, gripped the back of her t-shirt, and pulled her back into the room. Before she could regain her balance he hit her in the face, not with the flat of his hand as he usually did, but with his fist. Pain exploded in her head, silver stars shooting across her vision. His mouth opened and closed, and he gripped her by the throat, squeezing hard and shaking her like a rat. She managed to hit him once, her fist glancing off the side of his face, and then he let her go and punched her again, in the stomach this time, and she went down gasping for breath. He would stop now, surely he would stop now. He had never hit her this hard before.

"You're not leaving," he shouted from above her. "You're not leaving me, you can't, I won't let you." His voice sounded frantic, desperate; he'd realised that she meant it this time. He kicked her in the chest, hard, and she curled up, instinctively lifting her arms to protect her head. She felt his foot connect with her arm, then her shin, and she realised that he wasn't going to stop; he was going to kill her, as he'd threatened to more than once, and she felt a strange sort of peace descend on her, the pain of the blows diminishing, then vanishing altogether into a soft, velvety blackness.

* * *

When she came round she was lying on the floor at the side of the bed, and it was dark. She waited a moment until her eyes adjusted and in the dim amber glow from the streetlamp outside she could make out the wardrobe, the bedside table, her blouse still draped over the lamp, the open door. The house was silent; he must have gone out again.

She tried to lift her head. The side of her face seemed to be stuck to the carpet and it took her a minute to realise that it was because the blood from her nose had congealed under her cheek. She tried to uncurl her body, but a hot tearing pain shot through her chest and she subsided, afraid of blacking out again.

She was injured, badly, she realised. She remembered him hitting her in the face, the stomach, chest. Her nose was probably broken, and maybe her ribs. That would account for the pain. She couldn't just lie here and wait until he came back. She had no idea what he would do. She had to get help.

The phone was downstairs in the hall. She tried to move again, uncurling very slowly, fighting the pain that made her want to give up and lie still. It took an age to lever herself into a hunched sitting position on the floor, her back leaning against the bed. There was something wrong with her right arm too; the wrist was swollen. Waves of nausea and faintness washed over her, and she remained in her new position until they faded. Tears trickled weakly down her cheeks; she could not get downstairs.

She had to get downstairs. Her mobile was on the coffee table in the lounge, even less accessible than the house phone.

Infinitely slowly, she manoeuvred her way to the stairs, then shuffled down them on her bottom, gripping the stair rail with her left arm. The stairs swung dizzily around her, and she closed her eyes for a moment. It took an eternity to get to the hall, but she did it, and felt a faint sense of achievement in doing so. She would not be lying there where he'd left her, beaten and broken, when he deigned to return home and minister to her. All she had to do now was phone for help.

She picked up the receiver with her left hand and placed it on her knee while she dialled. Then she held it to her ear and listened as the tinny voice at the other end asked her which service she required.

"Ambulance," she said, and then slipped sideways and automatically tried to brace herself on her injured arm. She heard the phone hit the hall floor with a dull thud, and felt a vague sense of panic as she realised she hadn't given the operator her address, before she passed out again.

CHAPTER ELEVEN

It was Sunday lunchtime before Kate arrived at the hospital, dishevelled and clearly in something of a panic even though Joanne had asked the nurse who phoned her sister to explain that there was no need to worry, or rush.

"Hi," said Joanne somewhat indistinctly.

Kate took a long look at the purple swollen mess that was her sister's face, then sank down into the chair at the side of the bed.

"My God," she said. "Did Steve do this to you?"

"It looks worse than it is," Joanne said. "I should only be in for a couple of days."

"Why didn't someone phone me last night?" Kate said. "Have you been unconscious all this time?"

"No," replied Joanne. "I came round in the ambulance. There wasn't any point in waking you up in the middle of the night, or upsetting Amy. It's not as though I was dying or anything, after all. So I asked the nurse to wait until I knew Amy would be on her way home before phoning you."

"I know about it. About what he did to her," Kate explained. "Amy told me last night. Did you challenge him about it? Is that why he did this to you?"

"No, I didn't. There was no point. He came home as I was packing. He didn't want me to leave."

"Nice way he's got of putting his case," Kate said wryly. "Tell me he didn't change your mind, Jo. You can't possibly go back to him now. God, you look as though you've been hit by a bus!"

Joanne smiled lopsidedly.

"He didn't change my mind," she said.

"Have the hospital told the police?" Kate asked. "You did tell the doctors what happened, didn't you?"

"The hospital don't do that," Joanne said. "Yes, I did tell them. I asked them to ring the police this morning and they sent two officers down to see me. They left a few minutes before you turned up. They said that seeing as I'm safe in hospital and not going back to the marital home, they can wait until I get out before they take a statement. I assumed that you'd let me stay with you for a bit."

"You can stay with me for as long as you like," Kate said. "What happens once you've given your statement?"

"They'll charge him with assault. I don't really know any more than that at the moment. I should get a solicitor, they said."

"I can sort that out for you if you want." She looked at Joanne closely. "Jo, you're not going to change your mind in a couple of days, are you? You know he'll be round pleading with you to go back to him, telling you he loves you and can't live without you, don't you?"

"No he won't," Joanne said. "He doesn't know where I am, for one thing. But if he finds out, the hospital have said they won't let him in if he tries to come and see me. It'll be different when I'm out, I suppose. He'll guess I'll come to stay with you. The police said something about being able to stop him coming round, an injunction or something. I was a bit woozy with the painkillers they've given me, to be honest. I couldn't concentrate very well."

"You really mean it this time, don't you?"

Joanne nodded.

"Hallelujah," Kate breathed, leaning back in the chair. "Don't take this the wrong way, but I'm almost glad he did this to you, if it's finally made you wake up and see sense."

"It wasn't this, Kate," Joanne said. "I was leaving

anyway. It was what Amy told me that did it."

"Yes, she was very upset when she got home. I don't think she intended to say anything to me, but it sort of spilled out."

"I don't think she'd have told me if Steve hadn't come home unexpectedly," said Joanne. "She was frightened I wouldn't believe her."

"I believed her," Kate replied. "I told her that he'd tried it on with me once."

"With you?" Joanne exclaimed. "When?"

"Oh, it was ages ago," Kate said dismissively, "when Amy was a baby. He put his hand on my knee and said something suggestive, I can't even remember what it was now."

"What did you do?" Joanne asked.

"I told him I was fifteen and if he ever touched me again I'd have him done for child abuse. I didn't tell you because I didn't think it was worth it at the time. Maybe I should have done. I just knew he'd deny it, and use it as an excuse to stop me babysitting. I was hoping that by doing the night classes you'd get a bit more independence, and eventually leave him."

"Well, it worked." Joanne smiled weakly. "Eventually, I have."

"Are you really going to go through with pressing charges?" Kate said. "You might have to go to court, you know."

"I have to, Kate. I'll never be able to live with myself if I don't." A tear trickled slowly down Joanne's cheek, and Kate reached out to grip her uninjured hand.

"Don't you dare blame yourself for this," she said fiercely.

"I don't, not for him hitting me," Joanne replied. "But I should have seen it, I should have noticed, the way he was with Amy, I should…."

"Amy doesn't blame you," her sister interrupted. "She told me he never did anything when you were around, that's one of the reasons she felt uncomfortable about it."

"I know, but she should have been able to tell me about

it, and she couldn't. And it wasn't just Amy, he probably molested at least one of her friends as well. And you. God knows how many other children he's abused. And that *is* partly my fault. He thinks he can do anything he wants and get away with it, because he always has. I should never have given in to him like I did. I can't tell the police what he did to Amy, because she doesn't want me to, but at least I can make him see that what he's done to me is wrong. Maybe it'll wake him up, make him see himself as he really is."

"Do you really think so?" Kate asked.

"I don't know, but I don't know what else I can do," Joanne said. "I've been so blind. You were right, I should have left him years ago. I should have seen him for what he was. I just wanted Amy to have a father who loved her. I should have known Steve only cares about one person, and that's himself."

"What have you told the police?" Kate asked.

"I just told them that he's been violent to me for years, and he did this because I was leaving him. I haven't told any lies. And at least if he goes to prison it'll give him time to think about what he's done. And he won't be able to touch anyone else's daughter while he's in there."

"It's odd, though," Kate said. "You've threatened to leave him before, and he's never put you in hospital."

"I know," said Joanne. "But this time he knew I meant it."

It *was* odd, thought Joanne later, when Kate had left and most of the other patients had gone down to the dayroom to watch Coronation Street. Not that Steve had put her in hospital, but that twenty years of love could be wiped out in a moment. It was as though Amy had flicked a switch that had turned off everything she had ever felt for him instantaneously. One minute she believed herself still in love with him, still able to convince herself that all the sacrifices she'd made, all the times she'd given in to make him happy were worth something; and the next minute she knew that it had all been pointless, that apart from having her daughter, she had completely and utterly wasted twenty years of her life; and that by her feeble capitulation to his every wish she had also, albeit unintentionally, contributed to his abuse of Amy.

It was over, irrevocably, and Steve had recognised it in that moment when he had come home. That was why he'd beaten her so badly. She was lucky, the doctors had said; raising her arms to protect her head had possibly saved her life. The kick that had broken her wrist could have killed her if it had landed on her temple, where it had been aimed. He had fractured her cheekbone when he punched her in the face, and she had two broken ribs and bruising to her body and legs.

He hadn't intended to kill her, she knew that. He had just lost his temper, had seen that this time he wasn't going to get what he wanted, and had been unable to cope with it. In many ways he was still a child. She had never thought of him that way before, had always felt herself to be the immature one. Steve was the big man, the breadwinner, the payer of bills. It was only now, now the confusing emotions had been swept aside, that she could see him clearly for what he was; a child who was never wrong, who had to have everything his own way, and who threw a tantrum if he was challenged.

Would taking him to court make him wake up to what he was? Joanne had no idea, but at the least it might make him think twice about hitting his next partner. And he *would* seek another partner, she was certain, once he realised that she was definitely not coming back. He needed to be worshipped, to feel important; he was handsome still, and charismatic, and there were lots of women out there as naïve as she had been until last night. He would not stay single for long. *Whereas,* determined Joanne, *I will. I will never, never, let anyone rule my life again.*

It was time to learn how to look after herself. And what better way to start than by staying with Kate, the queen of independence and self-sufficiency? Joanne smiled to herself.

For the first time in years, she realised she was actually looking forward to the future.

It was a good feeling. A very good feeling indeed.

* * *

"I can't believe she's doing this to me," Steve muttered morosely into his pint.

It was the sort of grey chill November day which reminds people that winter is just around the corner, that makes them yearn for blazing fires and hot toddies. Consequently, the moment the wind had got up the four men had abandoned the muddy field, packed their planes away, and adjourned to the local pub.

"You know what women are like," said Terry. "They get hysterical over the slightest thing. You shouldn't have hit her though, mate."

"No, I know. I just sort of lost it when I saw her packing. She was so cold and nasty. And I only gave her a slap. I didn't mean to hurt her."

"Did she tell you why she was leaving?" Harry asked.

"No, when I asked her she just said 'you know why'. I think it's because I'm on the dole. She's used to having the best of everything. She can't handle it now that the money's tight."

"Has she got another fella?" asked Terry.

Steve looked up in genuine surprise. He hadn't thought of that as a possibility. He pondered for a moment, then shook his head.

"No, I don't think so," he said. "She's gone to stay at her sister's. In fact it's probably her sister that's put her up to calling the police in. She's always hated me, the bitch. She tried to get off with me years ago and she's never forgiven me for rejecting her."

"Women can be real bitches," Harry agreed. "My wife buggered off ten years ago. I gave her everything. Worked myself to the bone to give her a fancy kitchen, all the latest electrical stuff, and she took me for everything I'd got."

"She didn't get you done for assault though, did she?" Steve said.

"No, well, she couldn't. I never hit her, did I?" Harry responded.

Steve reddened.

"It wasn't *that* bad," he said. "She's making it out as though I tried to murder her or something."

"Have you got yourself a solicitor?" John asked. He was a clerk in a legal office and fancied himself an expert in the law.

"Yeah, my mum sorted one out for me. She's paying for him, thank God. I couldn't afford to, not at the moment."

"Who is it?"

"Patrick Hughes, his name is. He's supposed to be really good."

"What does he advise you should do?" Terry asked.

"He told me it's not his practice to tell me what to do. He just gave me all the options." Steve stopped, remembering his extremely uncomfortable hour under the scrutiny of a pair of shrewd grey eyes who saw straight through his blustering professions of innocence. Mr Hughes had told Steve he could only help him if he told the truth, and that he was not willing to stake his considerable reputation on defending a liar. He was not there to judge him, but he needed to know what Joanne might say in court so he could be prepared for it. Steve had wanted to punch him, but he was more frightened of going to prison than he was of telling the truth. So he did. Except about Amy. He would never tell about Amy, and was sure Joanne wouldn't either. Would she? He frowned.

"What were the options?" John broke in.

Steve thought for a moment about how to word things. He was enjoying the sympathy, but he didn't want to say too much.

"He said I could plead not guilty. But that would be difficult, because she could get her sister to say I'd hit her before. That bitch'd say anything to get one over on me. And it's not as though anyone else could have done it, a burglar or anything." He paused for a minute, getting his story straight in his head. "Or I could plead guilty but with mitigating circumstances. I could say that she provoked me, insulted my manhood, that I was unhappy because I was out of work, that sort of thing."

"Have you decided what you're going to do?" Terry asked.

"I'm not sure, but I think I'll probably plead guilty. That way Jo's not likely to come up with a load of lies about me, and because it's my first offence, if I can prove I'm really sorry, that I acted out of character because I was upset and depressed with being on the dole, I might get away with a fine or probation. Or at the worst, a suspended sentence."

The men digested this news for a minute.

"Couldn't you just go round and see her, try to persuade her to drop the charges?" asked Terry.

"No, she's got one of those injunction things out, so I can't go near her. Christ, you'd think I was Jack the Ripper or something!" Steve sighed. "It's my round," he said. "Same again?"

"Keep your money in your pocket, mate, I'll get these," Harry said. He stood up. "You know, you ought to get yourself down the docs, get some of them happy pills. And some sleeping tablets as well."

"I don't need stuff like that," Steve said. "There's nothing wrong with me."

"No, but if you can tell the judge you can't sleep at nights and you're taking antidepressants and trying to sort yourself out, he's more likely to let you off, surely?"

Harry was a boring old git, Steve thought, but he had some good ideas now and again.

* * *

"No," said Mike. "I'm not getting involved in this." He handed Steve a can of beer and sat down on the sofa.

"Oh, come on, when have I ever asked you to help me out before?"

"Never," agreed Mike. "And I've never asked you for anything, either. And I'd like to keep it that way. Go to your own doctor."

"I don't want to bother him. And I don't know if he'd be willing to come to court for me anyway."

"He doesn't have to," Mike said. "He can write a report to say you're depressed and are on medication, if your solicitor asks him to."

"So can you!" Steve pointed out.

"No I can't."

"You can't or you don't want to?"

"OK then, I don't want to," Mike admitted.

"Why not?"

"Tell me something. If I prescribed Prozac for you, would you take it?"

"No of course I bloody wouldn't!" Steve said. "There's nothing wrong with me."

"There's your answer then," Mike replied. "I'm not willing to perjure myself, not for you or anyone else. You're not depressed, Steve. You've got problems, sure, but you're not depressed."

"What's that supposed to mean?" Steve said, instantly on the defensive.

"Men aren't supposed to hit women, Steve. Did nobody ever tell you that?"

"She was going to leave me! I made a mistake, I lost my temper, and slapped her, once. I'm sorry I did it, but it hardly makes me a criminal!"

"You don't put someone in hospital for three days by slapping them once, Steve. And don't give me all that bollocks you gave Mum about it being the first time you've ever touched her. You've been hitting her for years."

"Did Jo tell you that?" Steve asked indignantly.

"No, I haven't been in touch with her. I told you, I'm not getting involved. But I've got eyes in my head. I've seen the bruises, and I've seen the way she behaves around you."

Mike let the silence spin out, watching as his brother

fought with his instinctive urge to deny everything.

"She's always nagging at me, winding me up," Steve said sulkily at last. "You know what women can be like."

"Yes, I do," agreed Mike. "I was married to the bitch from hell, remember. She drank too much, was never satisfied with anything, and left Bart, Jeremy and Rupert on their own while she went off and shagged anything wearing trousers. Yes, I know what women can be like."

"There you go, then," said Steve. "You can…"

"In spite of all that, I never laid a finger on Jenny," Mike interrupted. "I also know that Joanne isn't like that. You're bloody lucky she didn't leave you years ago. You're not depressed, you're just full of yourself, you always have been."

"For fuck's sake, Mike, you can't let me go to prison!" Steve said, his voice rising as he fought to control his temper.

"Oh I doubt you'll go to prison," Mike said nonchalantly. "Mum's paid a fortune to get you the best solicitor money can buy. You'll probably get off with a fine, and I'm sure Mum'll pay that for you too, if you ask her."

"At least she knows that families are supposed to help each other when they're in trouble," Steve spat.

"Yes, Mum always has thought that money can buy anything. She bought you everything you ever wanted, Steve. She even went over Dad's head to pay the deposit on your house when you and Jo got married, did you know that? But when has she ever shown you any affection, eh? Has she ever told you she loved you? Given you a cuddle?"

"You're just jealous because she never took any notice of you," Steve said triumphantly.

Mike looked at him, almost pityingly.

"Yes, well, you think that if you want. But the truth is that I'm glad she ignored me. Otherwise I might have grown up like you, with no idea that love means more than buying lots of things for people, ignoring their needs completely, and then punching them when they don't do exactly what you want all the time. You said families are supposed to stick together. Let me remind you that when you married Joanne she became part of the family too. Do you want me to stand up in court and tell the magistrate that you've made her life a misery for twenty years?"

"You wouldn't do that!" Steve gasped.

"No I wouldn't, because I'm not getting involved. But at least if I did it'd be the truth. Go to your own doctor, Steve. You're a good actor, when you put your mind to it. You should be able to convince him you're depressed. And then, if you've got any sense you'll go home and do some serious thinking about what you did to make her finally see sense and leave."

He wouldn't, thought Mike over another beer after his brother had walked out. He wasn't one for self-analysis of any sort. It was easier to blame someone else than admit that he might actually not be perfect. It always took two to wreck a marriage. Joanne had put up with Steve's abuse for far too long.

Just as he had convinced himself time and time again that Jenny's latest affair would be her last, that it had only been a meaningless fling, that she was bored because he worked long hours. His wake-up call had come when he'd come home early one evening expecting to surprise her, to find his three sons, the eldest Bart only seven, on their own in the lounge watching TV. Bart had told him that Mummy had gone to the shop and would be back soon. When she did come back four hours later, drunk, he had told her to pack her things and get out. It had been the best thing he'd ever done in spite of all the acrimony that had followed, and his mother's complaints that no one in the family had ever divorced before and he was bringing shame on the family.

What she thought of her youngest being charged with assault, Mike had no idea. He kept contact with his family to a minimum now. Christmas, Easter, the annual family party. It was much better that way. Even so, he liked Joanne, and would miss her. He wondered what her wake-up call had been. Whatever it was, he was heartily glad she'd finally got up the courage to leave.

Congratulations Joanne, he thought, raising his can in a solitary toast. *Just don't let him talk you into going back.*

* * *

It was amazing how difficult it could be to do the simplest things when you only had one functioning arm, Joanne thought as she struggled to fasten the button at the waistband of her trousers. Or rather Kate's trousers. Two weeks after her release from hospital, Joanne had still not been back to the house to collect her things.

I can't carry on hiding away like this, she thought. *I have to face the world again at some point.* It was so easy to just stay in the comfortable apartment all day while Kate was at work, convincing herself that she was not yet well enough to venture out. Her ribs were starting to heal now, although it still hurt to breathe, and the swelling on her face had subsided, the bruising turning a sickly yellow-green. The arm was a problem, but hardly enough to stop her going out. And she couldn't just sponge off her sister forever.

Tomorrow, she thought. *Tomorrow I'll go down to the social and sign on the sick.* At least she would then be able to make a contribution to the household. Kate was being wonderful, giving her time to heal, not just physically but emotionally too, and had said she didn't need to worry about money, that it hardly cost any more to support two than one. But that wasn't the point. Joanne knew she had to venture out into the world again, and it would be better if she could do it under her own volition instead of waiting until her sister thought she was ready.

She had telephoned her clients to tell them she was sick, and was relieved that none of them had asked her how she had broken her arm. They were all more worried about what they would do for a cleaner while she was off. Joanne wondered whether she'd have told the truth if asked, or just come out with another of her excuses; *I slipped in the shower;*

the stair carpet was loose, I've been meaning to look at it for weeks. She wasn't sure, and that bothered her.

She was losing her resolve, sitting around all day watching TV. She had to pick up the pieces of her life, or make a start anyway. The police had told her they would accompany her when she wanted to go back to the marital home and retrieve her belongings. She would do that in a couple of days. And she would open a bank account next week, even though she had nothing to put in it. It would symbolise the start of her independence.

She sat down on the couch and flicked the television on, then off again. *No*, she thought. *I won't watch TV at all today. I'll write a list of things to do, and then tick them off one by one as I do them.* It would be a somewhat illegible list, as she'd have to write with her left hand, but it would at least be a positive move.

She was halfway across the room in search of a pen and paper when the doorbell rang. Joanne's heart instantly started hammering, and she forced herself to calm down. It wasn't likely to be Steve; he wasn't allowed near her and she didn't think he'd break the injunction; his solicitor would certainly have advised him not to do anything that would jeopardise him in court. She could open the door on the chain; if it was him she would close it again and phone the police. The bell rang again and she steeled herself and opened the door the three inches the chain allowed.

"Hello Joanne," said Susan Harris. "Can I come in?"

Joanne fought down the urge to say no. That would be rude, and she had no quarrel with Steve's family. Even so, she knew why Susan was here; she should have expected it. Better to get it over with.

She opened the door and Susan walked into the hall, and looked around at the tasteful cream décor, the expensive abstract painting hung on one wall. Joanne had nearly had heart failure when Kate told her how much she had paid for what looked to her like a five-year-old's botched attempt at a landscape. Susan nodded her head towards it in admiration.

"Excellent taste your sister's got," she commented.

"Did Steve ask you to come?" Joanne replied. She was not going to waste half an hour in pointless small talk about abstract art. Her mother-in-law was not here for a social call, and Joanne had no interest in pretending otherwise.

Susan leaned on her stick and turned her attention from the painting to her daughter-in-law. Not her face, though. Her gaze settled somewhere around Joanne's collarbone.

"No," she said. "He doesn't know I'm here. David brought me. He's coming back for me in half an hour."

Joanne bowed to the inevitable and invited Susan into the lounge. She sat down gratefully but refused the offer of tea. She opened her mouth to speak, but Joanne forestalled her.

"If you've come to ask me to go back to Steve, you're wasting your time," she said. Susan bristled instantly at Joanne's brusque tone but made an effort not to show it.

"You've been married for over twenty years, Joanne," she said. "Surely you're not going to throw all that away for one unfortunate incident?"

"No I'm not, Susan," Joanne said, moderating her tone. She didn't like Susan; she thought her a pretentious snob, but she was also a frail old woman. "This isn't the first time Steve has hit me, but it is the last. There's nothing to throw away. Our marriage never meant anything. It's just taken me all this time to realise it, that's all."

"You can't mean that," Susan responded. "Look at the wonderful house you've got, the car, all that expensive furniture. I know Stephen's out of work at present but that's only a temporary situation, you know that. It's a wife's duty to support her husband through difficult times, not abandon him."

"And it's a man's duty to protect his wife and cherish her, not to use her as a punchbag every time he can't get his own way," Joanne retorted. "He nearly killed me this time, Susan."

Susan's glance flickered up to Joanne's face, then back

down to her collarbone, then away, coming to rest on the arm of the chair she was sitting on.

"Surely you exaggerate," Susan said. "Stephen told me that you were already packing to leave when he got home, and he lost his temper because he was so upset. You can hardly say you left him because he hit you."

"Did Steve tell you why I left?" Joanne asked.

"No," Susan said. "He doesn't know. He can't understand why you're being so vindictive, suing him for assault." Her confusion was clearly genuine.

Joanne sighed.

"Steve knows why I left him. That's between me and him. But it was serious enough to end the marriage. I won't go back to him, and there's nothing you can say to change that. I'm sorry if you're upset about it, but you'll get over it in time."

"But…surely at least you can drop these ridiculous charges you've brought against him?" Susan said. "He didn't mean to hit you. It was just an impulsive reaction, he was so upset at the thought you would consider leaving him."

"Susan, look at me," Joanne said gently. "Not at the chair, or my shoulder. Look at my face. This happened nearly three weeks ago and you still can't bear to look at me. I don't know what he's told you he did, but he's lying. He didn't slap me, he punched me in the face with his fist, and then he kicked me until I passed out. He broke my arm, my ribs and my cheek, and then he went out and left me lying in my own blood. I could have died, and he couldn't have cared less. I'm not trying to hurt you," she added, seeing Susan wince, "but if you're going to defend him, you should at least know what he's capable of."

"And what good will it do if he goes to prison?" Susan asked, anguished. "It won't make you well again. You want revenge, but all you'll do is ruin his life. And yours too. He won't be able to pay you maintenance if he's in prison!"

"I don't want maintenance off him. I don't want anything, except to move on and try to make a new life. I don't even want a divorce, although if he does I'll grant him one." Joanne hesitated, trying to find the right words to make Susan see where she was coming from. "Susan, can I ask you a question?"

Susan nodded. She was fighting back tears, and didn't trust herself to speak.

"Was Edward violent towards you?"

The question caught Susan off guard and Joanne had her answer even before her mother-in-law opened her mouth to deny it.

"It's all right," Joanne said quickly. "I shouldn't have asked you that. I just wondered if Steve had grown up thinking that what he was doing was right because he saw his father doing it. It doesn't really matter. But wherever he got the idea that men are allowed to hit women, he needs to learn that it's wrong. He never has, in all these years, Susan. I can't tell you how many times he's apologised to me and promised he'd never do it again. Maybe going to court will wake him up, make him take it seriously. I hope so."

"But you said you're not going back to him," Susan said. "What difference will it make to you?"

"I'm not doing it for me," Joanne said. "I'm doing it for him. And for the next woman he finds."

"He doesn't want any other woman," Susan said. "He's beside himself. It's you he loves, he always has done." She struggled to her feet, bracing herself on her cane and looked Joanne in the face for the first time since she arrived. "When he said he wanted to marry you, I did my best to put him off. I knew he could do better than some silly little girl from a council estate. But he was determined, and when Stephen had his mind set on something there was no talking to him. But I tried. I really tried. I wish to God I'd succeeded."

She turned around and walked out of the flat, closing the front door quietly behind her. Joanne leaned back and closed her eyes. *I should have expected Susan's visit,* she thought. *I must start anticipating things. Then I'll be better prepared.*

"Of course you're doing the right thing," Kate said when she'd swallowed her mouthful of pasta. "If you drop the charges now, he'll think he's got away with it."

Joanne toyed pensively with her dinner, mixing the sauce with the pasta, while Kate refilled her wine glass.

"Do you want me to cut it up for you?" Kate asked. "I should have thought, shouldn't I? Spaghetti's not the easiest thing for a one-armed person to eat."

Joanne laughed.

"No, I can manage," she said. "I'm just not very hungry, that's all. Susan seemed to think I'm taking Steve to court for revenge."

"So what?" Kate replied casually. "Who cares what Susan thinks?"

"What do *you* think?" Joanne asked.

"I think you're hoping it'll shock him into reforming, because that's what you've told me, and I believe you. I hope you're right and he will but I doubt it, because I don't believe in miracles. What's wrong with revenge, anyway? That's a damn good reason for charging him. You should have done it the first time he touched you. Stop brooding about it and eat your dinner."

"I wish I could see things in black and white like you do," Joanne sighed. "It would make life a whole lot easier."

"Life is full of colour," Kate replied. "But some things *are* black and white. He beat you up; you're letting him know he can't get away with it in the only way you can. With luck, he'll learn something. At the very least he'll learn that you're not a pushover any more. Move on Jo, it's time."

"You're right," Joanne said. "I need to start going out, and find something to do. I'm going to sign on tomorrow."

"Good. Don't give me any money, though. Save it, let it build up a little bit."

"I can't just live off you, Kate!" Joanne protested.

"No, well, I've been thinking about that. I've got a ten-thousand-word progress report to type up. I've been putting it off because I don't want to do it. You still remember how to type, don't you?"

"Yes, I think so," Joanne said. "Although I'm out of practice and I won't be very fast at the moment, with one hand."

"That's OK. You can take all week over it if you want. It's all in note form, and you'll need to add in graphs and stuff."

"What, you want me to draw graphs?" Joanne said. She wouldn't be able to do those, not with her left hand.

"Welcome to the twenty-first century, big sister." Kate laughed. "We have these amazing things called computers that do it all for you. You just have to put in the information. No messy carbon paper, no correcting fluid. It's easy, I'll show you. Let me have a shower while you finish eating, then I'll give you a crash course in IT. It'll be a good start to your new life in the real world. Computers are everywhere. You can't avoid them, so you might as well learn how to use them."

She drained her glass, refilled Joanne's, then stood up.

"I think Steve's bloody lucky myself," she commented as she reached the door.

"In what way?" Joanne asked.

"If it'd been me and my daughter whose lives he'd ruined, I'd have killed the bastard. Then I'd be sure he'd never mess around with any other women, or their children for that matter. If he does get a prison sentence he'll be getting off lightly, in my opinion. Very lightly."

She went into the bathroom, leaving Joanne to ponder her last words and to anticipate the terrifying mysteries of information technology.

* * *

Every little hurdle was an achievement, a step closer to independence and a new life. When she went to sign on for sickness benefit she was told that she needed proof of identity, like a birth certificate, and preferably a bank account which her benefit could be paid directly into. The bank needed two proofs of identity, but she explained that she didn't have a driving licence and had never had a passport of her own; Steve had included her on his as his wife. They finally agreed to accept her birth certificate alone, given the special circumstances.

Her birth certificate was at home, along with her marriage lines and all her clothes. Joanne toyed with the idea of applying for a new birth certificate, then abandoned it. She would never make a new life for herself if she refused to face up to her past. So she phoned the police and arranged to go round to the house and pick up her belongings.

She had hoped Steve would go out, but his car was in the drive and when she opened the door he came down the hall to meet her, smiling. He was politeness itself. He asked her and the two policemen if they would like a cup of tea, and even offered to help Joanne collect her things together and pack. She knew this Steve. This was not an act for the benefit of the law; this was the genuinely reconciliatory Steve, who truly believed an abject apology and friendly co-operation could make up for what he'd done. He had wanted to talk to her alone, she could see that, so she told him she would prefer it if he stayed downstairs with the police while she got her things together, and he had no choice but to obey.

Desperate to get out as fast as possible, she threw clothes haphazardly into a sports bag until it was full and then left, with the result that when she got home she found that she had a range of mismatched blouses, t-shirts and skirts, and had failed to pack half her underwear or her most comfortable shoes. But she did have her birth and marriage certificates. And after having succeeded in ignoring Steve's pitiful attempts to be friendly and engage her in conversation, signing on and opening a bank account were a piece of cake by comparison.

She had worried that the social security would try to pursue Steve for maintenance but they told her that in view of the reasons for separation and the fact that she had no dependants, they were not interested. It was an immense relief. Under duress Kate accepted £25 a week from Joanne as a contribution towards the household expenses. With the remaining money she bought some new clothes, and once she had a basic wardrobe she allowed the rest to accumulate in her account.

Once her plaster was off she returned to her cleaning job, although she was not really ready and the doctor had given her another sick note. Her arm was weak from disuse, but she felt that the exercise of cleaning would be an ideal way to build up her strength again. She went to the social security to tell them, and was amazed to find that the £50 a week she earned cleaning would be disregarded by them.

Life was getting better by the day. She kept Kate's flat immaculate, joined the library and started reading again, firstly novels, then books on computers. She learnt, with Kate's assistance, how to use the internet and to send emails, although she had no one to send them to. She even went to London to see Amy for a weekend, which caused her great anxiety; she hadn't been on a train since she was a teenager. She had set herself the challenge of finding her own way across London to Amy's flat in Highbury, but faltered when she saw the underground map. It was at first glance an incomprehensible electrical wiring diagram, but she forced herself to calm down, and found that it was relatively easy to follow when her mind wasn't fogged by panic. She felt a massive sense of achievement and pride in herself for not giving in and allowing Amy to pick her up from the train station.

Amy and Joanne spent Saturday afternoon at the Tower of London, which Joanne had always wanted to see. She had been interested in the Tudors for years, having devoured every novel she could find about the turbulent royal dynasty when she was younger. They ate ice-cream and went to Starbucks for a complicated coffee, and by unspoken agreement Steve, the separation and the impending court case were not mentioned. Instead they spoke about clothes and hairstyles, and the wedding, the date of which was now fixed for the following May. In the evening they went to a

Chinese restaurant in Soho, where Joanne finally met Zac.

This was one of the things Joanne had been dreading. She was terrified that she would dislike him, or worse, that she would see the seeds of a Steve in him; the subtle put-downs, the possessiveness, the obsessive, overblown romantic gestures that Amy might be mistaking for love, that Joanne herself had mistaken for love. How would she make her daughter see the danger signs that she herself had so blindly ignored when she was nineteen?

She had talked it over with Kate beforehand, who had listened to her worries, then dismissed them.

"Amy's not like you were," she had said. "She had a mother who really loved her. She knows what love is, and what it isn't. And she's sensible. From what she's told me about Zac, he sounds like the complete opposite of Steve. Stop worrying. And if you do see something that bothers you, we'll talk to her together."

"So then, tell all," Kate said the moment Joanne opened the door on her return, late on Sunday evening. "Is Zac the devil incarnate, or God's gift to women?"

Joanne dropped her suitcase in the hall and took her coat off, before sinking down gratefully onto the couch.

"God, I'm tired," she said. "We never stopped. We were up till three in the morning talking, and then Amy dragged me out of bed at seven so we could go to Hampton Court Palace before I came home. I wish I'd never told her I was interested in the Tudors. I nearly missed the train." She yawned hugely.

"You're not going to bed until you've told me what Zac's like," Kate said unsympathetically. "With work the way it is at the moment, I'm not likely to see him until the wedding. I've spent the whole weekend biting my nails, worrying."

Joanne looked down at her sister's tapering, perfectly manicured nails.

"Figuratively speaking," Kate added.

"He's really nice," Joanne said. "We went out for a meal

and I watched him like a hawk, looking for all the tell-tale signs. He was overly polite at first, but after a while he started to relax and open up a bit. His family are Jamaican, his grandparents came over here in the fifties. He was intelligent, friendly, and interested in what Amy and I had to say, but more important than that, he didn't order her meal for her without asking what she wanted, and when she went to the toilet he didn't watch her to make sure she didn't speak to anyone. In fact, at one point she saw some friends of hers and went over to say hello. He just carried on chatting to me, telling me that he was really glad to have met me after all this time. And then I asked about word processor programs, because he works in computers. He didn't show off his knowledge and try to make me feel ignorant, he just answered the questions I asked. I know all the shortcuts now, if I can remember them."

"Was Steve really like that?" Kate asked. "Showing off, watching you all the time?"

Joanne nodded.

"Yes. He couldn't help it. He had to show me how lucky I was to have him. He wanted me all to himself, and if anyone spoke to me when we were out he had to know everything about them. At the time I thought it was because he loved me and was interested in the people I knew. If Zac had been like that I'd have seen it. He'd have kept glancing Amy's way, weighing up the people she was chatting to, particularly the men. He didn't. I didn't see anything to worry about. He swears a bit, casually, like young people seem to nowadays. And he's got his nose pierced."

"A hanging matter, without doubt," Kate said, grinning. "No, seriously, I'm glad you like him. I wouldn't have noticed all that stuff about his eyes following her around the room. I didn't notice that with Steve. I just never liked him. It was an instinctive thing, not anything he did that I could put my finger on. Until he started hitting you, of course."

"That's all over now," Joanne said. "Well, it will be when the court case is over. I don't know if I'd have pressed charges if I'd known it'd take up to six months to get to court."

"You're not thinking of backing out now, surely?" Kate said.

"No. I don't want to see Steve again, that's all. And I'll have to, in court. I just wish it was over. Then I can forget him and get on with the rest of my life."

"At least you won't have to talk to him," Kate said. "And I'll come with you, if you like."

"No," Joanne said. "I want to do this on my own. Face him, just once more, and show him that it's really over between us, once and for all. He needs to know I really mean it."

"Maybe he does already," Kate observed. "He hasn't tried to get in touch with you at all."

"No, he hasn't," Joanne said thoughtfully. "Maybe you're right. Or perhaps he's frightened of breaking the injunction. Whatever it is, I'm glad."

* * *

Mrs Llewelyn, one of Joanne's clients, was excessively proud of her prize flowers, and it was while Joanne was trying to work the fiddly catch to close the garden gate to stop dogs getting in, that she saw him walking up the street towards her. She was half tempted to run back up the path, but she realised that if she did that he would know she was still afraid of him, and she didn't want to give him that satisfaction. So she stood, her hand on the catch, and waited for him to approach. He stopped a couple of yards away from her.

"Hello Joanne," he said brightly, as though surprised to have met her, although he must have been lying in wait for her to come out of her client's house. "You're looking nice."

She didn't respond to his compliment, which was a lie in any case. She wore no makeup, an unflattering lilac overall, and her hair was screwed up in an untidy bun. She was a mess, even by her standards.

What do you want, Steve?" she asked.

Her brusque manner unnerved him, and he looked suddenly uncertain.

"I…wanted to see you, to find out how you are. I miss you," he said.

"I'm fine," Joanne replied. "You're breaking the injunction, you know." She set off walking down the street and he followed.

"I know," he said. "Are you going to report me?"

"It depends on what you do," she replied. "If you touch me, yes, I will report you."

"I'm not going to touch you. I just wanted to talk to you, that's all."

She got to the zebra crossing and waited for the cars to stop, then crossed. At the other side she halted. Her way from here took her down a reasonably quiet lane, and she didn't want to be alone with Steve. She doubted he would attack her in the street, but it was better not to take chances.

"If you're going to ask me to come back to you, you're wasting your time," she said bluntly. His expression told her that was exactly what he had intended to say, although his next words contradicted that.

"I know you don't want to come back," he said. "I don't blame you. Are you all right now?"

"My right arm's weak," she said, "and my ribs still hurt if I take a deep breath. But the bruising on my face and legs has gone, as you can see. My cheek's still sore to touch though, but as it was only a hairline fracture, I won't be disfigured."

She spoke matter-of-factly and looked him straight in the eye while she was speaking, which unnerved him further, as she'd intended. She wanted to show him she had changed, was no longer the sort of person who would believe his lies.

"I'm so sorry, Jo," he said. "I'd give anything if I could turn the clock back."

"So would I," she replied. "Twenty years and nine months would be good. Or if not, at least back to the day before Amy left home."

He blushed scarlet and looked away. He seemed genuinely distressed. No, he *was* genuinely distressed. He always was. He believed his lies. That was why he was so good at them.

"I wanted to tell you that I've been to the doc's," he said. "He reckons I'm depressed. He's given me these antidepressants to take, and I've got an appointment to see a shrink."

"Well, good luck," Joanne replied. "Are they working, the tablets?"

"I don't know yet," Steve said. "The doctor said it'd be a month or so before I see a difference. I've been having trouble sleeping, too. It's not the same without you there."

"You'll get used to it, in time," Joanne said. "Look, I've got to go. I've got a client waiting for me."

Steve glanced at his watch.

"You don't have to be at the Philips's till half past," he said. "You've got fifteen minutes yet. I can understand why you don't want to come back to me, after I hurt you like that. But I wanted to ask you…Jo, can't you drop this court business? Mum's worried sick about it, and so am I, to be honest."

"I never intended to upset your mother, Steve, and I'm sorry for that," Joanne replied. "But I'm not dropping the charges."

"Please, Joanne. I know I was wrong to beat you up like that. I never meant to, you know that. I love you. You're everything to me. I just couldn't bear it that you were going to leave me, and I lost my temper. But I'm trying to change. I'm taking the tablets and I've got another interview tomorrow. I'm really changing this time. I'm just asking you to give me a chance to prove it."

"I've given you chances," Joanne said. "I've given you twenty years of chances. You say the same thing every time, Steve. And do you know what? I'm so stupid that if I didn't know what you'd done to Amy, I might even have forgiven you this time as well. But not now, not after that. You need to learn that you can't behave the way you do towards women and get away with it. Fathers don't do what you did to your daughter. No, I'm not dropping the charges. Tell Susan I'm sorry, but no."

She turned to walk away, and he put his hand out to restrain her, stopping just short of touching her. *He believes I mean it then,* she thought.

"Please," he said, his face a mask of distress. "Jo, I can't go to prison, you know that. I'll never touch you again. I'll never lie to you again, I swear, and I'll make it up to Amy somehow. I'd been drinking that night, I never would have touched her otherwise. I feel sick just thinking about it. I promise, if you'll just drop the charges I'll never drink again. Please, I'm begging you."

"How's the pool team doing?" Joanne asked.

Steve's face creased in bewilderment.

"What?" he said, completely thrown by the sudden change of subject.

"The pool team. For the Bull. You were doing quite well, the last you told me. I just wondered."

"Yes," he said. "We're doing OK. I haven't been for a couple of weeks. I've been too worried about the court case and everything."

Joanne nodded.

"I see," she said. "I'll think about what you've said. I've got to go now. Goodbye, Steve." She started walking away, listening for sounds of him following her. *If he does, I'll walk up the first path I come to and knock on the door,* she thought. *If he doesn't go away then, I'll phone the police.*

"Will you ring me when you've had time to think?" he shouted after her from the corner. She raised her arm in acknowledgement that she'd heard him, and carried on without looking back.

* * *

When it was over, she walked up the road to the coffee shop and ordered a cappuccino and a large pastry covered in chemically-sweetened white icing which she left after the first bite. She sat at a table by the window and watched the people walk by for a time, wondering how many of the women passing had secret bruises that they covered with foundation or carefully placed accessories. What was it the statistics said? One in four women has been a victim of domestic abuse.

Joanne sipped her coffee. Surely it wasn't possible for a quarter of the female population to be as stupid as she had been? Of course the figures included emotional abuse as well; undermining your confidence, making you feel inadequate, ugly, fat, inferior. Steve had done that too, she now realised. *Why don't you wait till you know what you're talking about before you open your mouth? I wouldn't wear that if I were you. You're too flat-chested to look good in a low-cut dress.* Little comments, insignificant if taken one by one, but together they had chipped away at what little self-confidence her father had left her with, until by the time Steve hit her she already felt that she deserved it; she'd been such a disappointment to him, had not lived up to any of his expectations.

Well, *he* had lived up to her expectations today in court, had exceeded them in fact. No wonder so few women pursued charges against their partners. She would never do it again, she vowed.

It had been a nightmare from the first moment, when she had been shown to an uncomfortable green moulded plastic chair in the waiting area. She had refused to let Kate accompany her; she had wanted to do this alone, to prove that she was strong now and needed no support.

She had taken a book to read, and had barely opened it before Steve was shown into the same area. He sat down as far away from her as possible. That was not in his nature, Joanne knew. His instinct would be to sit next to her, try to make small talk, to make her feel guilty for putting him through this ordeal, when everything he had done had been out of love for her. He had obviously been warned by his solicitor not to speak to her, but his presence filled the area, and she could feel his eyes burning into her as she tried desperately to concentrate on her book.

He was wearing a suit and tie; he looked the epitome of respectable middle-class manhood. She too looked the part, dressed in a grey skirt suit and cream blouse chosen by Kate, her hair twisted up into a chignon. One of the clips securing it was digging into her head, but she didn't dare loosen it for fear the whole style would fall down and make her look dishevelled.

She had been dreading hearing her name called, but in the end she was grateful; she thought it would be a relief to have Steve's looming presence diluted by the three magistrates, the clerk and the solicitors. But the atmosphere in the courtroom was oppressive, redolent of guilt and despair, and Joanne had a sudden urge to say that she had changed her mind; anything to escape this ordeal. Her solicitor's smile did nothing to counteract the impassive faces of the magistrates. She had to convince them that she was telling the truth. It was Steve's word against hers, and he was by far the better liar. He had had years of practice at it while she had cowered in the shadows, too afraid of his sharp tongue and later of his fists to contradict him.

He can't touch me now, she told herself. *He can't ever touch me again. He's dead to me.* But her thoughts rang hollow in her head, and she heard but did not register Steve's admission of guilt at first. When she did, she felt a wave of exhilaration flood her. She would not have to convince anyone after all; he had admitted he was at fault, had done the right thing.

Then she listened as Steve's solicitor continued speaking, and then Steve himself, and she realised that nothing had changed. Steve was guilty but it was nevertheless her fault, as always.

A picture was painted for the magistrates, in glowing colours, of a perfect marriage, a hard-working, dedicated man who had striven all his life to provide his wife with the very best of everything, who had worked long hours, driven himself to near collapse to fulfil her every wish. Then he had been made redundant. Adding to his sudden loss of self-esteem and sense of worthlessness had been the worry of the mounting bills, which had eroded his self-control. He had been unable to cope with Joanne's inability to understand that they had to retrench, but had not recognised that he was suffering from depression until he had come home to find his wife, the woman he expected to support him through this difficult time, packing and coldly announcing her intention to abandon him. He had lost his temper, and had regretted it bitterly ever since.

But this terrible, one-off assault against the person he loved most in the world had woken him up to the fact that there was something wrong, and he was taking every possible measure to ensure it would never happen again; he was now taking antidepressants and was awaiting an appointment to see a psychiatrist. Steve stood in the dock, his handsome face disfigured by misery, his broad shoulders stooped with the grief his cherished wife had caused him by her heartless lack of understanding of his plight.

It was a compelling picture, and as Joanne walked on shaky legs to the witness stand and took the oath, it took every ounce of courage she had to fight against twenty years of conditioning; she wanted nothing more than to just admit that it was all true, that she was at fault, that she had never been the wife he'd wanted, that she'd been a constant disappointment to him.

She thought again about Amy, about how terrified she must have felt to have the one man she thought she could trust abuse her in a way no one should have to endure, ever. He had done that, this weeping, distraught wreck of a man standing opposite her, he had done it coldly and calculatingly, and then had let his daughter walk out alone into the world, damaged and bereft, and he had let her go without a thought, and had blamed her for it for three years. He cared for no one but himself.

Joanne had a desperate urge to tell the magistrates the

truth about why she had left, but she could not do that to her daughter. She had endured enough. For Amy's sake she would have to perjure herself, and it was Steve's fault. For the first time she felt the seed of hatred put out its first fragile roots deep inside her, and she took courage from it. She placed her hands on the stand in front of her to stop them trembling and when she spoke her voice was clear and controlled.

She told them that she had endured years of violence, but that it had never seemed bad enough to call the police. He had slapped her, pulled her hair, banged her head on the wall, but she had put up with it for the sake of her daughter and for the sake of her marriage. Steve had been her first boyfriend, she explained; she had not known relationships could be otherwise.

She realised as she spoke, as she answered the questions put to her, that she sounded ridiculous, a pathetic apology for a woman who would put up with anything because she was too feeble to leave. Either that or she was lying. It would help if she could make her voice tremble, if tears could run down her cheeks, as they were running down the cheeks of her husband, but her body gave her only two choices; distance herself from everything and speak clearly and unemotionally, or collapse entirely into a weeping, shaking wreck. She would not, could not do that in front of him. She would never show weakness in front of him again. She would die first.

So she told the truth, as far as she could, and because of that she knew that her reasons for suddenly leaving after twenty years of alleged mistreatment, sounded false. She was already leaving before he beat her so badly; what other reason could she have than that she was unwilling to support him through this bad time?

Finally she sat down, aware that she had taken his beautiful picture of their marriage and daubed black paint on it, had tried, but not succeeded in obliterating Steve's vision of a perfect marriage from the magistrates' eyes.

Instead she had just shown herself to be a destroyer of perfection, a graffiti vandal spraying her petty spite across an exquisite work of art.

He did not go to prison, in the end, didn't even get a suspended sentence; instead, in view of the medical evidence of her injuries he was put on probation for one year, and ordered to attend a domestic violence programme once a week to learn how to control and eradicate his anger.

She hung around outside the courtroom, thanking her solicitor and listening as he told her that these therapy courses were proving very effective in amending the behaviour of violent men. She sensed that he was impatient to be gone, that he had another case in a few minutes and wanted to forget her so he could concentrate on his next client. Even so, she held him back, asking him irrelevant questions about his bill until Steve had left the court building completely, after which she said goodbye and watched the solicitor scurry thankfully away.

Would Steve wait for her outside? *No,* she thought, *the injunction's still in place. He won't break it where others can witness it. If he wants to see me he'll catch me between clients when I'm working, or on a dark evening when I nip out to the all night shop for some milk.* He had looked at her directly once, as he was leaving the courtroom, and she had seen the look of triumph in his eyes. He'd won, as far as he was concerned, and it would only be a matter of time before he came for her, pleading or violent, it didn't really matter.

There was only one way to really end it, finally, and that was what she thought about now, as she sat in the café and watched the office workers hurrying down Deansgate in the pale early spring sunshine, clutching plastic-wrapped sandwiches or pies in greasy paper bags.

Everyone was in such a hurry all the time, she noticed. Rushing to school with the kids, rushing to work, dashing out for lunch, rushing back again, running for the train, then throwing themselves in the shower, before hurrying out to the pub, or a club, or sitting in front of a TV, not to relax but to avoid having to think about how futile their lives were.

That was what she had done for all those years, she realised. She'd kept herself busy with pointless tasks; vacuuming her already immaculate carpets, polishing gleaming surfaces, spending hours concocting meals that had been shovelled down without comment.

It was lunchtime and the fashionable coffee place was full, but the young people, though sitting, were restless, perching on the edge of their seats, texting frantically on their mobile phones, their eyes darting round the room as though terrified of missing something, or talking twenty to the dozen in over-loud voices with disinterested companions.

The only people who appeared truly relaxed were the old. But it seemed to Joanne to be resignation rather than relaxation, a realisation that their lives were over, that all they had to enjoy now were memories of when they had had the energy to rush through life unthinkingly. Joanne was not old, she knew that; her life was not over yet and if she wanted to have happy memories to sustain her through her dotage, she had to start accumulating some, and fast.

I've got to get away, she thought. *I can't hide behind Kate any more. I've got to make a new start, go somewhere where I can have time to think, where no one knows me and I can reinvent myself.*

She sat and sipped her cooling coffee, listened to the hubbub of voices, and started to plan.

* * *

"You're mad," said Kate. "You don't have to go anywhere to get away from Steve. You've got an injunction out against him. If he tries to contact you, you can have him arrested."

"I can't keep getting injunctions out indefinitely," Joanne pointed out. "And anyway, it's not just that. I want to get away, to make a new life."

"You can make a new life here," Kate said. "You don't need to go to the back of beyond to do that."

Joanne sighed. How could she explain to her sister, who

had always known who she was and what she wanted and had gone straight out to get it, that she had to break away completely, away from anyone who knew her past? It was much harder to lie when there were people around who knew the truth. No matter how understanding and supportive those people were.

"I need to stand on my own two feet, Kate, and prove to myself that I can live on my own," she said.

"I can understand that," Kate said. "But why do you have to go to Aberystwyth to do it? There's nothing there, for God's sake!"

"Yes there is, there's a job," Joanne countered. She had applied for jobs in Wales, Scotland, the Lake District, and had taken the first one she was offered, seeing it as destiny.

"There are jobs in Manchester," Kate said reasonably. "Hundreds of them."

"I know, but I don't want to spend the rest of my life looking over my shoulder. And I don't want to live in the city. I know you love it, but I always did want to live in the countryside."

"Yes, I remember," Kate said. "You used to collect those little cottage ornaments, what were they?"

"Lilliput Lane," Joanne said.

"Yes. You had loads. What happened to them?"

"Steve threw them all out one day. He said they were cluttering the place up," Joanne said. She had been collecting them for years, and had been heartbroken at the time.

"Oh. Right. Sorry," Kate said uncomfortably. "Well, even so, you can't *really* want to live in the countryside. I mean it's not all thatched cottages with log fires and roses round the door, is it? It's cold and muddy and miserable, and there's nowhere to go, and no way of getting there if there was with one bus a week or whatever it is they have. And it's a long way away, Jo. What will you do if you hate it?"

"I can come back. I've not sold myself into slavery or anything." Joanne laughed. "If I hate it I'll quit. I can come back here, can't I?"

"Of course you can. Always," Kate said. "But you're taking a chance, aren't you? I mean, you've never even been to Aberystwyth!"

No, she hadn't, but she'd looked it up on the internet. It was near the sea, and it had a castle and a hill and a university and nobody, absolutely nobody she knew lived there.

Her employer was taking a chance too. The interview had been conducted on the phone; Joanne was to clean fifteen student houses owned by her employer, and while she was cleaning she was to report back any 'goings-on'. Drugs, men staying over, things like that, Mrs Jones had explained in her melodic Welsh accent. She would be paid minimum wage, but would have her own rent-free furnished room in one of the houses, which was mainly occupied by older students, postgraduates. All female. Mrs Jones didn't hold with men, she said, in a tone which implied the male of the species was only a notch or two above the cockroach, which suited Joanne fine.

"I'll be OK," Joanne assured her sister. "It'll be an adventure. It's about time I had one of those."

It was. The future opened up before her, bright and crisp and full of promise. She had already made a start. She had told Mrs Jones that she was divorced, and had reverted to her maiden name. It would be difficult at times, she knew that. There was so much she had to learn, stuff that other people took for granted. How to budget money, how to talk to people, make friends. She really could do with learning to drive. And she would be alone out in Wales, really alone.

But she would not be lonely as she had been for years with Steve. And most of all, she would be free, truly free. That would be the hardest thing of all to cope with, probably. Having to make her own decisions and stand or fall by them.

It was heady, exhilarating. She couldn't wait.

CHAPTER TWELVE

Aberystwyth, May 2006

Joanne stopped running just short of her destination, and walked the rest of the way to the top of the hill to allow her breathing to return to normal. She reached up to lift the weight of her hair off the back of her neck, and relished the feel of the breeze that cooled the sweat trickling down her back. In a moment her t-shirt would start to feel clammy and uncomfortable. She swung the small daysack off her shoulders and drew a towel and light cotton sweatshirt out of it. Deftly she stripped off her damp top and wiped herself with the towel before pulling on the sweatshirt.

She glanced back briefly at the way she had run, the ruins of the castle hazy in the pearly evening light, the curve of the promenade with its once-grand houses, all now either derelict or transformed with little more than a lick of paint into cheap hotels with unimaginative names. *The Seaview, The Grand.*

She walked over the brow of the hill and Aberystwyth disappeared from her view and her mind as she sought the little grassy hollow between two rocks, where she sat down, hidden from the sight of anyone except the most observant walker. Not that she expected anybody to be on the path; it was not the holiday season yet, and few of either the locals or the students ventured up here at dusk.

She took an apple from her bag and bit into it, savouring

its crisp sweetness, and gazed out across the sea, letting her mind drift free. She had found this place by accident the first time she had had sufficient breath after jogging the length of the promenade to attempt the hill at the end of it. She had arrived at the top with lungs burning and legs like jelly, and had staggered on a few more paces to get out of the wind. Then she had seen the perfect shielded hollow, and it seemed to have been designed just for her, a place where she could go when she wanted to be completely alone and undisturbed for a time. Like now, when she needed to think, to reflect on how far she had come in the last twelve months, and where she wanted to go from here.

It was difficult to imagine that she had once been so unfit. This time last year, fresh from the city, she would have had difficulty even walking up the hill, let alone jogging up it. Kate had insisted on taking a precious day off work to drive her and her meagre possessions to Aberystwyth, and had looked around the room that Joanne was to call home, eyeing the green paintwork and red carpet with horror.

"Christ, Jo, you can't live here!" she had said.

Joanne had looked at the clashing colour scheme, the scratched wardrobe and table and sagging single bed and had seen only one thing; freedom. The absolute certainty that however rundown this house was, she would never, never come home to find Steve waiting for her. She could walk outside confidently without fearing that every shadow or doorway might contain her husband. She had hung up her clothes, attempted and failed to open the warped sash window, and then had gone out to a café with Kate, where they had eaten a surprisingly tasty meal of pie and chips. Kate had spent a fruitless hour trying to persuade Joanne that she would be just as safe living somewhere on the outskirts of Manchester as she was in this hellhole.

"It's not a hellhole," Joanne had said laughingly. "It's lovely. Well, OK, the house isn't lovely, true, but it's only a few yards from the sea. I'll be able to swim in the summer!"

"You'll die of hypothermia if you try to swim in that!" Kate had said gloomily. "And the people don't even speak *English*, for God's sake!" The waitress had greeted them with a friendly "*Prynhawn da*," before switching smoothly into English on seeing their twin uncomprehending looks.

"Yes they do, but they speak Welsh as well. It's one of the oldest languages in the world, apparently," Joanne said, enjoying the opportunity to show off her research. "I expect I'll be able to learn it, if I want."

"You're mad," Kate had commented as she was driving off a couple of hours later. "I'll give you six months. No, three. Just ring me when you see sense and want to come home."

Joanne had waved her sister off gaily, but as soon as the car had disappeared round the corner she had felt the leaden weight of dread settle in her stomach. Would she be able to cope, completely alone? What were her housemates like? Would they all be young trendy types who spoke a teenage version of English almost as incomprehensible to her as Welsh? Would they ignore, or worse, deride her because she was old, yet had less experience of the world than they did?

She sat in the kitchen with a cup of coffee and tried to calm herself. She had her own room; she would only have to meet the other inhabitants of the house at mealtimes. It would be all right. She would take it one step at a time.

Her employer had turned up mid afternoon to meet her, walking in on Joanne as she was struggling to open the back door.

"It swells in the wet weather," the voice had suddenly come from behind Joanne, making her jump. "If you just give it a kick at the bottom left hand corner, that should do it."

Joanne had turned round to be confronted by a small elderly lady with a disdainful look on her face. Her eyes swept up and down her new employee, and seemed somewhat dissatisfied with what they saw.

"*Croeso y Gymru,*" she said, stony-faced. "That means

welcome to Wales," she translated. "You're younger than I thought you'd be."

"I'm forty-one, Mrs Jones," Joanne said, disliking the woman on sight but trying not to show it. "I told you that on the phone."

"Yes. Well, you don't look it," Mrs Jones said, managing to make the fact sound like an insult. "Will you be able to start tomorrow? I shall expect you to clean all the communal rooms in each house," she continued without waiting for a reply. "I have no male tenants. If you see any evidence of male occupation or presence, I expect you to inform me immediately. If you see any sign of drugs, syringes, burnt teaspoons, silver foil, white powder and such like, I expect you to tell me immediately. You will come to my house every Friday after tea, when I shall pay you what I owe you for the week. I will check to make sure your work is up to the standard I expect. I live in Borth," she said briskly, handing Joanne a paper with a list of addresses on. "My address is at the top. The others are the houses I own. Do you have any questions?"

"Yes," said Joanne, already resolved not to tell Mrs Jones even if she were to find an opium den or fully operational brothel at any of the houses on the list. "How do I open the window in my room?"

She shared the house with four other women, all of them training to be primary teachers, all of them in their early to mid twenties. At first Joanne had been wary of them, their exuberance, their detailed attention to fashion and overly dramatic reactions to the most trivial thing; someone had cut them dead in the street; the man of their dreams didn't even know they existed; they couldn't find a lipstick to match their t-shirt; *oh my God,* they'd put on a whole pound this week!

Joanne had smiled, introduced herself, and then retired to her room. For the first week she had hardly seen her housemates at all. She had to clean three houses a day, which she had thought would be easy; but the houses were large, the carpets were of colours which showed every scrap of dirt, and the surfaces were hard to clean; white pitted kitchen tops that had to be scrubbed with bleach, picture rails and deep skirting boards that harboured dust. Mrs Jones followed round behind her, poking her stick into the corners of rooms, sweeping her fingers across furniture looking for dust.

At the end of the week Joanne had taken the bus to Borth to be told that her work was satisfactory and she would do. Mrs Jones had given her an envelope containing her wages and had closed the door. To her dismay, Joanne discovered that the last bus back to Aberystwyth had already departed and she had had to walk back, arriving home completely shattered to be greeted by a kitchen full of young giggly females quaffing wine and eating crisps. She had been invited to join them and, too tired to resist, had been swept into their lives.

In the next weeks she had learned that 'totally' and 'like' were meaningless words inserted into every second sentence, that 'wicked' and 'bad' meant good, that 'whatever' meant you couldn't care less and that suddenly developing an American accent half way through a sentence was perfectly acceptable behaviour.

The girls separated out from a mass into individuals; Rachel, the gentle ethereal hippy who burnt incense in her room and smoked cigarettes that would have caused Mrs Jones to throw her out on the street, if Joanne had done her job properly; Siobhan, who really only wanted to teach until she married her long-term boyfriend and gave up work to have lots of children; Cathy, who read only feminist literature, disdained cosmetics of any kind and saw discrimination in the most innocent male gesture; and the monosyllabic antisocial Alice, who refused to follow the rota of chores the girls had established.

To avoid confrontation Joanne had done Alice's share as well as her own, until Cathy found out, and sweeping the previous evening's dirty dishes into the washing bowl before Joanne could stop her, had dumped the whole lot upside down on Alice's bed.

"Don't let her shit on you," Cathy had said while Joanne looked on in horror as the remains of yesterday's bolognese sauce soaked redly into Alice's pastel pink duvet cover, "because she will. She's like a man, the cow, thinks everyone else should fetch and carry for her. You've got to stand up for yourself."

Alice had stormed out of her room into the kitchen that evening to be met by a wall of cold accusing silence. Cathy had stared her down, and after a few moments Alice's eyes had dropped and she had retreated. From then on she did her share of the jobs, tight-lipped, and on the odd occasion when she didn't, Joanne forced herself to ignore the dishes in the sink and the ring round the bath, until it became easy to do so.

She settled into the community of the house, everyone adopting the role that suited their personality. Cathy stood up for everyone's rights whether they wanted her to or not, Rachel made the peace, Siobhan turned the house into a home with pictures and cushions, and Joanne became the agony aunt, listening and sympathising with broken romances and assignment deadlines that couldn't be met, providing a shoulder to cry on.

After a few weeks she realised that it was the sullen, unfriendly Alice who was the misfit in the house, not herself as she'd expected. The others delighted in her naivety, advising her on what to wear, how to apply makeup, which digital camera to buy, and how to use it when she had. She allowed Siobhan to trim and colour her hair, transforming it from a dull brown to a glossy mahogany; she learned to join in conversations, then, tentatively, to initiate them. They invited her to go with them to the pub, not because they pitied her but because they really wanted her company. They asked her advice, and sometimes followed it, and they laughed when she took up jogging and persisted in going out even when the wind was lashing the waves across the promenade, but their laughter was good-humoured and inclusive, not derisive as Steve's would have been.

Under their friendship and tutelage Joanne blossomed, far faster than she ever would have done if she'd followed Kate's advice and rented a flat in Manchester on her own, a fact which Kate acknowledged when she came to visit, one overcast day in September. They went to the same café as they had six months before, and ordered the same meal. Kate was uncharacteristically quiet while she ate.

"OK," she said, when she'd swallowed the last chip on her plate. "I admit it, I was wrong, and you were right. You look great. I hardly recognised you when you came to the door."

Joanne laughed.

"It's the other girls," she said. "They've decided to bring me into the twenty-first century." She gestured down at the floaty burnt-orange skirt and embroidered peasant blouse she was wearing. "This was Rachel's idea. I thought it was a bit too young for me."

Kate took in the sleek dark hair falling gently past her shoulders, the sparkling brown eyes, the toned figure.

"You look bloody marvellous, Jo," she said. "That colour brings out the gold flecks in your eyes and the copper highlights in your hair. You look ten years younger. It's amazing!" She leaned forward, propping her elbows on the table. "You have no idea how worried I've been about you," she said.

"But I've rung you every week to tell you I was OK," Joanne protested, "and you saw me at Amy's wedding."

"I did. But that was four months ago. You looked drawn. You had dark shadows under your eyes. You seemed happy enough, but you've had years of practice at pretending to be happy when you were miserable."

"I *was* happy at Amy's wedding, though. Zac and her are really well suited."

"I know," Kate replied. "But now you're different.

You're buzzing. You're becoming the sister I should have had, if that bastard hadn't squashed you." She smiled, but her eyes filled with tears. "I'm sorry," she said, embarrassed by this uncharacteristic show of emotion. "Christ, it's good to see you like this," she added, fishing in her bag for a tissue.

"He hasn't squashed me, Kate," Joanne said. "I just thought he had. But I was still here, underneath. The girls have brought that out, they've been wonderful. I couldn't have done it without them. They're all off on teaching practice next week, and I'm really going to miss them."

They talked for a while about the other girls, how different they all were, and how they'd all made compromises to co-exist in the same house.

"Except Alice," Joanne said. "The others don't like her at all, because she's lazy and doesn't speak much. I'm not so sure. I think she might be very unhappy, but I don't know how to help her. She won't talk to me."

She hasn't changed completely, after all then, thought Kate. *She still tries to understand people, even if they're not worth the effort.*

"Do they know about Steve?" Kate asked.

Joanne shook her head.

"No," she said. "They think I'm divorced, and they know about Amy and Zac, but I haven't told them anything about my marriage, and they're considerate, they respect my privacy. I just said I didn't want to talk about it, and they've never pressured me." She was quiet for a moment, thinking, her eyes suddenly serious. "Has he pestered you a lot?" she asked.

"No." Kate shook her head. "Not after I spotted him hanging around at the end of the street and confronted him."

"What did you do?" Joanne asked.

"I told him that he was wasting his time if he was waiting for you, because you'd moved out. He asked me where you'd gone, as though he thought I'd actually tell him! Stupid git. I told him to piss off, and he gave me this sad puppy look and started coming out with all the usual crap about only wanting to talk to you, to say he was sorry, that he'd learnt his lesson now, blah blah. I let him finish, and then I told him that if he was looking for a career in acting he was barking up the wrong tree, because that was the most pathetic performance I'd ever seen. Then he forgot he was supposed to be all repentant and got nasty."

Joanne's eyes widened.

"What did he do?" she asked. "He didn't hit you, did he?"

Kate grinned, a malicious sparkle in her eyes.

"No. He said that he hoped I was satisfied, that I'd spent my whole life trying to turn you against him. Oh yes, and that I was only jealous because I was a sad old dyke who couldn't get laid. I told him that having him for a brother-in-law would be enough to turn any woman into a lesbian. And then he grabbed hold of my arm." She smiled, remembering the moment with obvious pleasure.

"What did you do?" Joanne asked warily.

"What I've wanted to do for years," her sister replied. "I smacked him right in the mouth. Literally. I actually cut my knuckle on his teeth." She laughed. "God, it felt so good. You should have seen his face."

"You shouldn't have done that, Kate," Joanne said. "What if he'd hit you back?"

"You still don't know him, do you, after all these years?" Kate said. "He didn't hit me back, because he knew I wasn't afraid of him. He knew that if he did I'd have him in court so fast his feet wouldn't touch the ground. He's a coward, Jo, like most bullies."

Joanne thought for a minute. Steve was a bully, yes. But a coward? Was he?

"He might have hit you anyway, without thinking," she pointed out. "He's got a terrible temper. And he could have really injured you, Kate."

"True," Kate conceded. "I didn't think of that at the time. But he didn't, anyway. He just let me go and walked off. He bruised my arm a bit, that's all. I haven't seen him since. He's been round to Mum's a couple of times, though, with his smarmy act, but she doesn't know where you are anyway, so he didn't get anywhere."

"You haven't told anyone else, have you?" Joanne asked worriedly. She'd thought less and less about Steve as the months had gone by. Now he loomed large before her.

"What do you take me for?" Kate responded. "No. The only people who know where you are are me and Amy. You're safe. Stop worrying. Oh, by the way, I met Mike in Altrincham a couple of weeks ago."

"Mike?" Joanne asked, puzzled.

"Your brother-in-law. The nice one. He asked how you were, and I told him that I had no idea, I hadn't seen you for months. He just grinned and said that next time I didn't see you I should give you his love and say congratulations. How the same parents can turn out two such different sons is beyond me. You should have married him instead, if you had to marry anyone."

"I didn't meet him until my wedding day," Joanne said. "And anyway, I didn't fancy him."

"No, you never did have eyes for anyone except Steve, did you?"

"Not any more," Joanne said. "I'm just enjoying being single now. I'm enjoying it so much, I think I'll stay that way for the rest of my life."

Kate went back to Manchester, and Steve receded into the background again. At Christmas the girls all went home, and Joanne spent Christmas day alone. Amy had invited her to London but Joanne turned her down, saying that she wanted to spend this Christmas alone, to remind herself how wonderful it was to be free. Amy had tried not to sound relieved, but Joanne had known her daughter would want to spend her first married Christmas just with her new husband.

Kate had invited her too; she had to work on Boxing Day, so couldn't drive to Wales. Joanne had been tempted, but Steve would be expecting that. Kate might not have seen him since she'd hit him, but that didn't mean he'd given up.

So she had got up in the morning and gone for a jog along the deserted prom, and then had cooked herself a full Christmas dinner, left all the dishes unwashed in the sink because it would have annoyed Steve, and alternately dozed and watched rubbish on the TV all evening.

It was wonderful. No bickering, no tension, no violence, just the complete and absolute freedom of knowing that he was, finally, out of her life. She could do whatever she wanted, whenever she wanted, forever. It was like being a teenager again. She felt young and healthy, bursting with vitality. Her legs were toned and slender from the running, her stomach flat. Her arms could do with a workout though, she thought.

In January the girls came back, full of tales of the holidays, of drunken fumblings at Christmas parties, of overindulgence in food and wine, of unwanted Christmas presents and boring relatives, and having to pretend to believe in Santa for the benefit of much younger siblings and cousins. The house settled back into its routine, and Joanne started thinking about continuing her education the following September. She didn't want to clean houses forever; the money was poor, for one thing, and the work was boring. The exercise, combined with the headiness of her new-found freedom was invigorating her mind as well as her body. She wanted to do more with her life. It wasn't too late, but she would have to act quickly.

In January she joined a gym and was shown, along with five other women, how to use the weight machines by a bored employee who made it clear from his attitude that he expected to see them only a couple of times at the most before they abandoned their shiny new year's resolutions.

It was a small but well-appointed gym, with a treadmill, rowing machine and stationary cycle as well as a variety of weight machines. Joanne soon learned that Friday was the quietest time, as for most people that was the start of a weekend of partying in the surprisingly large number of pubs Aberystwyth boasted.

Although Joanne had enjoyed the conversation and pub music on the odd occasion she had accompanied the girls to the pub, the smoky crowded atmosphere made her feel claustrophobic after a while. She preferred the fresh air, and enjoyed the freedom of being alone, of not having to consider anyone else.

She started going to the gym regularly on Friday evenings. Occasionally the employee, Andy, who had given her her induction, also worked out; often she had the gym to herself. He had been right; the other women had appeared sporadically for two or three weeks, and then drifted away. Only Joanne attended regularly, and she had exchanged names with him, but no more. He was there to work out not to engage in conversation, which suited Joanne, who wanted the same thing.

She enjoyed the peace; focussing on the particular muscle group she was working acted as a sort of meditation for her, relaxing her mind. Sometimes she overworked, forgetting her age and how unused to exercise her muscles were, and the next morning would find herself so stiff that getting out of bed was painful. But this was good pain, telling her that her muscles were growing and toning. A far cry from the pain she had suffered after her arguments with Steve, when he had twisted her arms up her back until she screamed, or had pulled her head just a little too far back, cricking her neck in the process. After years of that she could bear any amount of healthy aches and pains. She was growing stronger, both in body and mind, and it was a wonderful feeling.

Most of the time after the brief hellos she forgot Andy was at the gym, so she actually jumped one evening in March when she heard his voice directly behind her as she sat at the bicep machine.

"You're not doing it right," he said, moving round into her line of sight. He was wearing black Adidas shorts and a sleeveless vest; his athletic body gleamed with sweat. "Do you mind me telling you?" he asked, misinterpreting her startled look for resentment.

"No, not at all," Joanne replied. "I'd appreciate it."

"You need to sit right back in the seat, keep your shoulders back and rest your elbows on the pads, so that when you lift the weight you work your biceps instead of your shoulders." He watched as she straightened her arms and lifted the bar.

"No, you're still using your shoulders. Drop the weight a bit." He moved the pin up the weight stack. "Right. Have another go."

Joanne took a breath and gripped the handles. She started to lift, and felt her shoulders automatically curve forward.

"It's difficult," she said, letting the weight go.

"It's because you've got into a bad habit," Andy said. "I never noticed before. Grip the handles again." He went behind her and she felt his hands grip her shoulders, gently pulling her against the seat back. "That's where you should be. Now lift again." He released her shoulders but stayed behind her, out of sight.

She pulled the handle upwards, felt her shoulders move; and then they were gripped firmly and held in place and she had to take the weight on her biceps. She lifted the weight and lowered it again, and felt the difference.

"Thanks," she said. She expected him to release her.

"Do another one, just to make sure," he said. His hands retained their grip, and she took hold of the handle again, started to lift, felt her shoulders curve to take the weight and his hands suddenly pressing her back, pinioning her so she couldn't move. Panic tore through her unexpectedly; she was trapped. She let the handle go, the weight dropped with a crash, and she tore herself forward out of his grasp.

He reappeared in front of her, his hands held up, palms forward. His face was wary, concerned.

"I'm sorry," he said.

She leaned forward, hands on knees, and forced herself to take deep breaths to calm down. *God, he must think I'm mad!* she thought.

"Are you all right?" he asked. "I didn't mean to…I shouldn't have touched you. I'm sorry."

She glanced up at him and realised that he was afraid. In his eagerness to help her he'd forgotten that any contact with a customer could be misconstrued. She could hear the fear of dismissal, of a possible assault charge in his voice.

"No," she said. "It's not your fault. It was nice of you to help me. It's nothing to do with what you did. I've had…a bad experience in the past, that's all. You…I just remembered it. It's OK. Really." She sat up, forced herself to look at him, and smiled. "Really. You didn't do anything wrong."

He went across the room, filled a plastic cup with water and handed it to her.

"Here," he said. She took a sip, felt the coolness of the water slide down her throat, and began to relax. "Is there anything I can do?" he asked. His eyes were grey, not blue, and the expression in them was one of puzzled concern, not amusement or contempt. This man was not Steve. He was no threat to her.

"Yes," she replied. "You can forget that I just behaved like a complete lunatic."

He grinned, relieved.

"Forgotten," he said, and moving away, adjusted the seat on the exercise bike and began pedalling.

Joanne didn't go to the gym the next Friday, and told herself that it was because she was too busy. Then she spent the rest of the week annoyed by her own feebleness. The following Friday she forced herself to go.

She half-hoped he wouldn't be there, or if he was that there would be other people working out as well, but he was running on the treadmill when she arrived, and the room was otherwise empty. She pulled her hair back into a ponytail and started to warm up, stretching the muscles out slowly to avoid injury. He raised his hand in acknowledgement of her presence and carried on running, his feet padding rhythmically on the machine.

They worked out for half an hour in silence, and then she stopped for a drink. He finished his set on the bench press and sat up.

"Do you know how to use the running machine?" he asked.

She looked across at him. He was smiling normally; no wariness, just a friendly question.

"Yes, I just don't see much point in them," she replied. "I'd rather go for a run outside. Then I can look at the scenery instead of having to watch my flab bounce up and down in the mirror."

He laughed.

"You haven't got any flab to bounce," he said. "There's nothing of you. They're good if you want to time how fast you're running, or to know how far you can go."

That was a point. Joanne had no idea how far she could run now. She had started picking her wages up on Saturday morning and regularly jogged to Borth to get them, getting the bus back. How far was it? The run up and down the prom was increasingly easy to her now, more a warm-up than serious exercise.

"Two miles," Andy said suddenly.

"What is?" Joanne asked.

"From the castle to the bottom of the hill and back. Probably half a mile or more to the top of the hill as well. I live in a flat on the seafront. I've seen you a couple of times. You've got a nice easy style. You look as though you actually enjoy it."

"I do," she admitted. "It's great when I get the rhythm right. My body just goes on automatic pilot and I can let my mind drift off."

"I'm training for the Cardiff marathon in October," Andy said. "That's why I use the treadmill, to see how fast I'm running. It's not so hard on the feet as tarmac, either. You should consider entering."

"A marathon? Me?" Joanne said incredulously. "I think *walking* twenty-six miles would kill me, never mind running them."

"You've got the right physique," he said. "Better than me. I'm a bit bulky for long-distance running. Not that I'm trying to beat any records, I'm just doing it for charity. But I'd like to do a respectable time, if I can. What's the furthest you've run, then?"

"Borth, I think," she replied. "I jog there every week to get my wages."

"How do you feel when you get back?"

"I get the bus back. And I feel tired. But not completely shattered like I used to. The first time I went I missed the bus and had to walk back and it nearly killed me. My legs ached for a week afterwards!" She smiled, remembering how far she'd come in ten months, and not just in fitness.

"If you can build yourself up to running back as well you'd be able to do a half-marathon, at any rate. It's over seven miles to Borth."

"Is it?" She was shocked. She hadn't realised it was that far.

We can train together if you want," Andy suggested casually, lying back down on the bench and gripping the weight bar. "It'd be nice to have a bit of company. Have a think about it and let me know."

She was suspicious. She felt guilty about it, but couldn't help herself. She waited to see if he would pester her to agree, if he would suddenly appear when she was out jogging, follow her up to her secret place on the hill, offer to give her a lift home, be over-friendly or proprietorial in the gym, show off his strength on the weights.

Three weeks went by and nothing happened. She was being ridiculous, she realised. Andy was just being friendly. How old was he? Probably in his late twenties, early thirties. Much too young to be romantically interested in her. He wanted someone to train with, that was all.

"OK," Joanne said the following Friday. "I've thought about it. I don't know about doing a half-marathon, but I'll come training with you if you still want me to."

"Great," he said. "Tomorrow morning at ten o'clock? I'll meet you at the ice-cream hut near the castle."

The first time they went out, they jogged steadily to Borth, where she collected her wages. Then they got the bus back together and went for a coffee.

"A little over an hour," Andy said. "Not bad. You kept up a nice steady pace, and you don't seem too tired."

"I'm not, but there was no wind today, which makes a big difference. Tell me something," Joanne asked. "If you hadn't been slowing right down to my pace, how quickly could you have done the distance?"

He grinned.

"And there was me thinking I'd been subtle," he said. "I don't know. Forty minutes, maybe a bit less if I pushed myself. But I've always been sporty. I swim twice a week, and cycle as well. I did a triathlon a few years ago."

"Did you?" she said admiringly. "How did you do?"

"I fell off the bike and broke my arm," he said. "I've never been so disappointed in my life. And humiliated. I'd told everyone I was going to come in the first ten. Didn't live that down for ages. It served me right too; I was a big-headed bugger when I was younger. I haven't told any of my mates I'm doing the marathon yet. I'll have to a bit closer to the time, because I want them to sponsor me."

"You've told me," she pointed out.

"True, but you look the trustworthy type," he said. "And anyway, you don't know any of my mates." He winked at her. "Do you want to go for another run midweek, a shorter one, or just stick to the weekends?"

Running with Andy became a pleasant routine, something to look forward to. She didn't want to let him down, which pushed her into exercising even when the weather was foul, or she was tired and might have found an excuse not to bother otherwise.

Afterwards they'd usually go for a quiet drink, and she found herself looking forward to that, too. He was easy to be with, friendly without being pushy. He treated her as an equal rather than some delicate flower that needed protection, and she found herself opening up to him a little. At first they talked mainly about training techniques, how to increase speed and endurance, and fired up by his enthusiasm, she found herself pushing her body a little harder every time she ran. She started walking back from Borth instead of taking the bus, letting Andy run on ahead. By the time she got back, he'd be halfway through his pint. Occasionally they had a pub lunch.

After a while their conversation turned to topics other than running. He wanted to open a private gym, he told her, and had started looking into possible locations.

"In Aberystwyth?" she asked.

He shook his head.

"No," he replied. "I like living here, it's pretty vibrant, with all the students. But they haven't got any money and there's not enough interest among the locals. No, I'd have to move to a city, I suppose. Birmingham, maybe. Or at least somewhere where there's plenty of money. I want to offer alternative therapies too, reiki, aromatherapy, that sort of thing. What about yourself? Do you intend to stay here for the rest of your life?"

"I don't know," Joanne said. "I'm just trying to find myself at the moment. I'm thinking of going back to college, part time. There's an IT course I'm interested in, but it doesn't start till September. It'll feel odd going back to school at my age."

"Better late than never," Andy observed. "How old are you, anyway?"

"Forty-one," she said. "I used to live in the city, though, and I don't think I want to live there again. A lot of people might find it boring, but I like the slower pace of life here."

"You know," Andy said, draining his cup and placing it back in the saucer. "That's one of the things I really like about you."

"What?" Joanne asked. "That I don't want to live in the city?"

"No. That you just told me how old you were, straight out. Most women would say 'that's a rude question' or 'how old do you think I look?'"

"Would they?" she said, genuinely surprised.

"Yes. You're the least self-conscious woman I've ever met. You don't care about getting sweaty and smelly, you never wear makeup, you're not on a diet. You don't need to be, by the way, but most women seem to be dieting, no matter how thin they are."

"I never really thought about it," Joanne admitted. "I've not really had many women friends, or male friends for that matter, till I moved down here. The other girls in the house are always on one diet or another, and notice every tiny detail about each other's appearance, but I just assumed it was because they were young."

"Were you like that at their age, then?" Andy asked casually.

"No," she replied. "When I was their age I was married with a baby." She stopped and looked away, biting her lip.

"I'm sorry," Andy said. "Shall I change the subject?"

She hesitated. Just for a moment she had the urge to confide in him, to tell him about Steve and her past. But then he would know how pathetic she'd been and their developing friendship, which was coming to mean a lot to her, would be spoilt.

"Yes," she said. "I don't want to talk about it. I'm not ready, not yet."

"OK," he said immediately. "What subject are you thinking of studying?"

It was as simple as that. No trying to probe further, to find out her secrets. No subtle questions or hints. He was a breath of fresh air, uncomplicated, good-humoured, relaxing.

"He's very fit, that bloke of yours," Siobhan commented one evening. "I saw you running down the prom together when I came out of the library tonight."

Joanne was at the stove stirring a huge pan of chilli con carne.

"Yes, he works down the leisure centre," she said. "He trains every day. And he's not my 'bloke', we're just friends."

"Yeah, whatever," said Siobhan. "You didn't tell us he was so fit, though."

"Yes I did," Joanne protested. "He's training for the marathon, of course he's fit."

Siobhan rolled her eyes to heaven.

"Not fit, *fit*," she explained. "Good-looking. Well, from what I saw as you both shot past, anyway. And he's got a lovely bum."

Has he? Joanne hadn't noticed.

"I thought you were happily engaged to be married," Joanne teased.

"I am," Siobhan said, turning the tap on to fill the kettle. "Doesn't mean I can't look though, does it?"

In April Joanne took up swimming at Andy's suggestion, and started getting up an hour earlier twice a week so she could swim for half an hour before the pool opened. He had the keys to the centre, and the manager had no objections to them swimming out of hours. It was lovely not having to avoid splashing kids and people swimming breadths. She practised her backstroke, impossible in a crowded public session, enjoying her new-found strength as she powered up and down the pool. When she'd done twenty lengths she pulled herself out and sat on the side, squeezing the water out of her hair. Andy was already out of the water, and had gone to get changed. She stood up and turned round, to find him standing a few yards behind her.

"You've got a gorgeous figure, you know," he said admiringly.

She blushed crimson and felt suddenly naked, vulnerable.

She had a ridiculous urge to fold her arms across her breasts to hide them from him, and fought it down. She turned away.

"I'd better get dressed," she said, and walked off before he could say any more.

Andy waited for another two weeks before he broached the subject again. They'd been for their customary Saturday run to Borth, and had succeeded in shaving another couple of minutes off their time. Then they went to the wholefood café in the centre of town. He ordered their coffees and slices of pie, and then sat down. He was silent while she re-tied the laces of her trainers, and then as soon as she'd finished he spoke, before she could start a conversation about marathons or fitness training.

"Joanne, can I ask you a question?" he said. His tone was serious, and she felt her body tense.

"Yes, if you want," she said warily.

"Why do you find it so hard to accept a compliment? The other week at the pool, I was just being honest, and you made me feel like a pervert."

She looked at him, shocked.

"Did I?" she said.

"Yes. You ran into the changing room as though you thought I was going to jump on you or something."

"I'm sorry," Joanne said. "I didn't mean to. I just...I'm just not very good with compliments, that's all."

"You can say that again," Andy replied, "but it's more than that, isn't it? That first time, when I showed you how to use the weight machine, when I touched you, you were the same then."

"I know. I told you, I've had a bad experience in the past. It's nothing you've done."

"Yes. I realise that. But it's getting harder for me. I like you, you know that."

"Of course I do." She smiled. "We're friends."

"Friends," he repeated. "Yes, we are. But I like you more

than just as a friend. Surely you've seen that?"

No, she hadn't. All she knew of men she'd learnt from Steve. Andy hadn't smothered her with presents. He didn't ring her ten times a day to see how she was, and tell her he loved her. He didn't turn up outside her house to take her out on a date she was sure he hadn't mentioned before, and then get upset because she'd forgotten.

"No," she said. "No, I haven't seen that. I'm sorry if I should have done. I'm a lot older than you, and it never occurred to me that…"

"I'm thirty-seven, Joanne," he interrupted. "Four years is hardly an enormous difference."

Steve was nine years older than her. No, it wasn't much.

"I'm not very good at relationships," she said quietly. "I married my first boyfriend, and he's the only…er…" she stopped, trying to think of the right words.

"Man you'll ever love?" Andy suggested. "Do you wish you hadn't got divorced?"

"No!" she exclaimed, not noticing his eyes light up at her immediate response. "No, I don't love him, not at all. No, it's just that he's the only man I ever had a relationship with. I'm not good at reading signals."

"This bad experience you mentioned then," Andy said. "Was it to do with him?"

He genuinely cared. He was a lovely person. In three months he'd never done anything other than treat her with the utmost respect, as an equal. He deserved the truth. Or a little of it, at least.

"Yes," she said. "He was…he was…violent. And possessive. And a lot of other things. I put up with it, for too long, and then I stopped putting up with it and left. And now I'm here, and trying to make a new life for myself. And I like you, I really do."

"But you don't want to go out with me?"

"I don't know," she replied honestly. "I haven't thought about you in that way. I just enjoy being with you. You're very different to Steve."

"I should think I am!" Andy said vehemently. "I've never hit a woman in my life!"

No, she thought, *I don't think you have. And I don't think you would, either.* She had a sudden urge to please him, to say yes, she would like to go out with him. But it was wrong. She needed to think about it.

"I don't know if I'm ready," she said. "I don't care about Steve anymore, but I'm not over what he did to me, yet. I don't know when I will be."

"I don't want to pressure you into anything you're not ready for," Andy said. "I just want to see more of you. I want to take you out for meals, go to the theatre, that sort of thing. I want to…it's just getting harder not to put my arm round you, kiss you. Maybe I can help you to get over what he did. Not all men are like him, you know."

"I know," she said. "In my head, I know that. But…I need to think about it. Can you give me a little more time to sort things out in my head?"

"Sure," he agreed. "Take as much time as you like. Can we carry on as we are in the meantime?"

"Yes," she said, relieved beyond measure that he hadn't taken it the wrong way, walked out, sulked.

"Right then," he said. "Let's talk about ways to improve our running speeds."

* * *

Sitting on the top of the hill, she bit into her apple again and watched as a lone gull lazily rode the thermals over the sea. The sun was almost set now, the waves sparkling gold-tipped. She wrapped her arms round her knees and turned her mind to her dilemma.

Did she want to get involved with someone again? Life was simple at the moment; she went to work, came home, chatted with her housemates, went training, and then to bed. She could do what she wanted, when she wanted, with no ties. It was wonderful, after years of tiptoeing around terrified of saying or doing anything that would set Steve off.

She wasn't ready to start considering someone else's feelings. She wasn't sure she ever would be.

Andy would not be like Steve; she was sure of that. But if she agreed to go out with him their relationship would change. He would expect her to consider him when making arrangements, would want to spend more time with her, would make demands, however innocent, on her time. She didn't want that. But Andy was lovely. She didn't want to lose his friendship by refusing him either.

She thought for a while longer, made her decision, threw the apple core away, stood up and flexed her limbs for a moment, then set off straight away for his flat on the seafront before she could change her mind.

Andy opened the door dressed only in a pair of shorts. His eyes widened when he saw who his visitor was; she had never called on him at home before. Her hair was dishevelled, her face flushed with exercise and the wind off the sea. She looked lovely.

"Is it a bad time?" Joanne said.

"No, I was just going in the shower. Come in."

He led her upstairs into his flat. It was small but well-kept and reminded her of Kate's first place, the one she had stayed in for a week with Amy the first time she left Steve. Andy beckoned her to an armchair, then busied himself making tea.

"I've been sitting on the hill, thinking over what you said," Joanne began as soon as he returned with two steaming mugs. "And I wanted to come and see you while everything's clear in my head. I haven't been completely honest with you." She looked at him, trying to gauge his reaction; but his face was unreadable.

"I'm not divorced, like I told you I was," she continued. "I've been married to Steve for over twenty years, and looking back, it was hell, all of it, although I didn't see it like that at the time. I let him walk all over me from the moment I met him. He used to hit me now and again, but that's not the worst thing he did. He messed with my mind, too so I didn't know who I was anymore. I was pathetic, and I'm ashamed of myself for letting him do that to me for so long. Last year I found out about something he'd done. I won't tell you what it was, because it affects someone else, but it was enough to make me leave. He beat me up, quite badly, and I took him to court over it. Then I left Manchester and came here because I wanted to make a new start."

Andy smiled.

"That's not pathetic," he said, "that's admirable. It takes a lot of courage to leave everything that's familiar behind. Particularly after twenty years."

"Maybe, yes," Joanne agreed. "But I should have done it a long time ago. I had hundreds of reasons for staying with him, but they all came down to the fact that I was too cowardly to leave, really. I can see that now. I've spent the last year trying to find myself, and I'm starting to do it."

"But you're not there yet," Andy finished.

She sipped her tea.

"No. I'm not. And until I am I don't think it would be fair to start a relationship with anyone else. I need to be absolutely sure of myself, so I won't ever let anyone do what he did to me again." She looked up at him and saw the hurt in his eyes.

"I know you're not like Steve," she said. "And our friendship means more to me than you can imagine. Part of me wants to give it a go, and see how it works out."

"Why don't you, then?" Andy asked, brightening.

"Because right now I'm completely relaxed with you as a friend. I wasn't at first. I kept looking for signs of you being like him. If I start a more intimate relationship with you, I'll be tense, seeing ulterior motives in the most innocent gestures, and it just won't work. I need to be really confident in myself before I can go any further. I don't know how long that will take, it could be years. I never had any friends after I met Steve. He cut me off from everyone. With you I'm learning about friendship, and it's wonderful. I don't want to lose that, but it wouldn't be fair to agree to something I'm not ready for, just because I don't want to lose you as a friend."

"I can understand that," Andy said. "I don't *like* it, but I can understand it. And I admire your honesty. I'll be honest with you, too. I can carry on being your friend for now, and push the fact that I want more to one side. I don't know how long I can do that, but I want to be able to tell you if it's getting too difficult for me. Is that fair?"

"Yes," she replied. "It's fair." She smiled. "I can't believe how well you're taking it. I was frightened you'd tell me you didn't want us to be friends any more. That would have been terrible."

"I couldn't do that. Your friendship means a lot to me too. Why haven't you divorced him?"

The question took her by surprise. No one else had asked her that. But then most people thought she *was* divorced.

"I don't want any more contact with him," she said after a minute. "I never thought about having another relationship. I planned on staying single for the rest of my life. And I'm terrified that if I file for divorce he'll find out where I am. I don't want him to find me, ever."

"You don't still love him, just a little bit?"

"No," she replied without hesitation. "I don't love him at all. And I'm trying not to hate him, which is harder. I don't want to feel anything for him."

"What will he do if he does find you? What will you do?" Andy asked.

Joanne shuddered.

"I don't know," she said. "I don't intend to find out. Only my sister and my daughter know where I am, and they'll never tell him."

"How long do you think it'll be before he gives up on you?" Andy asked.

"When he's dead," she said. "That's when I'll finally be free of him. Until then he'll always want revenge for me leaving him. He'll always be a shadow in the background somewhere."

"I think you're wrong," Andy said. "I think you'll be free of him when you realise how special, how strong you really are. And when you realise that you don't give up friendship when you fall in love with someone, you just enhance it." He smiled across at her. "And when you do find that out, I hope I'm around to take advantage of it."

"So do I," Joanne said. "But if in the meantime you find someone else, go for it. I'm serious when I say I may never feel able to commit myself to anyone else."

"I doubt that, somehow. I think you will, in time. I've had several disastrous relationships too. Not like yours, but I know a bit about hurt. I was even engaged once, when I was young and stupid. I thought I was going to die of misery when we broke up. I'm older now, and wiser, I hope. You're the first person I've met in years that I really think it would work with. That's worth waiting for, I think."

He reached across, and pulling her to her feet gave her an unexpected hug, which was over before she could react to it. Then he let her go and stepped back, smiling, although his eyes were serious.

"Right," he said, picking her empty cup up and putting it in the sink. "When you knocked, I was reading an article about diet and how it can make a huge difference to your performance. It's over here somewhere." He picked a magazine up off the table and began leafing through the pages, tactfully closing the subject in the process.

CHAPTER THIRTEEN

Manchester

The five men attending the perpetrators' course filed into the classroom in the local comprehensive school and settled into their customary seats, which were arranged in a semi-circle around the flipchart at the front of the class.

Before Steve sat down he ran his fingers carefully round the edge of the chair. The last time he had been here he'd stood up at break time to find that he'd been sitting on a piece of bubble gum for the last hour and a half, which had softened with the warmth of his body and stuck to his new Armani trousers. He had managed to scrape it off in the toilet, but it had left a nasty pink stain on the beige material.

He had spent the second half of the session raging inwardly at the pimply-faced little shit who must have left the gum there, and thinking what he would do to him or her if he could get his hands on them. As a result he'd hardly registered any of the other men's responses to the case study they were supposed to be looking at.

It was a fictional story about a man who'd had a bad day at work and then came home to find the kids playing up and his wife moaning on about the leaking dishwasher and telling him that he should have fixed it but he hadn't because he was so useless. She wouldn't shut up when he told her to so he belted her one. *And serve her right too,* Steve felt. *If a man worked hard all day to put food on the table, he deserved a little peace when he got home at night.*

The other four men in the group didn't feel this way about the story, although they would have done a few weeks ago, before they'd been brainwashed by the smarmy do-gooders running the course.

At the first session Steve had thought it would be plain sailing. There were two social workers running the sessions, Tony and Claire, and they had explained that although the five men attending were all from very different backgrounds, they had one thing in common. They had all been violent towards their partners and as a result were attending this course to learn how to change their behaviour. They probably felt confused, Tony said, and that they were sick, or there was something wrong with them.

What a load of bollocks. The only thing wrong with them was that they'd all married women who didn't understand them, bitches who'd taken them to court. None of them really wanted to be on the course, even though they'd signed a paper agreeing to attend it if the courts ordered them to. It was a way of avoiding a custodial sentence, nothing more.

In the break they'd huddled together in a corner, away from the other people attending evening classes in pottery, French and IT, and had talked together in low voices over plastic cups of revolting instant coffee. Not about their marital situations, of course. Instead they'd exchanged a few politically incorrect jokes, agreed that this course was going to be a pile of shit, and then had settled into a conversation about how United were doing, until they'd been summoned back by a smiling Tony to the second hour of crap, after which they were all asked what they hoped to get out of being on the programme.

Fuck all, Steve thought as he stood up and said what he was sure the do-gooders wanted to hear, that he hoped to learn how to control his temper, to learn how to understand his wife better so that she would come back to him and they could make a success of their marriage. The other men had all come out with similar sorts of statements, and Steve could tell that they were all every bit as sincere as he was.

Tony had sweetly pointed out that it was commendable that they all wanted to change, and that this course would help them to learn about their emotions and how to manage them, but that they should not hold out any hopes that it would influence their wives to come back to them.

That last comment was directed at Steve, he knew that, because his wife was the only one who *had* left. Steve wanted to plant one right in the mouth of the scrawny little fart, but instead he'd said of course he understood that, that he wasn't trying to force Joanne to come back to him.

Well, that bit was true at any rate. He couldn't get her back unless he could find out where she was. The only person who seemed to know her whereabouts was that fucking cow of a sister of hers. The last time he'd seen her she'd punched him right in the mouth, splitting his lip and loosening one of his teeth. How he'd restrained himself from battering her face to a pulp he had no idea. Only the thought of the satisfaction she'd get out of seeing him go down for it had stopped him. He didn't dare talk to her again for fear that he wouldn't be able to restrain himself next time.

But he'd watched her flat regularly, especially on special occasions such as Kate's and their mother's birthdays, certain that at some point Joanne would come back for a few days from wherever she was hiding.

Nothing. Wherever she was, she was keeping her head really low. And in the meantime he was stuck with this pointless course, which he'd agreed to mainly so that he could convince her he was changing. It was her fault that he had to endure two hours of bullshit every week. Her and that fucking Kate, who'd put her up to the whole thing about leaving him and prosecuting him in the first place.

Left to her own devices Jo never would have had him arrested, he knew that. She wouldn't have had the guts. And she loved him. They loved each other. One day he would find out where she was, and when he did he'd be able to talk her round, make her see sense, he knew he would. In the meantime he vowed to get through the course, to grin and bear it. At least all five of them attending felt the same way.

But over the weeks he had watched incredulously as the others had fallen one by one under the spell of the mumbo-jumbo that they were being taught. Instead of discussing Man U or the Grand Prix in the breaks, they now discussed the family outings they'd had at the weekend, and how much happier the kids were now they could see Mummy and Daddy were getting on better. It was enough to make you vomit.

Of course there was something in some of the stuff they'd learnt, but then there always was a grain of truth in all brainwashing techniques, wasn't there? That's why they were so seductive. Take the sixth (or was it the seventh? he'd lost count) session, for example. They'd made a list of the emotional feelings men find difficult to express for fear of being thought a wimp, such as fear, loneliness, anxiety.

Steve had gained brownie points by revealing that he had become depressed after he lost his job because he felt useless, and had agreed with Tony that part of the reason he felt so low was because he was suppressing his feelings of uselessness and insecurity about being unemployed. That had gone down well, and Steve had felt quite proud of himself. Tony and Claire seemed to think it a positive sign that he'd admitted he was depressed and had even done something about it, going to the doctor's and getting antidepressants. They didn't need to know that he wasn't taking them, although he religiously went back to the surgery month after month for a repeat prescription, telling his GP that he was feeling a little better, but not enough to come off them.

The overworked doctor couldn't really care less. He was almost writing the prescription before Steve walked in the surgery. He'd even had a couple of lots of sleeping tablets.

That had been before he'd been to court, of course, when he thought that mental frailty and insomnia might influence the magistrates to acquit him. He'd taken one of the tablets once, one night when he couldn't sleep for thinking about Jo and wondering where she was, what she was doing and who she was doing it with. But he'd felt like shit the next morning, all groggy. After that he hadn't taken any more, finding that a good shot of whisky helped him to sleep and tasted a lot better too.

In the following week's session they'd discussed what it was like to be a child, small and vulnerable, able to cry without being derided, dependent on others for everything, and how from being young boys they'd then made the transition into manhood by excelling at sport, drinking, smoking, getting into fights. They discussed who gave them the idea that 'being a man' meant never showing weakness.

The men gave various examples which were written up on the flipchart by Tony, such as macho films, gangs at school, and Steve had, to his surprise, got caught up in the session and found himself revealing that his dad had told him he was a poof. As soon as the words were out of his mouth he'd regretted it, but Tony had pounced and there was no going back.

"Why do you think your dad said that?" he asked.

Steve had felt his face blazing. He tried to think of a way to back out, but couldn't come up with one. So he ended up telling the truth instead.

"I was the youngest," he said. "And when I was a little kid I was really cute. My mum kept my hair in ringlets until I was five. I think she wanted a daughter really."

"Can you remember how it felt?" Tony asked.

"Yeah," said Steve, his eyes misting as he cast his mind back. "It was great. Dave and Mike – my brothers – were jealous because I used to get more sweets than them, and I could get away with murder. But then I went to school and the other kids started calling me names and hitting me because they said I was a girl. When my dad found out he took me straight to the barbers and had my hair cut. Then he told me that if he caught me snivelling about kids calling me names he'd give me something to cry about, and if any of the kids tried to bully me again I should hit them."

"And did you do what your dad said?" Tony asked.

"Not at first, because at school the teachers told us we should tell them if someone was nasty to us, not hit them. So I did. But it didn't do any good. They still called me names, even though I'd had my hair cut. They said I had nits. So then one day I just lost it and laid into this kid. He was a lot bigger than me." He smiled, remembering. "God, it felt good watching him crawl around on the floor, snuffling and crying that he was going to get his dad on me. No one ever touched me at school after that. I told my dad when I got home and he said he was proud of me. It was the only time he ever said that to me."

Steve looked up, suddenly aware of where he was. Shit! What was he doing? He wanted the floor to open up and swallow him. "I mean, I know it wasn't right to hit the kid, but…" he blustered, mortified.

"You were a little boy," Tony said. "It's only to be expected that you'd do what your father said. Parents are a huge influence on children. We learn a lot about how we're expected to behave as adults from them. Why did your dad call you a poof, then? Do you want to tell us about that?"

No, thought Steve, *I don't, you nosy bastard.* But if he held back now, no doubt it would be reported back to his probation officer, and he wanted to do well on the course.

"It was a lot later, when I was fifteen. I was good at drawing, and I told him I wanted to do art O level and maybe go on to university. He went ballistic. He wanted me to go into the law, you see, be a copper, or better still a lawyer. That's what he'd wanted to be, but he didn't get the qualifications. Dave was already working as an accounts clerk and Mike had decided he wanted to be a doctor, so I was the only one left who could follow in Dad's footsteps.

But I wasn't interested. I never was one for reading at all, let alone bloody law with all those long words and stuff. I told him I wanted to be an artist, not wear a stupid wig and ponce about in a room crammed with dusty old books full of shit. I remember those were exactly the words I used."

The other men in the room laughed, and Steve smiled at them, relaxing a little. "Probably not the most tactful way to talk to someone who was bigger than me and who could make me do whatever he wanted. Anyway, he told me that he wasn't having any son of his growing up a nancy boy, and that I could do law or nothing."

"What did you do?" Daniel, one of the other men, asked.

"Nothing, as far as he was concerned. I left school when I was sixteen and set up my own decorating business. I managed to talk Mum into lending me the money to get started. I was determined to prove to him that I could be successful doing something artistic without being queer."

"And did you?" Claire asked. Trust it to be a fucking woman that asked him that.

"No. The bastard died just after I'd gone bankrupt, and I swear he was happy because I'd proved him right. Not about the queer bit, I was already married with a kid by then, but about the success."

"How did that make you feel?" Claire persisted gently.

Bitch. She was just trying to humiliate him in front of the others. He felt the temper surge up in him, and wanted to give her a slap, wipe the pitying look off her smug face. What right did she have to feel sorry for him? He glanced at her left hand. Bare. She was just a dried-up spinster, too fucking ugly to get a man, so she got her kicks out of lording it over them on courses like this, making them feel small.

He swallowed the rage down and looked at her challengingly.

"How would anyone feel?" he snapped. "Angry. Frustrated. At the time. It doesn't matter any more." He kept his gaze locked with hers and felt her back down, recognise his superiority, and turn her attention to the next man.

Since then he had kept himself under better control, had not let himself get drawn into revealing anything embarrassing. Of course he couldn't just sit silently through the sessions; none of the men were allowed to do that. If they tried, Tony or Claire would question them directly, forcing them to participate. So he took care to interject responses where he felt fit, taking his cue from the other men, who were being seduced by the psychological claptrap into revealing all sorts of humiliating things about themselves. But never again had he revealed himself as he had that night, nearly three months ago.

And now they were in the sixteenth week, and this was the session he'd been dreading, the one where each man in turn talked about the events which had led to his arrest and conviction for assault. This time he couldn't just contribute a few casual observations. All the men had been given a sheet with questions about their arrest event and had been told that they would be expected to talk about this, using the sheet for reference, one at a time.

This was a crucial exercise, Tony had said. It helped men to face up to their bad side and look at it in depth, working out the reasons why they became violent. In future sessions they would use the men's experiences to see how the women in their lives were affected by their behaviour, and to learn how to develop empathy for others and acquire individual skills for non-violence.

Steve was praying that one of the other men would be chosen to go first; then he could observe the social workers closely to find out what they wanted, and base his answers on that. But of course Sod's Law was in operation, and no sooner had they got settled in their seats than Tony had asked Steve if he would like to start.

He sighed, and picked up his paper. The first question was easy enough. 'When did the incident happen?' He'd written only three words in answer; 'On Saturday evening'.

"Did you have an argument?" Tony asked.

"No," Steve answered. "When I came home I went upstairs and I found her packing her case. She said she was leaving me."

"Did she say why?"

Shit. What had he told the magistrates? He was sure Tony would have read the court transcripts.

"She just said she'd had enough of living like this, worrying about money and stuff, you know, with me being unemployed. She was used to having whatever she wanted, I suppose. I told her I didn't want her to leave and she said that she didn't care what I wanted, she was leaving anyway."

Tony nodded.

"How did that make you feel?"

"Angry," said Steve. "And frustrated. I suppose I thought that she didn't think of me as a man anymore, because I wasn't bringing any money home."

"You'd been unemployed for a while, though," Tony observed. "Can you think of any reason why she chose that particular moment to leave?"

"We'd had a bit of an argument earlier on in the day." Bollocks! He hadn't meant to say that. He was sure he hadn't mentioned that in court. Joanne hadn't either, as far as he remembered.

"And had you hit her then?" Tony asked.

"No," said Steve, trying to salvage something. "No, I took a time-out thing, like we talked about a couple of weeks ago, although I didn't know what it was then, of course. I went out for a bit to cool down."

"Good," said Tony, and for a moment Steve thought he was going to get away with it. "So what did you argue about in the afternoon?"

Fuck. He'd have to tell the truth, or part of it at any rate. It would be easier to remember later.

"My daughter had left home when she was sixteen," he said. "She didn't like being told what time she should be home, that sort of thing, you know what teenagers are like. Anyway she left, and we hadn't heard anything from her in three years. On Saturdays I usually spend the whole day at the flying club, but on that day it was windy so I came home early and found my daughter there."

"What's your daughter's name?" Tony asked. Of course, they had this rule about always calling your family members by name to make them individuals, or some crap like that.

"Amy. Anyway, I was really angry that Jo hadn't told me she was visiting, or even that she was in touch."

"Can you think of any reason why she wouldn't have told you?"

"No," Steve said immediately. "That's why I was mad. I guess I didn't handle it very well, but I didn't throw anything or hit anyone. I just went out to the pub for a while to calm down and when I came back Amy had gone and Jo was packing."

"OK. So what did you do?"

Steve breathed a sigh of relief. Back to the truth; he could remember everything he'd told the court now.

"I threw her case across the room. I thought that would stop her leaving, if she couldn't take her clothes with her, but she just looked at me and then walked past me anyway and I realised that she was really going to go, and then I…lost it. I remember punching her in the face, I didn't usually do that, not with my fist closed. She tried to hit me back and then I just laid into her, I don't remember exactly what I did. I know I kicked her a couple of times. I just saw red. I could see that nothing I did was going to change her mind about leaving, and I just couldn't bear it."

"Why did you stop hitting her?" Tony asked. "If you just lost control, what stopped you from killing her?"

They'd discussed this as a general concept before, the fact that if you really lost control you wouldn't be able to just stop, and the fact that you did before you killed the person showed that you had control over what you were doing but just chose at some deep level not to exercise it.

"I don't know," Steve said. He cast his mind back. No harm in telling the complete truth here. Maybe it would distract Tony from asking any more questions about Amy.

"I remember just suddenly kind of coming round and seeing her lying on the floor, curled up in a ball. There was a lot of blood on her face and I couldn't bear it, to see her like that, so I went out. I thought that when I came home, she'd have cleaned herself up and it'd be alright."

"Is that what she usually did after you'd been violent to her?"

Steve nodded.

"But usually I just gave her a slap, you know, or pushed her around a bit, that sort of thing. I know it's wrong, even to do that," he added quickly before Tony could jump in, "but this time I'd gone too far. I didn't know that until the police came round. I just thought she'd left anyway. I didn't realise I'd hurt her enough to put her in hospital." Tears sprang to his eyes, and instead of swallowing them back he let them spill down his cheeks. It would give a good impression of remorse. He *was* remorseful. He really hadn't intended to hurt her so badly. He just needed to find her, and make her realise that he'd learned his lesson. He'd never lay a hand on her again.

"How did you feel, after the violence?" Tony said.

Steve sniffed and swallowed.

"Terrible. Guilty. I shouldn't have done that, even if she was going to leave me. It didn't stop her leaving anyway. And frightened, that she wouldn't come back. I love her, and…"

He stopped.

"And…?" Tony prompted.

"I don't know how to live without her. She's always been there for me. I guess I should have listened to her more, then I would have realised how unhappy she was with me being unemployed and everything, but I didn't. At least now I'm learning how to change. If she *does* decide to come back one day, we might be able to make a go of it. We had a lot of happy years together."

After the break they talked about Daniel's experience. He'd only slapped his wife once, and she'd had him arrested for it. True, he had smashed the house up as well, and he'd threatened her with a knife too, but even so, he hadn't *used* it. It was a bit over the top to threaten a woman with a knife, in Steve's opinion. Women were weaker than men; you didn't need to resort to weapons to control them. But then Daniel was pathetic, a skeleton of a man. His wife probably ruled the house.

She certainly would now, anyway; he'd gobbled up every ounce of the shite they'd spent the last months listening to. Still, Steve thought, his mind drifting even though they had been asked to try to focus on what the others were saying, at least the ordeal was over, and Tony had been too thick to realise that there was more to the situation with Amy than met the eye.

* * *

"So, what do you think?" Claire asked while they were putting the classroom back into order after the session. Tony collected the men's homework papers together and put them in his briefcase.

"I think Daniel's doing well," he said. "He's very enthusiastic. The feedback from his wife is very positive as well. He's probably going to be our success story this time. I'm not so happy about Steve, though. I think he's coasting."

"I know," said Claire. "I get that feeling too, that he's looking for the right thing to say to impress us. When you were talking to him about his arrest event, I felt as though he was hiding something."

"Did you?" Tony asked. He hadn't noticed that, but then he'd been fully preoccupied asking the questions. That was one reason why there were two of them running the course. "Like what?"

"I don't know. I can't put my finger on it. Something to do with the daughter, maybe. He never talks about her, and when he did tonight he changed the subject as quickly as possible. What does his wife say?"

"That's one of the problems with this case," Tony said.

"We've only got her initial account from our first contact with her. She disappeared not long after that, so we can't get any more feedback from her. But what she said pretty well ties in with his account of that evening."

"Hmm." Claire finished stacking the plastic chairs in the corner of the room. "It's not just that, though, is it? He never engages fully with any of the sessions."

"No. Maybe he feels a bit of a misfit. After all, all the others have still got their partners living with them. They've got an immediate reason to want to change their behaviour. He hasn't. His marriage is over, from what I gather."

"He doesn't seem to think so, though, does he? Almost every week he mentions what it'll be like when Joanne comes back."

"He's on antidepressants as well, though. And he's still unemployed. I suppose the poor sod's got nothing else to hope for. Maybe when he starts to lift out of the depression and gets a job he'll be able to move on."

Claire smiled. Tony always did look for the best in everyone. Personally she didn't like Steve; she thought he was an arrogant, vain man who didn't think he had a problem with his temper, in spite of what had happened. But she knew she was supposed to keep her personal feelings out of it, and in spite of their easy relationship Tony was her immediate superior, and perhaps it was better not to say any more.

Susan asked Steve if he wanted to come to her for Christmas, but he turned her invitation down. In one way it would have been nice to have someone to talk to, to take his mind off his problems, even if it was only his mother. And she would come up with a good dinner, turkey, stuffing, mulled wine, the works.

But the trouble was, there wouldn't be only his mother there. Dave always dropped in at some point with his anorexic wife, and would be sure to make some snide remarks about his conviction and Joanne leaving. And Mike would definitely be there with his three brats. Mike was on Jo's side, he'd made that very clear. Come to think of it, at every family gathering they always found a reason to wander off together for a chat. He'd probably encouraged Jo to leave as well. He probably fancied her. She was a very attractive woman when she made an effort.

He sat at home on his own instead eating a microwave turkey dinner for one, imagining Joanne in London or Birmingham or Newcastle or wherever the hell she was, sitting at a table with her new boyfriend, eating mince pies and drinking wine by the light of an enormous Christmas tree and a blazing log fire.

Bitch! How could she do this to him? He'd got her away from that bastard of a father of hers, and given her everything, a lovely house, holidays abroad. He loved her, she knew that, and if he'd been a bit hard on her at times, it was only because he wanted a little respect from her. It wasn't much to ask for. And then just because of one mistake, she'd left him.

True, he shouldn't have touched Amy, there was no excuse for that. But she had provoked him, leaving the door unlocked whenever she was taking a bath, and then deliberately letting the towel drop to the floor…no doubt she'd learnt that from her friends.

They grew up so fast these days. At twelve or thirteen they were already wearing makeup, flashing their bodies at you in tiny skirts and cropped tops that left nothing to the imagination. Innocent kids, bollocks, they knew what they were doing, coming on to you like that, smiling seductively and casting meaningful looks at you. And then the minute you touched them, what did they do? Started crying and saying they didn't mean it. Well, they shouldn't offer if they didn't want it. They all wanted it at that age, with their hormones running riot.

Of course he hadn't let Amy wear makeup and provocative clothes, but even so, she'd obviously learnt how to flirt from the other sluts anyway. He knew what women were like. Well, he'd taught Amy what men were like too, if you pushed them. Better *he* show her than she end up raped and murdered in a back alley by some thug that she'd pushed too far. He should have explained that to Joanne when she'd been packing, instead of losing it and beating her up like that. Maybe she wouldn't have left if he had.

Well, really there had been two mistakes, but Jo didn't know about Christine, and there was no reason she ever should. He'd only started seeing her because Joanne had let herself go, and didn't seem very interested in sex any more. Christine had been the opposite of Joanne; blond, plump, and very willing. A slag, really, the way she'd thrown herself at him in the pub, but it had been fun. Until he'd made the mistake of telling her Jo had left; then she started to take things too seriously, and actually suggested that she might move in with him! Christ, she wasn't even fit to kiss Jo's toe, let alone replace her! Still, that was all over now.

There was only one woman for him, there only ever had been. They were meant to be together, he knew that. Jo did too, deep down. If only he could have one more chance, he'd make it work this time.

In the afternoon he drove into Manchester and hung around Kate's apartment block for a time, just in case. There was no sign of Jo, but maybe she was staying in the flat. It was impossible to tell; the lights were on and the curtains closed.

At daybreak on Boxing Day he was back, and after an hour or two of hanging around in the freezing cold he saw Kate drive out of the underground car park in that flashy convertible of hers. Alone.

Steve waited five minutes to be sure she'd gone, then went and rang the doorbell, hoping that Joanne would think Kate had popped back for something she'd forgotten. He rang and knocked for five minutes, but there was no answer and no sound from inside. He stayed outside for a couple of hours listening for signs of life, then gave up and went home.

On New Year's Eve he went to his local pub. The place

seemed to be full of couples, all taunting him with their jollity and closeness. He tried to get into the spirit of things by drinking too much, but instead found himself feeling morose and tired. There was nothing that made you feel lonelier than being with a crowd of strangers who were all having fun.

He left just before midnight, weaving his way home unsteadily, and fumbled with his key in the door for a full five minutes before he gained entrance. The house was dark and cold and empty. Unbearably empty. She should have been here. He sank down on the stairs and put his head in his hands, waiting until the room stopped spinning. Then he picked up the phone.

He had to dial the number three times before he got it right. When she picked the phone up he felt suddenly nervous.

"Hello?" she said.

He could hear music and chatter in the background. She was having a party, by the sound of it. His heart soared.

"Kate?" he slurred. "Is she there?"

"What? I'm sorry, I can't hear properly, hang on a minute."

There was a pause, and he heard a door slam. The noise became muffled.

"Who is it?" Kate asked.

"It's me, Steve," he said slowly, trying to sound sober. "Is Jo there?"

"No, she isn't," Kate replied. Her voice was icy now she knew who she was talking to.

"Please, Kate, I need to talk to her, just for a minute." He sounded pathetic, but he couldn't help it. The need to talk to her was a physical ache. He had to make Kate understand how he felt.

"Give it up, Steve," she was saying. "She's not here. And if she was, she wouldn't want to talk to you."

"You don't know that, you don't know what we had together," he said, his voice rising hysterically. "Tell her I'm on the phone, she'll want to talk to me, I know she will."

"She's not here, I've just told you that," Kate said. "Now..."

"Tell me where she is, then. Just let me talk to her, just once. Then if she doesn't want to come back I won't bother her any more, I promise I won't. Just tell her..."

"Steve." Kate cut through his drunken rambling.

"Yes?" She was going to give him Jo's address. He scrabbled around on the shelf for a pen and paper.

"Piss off."

He listened to the dialling tone in disbelief for a few seconds, his fingers still searching for a pen. Then he tore the phone out of the socket and threw it across the hall. It bounced off the wall and landed on the floor near his feet.

"FUCK!" he shouted. "FUCK, FUCK, FUCK!"

He stood up, his fists clenched, his temper boiling. How dare she put the phone down on him? He'd kill her! He would go round there, right now, and he'd wipe the smug smile off her face, the fucking bitch. Where were the car keys?

He tried to open the kitchen door, fumbling with the faulty doorknob for a moment, then gave up and punched it as hard as he could, splintering the plywood of the door panel and cutting his hand in the process. Then he sank slowly down the wall, pressing his injured hand to his chest. It wasn't fair, it just wasn't fair! He didn't deserve this, he'd tried his best, he'd always tried his best, everyone knew that. It wasn't his fault.

When he woke in the early morning he was stiff and cold, his neck sore from being twisted at an unnatural angle against the wall. His hand was cut and bruised, and the blood had congealed, cracking as he gingerly stretched his fingers out. He made his way blearily up the stairs and lay on the bed still fully clothed, staring at the ceiling until his eyes grew heavy and he slept.

The perpetrators' course finished at the end of January. Steve was given a 'satisfactory' report, which disappointed him a little. He'd done his best to make all the right responses, and he felt that some allowance should have been made for the fact that he couldn't prove he'd learnt to control his temper like the other men had, because his wife wasn't there. Still, at least it was over and with the help of his probation officer, he finally managed to get a job, albeit a crap one stacking shelves at the local supermarket.

Winter turned to spring and then summer, with still no sign of Joanne. In May his probation finished, and in July he finally managed to get a better job, working for a small decorating company who'd gained a contract to repaint an office building.

At last the techniques he'd learned at the perpetrator's course came in handy. When his boss told him that he needed to be a bit more careful masking off the woodwork, he didn't tell him to piss off like he might have done a couple of years ago. Instead he got the roll of masking tape and started again.

At home he'd turned the spare room into a sort of mini-gym, with weights and a punchbag, and when he got in he spent a satisfying five minutes laying into the bag, pretending it was his boss. He doubted Tony and Claire would approve of this tactic; they would say that his wife would still be intimidated if her husband went off and thumped a bag every time he was annoyed.

But his wife wasn't here, and neither was his boss, and knowing he could come home and release his aggression helped him to control his temper at work. He had to keep this job, if he was to persuade Jo to return to him.

There were just so many arseholes in the world, who made a point of winding you up. A man had to get rid of his aggression somehow. It was cheaper than replacing a door every few weeks, anyway.

He'd visited Jo's pathetic little mother a few more times, taking flowers and being his most charming, but it had got him nowhere. He had finally come to the conclusion that she genuinely had no idea where her eldest daughter was.

She liked him, he knew that by the way her eyes lit up when she saw him. She even flirted with him a bit, running her hand down his arm when she was talking to him and telling him how good-looking he was, and he played up to the old crone a bit, hoping she'd let something slip. But she didn't know anything to *let* slip, and eventually he'd given up and stopped visiting.

Steve could think of only two ways of finding Joanne now. The first was to waylay Kate one night and force her to tell him where her sister was. He spent many happy hours at home fantasising about what he would do to her, how she'd end up grovelling at his feet, begging for mercy. But, pleasant as the thought of teaching the cocky bitch a lesson was, it was only a fantasy. He could make her tell him where Joanne was, he knew that, but he was hardly likely to persuade his wife that he'd changed and get her to come back to him if he'd beaten her sister up.

The other way was to employ a private detective to find her. It all seemed a bit Hollywood to him, but to his surprise when he looked in the Yellow Pages there were several listings, which made it all seem more homely.

He thought up a convincing story about wanting to get a divorce and needing to find his wife to serve papers on her, then rang a couple of agencies, just to get an idea of prices. They were not cheap; but it would be worth saving for, he thought. He was getting his life back together; his probation was over, he'd got a steady job, all he needed now was to convince Joanne that he'd changed. That would be easy, once he'd found her. His credit card allowance had all been used up buying model planes, so he couldn't pay for a private eye with that.

He started looking for small decorating jobs on the side; they occupied the time and all the money he earned from those he saved. It would be a few months before he had enough money, but it would be worth it. Any amount of sacrifice would be worth it, if he got Joanne back.

CHAPTER FOURTEEN

September 2006

"I saw your wife the other day," Harry said. "Judith, isn't it?"

Steve froze in the act of putting his channel peg in the pegboard.

"Joanne," he corrected, forcing his voice to remain calm.

"Joanne, that's it. At least I'm pretty sure it was her. She looks really different. Has she dyed her hair?"

Had she?

"Yeah, she fancied a bit of a change," he said vaguely, pretending to be preoccupied with his plane. His body was tingling with sudden exhilaration. "Where did you see her?" he asked nonchalantly.

"She was jogging down the prom. I thought she looked familiar, but I was so surprised to see her there that I didn't recognise her at first."

Jogging? Joanne? What prom? Blackpool? No, surely not. The stupid old fart must have mistaken someone else for her. He'd only met her a couple of times, after all.

"It was only when she turned round and started back that I was sure it was her. She looked gorgeous. Christ, I wish my wife looked like that, you lucky bugger. Anyway, I shouted after her but she didn't turn round. Probably because I called her Judith." Harry laughed, and bent down to put his own peg in the pegboard. "Have you managed to sort out the problem, then?"

Steve wanted to leap up and grab Harry by the throat, make him tell him where Joanne was. Instead he took a deep breath and counted silently to ten.

"Yeah, it was just the engine running lean, that's all. Couple of clicks on the needle valve to richen it out and it seems fine now," he explained. "Having a day at the seaside, were you?"

"No such luck." Harry laughed. "My youngest is starting teacher training in a couple of weeks. I was helping her to move into her digs at the weekend. Poky little room she's got, as well. Don't know how she's going to fit all the stuff she took in there. Still, it's only for nine months. Do her good to rough it a bit."

Steve gritted his teeth in frustration. How could he get Harry to tell him where she was? He hadn't told the blokes at the flying club that Jo had left. They'd think it suspicious if he revealed that he didn't know where his own wife had been last weekend.

"Has your daughter got anyone she knows out there?" he asked.

"What? God, no. It's beyond me why she chose to go to Aberystwyth. Back of beyond it is. I was telling her when we were driving there, through miles and miles of nothing, 'you'll be sorry come winter, my girl,' I says, 'when you're all snowed in and can't get home for Christmas…'"

She probably wanted to get as far away from you and your bullshit as possible, Steve thought uncharitably. He listened with half an ear to Harry's voice droning on about the journey, his mind racing. Aberystwyth? Where the hell was Aberystwyth? Wales, somewhere. And what was Jo doing there? She didn't have any connections with Wales, as far as he knew. They'd been to Rhyl for the day once, when Amy was little. That was it. The senile old bastard had probably mistaken someone else for her. Joanne had never been jogging in her life. She wasn't one for exercise. He became suddenly aware that Harry had stopped talking and was waiting for an answer.

"Sorry, mate, I was miles away. I'm a bit worried about crashing the plane again," Steve improvised. "What did you say?"

"I was asking what she's up to in Wales. Your wife," Harry said.

"She went out to visit some friends, "Steve said. "We met them on holiday, and she's kept in touch. She fancied a few days away before the weather turns. I'd have gone with her, but I couldn't get the time off work. You know how it is, new job and all that."

"Yeah, got to make a good impression, eh?" Harry said. "While we're on the subject of work, when are you going to get round to tiling my bathroom? Next weekend'd be good for me, if you're free."

"Can't make it then," Steve said. "I'm away at the weekend. Should be able to make a start one evening during the week, though."

If it was *Joanne*, he thought, *I'll do your bathroom for free, as a favour. And if it isn't, and I drive all the way to fucking Aberystwyth for nothing, I'll shove the tiles up your arse myself.*

It was worth checking out though, he decided later at home over a beer, the road atlas spread out on the dining table. Harry was right; Aberystwyth *was* at the back of beyond. Never in a million years would he have guessed that she might go there. Another big city, yes, where she could be anonymous, but not a little shithole miles from anywhere. Having said that, she always had loved the sea and the countryside. Hadn't she told him once that when they retired it'd be lovely to buy a little cottage in the country somewhere? That had been years ago, but she probably still felt the same.

It had been over a year now. Fifteen months, to be precise. If it *was* Joanne Harry had seen, she'd think she was safe by now. She'd never expect him to turn up after all this time. She's changed, Harry had said.

Well, so have I, thought Steve. *I've done that course now, and learned how to control my temper. I've got a job. What a surprise she'll get when she sees me.*

Just as well Harry had got her name wrong. If she'd recognised him, she'd have been bound to realise he'd tell her husband he'd seen her. She might even have upped and moved on, without him getting the chance to show her how he'd changed. As it was she'd never suspect a thing, and once she saw him again, she'd remember how good it had been between them.

No doubt she'd been lonely, and was missing him as much as he'd missed her. It'd be easy to persuade her to come back. She probably would have come back already of her own accord if her sister hadn't kept on at her, turning her against him. Kate had never liked him, even though he'd tried his best to win her round.

He got the jar out that he'd been saving money in, and counted out the notes. Four hundred quid. More than enough to pay the petrol to Aberystwyth and back, and a few nights in a B&B, if necessary. If it wasn't Joanne, then he'd charge Harry the same amount for tiling the bathroom that he'd wasted on his wild goose chase, so he wouldn't be out of pocket.

That night he couldn't sleep at all. Even a six pack of beer and a hefty shot of whisky didn't do the trick. He ended up getting up at four in the morning and planning his route in detail. It was Tuesday. Four days until he could go. Forever. Still, he had waited over a year. Another few days wouldn't make any difference.

* * *

On Saturday morning he was up at dawn. He'd booked two nights at the Sea Breeze Hotel, a rambling Victorian building which had no doubt been a salubrious establishment in the heyday of Aberystwyth's popularity, before the tourists had forsaken its bracing sea air in favour of more sultry foreign climes. Now its high-ceilinged rooms smelt of damp and rot, and the wallpaper was faded and peeling. Even so he'd had to fork out sixty quid for two nights, *and* the landlady had tried to charge him extra when he'd insisted on a room overlooking the sea. He'd stated coldly that although he was paying for it, he wasn't having breakfast, and when she had opened her mouth to point out that breakfast was included in the price whether he took it or not, he'd given her a look which had withered her complaint before it was uttered, and she had taken his money without further comment.

He'd told the landlady he didn't want to be disturbed in the morning, and trusting that she'd make sure the chambermaid didn't clean his room, he made a cup of tea and settled himself in front of the window to wait, a packet of biscuits and his binoculars on the rickety wooden table by his side.

God, what a dismal place, he thought as he surveyed the deserted prom in the grey early morning light. *Everything* was grey; the sea, the sky, the empty road and wide pavement of the prom. There wasn't even a proper beach, just shingle, which shifted constantly as the waves washed back and forth over the grey stones. He'd opened the window the previous evening to get rid of the smell of mould, but had had to get up and close it in the night because the bloody shushing noise had been driving him mad.

It was a dull blustery day, and every few minutes a shower of raindrops would patter against the window. Steve wondered if the place would look better in the summer, and tried to picture the view before him bathed in sunshine, the sky and sea blue, and lots of people strolling along the prom eating ice-cream. And failed.

What the hell had possessed Joanne to move here? If it *was* Joanne that Harry had seen, of course. It probably wasn't. He was going to spend the shittiest weekend of his life sitting in the most uncomfortable chair ever made, staring at the most boring view in the world, and see nothing.

Two hours passed and the only person he'd seen was an old lady in a shapeless brown mac hurrying along as quickly as her arthritic legs could carry her. He watched her anyway, just to relieve the boredom. When it started to rain she pulled an umbrella out of her shopping bag and turned into the wind to put it up, only for the wind to immediately change direction and blow it inside out. She struggled with it for a few more minutes, then gave up and hurried on, turning off down a side street. Steve sighed, and made himself another cup of tea. God, he felt like he'd been here a week already, and it was only nine o'clock!

As time wore on more people appeared, a couple with three children who walked along the prom before disappearing down some steps to the beach, a man walking a dog, a group of young girls in jeans, laughing as they strolled along. The rain stopped, and the sky lightened a bit, but it was still cold and gusty, and Steve began to think that even if it had been Joanne that Harry had seen, she might decide against jogging in this weather. Or maybe she didn't have a regular route. Maybe at this very moment she was jogging along the road at the back of the hotel, if there was one. Or was shopping, or working, or any one of a million other things.

I must be nuts, he thought, *to have wasted my money coming here.* He should have had more patience, and waited till he had enough money to employ people who were skilled at locating missing persons, not charged off all gung-ho at the first vague possibility of a sighting. Harry was an unreliable tosser at the best of times.

He was so engrossed in his thoughts that he didn't see the couple running down the prom until they were almost passing the hotel. They were both dressed in shorts and t-shirts, and the man was young, with a very athletic build and short red hair. The woman had dark brown hair cut in a bob, much shorter and darker than Joanne's. Even so she was about the right height and build, and Harry had said he'd hardly recognised her.

Steve picked up his binoculars, but the couple had already passed by the time he'd got them properly focussed, so he couldn't see the woman's face. He opened the window and leaned out, watching as they ran along the curve of the prom and disappeared from sight. They both had the look of habitual joggers; an easy regular stride. If it *was* Joanne, she'd changed, put on weight. Harry hadn't said anything about her running with a man, though. Maybe she'd been alone last week. *Or maybe I'm so pissed off with sitting here like a lemon, that I'm seeing Jo in the first woman who looks vaguely like her,* he thought.

Even so, he put his shoes and socks on, and his leather jacket, and waited. Harry had said she'd come back the same way. If this was a regular run, she'd no doubt do the same this time. He popped a biscuit into his mouth and leaned a bit further out of the window, hoping to see them in plenty of time to get a good look at them before they were close enough to maybe spot him.

Another hour passed before his patience was rewarded and they reappeared, at first mere specks in the distance. He trained his binoculars on them, following them as they got closer. The man's gait was still easy and relaxed, but the woman was flagging a little now, her stride less fluid. When they were about a hundred yards away she stopped for a moment, her hands on her hips, and the man stopped with her. Then they carried on towards Steve, walking now, and he had plenty of time to observe that in spite of the colour and style of her hair and the toned body, this woman was, most definitely, Joanne. Her face was flushed with exertion, but it was her; the same brown eyes, high cheekbones, generous mouth.

He felt like a striker who'd just scored the winning goal in the cup final; he wanted to run round the room shouting with joy. Instead he forced himself to sit still, and turned his attention to the man. About five-ten, he'd say, not so tall, but very well built, and young. Early thirties maybe. Open, friendly face, not handsome but pleasant, light-coloured eyes, and the freckled complexion that went with ginger hair.

Steve put the binoculars down on the table, waited until they'd walked past the hotel, then exploded into action. He grabbed the hideous woolly hat he'd bought just for this occasion, pulled it on his head and shot down the stairs and out the front door of the hotel.

And froze. Instead of being a hundred yards or so in front of him as he'd expected, they'd stopped just two buildings along. Steve turned abruptly and walked off in the opposite direction for a short way, before bending as though to tie his shoelace. He looked through his legs at the couple. The man was swinging a key from one finger. He must live in that building, then. A stroke of luck. Steve turned sideways, still crouched down, trying to keep his face averted while continuing to observe them. He doubted Joanne would recognise him; she wasn't expecting to see him, and he never wore a hat normally. He was proud of his full head of thick, still mainly blond hair.

They hadn't seen him. They were still talking, then Joanne laughed and turned as if to go, but the man said something that made her turn back, her face lifted up to his.

If he kisses her, Steve thought, the adrenaline coursing through his body, *I'll go over and deck him, right now.*

But he didn't kiss her. He just said a couple of words, then she smiled and walked away. Steve straightened up and waited until the man had opened the door and gone in, before he set off in the direction of the castle ruins, following his wife, keeping a good distance between them so there was no chance she would see him before he wanted her to. All his nerves were tingling with the impulse to rush after her and grab her, force her to come back with him if he couldn't talk her into it. It would be easy to do that; in spite of her new fitness, he was still twice her size.

But if he frightened her she would just run again the first chance she got, and the likelihood of him finding her by chance again was virtually nil. The course had taught him not to act on impulse, to take a time out and think things through before acting. It was good advice.

So after watching Joanne enter the terraced house on High Street, he made a note of the number then carried on walking, quickening his pace to burn off the excess energy and render himself calm enough to think rationally. Then he went back to the hotel to think about what to do next.

* * *

Every Saturday night the girls took it in turns to cook the dinner for everyone else in the house, while the rest of them showered and got ready for the night out. It was Joanne's turn this week, and she was stirring an enormous pan of chicken curry when the doorbell rang.

"I'll get it!" one of the others shouted from the hall. Joanne turned the light down under the curry and picked up the packet of rice. A few seconds later Cathy appeared in the kitchen doorway. "It's for you," she said.

"Who is it?" Joanne asked, turning round.

"I don't know, he…" Cathy started, then stopped as Joanne's gaze came to rest on a point above her right shoulder. She looked round and, smiling, stepped forward into the room to let the man past her.

"Hello Jo," he said pleasantly. He had a bouquet of flowers in his hand, which he held out towards her. Joanne's face drained of all colour instantly and the bag of rice fell from her hand and burst, scattering white grains all over the floor.

Cathy had been about to leave the room to give the couple a bit of privacy, but seeing her friend's reaction to the visitor, hesitated in the doorway instead.

"How did you…?" Joanne began, the words drying up in her throat as she tried to fight the panic that was welling up inside her.

"Find you?" Steve finished helpfully. "I've known where you were for a while. I just thought I'd give you a bit of time to think. It's been over a year now, though. I thought it was about time we met up and talked things through."

Her mind raced. Who would have told him where she was? No one knew. No one who would tell him, anyway.

"Don't worry, your precious sister didn't tell me," he said, reading her mind. "She wouldn't tell me the way out of a burning building, would she? I've got contacts, Jo, you know that. My dad was a copper. Surely you knew I'd find you, wherever you went? You must have been expecting me to turn up at some point?"

She had, when she'd first left. For a few months her heart had raced every time she saw a burly blond-haired man. But over time she'd started to relax. She'd felt safe for at least six months. Until now.

She took a deep breath, tried to force her heart to slow down. He was a man, just a man. He couldn't make her do anything she didn't want to do. He no longer had any power over her. She was free.

"There's nothing to talk about, Steve," she said. "You've had a wasted journey."

"You're wrong, Jo," he said gently. "There's a lot to talk about. Things have changed since you left. I've changed."

He put the flowers down on the kitchen table and looked at her, still smiling. He was huge; she had forgotten how big he was. He dominated the room, and she fought the instinctive urge to shrink back against the cooker.

"Good," she said. "Then if you have, you'll go away and leave me alone. I'm happy here. I'm not coming back to you."

"Fair enough," he replied, surprising her. "But we still need to talk, surely you can see that?"

"No." She shook her head. "We don't. It's over. If you want a divorce I'll grant you one. Just send me the papers to sign."

He took a step forward and she flinched backwards automatically.

"Jo…" he began.

"I think you should go now," Cathy interrupted from behind him. He stopped and half turned to face her.

"Do you?" he said contemptuously. "And who are you?"

"I live here," she said evenly, unperturbed by his disdain. "I'm one of Joanne's friends."

"Right. Well, 'one of Joanne's friends', I'd appreciate it if you'd piss off for a few minutes so I can talk in private with my wife," he said, straightening up to his full height.

"You want him to leave, right?" Cathy said to Joanne, ignoring him completely. Joanne looked at her, amazed by her fearlessness. But she didn't know him. She had no idea what he was capable of.

"No, it's all right, Cathy. I'll talk to him," she said.

"What?" Cathy's face was incredulous. "But you said..."

"You heard her," Steve interposed. "Out."

Cathy turned, reluctantly, and went to the door. She obviously didn't want to leave her friend alone with the unwelcome visitor, and Joanne felt touched by her concern.

"I'll be OK, honestly," she said.

"Yeah, whatever," Cathy replied. "If you need me, shout. I'll be just outside."

She went out, and Steve closed the door behind her.

"I don't want a divorce," he said. "Surely you know that?"

Yes, she did. She knew what he wanted. What he would always want.

"I'm not coming back," she repeated. She started to bend down to pick up the bag of rice, then changed her mind, not wanting to put herself in a subordinate position. In a more subordinate position. She could do nothing about their height disparity. But she had to show him that she meant what she said.

"Why didn't you sue me for divorce, Jo?" he asked suddenly.

"What?"

"I thought about that a lot, after you disappeared. I kept waiting for the solicitor's letter to land on the mat. And when it didn't, that was when I knew. I knew that deep down inside you feel the same as me. We can't live without each other."

She looked at him in horror. *Is that what he really thinks?*

"Steve, that's not...." she began, but he held his hand up imperiously. Years of indoctrination triumphed and she shut up instantly.

"I know I did some bad things," he continued. "I'm not going to deny that any more. What I did to Amy was wrong.

And I never should have hit you, not just that last time, but ever. I guess I felt frustrated a lot of the time, because I didn't make a success of the business like I wanted to. And I've been depressed too, probably for much longer than I realised. But I shouldn't have taken it out on you." His eyes were earnest; he really meant it. He always meant it when he apologised, she remembered.

"No, you shouldn't," she said.

He pulled a chair out and sat down at the table, which surprised her. He usually preferred to loom over her when he was lecturing her.

"You were right to have me arrested," he said. His ran his fingers lightly over the cellophane covering the flowers. "I didn't think that at the time, I was really angry with you. But it was the right thing. It woke me up, made me realise what a bastard I've been all these years. But I've never stopped loving you, Jo, you know that, don't you?"

"No, I don't know that," she said, gathering all her courage to contradict him. "It's not love when you have to control everything your wife says, does, thinks. I loved you, at one time, but I don't think you ever loved me, not really. You just wanted someone you could walk all over, to make you feel more important."

Now he would lose his temper, and would hit her, or leave, or both. And she would call the police again. She wouldn't let him get away with it any more.

But he didn't do either of those things. Instead he bit his lip and looked away.

"I know that's how it seems, and I can understand why you feel that way. But it's not true. I *do* love you, I always have. I just never knew how to show it before. Instead of sharing my frustrations with you, I took them out on you. I learnt that on this course I had to do. It was brilliant, Jo," he said, looking up at her, his eyes eager. "There were five of us on it, and these two social workers. And they taught us all about what we're expected to be like as men, you know, tough and all that, and that it was wrong, that it's okay to cry and show weakness sometimes. And we learnt how to recognise the early warning signs that we were getting angry, and to take time outs and stuff like that."

"I'm glad the course went well," Joanne said. She turned the light out under the curry and sat down opposite him. She would pick the rice up later, when he'd gone.

"Yeah. It was hard for me, though. All the other men still had their wives living with them, you see, so they could prove every day that they were changing. But I couldn't, because I didn't even know where you were. I really wanted to talk to you, but Kate wouldn't even give me your mobile number."

"I haven't got a mobile any more," she said. That was one of the first things she had done, throw away her mobile phone. It was part of her bid for complete freedom. No one, ever again, would be able to monitor her movements twenty-four hours a day.

"I wanted to show you how much I've changed. I love you, Jo, and I just want a chance to prove it, to make up for all the bad times. We did have good times together, didn't we?"

"Yes we did," she agreed. "But you can't make up for the bad times, Steve. There were too many of them. I spent years tiptoeing around, trying to anticipate your every want, to make you happy, but I couldn't. I never knew what I was going to do that would set you off. It was hell."

"It won't happen any more. I realise now how much you mean to me. You've no idea how desperate I've felt at times. It was only the hope that one day you'd come back to me that stopped me from killing myself. But I'm taking antidepressants now. They're helping. I've got a job. And I know how to control my temper now." He started to reach his hand across the table but she moved hers out of the way, and he pulled back. "We've been together for twenty years, you can't just throw it all away. I couldn't bear it if you said no, I think I *would* kill myself then. Just give me one more chance, that's all I want. If it doesn't work out you can leave, and I won't ever bother you again."

"It's too late," Joanne said. "I've changed too. I know what it's like to be able to do whatever I want, not to live in constant fear of what mood you'll be in when you come home. I'm happy. I don't want to come back."

"Is there someone else?" he asked. He looked at her intently. "Another man?"

"No," she replied instantly, meeting his gaze. "I don't want another man. I'm happy on my own."

He smiled. She was telling the truth. She never had been able to lie to him when he stared at her like that. He took his eyes from hers and looked around the kitchen, taking in the worn linoleum, the formica-covered table, the ancient cooker.

"You can't be happy here," he said. "It's a dump. And you've got to share it with, how many others?"

"Four," she said. "But they don't tell me how to live, what to think, when to breathe."

"I won't, either. Not any more," he affirmed. "You can do what you want. Go back to college, anything, anything at all."

"Anything? Do you mean that?" she asked.

"Of course I do," he replied.

"Then I'll tell you what I want," she stated. "I want you to go back to Manchester and leave me alone. It's over between us. I don't love you any more. I'm not coming back."

He looked at her in disbelief for a moment, then stood up.

"You don't mean that," he said confidently. "We love each other. You can't turn love off and on when you feel like it. You're just a bit shocked, that's all, because I turned up so unexpectedly. I'll leave you alone now, give you a bit of time to think about it. I'll come back in a few days and we can talk again." He turned and walked out of the room before she could find the words to convince him that she didn't need any time to know what she wanted. She'd always known what she wanted; she'd just never had the courage to take it before. But now she had, and there was no going back.

The door had barely closed behind him before Cathy was back in the kitchen.

"Are you alright?" she said, eyeing Joanne with concern.

"Yes," Joanne answered. "I'm fine." She started to stand, intending to pick the rice up, but Cathy motioned her to stay where she was.

"You don't look it, you're white as a sheet," she observed. "So, that was the husband then?"

"Yes, that was the husband."

"Nasty piece of work, isn't he? I wouldn't like to meet him in a dark alley."

Joanne laughed humourlessly.

"No, you wouldn't. He was being nice just now. He wants me back."

"Tell me you're not going," Cathy said.

"I'm not going." Joanne stood up. "The dinner's going to be a bit late. I'm sorry," she said.

"I'll finish it," Cathy offered.

"No, it's my turn to cook," Joanne protested weakly.

"Stay where you are. You've had a shock." She turned the light back on under the curry, picked the bag of rice up off the floor and tipped the remaining contents into the waiting pan of water. Then she turned and saw Joanne watching her warily. "What?" she asked.

"I just don't want to come home tomorrow and find a pan of curry upended on my bed," Joanne said.

Cathy laughed.

"It can't be that bad, if you can still make jokes." She nodded at the bouquet on the table. "Nice flowers."

"You can have them if you want," said Joanne. "Or throw them in the bin. I don't want them."

Cathy picked them up.

"I bet he wouldn't like it if he knew you'd given them to me, would he?" she said.

"No, probably not."

"Well then, thanks." She went to the cupboard to find a vase. "I thought you said you were divorced?"

"I lied," Joanne admitted. "I wish I had divorced him. I just wanted to forget about him, start again."

"Well, if he comes round again, we'll tell him to get lost. I'll warn all the others not to let him in."

"It won't make any difference," Joanne said. "Now he knows where I am, he won't give up until I go back." She rubbed her hand over her face. "Oh Christ," she said shakily. "What am I going to do?"

Cathy stopped stirring the pan.

"You're going to tell him to piss off, and keep on telling him until he gets the message," she said.

Joanne looked up at her, her eyes glittering with tears.

"It's not as easy as that. You don't know him," she said. "He won't take no for an answer. He'll never leave me alone. He'll keep on and on until I give in. God, he's really making it hard for me not to hate him."

"I'd just go ahead and hate him, if I were you. Sounds like he deserves it. Do you think he'd really kill himself if you didn't go back?" Cathy asked.

Joanne looked up at her, surprised.

"You were listening," she said.

"Yes. Well it's hard not to, in this place. The walls are like paper," Cathy replied unrepentantly. "I thought he might hit you. I wanted to hear if he did."

Joanne smiled. It was nice to have people around who cared about you.

"He's threatened to kill himself more than once, when I've said I wanted to leave," she said. "I don't think he'd really do it, though. At the most he might take a few tablets, just enough to make him groggy, something like that, to try to blackmail me into doing what he wants."

"There you go, then," said Cathy. "Let's look on the bright side. With a bit of luck, if you don't go back to him he might try it and be more successful than he expects! Then you can do whatever you want."

"I wish life was that simple," Joanne said. "I knew someone who killed herself. It's horrible, much worse than if they'd died of cancer or got hit by a car or something, because you always feel as though you're to blame, that you could have done something to stop it."

"Could you? Have done something to stop the person you knew killing herself, I mean?"

Joanne thought for a minute.

"No, I suppose not," she admitted finally.

"Well then, why feel guilty?" Cathy said. "You should never feel guilty, if you've done your best. If your husband really loved you like he says, he'd leave you alone if it made you happy, wouldn't he? He wouldn't try using emotional blackmail to get you back. He's pathetic."

Maybe he was. But he was also ruthless, and used to getting his own way. The only way she could fight him was to be as ruthless as him. And she didn't know how to be like that. She'd spent the whole of her adult life giving him what he wanted, and the urge to give in to him, even now after a year of freedom, was still strong. She had to fight it, to stand up for what she wanted. It would be easier if she could do as Cathy said and actually hate him, instead of just not loving him any more.

It would have been easier if she could have fallen in love with Andy, too. He deserved to be loved. But you couldn't help the way you felt or didn't feel for people. Life just didn't work like that.

On Sunday Joanne waited all day for a knock on the door. Every time she heard an unfamiliar noise she tensed, expecting to see his bulk in the doorway, to hear his voice. By the late evening when it was obvious he wasn't going to call, she was a wreck. She spent the best part of the night awake, telling herself off for being so stupid. She'd been independent of him for more than a year. She'd proved to herself that she was strong, strong enough to live without anyone else. Now she had to prove it to him, and stand her ground.

When the alarm went off at seven o'clock she'd only been asleep for two hours. She resisted the urge to turn over and go back to sleep, and got up. She had to work. Life had to go on. She got up, dressed, and forced herself to eat a good breakfast.

Then she went out, looking up and down the street to see if there was anyone lurking around. No one. But there were cars parked the whole length of the street. He could be sitting in any one of them, waiting for her to turn the corner before following her. She'd never paid any attention to them before, had no idea which cars belonged to residents, and she could hardly check inside every one.

She was being ridiculous. If she let him get to her like this, then he'd already won. She straightened her shoulders and walked off down the street without a backward glance, trying to look as relaxed as possible.

* * *

Andy was keeping one eye on the two women pedalling away on the stationary bikes, while leafing through a back issue of Ultrafit magazine, when the gym door swung open and Dewi's head popped through.

"Have you got time to fit a quick induction in before you go?" he asked.

Andy looked at his watch. Wednesday. They were due to close in half an hour.

"This chap's very eager," Dewi added. "Says he's already used to weight machines, so shouldn't take up much of your time."

Andy closed the magazine.

"Yeah, go on then," he said. It would pass the time. Dewi gave him the thumbs up and disappeared. A minute later the inductee came in. Andy introduced himself and shook the man's hand, giving him the once-over in the process. Mid-fifties, roughly. Brand new tracksuit and trainers, which meant he'd probably not been to the gym for a while. Very firm handshake. Six-two, six-three perhaps, very well-built, big arms and shoulders, but running to fat round the gut. Probably did a lot of weight work but little or no cardio-vascular stuff. He smiled.

"Dewi tells me you're already familiar with weights," he said.

"Yeah, that's right. I go to a gym at home," the man said. He glanced round the room. "I recognise most of the stuff here. It's probably a waste of time, you explaining everything to me."

"There might be the odd machine you're not familiar with," Andy pointed out. "Everyone has to go through an induction anyway, for insurance purposes."

"Right. I assume that's so if some stupid cunt brains himself with the weights, he can't sue you." The man laughed.

Andy stiffened and glanced across at the women. He was old-fashioned in that respect, didn't like men using bad language in front of women. But they didn't appear to have heard; they were chatting about last night's *Big Brother* and getting ready to leave.

"Something like that," he said.

They worked their way round the gym, starting with the running, rowing and cycling machines.

"I don't normally bother with this sort of stuff," the man admitted as he walked briskly on the treadmill. "Seems a bit pointless, running or cycling for miles and never getting a change of view. I prefer the weights myself."

"Yes, I see your point, but it's great if you want to lose weight. The heart's a muscle too, don't forget, and cardio stuff like this is the best way to give it a workout."

They moved on to the bench press. Andy pushed the key in the weight stack, and the man lay down on the bench.

"You probably know how to use this," Andy said. "Do a few reps though, and I'll tell you if your technique's OK."

The man lifted the weight easily, then lowered it again and sitting up, moved the key down the weight stack. Then he lay down again, and taking hold of the bar, lifted it, keeping his gaze locked on Andy's face the whole time. Twenty reps at a hundred and fifty pounds was pretty impressive, although it was obvious to Andy that the man was trying to impress him with his strength. He hated showoffs, and that, coupled with the expletive the man had uttered earlier, stopped Andy from complimenting him as he normally would have done. Instead he smiled politely and turned to the next machine.

"Have you recently moved to the area?" he asked, hoping the man was only passing through.

"No, I'm here on family business," the man said, smiling. "Things weren't going too well for me and my wife, so we had a trial separation. But we've decided to get back together now. I might be here for a week or two though, while she ties up loose ends, and I didn't want to leave off the training. You know how hard it is to get back into the routine."

"Yes. Well, congratulations," Andy said. They moved on to the last machine.

"Thanks. You might know my wife actually," the man said. "She does a lot of exercise, running and that. Small, pretty. Her name's Joanne."

Andy froze in the act of adjusting the leg press machine and looked up at the man. He was still smiling, but Andy now noticed that the blue eyes intent on his were cold, hostile. He straightened up, the weight key still in his hand.

"You're Steve," he said.

"That's right." The man nodded. "I see Jo's told you about me. I just wanted to meet the man who's been screwing my wife for the past year."

"I haven't been screwing your wife, or anybody else's for that matter," Andy said tightly.

Steve nodded.

"You'd like to though, wouldn't you?" he said quietly.

Andy felt the blood flood his cheeks, and cursed his fair complexion. Steve smiled.

"No, well, now we've met I can see I've nothing to worry

about. You're not her type at all. Still, now we're getting back together, probably better if you don't meet her any more, not even to go running, right?"

"I think it's for Joanne to decide that, not you," Andy said.

Steve ran his hand across the padded back of the leg press.

"No, you're wrong. It's for you to decide," he said. "Either you leave her alone, or I'll break your fucking legs."

Andy fought the urge to smack him straight in the teeth. The other man had the advantage in height and weight, but Andy had fifteen years on him. They were pretty evenly matched, overall. But there was a reason Steve had chosen to confront him here, the devious bastard. If Andy planted one on him now, as he so wanted to do, he'd lose his job. At the very least. And it would just make him as bad as Steve if he resorted to violence at the first provocation. It was what the other man wanted. He turned away, rammed the key in the machine and forced himself to remain calm.

"The leg press is very good for the quads," he said. "But you have to be careful if you have knee problems, arthritis, rheumatism, anything like that."

Steve laughed.

"It's nice of you to be concerned," he said. "But I haven't got arthritis or rheumatism. Or anything. It's OK, I won't take up any more of your time. I know how to use the leg press."

At the door, he turned back. Andy was still standing by the machine, his fist curling and uncurling by his side.

"See you around, maybe," Steve said, then pushed his way through the swing door and was gone.

* * *

After three days of looking over her shoulder Joanne had finally started to relax. Steve had told her he had a job now. Surely that meant he'd have to go back home to work during the week? At the worst, that would mean that he'd only be able to annoy her at weekends. If she could relax in the week, she could cope with that. It was a long way from Manchester to Aberystwyth. Surely he wouldn't persist in driving backwards and forwards every weekend once he realised how determined she was not to go back to him?

Even so, when the doorbell rang on Wednesday evening, she jumped. The other girls had all agreed that they'd open the door if anyone called, and if it was Steve, would tell him she was out. She opened her bedroom door and listened.

"It's Andy, Jo," Siobhan called up the stairs.

Joanne let out the breath she'd been holding, and closed her eyes for a moment.

"Tell him to come up," she said. He'd never been in her bedroom before, but she needed to talk to him in private. She'd been putting it off, but he needed to know.

"Hi," she said as he appeared at the top of the stairs.

"Why didn't you tell me that your husband was here?" he said without preamble.

"How do you know that?" she asked.

"He came down the gym pretending he wanted to join," Andy said. "He showed off his muscles on the weights. Then he told me you were getting back together and threatened to break my legs if I saw you again."

Her eyes widened.

"Does he know you've come here?" she asked.

"I don't know, and I don't care," he said. "Is it true?"

Instead of answering, she dashed into the bedroom and pushed the window open, looking up and down the street.

"When did you see him?" she asked. Andy had followed her into the bedroom.

"Just now. I came here as soon as my shift finished."

"God, I hope he didn't follow you," she said, shutting the window. "I can't see anyone hanging around, but it doesn't mean…"

"Joanne!" Andy said urgently. "Is it true? Are you going back to him?"

She looked at him and blinked. He was really upset. She

was so happy with things the way they were, she often forgot how much he wanted to be more than just a friend to her.

"No," she said. "No, I'm not. Is that what he told you?"

Andy sat down on the edge of the bed.

"Yes," he said. "He made out that it was you who'd decided you wanted to get back together. He said he might be up here for a few weeks until you got things sorted out, and then you were going back to Manchester."

"No," she said. "I never said that. He came to see me on Saturday. I told him I didn't love him any more. I haven't seen him since. I thought he'd gone home."

"How did he find out where you were?" Andy asked.

"I don't know. I don't know how he knows about you, either," Joanne said. "I didn't tell him." God, how long had he been watching her without her knowing? All these months she'd thought she was safe, and he'd been there, in the shadows, watching her every move. She shivered suddenly.

"Are you cold?" Andy said. "You can have my jacket."

"No, I'm not cold. I'm…" She hesitated. "Perhaps it'd be better if we don't train together, just for a while," she said.

"Is that what you want?" he asked.

"No, of course it isn't," she said. "But I don't want you involved in this."

"I am involved," he replied. "I'm your friend. And anyway, if I stop seeing you now he'll think I'm frightened of him, and what's worse it'll encourage him to think you will go back to him, if you start letting him dictate to you again."

"You're not like him," she said frantically. "You're gentle, and kind. He's not. If he said he'll break your legs if you keep seeing me, he probably will. I don't want you to get hurt."

Andy stood up and took her gently by the shoulders.

"Joanne, I'm not frightened of him," he said. "Just because I don't go round threatening people and beating women up doesn't mean I can't handle myself. Do you think he might hit you if you carry on seeing me?"

The fact that she had to consider it for a minute made him want to go and kill the bastard now. How could someone his size think that terrifying a tiny woman like her made him a man?

"No, he won't hit me," she said after a long enough pause for Andy to have murdered Steve in his imagination in a variety of ways, each more gory than the last. "No, he's trying to prove he's changed, that he's learnt how to control his temper now. In fact, he must have done to some extent if he only threatened you. He's punched men in the past just for looking at me in the wrong way. He never was one for making threats. He always said the first punch was worth ten."

"If you ask me, all he's learned is to be more devious," Andy said. "You've got to stand up to him, Joanne. If you give in to him on this and stop seeing me, he'll think he's won."

He was right. She couldn't dispute that. But this was her fight, no one else's. And Steve was murderously jealous, she knew that. She couldn't count the bruises he'd given her for flirting with men she'd done no more than glance at on her way to the pub toilet. Or the times he'd waited outside the pub to beat up an imaginary lover. She'd been seeing Andy for months. If Steve had been watching, he'd have seen them going out for meals, to the cinema and the theatre together. That was a lot worse than just smiling at a man in a pub. She wouldn't put it past him waiting for Andy one night with an iron bar or something. No one could defend themselves against that.

She just couldn't take the risk. She had enough to worry about, she couldn't be constantly worrying about Andy too. She had to cut herself off from anyone Steve could use to manipulate her.

"I'm sorry," she said, moving out of his grasp. "I see your point, I really do. But I think it's better if we stop seeing each other, just for a while."

"You can't mean that," Andy said. "You're just upset. You can't let him decide who you see and..."

"It's not Steve's decision, it's mine," she said firmly. "I want us to stop seeing each other. I need to sort out what I want to do, and I need to do that on my own. I can't afford to let anyone influence me, not you or anyone else. I'm sorry."

He looked at her, pain in every line of his face.

"You're wrong," he said. "I'm your friend. I wouldn't try to influence you to do anything."

"Good," she said. "Then you'll respect my decision and leave me alone, just for a while. I think you should go now."

He stood up.

"Will I at least see you at the gym?" he asked. He was trying to sound casual, as though he wasn't devastated, but his voice trembled and she wanted to reach across and hug him.

"I don't know," she said instead. "We'll see."

She half-expected Andy to phone her after a few days, or at least turn up for the regular run to Borth. But he didn't, and she jogged the whole way alone, feeling strangely bereft and wondering whether Steve was watching her or not. Well, if he was at least he'd know he didn't need to worry about Andy any more, and hopefully would leave him alone.

Of course Andy had been right; he'd also think he'd won, but she couldn't help it if he misinterpreted her actions. She wasn't going back to him. He couldn't stay in Aberystwyth indefinitely. He'd lose his job if he did. He must have taken some leave or rung in sick, or something. He'd have to go home at some point. She could wait. What else could he do? He couldn't talk her round; she didn't love him any more. She was past that. She'd changed too; he hadn't allowed for that. He meant nothing to her. He was just a nuisance, and she would have to put up with him shadowing her and pestering her with unwanted presents until he gave up.

The thought lifted her spirits a little, and she sped up as

she entered Borth. If he was watching he'd see how fit, how confident, how independent she was now.

She paused at the gate to slow her breathing, then walked up the path and rang the bell. It always took Mrs Jones a minute to open the door; her rheumatism was worse in the cooler weather. Joanne glanced up and down the road, then cursed herself. She'd made a resolution not to do that; it made her look edgy and nervous.

"Hello," she said brightly as the door opened. "It's only me. I've come for my wages."

Mrs Jones looked at her coolly.

"Come in a moment, would you?" she said.

Joanne stepped into the hall, a little puzzled.

"Your wages are in the envelope on the table," the old lady said. "If you count them, you'll see I've included an extra week. Which is more than you deserve, I might say."

Joanne picked up the envelope. What was she talking about?

"I haven't asked for any holidays," she said.

"No, I know," Mrs Jones stated briskly. "Call it severance pay."

"What?" Joanne asked, stunned.

"I require my employees to be honest, *Mrs Harris,*" she said.

Joanne closed her eyes, opened them again.

"Steve's been to see you," she said.

"Your husband. Yes. A most pleasant man. He told me that you are not in fact divorced, as you told me you were. Is that true?"

"Yes," Joanne said. "But…"

"So you lied to me. What else have you lied about?"

"Nothing," Joanne said, trying not to feel like a naughty schoolgirl being reprimanded by the head. "Nothing else. We are separated."

"Yes, your husband told me that. He told me that he had been less than fair with you over the years, and blamed himself entirely for you leaving him. A very honest admission, I felt. However he now says that he has had time to think and wishes to try again."

"Yes, he would say that," Joanne said. "But.."

"If you recall, your marriage vows stated that you took each other for better or worse. In my day that actually meant something. Young people nowadays are so impatient, they walk out over the slightest thing."

"Mrs Jones," Joanne stated firmly. "I did not walk out over the slightest thing. I stayed with my husband for twenty years. I finally left him when he beat me up and nearly killed me."

"Yes, your husband said that he'd lost his temper and slapped you across the face once. He seems very penitent."

"My husband is a liar, Mrs Jones," Joanne said. "He didn't slap me once, he beat me up on a regular basis. He…"

"So you say. But I have only your word for that. And as you have just confessed, you are a liar. Why should I believe you?"

Andy was right, Joanne thought despairingly. *He* has *learned to be more devious.*

"I was married for forty years," Mrs Jones continued. "And it was not always plain sailing, I can tell you. Far from it. But we stayed together. A woman's place is with her husband. Mr Harris really wants you to go back to him. He was very upset. I think you owe it to him to give him another chance. I suggest you do that. But whatever you choose to do, I cannot continue to employ someone I do not trust. I am not unreasonable, however. I will give you until the end of the month to move out of your room in High Street. And now, if you will excuse me, I am expecting visitors shortly."

* * *

She sat curled up in her favourite little hollow at the top of the hill, the place she had made her own, the place where she came when she needed to think. Steve didn't know she was here; no one did, she was certain of that. She had waited until all her housemates were in bed. Then she had waited a little longer until she was as certain as she could be that she would encounter nobody. Then she had put on her warmest clothes and gone out, dropping down to the beach by the castle and walking along the shingle, so that anyone observing from the buildings along the prom would not see her. Once at the hill she made her way carefully up the path. Her eyes had acclimatised to the dark and the path was so familiar that she didn't need the torch she'd brought. She looked out across the inky blackness of the sea, and let her mind drift back over the afternoon's events.

After leaving Mrs Jones's she had walked across the road to the beach, tears of rage and misery rolling down her face, heedless of who saw her. What Steve had done to Amy had killed all the love Joanne had ever felt for him. Amy hated him; it was how she'd found the courage to make a new life for herself. Now, for the first time since she had been in court, Joanne could feel the hate too, writhing deep inside her like a demon, and this time she made no attempt to subdue it.

She had stood for a long time, ostensibly looking out to sea, relishing the emotion and feeling it grow until it had infused her whole being with a new energy and determination. Then she had started to walk back to Aberystwyth.

She had got nearly halfway back before the car pulled up just ahead of her, the window on the passenger side winding down as she approached. He would expect her to run away, she thought, or at best ignore him and continue walking. She stopped and bent down to the window. He smiled at her.

"Get in," he said pleasantly. "I'll give you a lift back."

"I'm not coming back to you, Steve," she said. She saw his mouth tighten momentarily as he realised he had not subdued her by taking her job and her home away from her. Quite the opposite, in fact. "Give it up, it's over."

She straightened up and started walking down the road, briskly, but not hurrying. She didn't want him to think she was frightened of him. She wasn't frightened of him. At that moment she thought she would never be frightened of him again.

"What are you going to do?" he called mockingly after her. "Run away again? I can find you, wherever you go, you know that. I've got contacts." She ignored him and carried on. She could hear the car engine ticking over as it kept up with her. He could follow her all the way back to Aberystwyth if he wanted. She had nothing to say to him, and he had nothing to say to her that she wanted to hear. "Or maybe I'll just ask that bitch of a sister of yours instead," he added, "only a bit more forcefully next time, if you know what I mean."

Joanne stopped so abruptly that he actually drove past her before pulling up sharply. He leaned across and pushed the passenger door open, obviously expecting her to get in the car. Instead she bent down again so her face was at a level with his.

"You listen to me," she said fiercely. "You ruined my life for twenty years, and you tried to ruin Amy's too. And God knows how many other little girls you've damaged, you sick bastard. I can't do anything about that, it's all in the past. But you touch Kate, and I swear to God you'll be sorry."

She stepped back and slammed the passenger door so violently that the whole car shook. Then she strode off down the road, her body fizzing with rage. At that moment she had wanted to hurt him so much she could almost taste it.

Now, sitting on the top of the hill reliving the event, she felt the rage rise in her again. How dare he come here and in one week take away everything she had spent the last year building so carefully; her home, her job, her friends?

No, she thought, he hadn't taken everything; there was one thing he couldn't take away from her. She knew now what he had done to Amy, and had tried to do to Kate.

And after seeing the look of shock and guilt on his face this afternoon when she had confronted him, she was certain that he had also assaulted others, probably that friend of Amy's, what had her name been? Emma? Gemma? Yes, Gemma, that was it. And others; no doubt there had been others. She knew Steve, better than she knew herself, even. She had had to, to be able to anticipate his moods for twenty years. He had got away with what he'd done to Amy, and to Gemma. He wouldn't stop until he was caught, and even then he'd blame others rather than himself. How many other children would he molest before one of them got the courage to report him? And even if someone did, what would the law do then? He had nearly killed her, and by way of punishment they'd sent him on a course, at which he'd clearly learnt nothing apart from how to be more devious.

She'd read about them in the papers, of course. Paedophiles who'd molested hundreds of children before being caught. And after all that, after lengthy court cases in which the children went through hell testifying, they got stupid sentences. Six years, she remembered reading about recently. Out in four, with good behaviour. It was ridiculous.

She sipped coffee from her thermos flask, and considered her options. She could run away again, try to start over once more, knowing at some point he would find her again. She had no doubt that he was capable of carrying out his threat to hurt her sister. He hated Kate, he would enjoy beating her up. It was a miracle that he hadn't already done it. He might even kill her, and if he did, it would be hers, Joanne's fault, because she knew how dangerous he was, even if Kate didn't.

And even if he didn't find her, even if all her prayers were answered and he gave up on her, let her get on with her life, then what? Steve was not a man to live alone for any length of time. He would take up with another woman, probably one with young daughters. He would insinuate himself into their hearts with his looks, his overblown romantic gestures, and then…

Joanne shuddered. No. She could not let that happen. She had been wrong to run away from him. She had thought she was strong, leaving him like that, making a new life for herself. But all the time she had been ignoring the truth, had been as big a coward as she'd been when she let him take over her life.

But at least this year away from him had given her the courage to see things clearly, to realise that, really, since Amy had revealed to her what Steve was, she had only ever had one option where he was concerned; by running she had merely postponed it for a while. But now the moment was here and she had to take action, because if she didn't no one else would. And in realising that, she felt suddenly calm, strong, imbued with purpose.

It was only fitting that she should be the one to do this. She had, after all, helped to make him what he was, by giving in to him all the time, by encouraging him to believe that whatever he wanted he could take, regardless of the damage it would do. It was only right that she do what the law would not do, and no one else could. Her life was ruined, irrevocably; the only thing she could do now was make sure no one else's would be.

She had to kill him. Only that way would she be certain that he would never get the chance to ruin anyone else's life. It was that simple.

The decision made, she felt a great weight lift from her mind, leaving her oddly detached and at peace. There was a lot to think about and to do, but her life now had a purpose, an importance that it had never had before.

She had wanted to be of use to society by being a psychologist, to help victims. But her father and her husband had taken that away from her. Now she could fulfil her destiny, a little late and not quite in the way she had anticipated, but even so...she sipped her coffee and sat, and thought. She thought until the sky turned from navy blue to pearly grey, until the streetlamps below on the prom were extinguished and she could hear the sounds of distant cars mingling with the soothing ebb and flow of the sea.

Then she stood up, stretched her cramped, cold limbs,

packed away her empty flask, and made her way slowly down the hill and back to her room, where she curled up in bed and, for the first time since Steve had come back into her life a week before, fell asleep immediately.

CHAPTER FIFTEEN

It was ten days before Joanne could summon up the courage to phone her sister and tell her that she intended to return to Steve. She had already told her housemates, dropping it casually into the conversation over dinner on the Monday evening. She thought she had got away with it at first; the girls were so engrossed in their current assignments on child psychology that, whilst expressing surprise and regret that she was intending to leave them and arranging a farewell drink down the pub on the night before she left, they hadn't asked any intrusive questions.

It was later, when she'd retired to her room with the intention of reading a novel, that there had been a knock on the door. The novel had remained unread; instead Joanne had spent an hour trying to make Cathy understand why she had made the decision she had, which was difficult when she couldn't tell the truth.

It had been even harder to tell Andy. His eyes had lit up when he'd seen her waiting for him outside the gym after work, and she'd accepted his suggestion of a drink, knowing that he was too civilised to make an awkward scene in public when she told him of her intentions.

She had been right; he had expressed his anger in a subdued manner, but the hurt and disappointment she had seen in his eyes as she'd left him would stay with her for a long time. She had not meant to betray their friendship. It had meant a lot to her, and still did, but her decision had damaged it beyond repair. There was nothing she could do to make him understand her logic. She had known there would be casualties and that Andy would be one of them; all she could do was try to keep the damage to a minimum.

She waited until all the girls were out frantically typing up their assignments on the computers in the dry and stuffy basement of the university library, before she put three pounds in the little box at the side of the phone and dialled her sister's number. It rang for a long time, and Joanne was on the point of replacing the receiver when Kate picked up, her greeting breathless as though she'd been running.

"Is it a bad time?" Joanne asked, half-hoping her sister would say yes and give her an excuse to postpone her unpleasant task.

"No, it's fine," Kate replied. "I was just coming in when I heard the phone. It took me ages to find my key, with all the bags I had. There's a sale on at Kendals, and I went a bit mad with the credit card. But I bought nearly all my Christmas presents!"

"Christmas! But it's only September!" Joanne said.

"It'll be here before you know it," Kate said breezily. "But I assume you haven't rung me up to talk about Christmas presents. You'll love yours, by the way. How are you?"

Joanne took a deep breath and told Kate part of what she intended to do. When she'd finished, the silence on the other end of the phone went on for so long that Joanne started to wonder if they'd been cut off.

"Kate?" she asked tentatively.

"Why?" her sister asked abruptly.

"I don't have any other choice," Joanne said. "I can't stay here. I've got no income any more, and at the end of the month I'll have nowhere to live either. I thought about disappearing again, finding another job and somewhere else to live, but if I do that he'll find me again. I'll always be expecting him to appear round every corner, and I'll never be able to relax. I can't live like that."

"Why are you so sure he'll find you, if you go somewhere else?"

"Because he did this time, even though I haven't told anybody except you and Amy where I am. He's got connections, he told me that. He'll find me wherever I go, I'm sure of it." Joanne could feel her heart thumping hard against her ribs, even though she hadn't told any lies yet.

"OK then, don't run. Come back to Manchester. You can move back in with me and face up to him. Get another injunction. I'll help you in any way I can."

"I can't keep burdening you, Kate. You've got your own life and I've got no right to keep disrupting it."

"You're my sister, for Christ's sake!" Kate countered. "It's no burden to help people you love. You'd do the same for me, wouldn't you?"

"Of course I would," Joanne replied. "But it's not just that."

"What is it then?"

Joanne paused to get her courage. It had to sound right. Her sister knew her better than anyone.

"I need to sort my marriage out on my own, Kate. I don't want to hide behind you or anyone else any more."

"And you think going back to him is 'sorting your marriage out'?" Kate's voice was incredulous. "It sounds like giving in to him to me, and that's what it'll sound like to him, too."

"I don't know," Joanne said. "He came round last night and we had a long talk. He really seems to be trying this time. He's got a job now, and he's taking antidepressants."

"Antidepressants?" Kate snorted. "If he's depressed, I'm a Dutchman. He's just sorry for himself because you buggered off, that's all. He isn't deep enough to get depressed."

"I'm not so sure, Kate. Me leaving and having to go to court and everything really shook him. He's threatened to kill himself if I don't go back to him."

"Well, it'd certainly solve your problems if he topped himself, wouldn't it?" her sister observed coldly. "But he won't, of course. He's just using emotional blackmail to try to get you back, that's all. Don't fall for it."

"He talked a lot about this course he had to do, as well. It seems to have helped him to manage his temper. He said he's learned how to recognise the early signs now, and can walk away before he loses control."

"Jo, you're an intelligent woman. You don't believe all this bullshit, surely to God? He's been promising to change for twenty years, and he never has. What makes things different now?"

"I've changed. I'm not dependent on him any more."

"You will be if you go back to him."

"No I won't," Joanne insisted. "I've started a computer course at college, and I've told him I'm going to carry on with it in Manchester. I've told him that I'm going to get another part-time job, and I'm not getting another mobile phone. I won't let him walk all over me this time."

"I don't believe you," Kate said flatly.

Joanne's heart plummeted. She had to make Kate believe her. Her mind raced, trying to think of what else she could say to convince her sister that she really thought her marriage was worth another chance. But before she could speak, Kate continued.

"I think you mean it now, I really do. But you know what'll happen once he gets you back. Everything'll be wonderful for a while, and then it'll start all over again. You've made the break, and you've done really well. You've made a new life for yourself. You know you can do it now. Don't go back to him. He's like a drug to you, he just takes you over and destroys you. I've seen it happen. You've broken the addiction, don't let him get to you again, Jo, for God's sake."

Kate's voice, normally cool and controlled, broke on the last word and Joanne felt the tears rush to her eyes. She had no wish to hurt her sister. But she had to do this. It was the only way.

"I'm sorry, Kate. I have to give him one more chance," she said, blatantly lying now, for the first time. "But this is absolutely the last one, I promise. If he doesn't change this time, then that's it. I will leave him then, for good."

"You're fooling yourself," Kate said desperately. "I can't believe you're doing this. What will Amy think?"

What would Amy think? She would find out soon enough. Amy was the next, and the last on her list to call, and she was dreading it.

I have to think of myself and of others he could hurt, Joanne thought. *Amy has her own life, with Zac. I'm the only one who can do this. I have to do it, I have to. I can't keep running away.* Her hands were trembling, and she could feel the blood on her lips from where she had chewed at them in her nervousness. She was so glad she had decided to do this over the phone. By the time she met her sister in person, she would be under control. This was the best way. But even over the phone she couldn't answer Kate's question about her daughter. It was too painful.

"Do you hate me?" she asked instead, her voice small and shaky.

"No, I don't hate you, Jo," Kate's voice was weary now, resigned. "I'm disappointed in you, but I don't hate you. I want you to promise me something, though, and if you don't keep your promise, I swear I'll never speak to you again."

"What is it?" Joanne asked.

"The next time he hits you, day or night, you walk out on him and you come to me. And you don't go back, ever again."

Joanne could have wept with relief. She had done it.

"If he hits me again, that's it. I promise," she said.

After she had put the phone down, she stared blankly at the chipped paint on the skirting board, and tried to summon the courage to phone her daughter. The first hurdle was over. She had told Kate. She could do this, she knew she could.

She picked up the phone, put it down again and ran for the bathroom, and just made it before being violently sick. Afterwards she put the toilet seat down and sat for a while, leaning back against the cistern while the waves of nausea washed over her. *I have to face her*, she thought desperately. If she couldn't even summon up the courage to phone her daughter, how would she manage to lie to Steve, and kill him?

It was different, though. She hated Steve. She had thought the hatred she had felt for him at the top of the hill would wane, but it hadn't. It was still burning in her, a steady flame, keeping her firm in her resolution. But she loved Amy, and cared desperately for what her daughter thought of her. There was no other way. She could hardly tell her the truth. This was her burden, and hers alone.

She rinsed her mouth out with water and went back to the phone.

"No, I don't understand," Amy said. "You've been away from him for over a year."

"You know what he's like," Joanne replied. "Now he knows where I am, he won't leave me alone."

"Come here then," Amy said suddenly, throwing Joanne completely.

"I can't," she stammered. "I…I'd be in the way. What would Zac say?"

"He wouldn't mind at all," Amy said confidently. "He likes you. And I've lived in London for over three years now, without Dad finding me. You'd be safe here. Just until you find somewhere of your own."

Joanne closed her eyes. Amy was only safe in London because Steve hadn't wanted to find her. He had no desire to ever see his daughter again. That would all change if Joanne went there. She couldn't anyway. She had a plan, and had to stick with it.

"You have your own life now with Zac," Joanne said. "And I have to go back to Steve. It's difficult to explain….it's complicated."

"That's all right, I've got all evening," Amy said. "Go for it."

"I can't," Joanne replied.

"You don't believe me, do you? He's managed to convince you that he didn't do anything to me, or that I came on to him or something, hasn't he?"

"No!" Joanne almost shouted into the phone. "No, you mustn't think that, not for a minute!"

"Do you still love him, then?" Amy asked.

"No."

"Then why? If you don't love him, and you believe that he…did what he did to me, how can you go back to him? How can you even look at him!" Amy's voice rose shrilly, and Joanne's eyes filled with tears.

"I just have to do this," Joanne said shakily. "I can't tell you why. But one day you'll understand." In a couple of days, in fact.

"No," Amy said. She gulped audibly and sniffed, clearly fighting for control. "No. I don't understand. I'll never understand how you can go back to him now you know what he is. I don't want to understand." She choked, and stopped talking abruptly.

"Amy, I…" Joanne began, but the line had gone dead.

She had expected it to be hard. Amy thought her mother had betrayed her. Of course she did, how could she think any other way? Unless Joanne told her the truth: *"Why am I going back to your violent, perverted father? I'm going back to him to kill him, so he can never do this to anyone else, ever again."*

No. She couldn't expect Amy to shoulder that burden. She'd suffered enough, and it was as much due to her mother's weakness as it was to her father's perversion. It would be bad enough when it was over, and Amy found out the real reason why Joanne had gone back to Steve.

For the first time since she had made her decision, Joanne realised that finding out her mother was a murderer, and why she had murdered Steve, could be more damaging to Amy than her father's assault on her had been. It might, no, it *would* make things worse, much worse, rather than better.

Joanne dropped her head into her hands. She had to do

this. She couldn't let him go on assaulting little girls. Even going back to him and living in misery and fear for the rest of her life wouldn't guarantee that he wouldn't do that again. After all, he'd done it at least twice, right under her nose, and she'd never guessed a thing.

It was a no-win situation. Or was it? Something that Kate had said during their earlier conversation came back to her. Could she do it differently? She had planned to go back to Manchester with Steve, kill him that night while he was asleep and vulnerable, and then phone the police immediately and tell them what she'd done. She hadn't thought she could sustain her pretence with Steve for longer than a few hours. Now she realised that she hadn't thought beyond the act itself, but she had to. She had to consider the others who would be affected by what she did. Having a murderer for a mother could destroy Amy, who would probably blame herself, to some extent at least, for Joanne's actions. And it would reverberate down the generations. Amy's children would have to live with the stigma of having a murderer for a grandmother.

Joanne stood up and went to her bedroom, where she put on her running shoes. She would go back up to her special spot on the hill. She could think clearly there, without any risk of being disturbed. She could not just go at this all gung-ho. If she was going to do what she had to do without ruining her daughter's life completely, she had to plan it far more carefully. It would be a lot more difficult; she would have to live a lie for much longer than she'd planned. But she could do it, she knew she could. She had to, for Amy's sake. She just had to plan it properly, down to every last detail, then stay focussed on her objective and let nothing dissuade her, that was all.

* * *

Steve was ecstatic on the way home. Joanne had never seen him so upbeat. He had a burgundy Land Rover now, the back stuffed with Joanne's possessions. She didn't ask why he wanted a gas-guzzling four-wheel-drive vehicle, when the nearest they ever got to the countryside was their twice-yearly visits to his mother in Hale. No doubt it was the latest fashion accessory and therefore essential.

He talked about his latest job, how well he was doing. His boss was pleased with him, Steve said, and had hinted at a promotion to foreman if he continued to work so well.

"Didn't it cause any problems, you spending three weeks in Aberystwyth?" Joanne asked.

"No, I took annual leave and I gave plenty of notice, so it was fine," he said. He glanced across at her, eyes gleaming. "You can't imagine how happy you've made me, agreeing to come back to me. You won't regret it, I promise you won't." He took one hand off the steering wheel and gripped hers, which was lying in her lap. She resisted the urge to pull away, and instead watched her hand disappear, engulfed in his much larger one. "I've changed, I really have this time," he continued. "I realise now how much I took you for granted. I won't make that mistake again. You don't have to go out to work if you don't want to, you know. I'm earning enough, especially now the mortgage is paid off."

She'd forgotten that. They'd had a twenty-year mortgage. So they now owned the house outright. Or rather Steve did. The house was in his name.

"I want to work," she said. "It's not the money. I'll get bored if I'm just sitting at home all day. And I've already enrolled on the computer course in Manchester. They said it's OK, they follow the same programme throughout the country, so it won't really matter that I'm transferring from Aberystwyth."

She watched the barely perceptible tightening of his mouth as he digested this information, and then it was gone and he was smiling again. He squeezed her hand, then released it.

"That's good," he said. "What do you want to do, then, get an office job or something, or do you want to go back to cleaning?"

"I don't know yet. I might sign on with a temping agency. I'll see, when I'm settled in again."

"I thought we could go out for a meal tonight, to celebrate," Steve suggested. "I've booked a table for eight. If you're not too tired, that is."

"No, I'm not tired at all," Joanne replied. "A meal would be lovely. But isn't it your pool night tonight?"

"I've stopped playing pool," Steve said smoothly. "I got bored with it. The same old stuff, week after week. I gave it up just after you left. I'm still flying the planes, though."

It wasn't worth telling him that she knew he hadn't been playing pool for six months before she left. He was such a good liar. Not even a slight hesitation, nothing. She could learn from his example. She sat back and relaxed, determined to take advantage of the honeymoon period. It would probably last quite a while this time. She'd shocked him badly by leaving him like that. Hopefully it would last long enough. There was a lot to do, if her new plan was to go right.

She had expected the house to be untidy at least, if not downright dirty, when she got home; housework was a woman's job, in Steve's opinion. But considering he'd lived alone for almost a year, the place looked good. Either he'd employed a cleaner, she thought, or sweet-talked another woman into doing the basics for him. The furniture was dusted, the carpets vacuumed; on the surface everything seemed neat and tidy.

Steve had booked a table at a small Italian restaurant. The food was delicious, the atmosphere intimate. They ate and talked. Or rather Steve talked, about how much he'd missed her, how beautiful she looked, about his hopes for their future together, and, as he grew more intoxicated on the red wine, about how much he wanted to make love to her. He didn't ask her anything about her time in Aberystwyth and she didn't volunteer any information. She knew him; right now, from his point of view, which was the only one that mattered, that part of her life was over. She was his wife again and the slate was clean. Accusations and recriminations would come later. For the time being everything was perfect as far as Steve was concerned, and Joanne had no interest in rocking the boat.

She had no interest in having sex with him either, and half-hoped he would be too drunk to insist on his conjugal rights when they got home. *On the other hand*, she thought, when it was clear that his desire had in no way been dampened by the alcohol, *better to get it over with*. He could be a good lover when he wanted to, although in the latter years of their marriage he had generally been too interested in pursuing his own satisfaction to notice whether she was enjoying it or not.

Tonight, however, he took his time, kissing and caressing her so expertly that, deprived of sex for over a year, she found it easier than she'd expected to detach her mind and let her body respond to him, even achieving orgasm, which made her feel both uneasy and relieved.

Afterwards, when he was sleeping, one arm flung across her, she lay and thought for a while. It was a bonus that he could still arouse her sexually, she realised. It would make things easier if she didn't have to pretend in bed, or not all the time, anyway.

You could still see that he'd been a handsome man in his youth; his arms and legs were very muscular, although he'd put on more weight around the stomach and had a definite paunch now, which was pressing into her back. She remembered when it had been flat, solid. He had been very proud of his six-pack; had done countless sit-ups daily to maintain it. That had been a long time ago, when his hair had been wheat-gold instead of the grey-streaked dirty blond it was now, and before his personality had etched deep scowl lines into his forehead and had turned the corners of his mouth petulantly downwards. His skin had coarsened and his face was slackening; he had the beginnings of jowls, which would one day soon obliterate the remnants of his good looks. How could he have changed so much in just a year?

With a jolt she realised that he hadn't changed – she was just seeing him as he really was, instead of how he wanted her to see him. It was she who had changed, and no amount of wishing on his part could turn her back into the doormat she'd been until a year ago. That old Joanne was dead, and there was no way to return to how it had been before, although it suited her to let him believe otherwise, for now.

Over the next couple of months life settled into a routine. Joanne signed on with a temping agency, and after her typing test was told that her speed was not high enough for her to obtain secretarial or PA work. Instead she was offered clerical work; filing, answering the phone, with some basic computer input duties occasionally. The pay was poor; only a little above the minimum wage.

Joanne wished briefly that she hadn't abandoned her accounting course on finishing her job. But she hadn't been really interested in accounts at the time; she had been too set on getting a degree and becoming a counsellor. In the end Steve had stopped her doing either.

Times had changed anyway and accounts were all computerised now. A twenty-year-old qualification would be worth nothing. No, she would stick with the European Computer Driving Licence. Computers were the future, and she was, hopefully, if her new plan worked out, going to be a part of it.

Her new employment suited her purposes; whilst the work itself was unchallenging, often boring, she enjoyed meeting people and learning about the similarities and differences between varying office set-ups. She still had a sympathetic face; people gravitated towards her to discuss their dreams and ambitions, and often their problems, with her. It was pleasant and saved her having to talk about her own situation, which she had no intention of doing.

The transitory nature of the job suited her too; as a temp she rarely spent more than a few days in any one place, which meant that she could be more warm and friendly towards her colleagues than she would otherwise have been, knowing that she would soon be leaving. She needed to stay detached, focussed on the bigger picture.

During the first weeks Steve would telephone the agency regularly on various pretexts. She had expected that, had known he would check up on her, and took pains to always let him know where she would be working. Often he would turn up unexpectedly at the office to take her out to lunch, which was a nuisance; she had other plans for her lunch hours, which did not involve spending them in a café. But she expressed delight whenever she saw him and would accompany him to the eatery of his choice where she would talk in detail about the tedious routine of her day with its minor emergencies and dramas, until he grew bored and stopped coming to meet her.

She had estimated it would be about four weeks before he became sure enough of her to reduce the phone calls to his normal one or two a week. In the end it took over eight weeks, which showed how insecure he was. In a way that was good; while he was insecure he would be on his best behaviour. On the other hand, it was a relief to have some time to herself again.

From mid-November when Steve's surprise visits tailed off, she took to buying a sandwich on her way to work and eating it in her spare moments. This left her free to spend her lunch hour in the public library, if there was one within easy reach of whichever office she was working in. She had no desire to draw attention to herself by joining the library, nor did she wish to check any books out; she couldn't take them home, where Steve might see them, and she had no regular desk at work where she could secrete them. Instead she sat at a table in the furthest corner of the library, one eye on her watch, reading and taking brief notes, which she would later memorise before shredding.

On Monday evenings she went straight from work, if she was working, to her night class in Urmston. She enjoyed this; you worked at your own pace, following a module coursebook, with a tutor on hand to answer any questions. The class was from six until nine in the evening, with a fifteen minute break in the middle, during which time she chatted with her classmates, drawing out information about them whilst revealing little or nothing about herself.

Steve insisted on picking her up from the course, which allayed his suspicions that she might be contemplating an affair with the seventy-year-old ex-gardener or the middle-aged overtly gay man who comprised the male component of the class. This suited her perfectly; she wanted Steve to believe she had nothing to hide, and there was no direct bus route from Urmston to her home in Sale anyway.

One night a week Joanne went to Kate's, where she made use of her sister's laptop to practice her new computer skills. The night that she went varied according to Kate's hectic work schedule, but Joanne looked forward to these meetings, where she could relax to a degree and chat.

They had agreed not to talk about Joanne's marriage unless she wanted to. Kate had made it clear that she didn't approve of Joanne's decision to return to Steve, and was not the sort to labour the point. If Joanne had a problem, Kate would be there for her; while things were running as smoothly as they were, the topic didn't arise. Instead they talked about Joanne's course, their mother's slowly failing health, Kate's latest business trip to Paris or Rome, and current affairs.

Yes, overall things were going very well. Steve hated Kate and would have preferred it if his wife had no contact with her; but he was not yet at the point where he felt able to put his foot down, and Joanne was taking full advantage of that. She knew he sometimes sat outside Kate's flat when she was there to make sure that she was not meeting anyone else. She had seen his car cruise past on more than one occasion, and once had watched him surreptitiously from between the curtains as he paced up and down the street below. She didn't tell Kate; it was not worth the resultant explosion and possible confrontation between him and her sister.

Steve was happy; he had got his wife back, had monitored her to make sure she wasn't up to anything he disapproved of, and now was starting to relax. Everything was going perfectly.

Except for one thing; whilst she now knew a great deal about the toxicity of various medicines, the most dangerous ones were prescription drugs and she had no way of obtaining those without arousing suspicion. A paracetamol overdose might work, but paracetamol was horribly bitter, which meant it would be difficult to administer to him without him tasting it, and it killed slowly, destroying the liver over several days. If her plan was to work it had to look as though he'd committed suicide, and whatever he took had to work quickly. Could she go to the doctor, tell him she was having trouble sleeping, maybe? And if she did, would he give her enough sleeping tablets for Steve to kill himself with? She doubted it. You couldn't even buy more than two packets of aspirin at a time from the supermarket now. The increasingly litigious society meant that doctors no longer dished out several months' worth of drugs at a time.

There had to be a way round it, but she couldn't think of one yet. In the meantime, life was settling into a routine, and she was aware that her initial resolve was starting to crumble away. She couldn't let that happen, but had no idea how to stop it.

On Saturdays when Steve was at the flying club, Joanne caught up on the housework. The superficial cleanliness that had confronted her on her return home in September had been just that; superficial. The kitchen cupboards had not been cleaned since she left, the oven was filthy, skirting boards and picture rails were thick with dust and cobwebs. In spite of Steve's insistence throughout their marriage that the contents of cupboards and drawers be neatly arranged, during her absence things had just been crammed into them haphazardly.

She tackled one room at a time, emptying out the contents of drawers and cupboards, discarding rubbish and rearranging the rest. She took her time, and as a result it was November before she finally got round to the bathroom.

She unhooked the shower curtain, took one look at the ingrained soapy scum encrusting the bottom, and put it in the washing machine, ignoring the 'handwash only' label. The contents of the bathroom cabinet were placed in the sink whilst she cleaned it out, then empty containers of deodorant and mousse were thrown away, the rest arranged neatly in size order on the sparkling shelves.

In the corner of the room was a small chest of drawers, mainly used to store medical items and Joanne's small collection of cosmetics, hair ties and slides. She added a couple of tubes of dried-up mascara to the rubbish bag, along with some glitter hairspray she'd bought for a Christmas party two years ago. She'd never got to use it in the end; instead she'd spent Christmas Eve applying arnica cream to the bruises on her arms while Steve sulked in the pub.

The bottom drawer contained a jumble of painkillers, tubes of cream and sticking plasters, a half-empty bottle of antiseptic, and a collection of small rectangular boxes, each wrapped in a chemist's paper bag. She took them out, curious. There were fifteen little bags in all, thirteen of them containing two packs of twenty-eight pink and brown capsules. They were prescription tablets. A sticky label on the front contained Steve's name and dosage instructions; two to be taken nightly. There was also a warning that they might cause drowsiness, and to avoid alcohol.

Joanne sat on the side of the bath and opening one packet up, read the information leaflet accompanying it. Then she folded it up and replaced it carefully back in the packet. Two of the bags contained a small brown bottle of sleeping tablets, fourteen in each.

Fifteen months supply of antidepressants, and four weeks of sleeping tablets, nearly all of them untouched, thrown into the drawer straight from the chemists and forgotten about. She looked again at the labels; the last one was dated two weeks ago. The earliest prescription had six capsules missing from its blister pack; he must have tried them for a few days and stopped because he'd experienced the side effects she'd just read about; dry mouth, nausea, drowsiness, amongst others.

He had never considered himself to be depressed, she realised, in spite of what he had told her. Or in need of sleeping tablets. So why had he continued collecting his prescription, month after month? He must have thought it would help his court case and give him a better assessment mark on his perpetrators' course if he could say he was seeking treatment for depression and had insomnia. He had certainly used it to persuade her into giving him a second chance.

She knew why he hadn't thrown the tablets away. Steve never threw anything away; that was her job. And he was a creature of habit. Medicines belonged in the medicine drawer, so that was where he'd put them. She sat there, her salvation sitting on her lap, and actually cried with relief. She could do it after all. By lying, Steve had actually given her the ammunition to kill him with. There had to be enough here, had to be.

She memorised the names of the drugs, replaced the tablets in their bags, and placed them right at the back of the drawer, hiding them with the bandages, plasters, tubes of ointment and packets of painkillers.

Kate had been right; he wasn't depressed, had never been depressed. But the doctor thought he was. And so, no doubt, did his probation officer and the social workers who ran the course. What about his family, though? Had he mentioned anything to them? He might not have done; whilst he would relish the attention and sympathy he'd get from his mother, he'd also have to suffer the derision of his older brother, who would consider depression a weakness rather than an illness and would lose no opportunity to tell anyone willing to listen how feeble his little brother was.

Joanne bent down, checked once more to make sure the packets weren't visible on casual inspection, closed the drawer, and set to work on the rest of the bathroom, her mind miles away, galvanised once more. She could do it. But she must not rush now, in her excitement; she had to plan it carefully.

The following week found her sitting in the library in Stretford, thinking. Many of the books she'd looked at in her weeks of research had been printed in the eighties; times had changed since then, and it was crucial that she have up-to-date information. She hadn't wanted to draw even the slightest attention to herself, but realised now that she had no choice. Anyway, she recognised she was being overly cautious, paranoid even.

She stood up and went over to the front desk. The librarian was pretty, young, and deeply engrossed in a magazine article. She looked up and flashed Joanne a brief insincere smile.

"I wondered if it would be possible to use the computers," Joanne said tentatively. "I'm doing research, and I thought there might be some useful information on the net."

The librarian shuffled through some papers on her desk and came up with an A4 notebook.

"Let me see," she said. "Really, you have to make an appointment unless it's a quiet period. I can let you have number nine, but only for twenty minutes, I'm afraid."

"That'd be fine," Joanne replied.

"Are you a member of the library?"

"No," Joanne answered. "Is that a problem?"

"No, we can sign you in as a visitor for today. But if you're going to be using our facilities on a regular basis, you'll have to join."

"No, I don't live round here, I'm just passing through," Joanne said.

"Right," the librarian said, picking up a green card from

a small pile stacked on the desk. "OK then, your name?"

"Johnson," Joanne answered. "Stella Johnson. Er…I wondered if perhaps you could help me to get started? Only I'm not very familiar with the internet."

The librarian accompanied her to her machine and Joanne watched carefully as she logged her into the system. Then she stood behind Joanne's chair and talked her through the basics.

"The most popular search engine is Google," she said, while she was waiting for the screen to appear. "These computers are a bit slow, they're like, five years out of date. We're waiting for them to be upgraded. Right. What subject are you after?"

"Law," Joanne said. "I'm doing some research for a project."

"You could do with being a bit more specific than that," the librarian suggested. "The internet's enormous. If I type in law, it'll bring up millions of sites. The more you can narrow it down, the better."

"Oh. Divorce law, then," Joanne said.

"In the UK?"

"Yes." She could have said axe murders or bomb making, she realised. The young woman couldn't care less about what she was researching. All she wanted to do was deal with this annoying customer and get back to her magazine.

The librarian's fingers flashed over the keyboard, then she pressed enter.

"The engine'll look for every site with those key words as main features. Then you can click on whichever ones you think might be relevant, and it'll take you to the site. If you right click on the mouse, you get this screen, see? If you open the sites you want in a new tab, you can click between the different windows. It's quicker than having to keep doing the search again."

Joanne spent her remaining fifteen minutes practising how to use the search engine, and how to open up various sites, until she had the relevant sequences of keys committed to memory. As she left she thanked the librarian, who smiled distractedly, having already forgotten her.

It was her last day working in Stretford. Tomorrow she would be at an office in Rochdale, and hopefully would be able to use the library computers without asking for help and drawing any attention to herself. Then she could look for the information she really wanted to know about. If later, by some remote chance the Stretford librarian remembered her and told the police, she could say she'd looked up divorce law under a false name because she was frightened of Steve finding out she was contemplating leaving him again.

She was being overly careful, she knew that. But even though her knowledge of crime was completely based on Hollywood movies and TV crime shows, common sense told her that it was the tiny details, the unexpected coincidences that led to criminals being caught. She had no intention of being caught, and it was no longer just for Amy's sake. She had suffered more at Steve's hands during her marriage than murderers ever did in prison. She had just served her sentence before committing the crime instead of afterwards, that was all. She had had a taste of real life now, and she was greedy for more. She could never have that while Steve was alive. But she hoped to have it after he was dead. Which meant she must not be caught. And in order not to be caught, everything had to be planned to the tiniest detail.

* * *

"You know when you look up stuff on the net," Joanne shouted, "does the computer keep a record of the sites you've looked at?"

There was no reply for a few seconds, then Kate appeared in the study carrying two wine glasses in one hand and an open bottle of Chardonnay in the other.

"Yes, it's stored in a temporary internet folder file," she said. "Why?"

"Steve's offered to buy me a laptop to help me with my course, and I just wondered if he'd be able to see any websites I looked at."

"He wouldn't if you used Crap Cleaner," Kate suggested, filling the glasses to the brim. "It's a program you can download," she continued in response to her sister's quizzical look. "If you run it whenever you've been on the net, it'll get rid of all the temporary files, history, everything you don't need."

"So if I did that, no one would ever be able to see what I'd looked at?" Joanne reached over for her glass and took a sip.

"Well, of course everything is all still stored somewhere on the hard disk, even after you've deleted it all. That's how the police catch paedophiles. But it takes a computer expert to find the hidden files then. A program like Crap Cleaner would stop Steve knowing what you were up to."

"Mmm. Right," said Joanne thoughtfully.

"What *are* you up to?" Kate asked.

Joanne seemed to come back from a long way away.

"Nothing," she said cagily. "Well, I've been looking into the laws about divorce a bit."

"Divorce?" Kate said brightly. "That's great! Why didn't you tell me? I've got a friend who's a solicitor. Well, more of an acquaintance, and he's a criminal lawyer, but I'm sure he could recommend someone in the matrimonial field, if you're interested."

"That's why I didn't tell you," said Joanne. "I knew how you'd react. Everything's going well at home at the moment. I just wanted to find out a bit about the law, just in case, well, you know. I'm not actually thinking of doing anything about it. Not right now."

"OK," Kate said. There was a pause in which Joanne emptied her glass and Kate fought to control the urge to pursue the subject of divorce.

"So," she said finally, "Steve's offered to buy you a laptop. That's very generous of him."

Joanne smiled wryly at her sister.

"It nearly killed you to say that, didn't it?" she said. "No, it's not generous, as you well know. He's hoping that if I don't have to use your computer to practice on, I won't come round as often."

Kate nodded, and opened her mouth.

"And before you ask, no, it won't work. Even if I didn't need to come round to pick your brains I still would, because I want to. I told you, I'm not going to let him stop me seeing you, or working, or going to night school. And I meant it." She looked at the screen, on which she'd typed a sample letter. "Speaking of picking your brains," she continued, "how do I reduce the whole text of this from twelve to ten point, without using the mouse?"

"Control and A first," Kate said, sighing inwardly. Her sister was a much stronger person now, more determined, more insular. Which was good in one way. But she'd also become an expert at deflecting questions about subjects she didn't want to talk about, and no amount of persuasion would get her to reveal what she was up to. And she was up to something; Kate was sure of that.

"Then control again, and if you press the left square bracket key it reduces the font, the right one increases it. That's it." She perched herself on the edge of the table. "Rob rang last week," she said.

Joanne stopped typing.

"How's he doing?" she asked.

"Great. He's running a clinic at a Buddhist Centre in Bodhgaya now. They run courses for Westerners who want to know more about Buddhism. He's asked me to go over for a few weeks."

"He's invited you over every year since he moved to India," Joanne reminded her.

He said I could do a course if I want, or just help out a bit. They always welcome volunteers," Kate said, refilling the glasses.

"You're going to have to bite the bullet and actually go one day, you know," Joanne teased.

"Hmm, I know, that's what I thought. I've booked a

flight for the middle of February."

"You have?" Joanne said, stunned. "That's brilliant! You'll love it. It'll do you good to get away and learn something about another culture."

"That's what Rob said. No, well, to put it more accurately, he said it'd do me good to realise how little material possessions are worth, and how spiritually bankrupt we are here in the West."

That sounded exactly like Rob. He hadn't changed, then. Joanne had really liked him, even though he was the polar opposite to Kate. They had been good for each other. Rob had taught Kate to be less uptight about things, Kate had given Rob the drive he needed to make his dream a reality. Steve had dismissed him, calling him a hippie fairy to his face, which had left Kate raging, Joanne squirming with embarrassment, and Rob completely indifferent.

"Are you going to do a course, then?" Joanne asked. She couldn't imagine her elegant, energetic sister meditating on a dusty floor somehow. She couldn't sit still for more than two minutes without fidgeting.

"I'm just going to go and play it by ear," Kate said. "I've taken my whole year's leave in one lump, so I'll have five weeks out there."

"Oh, that's wonderful news!" Joanne exclaimed. She wanted to jump up and give her sister a hug, but they had never been a particularly demonstrative family, so she settled for grabbing her hand and squeezing it instead. "I'll miss you," she added.

"Will you water my plants while I'm away?" Kate asked.

"Course I will."

"I've had a key cut for you," she added. "Remind me to give it to you before you go."

"There's no rush, you're not going for three months," Joanne pointed out.

"No, I know, but I've been meaning to give you a key anyway. Just in case you needed to get in when I wasn't here."

"There's nothing wrong at home, I'd tell you if there was," her sister said.

Would you? Kate wasn't so sure any more.

"I know," she answered. "But I also know how quickly things can change. Better to be prepared, just in case. Like you with your research on divorce."

Steve insisted on going to visit his mother on Christmas Day, which initially surprised Joanne. She'd expected him to want a quiet traditional day, just the two of them curled up together watching repeats of James Bond and Indiana Jones films on TV. Personally she wasn't really bothered either way; any relief she might have felt at diluting her husband's company with others was negated by the thought of the others who would be diluting it.

It was only as they were crunching their way up the gravel drive in the Land Rover that she realised why he was so eager to spend the afternoon with his family. He wanted to show her off. Mike was acrimoniously divorced; Dave and Evelyn were terminally bored with each other and no longer attempted to hide it, even in public. Steve wanted to show that his marriage, in spite of the recent blip, was not merely back on track, but was now perfect, of the fairy tale, happy-ever-after kind.

She would be expected to play the part of the blissfully happy wife, she realised, hanging on his every word, expressing delight that everything was now going so well. *That much I can manage,* she thought.

She would not, however, agree that she had made a mistake in prosecuting him, or in leaving. She sighed. Perhaps she should have pushed for the intimate afternoon in front of the TV after all.

On entering, she brightened up when she discovered that Dave and Evelyn had already been and gone. At least she wouldn't have to put up with his sarcastic jibes.

Susan greeted them at the door, offering her cheek coolly to her daughter-in-law and pulling it back out of range just as Joanne's lips were about to make contact. She waved them into the lounge, and went off to get them glasses of mulled wine.

The lounge was decorated in warm shades of red and gold, and a real log fire crackled merrily in the grate. A tastefully decorated Christmas tree dominated one alcove. Superficially it was the epitome of festive perfection. Mike was sitting on the sofa, dressed in faded jeans and an aran jumper, a glass of plum-coloured steaming liquid in his hand, a green paper hat perched at a rakish angle on his head. His three sons were nowhere in sight. He waved his glass at the newcomers.

"Merry Christmas to one and all," he said. "Have a seat. This mulled wine's not half bad. Bit heavy on the cloves, perhaps. How are you both, anyway?"

"Fine," said Steve and Joanne together.

"Ah, of one accord, I see." Mike grinned.

"Has Jenny got the boys, then?" Joanne asked.

"No, they're upstairs. Playstation," he said, as though that explained everything. "Won't see them for hours, I expect."

Susan returned with three glasses on a tray, and the temperature in the room plummeted.

"So," she said crisply. "How are you two getting along?"

The conversation pattered along fitfully, with short uncomfortable silences periodically, as occur between people who do not much like each other but are forced to pretend they do for a time.

"What do you intend to do with your computer qualification, if you get it, Joanne?" Susan inserted into one of these pauses.

"I don't know yet," Joanne responded, ignoring her mother-in-law's conditional clause. "I could carry on to do web design if I want."

"It can be very lucrative, web design," Mike put in.

Steve's expression wavered between pleasure at the thought of the possible extra income and annoyance that his wife might, one day, earn more than him.

"I've got a long way to go yet, though," Joanne said. She glanced out of the French windows and her face suddenly lit up. "Oh, look!" she exclaimed delightedly. "It's snowing!"

It was, big fat flakes that drifted haphazardly down, coming to rest gently on the green lawn and neatly-pruned shrubs of the garden. Within ten minutes the gentle drift had turned into a blizzard, and ten minutes after that the three boys came thundering down the stairs, their Playstations abandoned in favour of building a snowman.

"It's certainly sticking," Mike said, standing by the window. "But it'll be hours before there's enough to build a snowman."

The boys' faces fell in unison.

"Might be enough for snowballs though," Joanne said mischievously. She wasn't sure there would be, but was desperate for any excuse to get away from this stilted conversation. "I'll get my coat," she said, jumping up and following the boys before Steve could raise any objections. Susan wouldn't, Joanne knew that; her mother-in-law's contempt for her had bloomed into barely concealed hatred since her precious baby son had been dragged through the court.

They'd been outside for no more than five minutes, holding their faces up to the sky and feeling the icy kiss of snowflakes melting on their warm cheeks and tongues, before Mike joined them.

"Any port in a storm," he said.

"You don't have to come out," Joanne suggested. "I'll keep an eye on them."

"Are you kidding?" Mike replied. "If you'd said a portal to Hell had opened up on the lawn I'd have willingly come running out to investigate. Sitting in there puts me in mind of having my fingernails pulled out with a pair of pliers."

Joanne giggled. Her dark hair was frosted with snowflakes. As he looked at her one landed on her eyelashes, and she blinked it away. Mike toyed with the idea of telling her how lovely she looked, then dismissed it. He didn't want to embarrass her.

"Thank God for my kids," he said instead. "They manage to always give us a reason to get away for a chat. How are you doing, really?"

Joanne glanced at the French windows. Steve was sitting on the sofa, in animated conversation with his mother.

"They're not looking at us," Mike said, following her gaze. "Mum'll be talking about what a disappointment I am to her, not going into private practice."

"I don't know," Joanne said. "More likely she's telling Steve what a working-class bitch I am, and remonstrating with him for taking me back after what I did to him."

"Does it bother you?"

"No," Joanne said. "Not at all. At least the dislike's mutual. It's easier that way."

"You've changed, you know," Mike said. "You're more confident, somehow."

Joanne smiled at him.

"I had over a year of living on my own before Steve found me. I know I can do it now," she said.

"You can. So why did you go back to him?" Mike asked.

"It's complicated," Joanne said. "I didn't want to spend the rest of my life running away. And I think me standing up for myself and taking him to court shook him up a lot."

"You should have done it years ago," Mike said. "You do know he won't change, don't you? It's only a matter of time before it all starts again."

"I don't know," Joanne said thoughtfully. "He *is* different. I can't really put my finger on what it is." She paused for a moment, as if considering. This was an ideal opportunity to plant the seed. She couldn't turn it down. "Can I ask you something? In confidence?"

"You know you can," Mike replied. They turned as of one accord and walked away from the house in the general direction the three boys had taken.

"Has he mentioned anything to you about being depressed?"

"Why do you ask?"

"Well, he's taking antidepressants, for one thing. He told the court he was, but he's still on them, which bothers me a bit."

"Are you sure?" Mike asked. "Or is he just telling you that to get sympathy?"

He really does know his brother, Joanne thought.

"No, I've seen the prescription. Dothy-something," she said, sounding deliberately vague.

"Dothiepin."

"That's it."

Mike raised his eyebrows.

"What is it?" Joanne asked.

"Nothing. We don't tend to prescribe Dothiepin much anymore. There are other pills on the market with fewer side-effects now. He might have told his doctor he was having trouble sleeping. Dothiepin acts as a sedative too. And it's cheaper than the modern drugs, which is always a consideration for the good old NHS." Mike smiled. "Is he seeing a counsellor?"

"He had to do that anger management course, but apart from that, not as far as I know. Why?"

Mike gazed down the garden for a minute, considering. Then he seemed to come to a decision.

"He came to me, not long after you left," he said. "He asked me to tell the court that he was depressed and was taking medication. I told him he wasn't depressed, he was just full of himself, and that if I went to court it'd be to tell the truth about what he'd been like to you. We haven't spoken to each other much since then. I guess he was upset that I took your side."

"You didn't need to do that," Joanne said.

"I know I didn't. I wanted to. He must have gone to his own GP. Maybe he is depressed, after all, if he's been taking tablets all this time."

"He threatened to kill himself if I didn't come back to him," Joanne said. "He said he couldn't live without me."

"That's not why you went back to him, is it?"

"No. Well, not the only reason. I told you, I didn't want to spend the rest of my life running, and I thought it was worth one more chance. I told him that if he hits me again, that's it."

"And has he?"

"No, but you know what Steve is like, he wants to know what I'm doing every minute of the day. I'm finding it a bit restrictive, that's all. But it's OK. I have looked into the procedure for divorce, though, just in case."

"Joanne," Mike said firmly, "you mustn't stay with him if you're not happy."

"Yes I know," she said wistfully. "Do you…do you think he would kill himself, if I left?"

Mike's first instinct was to say no, to encourage her to end this farce of a marriage. But that wouldn't be fair. He bent down and scooped some snow up off the grass. It was sticking well, but there still wasn't enough for a decent snowball.

"I don't know, to be honest," he said after he'd straightened up again. "I'd tend to say no, but then I thought he wasn't depressed either. But I can't think of any reason why he'd still be taking antidepressants eighteen months after the court case unless he was. I wouldn't say Steve was the suicidal type, but it's impossible to say."

He might attempt it, take a few tablets in a bid for sympathy, Mike thought, but he wasn't going to tell Joanne anything that might make her put up with Steve ill-treating her again. "What I am sure of, though, is that you spent twenty years considering his happiness, and it got you nowhere. Whatever Steve does or doesn't do if you leave will be down to him. You've got to think of yourself now."

"Yes, I have," Joanne murmured to her boots. Then she looked up and smiled, a brilliant smile that made her eyes light up. "You're right. I'll give him this one chance, though, like I promised him. But if he messes this up there's no going back."

Mike looked back towards the house. They were out of sight of the French windows now. He took a step toward his sister-in-law.

"Joanne," he began. "I…"

A cold wet thud on the back of his head and a whoop of boyish triumph stopped him from continuing what he'd been about to say, and resulted in an energetic battle between adults and children, ending in a good-humoured truce ten minutes later when the ammunition ran out.

Later at home, the boys tucked up in bed, Mike was grateful for Rupert's well-aimed snowball. He was far too old to start falling in love, particularly with his own brother's wife. Christ, he was looking to retire in a couple of years. What had got into him?

Joanne, he realised, that was what had got into him. He had always had a soft spot for her, but had loved her almost as he loved his sons, as he would any vulnerable innocent child, had wanted to protect her, shield her from his brother's selfish, violent tantrums. But today, for the first time, he had seen the beautiful confident woman she had metamorphosed into in the last year, and it had transformed his love into something far more dangerous. And forbidden. She was not for him, he knew that.

But then, she was not for Steve, either.

You poor bastard, Steve, he thought. *You haven't got a hope. She's the strong one now. She's already finished with you. She just hasn't realised it yet.*

When she did, Steve would be devastated. He saw violence as the ultimate solution to everything. What he would be capable of when he realised it was truly over didn't bear thinking about. And if he *was* depressed, that could make him even more volatile.

What Mike could do about it, he didn't know. But he resolved to keep an eye on them, at least.

CHAPTER SIXTEEN

January 2007

She was procrastinating. She knew it, and hated herself for it. She had researched the effects of an overdose of Dothiepin and sleeping tablets in depth, she had gone over her plan in her mind, step by step, searching for flaws and had found none. Everything was ready, but she just couldn't summon up the courage to act. She knew she should be able to get that courage from what he'd already done to her, and to Amy. Especially to Amy. She had been telling herself that every day for weeks, to no effect.

She had forgotten, in her time away from him, just how charismatic he could be when it suited him. Even with all that had happened, she found herself being sucked into the emotional whirlpool again, overwhelmed by his consideration, the small but thoughtful presents, the declarations of love. It was easy to tell herself he had no control over her any more when he wasn't around all the time, chipping away at her will to resist him. Kate had been right; he was like a drug to her.

She had managed to hang on to the small freedoms she had promised herself; the night classes, the visits to Kate, but it had taken all her energy to do that in the face of his objections.

It had started subtly. He'd bought tickets for the theatre for a Monday performance, but she had insisted on attending her evening class instead, ignoring the hurt in his eyes as she'd rejected his treat. Two weeks later he'd booked a meal for the same night, and she'd known she was right; he was trying to stop her attending her computer course. She'd turned that down too.

The following week he had been nearly an hour late picking her up from the course, telling her he'd had a puncture, and complaining that if she'd had a mobile phone, he'd have been able to call her.

"It's all right," she'd said casually. "It wasn't raining."

"That's not the point," he'd replied. "I was worried about you standing outside by yourself in the middle of the night. It's not safe."

"It's only nine o'clock. I was fine," she'd insisted. "I'm not getting a mobile phone. I told you that when we got back together."

He had not pressed the matter, but hadn't spoken to her for the rest of the evening.

The little presents had stopped, and the endearments and compliments were now few and far between. He was getting impatient. Soon he would put his foot down and start demanding. She should act now, she knew that; she had told Mike that Steve was depressed, and had mentioned it to her work colleagues too. Everything was in place.

She could have done it last September, killed him while she was fired up with hatred when he had just taken her new life away from her; but she just couldn't find it in herself to be that cold-blooded now, months later. She needed an immediate reason, something that would rouse her hatred and anger and galvanise her into action, and she just didn't have one.

* * *

"Why not? You're just being stubborn for the sake of it," Steve said hotly.

"No I'm not," Joanne replied. "I told you when I agreed to come back to you, I've changed. I need more freedom now. You agreed to let me have it."

"I have!" Steve protested. "I'm letting you do your night class, aren't I? And visit your bloody sister all the time. I hardly see you anymore!"

"That reminds me," Joanne said. "I must pop round there on Saturday."

"Why?" Steve asked. "She's not even there, for Christ's sake! She's in India!"

"I promised I'd water her plants for her and keep an eye on the place," Joanne said. "I'll only be there an hour at the most. It won't make any difference to you. You'll be out at the flying club, anyway."

"Don't change the subject," Steve said, his colour rising. "You need a mobile phone for emergencies. If you insist on being out all hours of the day and night, it's the least you can do. I'm going to buy you one, and that's that."

Joanne looked out of the window. They had new neighbours, a recently married couple. She could see the man now through the trellis fence that separated their gardens, pruning the leggy, neglected rose bushes. His name was Kevin, Keith, something like that. He had already dug over the borders. It looked as though they were going to make something of it. It would be nice to have decent neighbours, a change from the surly old couple who'd lived there before. She wondered idly how much they'd paid for the house.

Steve's fist banged down hard on the coffee table, and she jumped.

"Are you listening to me?" he shouted.

"Yes," she lied. "I was just thinking about the new neighbours. They're…"

"Fuck the new neighbours!" Steve said. "I told you, I'm buying you a phone."

Joanne looked at him. His face was red, and his hand, lying on the table, was still curled in a fist.

"OK," she said. "If you're so worried, I'll get a pay-as-you-go phone and keep it with me, for emergencies. Switched off," she added.

"What are you up to?" he asked, eyeing her suspiciously.

"I'm not up to anything, Steve," she said. "You know that."

"Do I? Then why don't you want a mobile phone, if you've got nothing to hide?"

"I don't want a mobile phone because I don't want you ringing me morning noon and night, checking up on every step I take, like you used to."

"And why should that bother you if you're not doing anything you don't want me to know about?" he asked.

"You know what I do when I'm out," Joanne said reasonably. "You ring me at work to make sure I'm there, you pick me up from my computer class, and the only other thing I do is go to Kate's."

"How do I know you're not sneaking out from work and getting someone to cover for you?" he said. "How do I know you're not going off to meet some bloke instead of going to Kate's?"

"I'm not, and you know it," Joanne replied. "You just want to control me all the time, like you used to. A mobile phone's just the start of it. I'm not having it, Steve. I'm not going back to how it was before. You have to trust me."

"Trust you?" Steve snorted. "You had me arrested, then you pissed off and left me. I went through hell worrying about you, wondering where you were. And when I found you, you were screwing around with some muscle-bound freak. And now you expect me to trust you?"

He'd moved forward, hands on the arms of the chair ready to leap up. Joanne felt her stomach twist and the adrenaline flood her body. She bit her lip instinctively and saw him register it, saw the flicker of triumph pass across his face. He thought she was afraid of him. She should be, she knew that, but she wasn't. What she was feeling was, strangely, excitement, exhilaration even.

"I'm sick of it," he continued, confident now. "I've waited for months for you to see sense. You think I've gone soft, that you can do anything you want, don't you? Well, you're wrong. I've had enough."

She suddenly realised why she was feeling exhilarated. This was it, the reason she'd been waiting for. She needed to make this public, if possible; that way afterwards people would say she'd had good reason to leave him. And it would stop him hurting her too badly, as well.

She glanced out of the window. The neighbour was still in the garden, pruning. She turned her attention back to Steve and looked him straight in the eye, amazed by how calm she felt.

"No, *I've* had enough," she said. "I want a divorce." The sentence dropped from her lips into the lounge like a grenade.

There was a moment's silence while he absorbed the words, in which she saw everything in slow motion; she watched his eyes widen, his fingers clench, his leg muscles tense ready to take his weight, and then she was up and out of the room in a flash.

He expected her to make for the front door, and she gained a few seconds on him by veering to the left through the kitchen and out into the back garden. She tore down the path, and was fighting to draw back the rusty bolt on the gate when he caught up with her. Grabbing her by the arm and pulling her round to face him, he lifted his other hand and slapped her hard across the face, sending her sprawling backwards onto the grass. She sat up, her head reeling, and looked up at him as he bent over her.

"You fucking bitch," he spat. "You're not leaving me again. I told you what I'd do if you left me. You think I was joking?" He reached down to get hold of her hair, and she lifted her arm up defensively, and then he stopped, his hand still outstretched to her, and she knew he'd seen the neighbours. He wouldn't beat her up in front of witnesses, she was sure of that. She was banking on it.

She turned and followed his gaze. The young man was looking at them, his eyes wide with shock, the secateurs still clutched in his hand. On the back step his wife was watching too, clearly uncertain as to what to do.

Steve straightened up and glared at the couple.

"Seen enough, have you?" he said.

The young man looked from Steve to Joanne, who was struggling to her feet, and back at Steve again.

"I don't think…" he began tentatively.

"Good," Steve interrupted. "Because it's none of your fucking business. Keep your nose out, pal, or I'll fucking break it for you."

He turned and strode back down the path and into the house, leaving the ashen-faced couple staring after him.

"I'm sorry," Joanne said shakily, clinging to the fence, the blood roaring in her head, the right side of her face burning. "He…he didn't mean it. He's…not well."

The woman came down the step into the garden.

"Are you all right?" she asked, although it was clear that Joanne wasn't. The young man looked towards the house uncertainly, clearly torn between the impulse to help her and the fear at what his enormous neighbour might do to him if he did.

Joanne tried to smile, then winced as the skin tightened over her swelling cheek.

"I'll be fine," she said. "Your snowdrops are lovely."

The man looked at them as though he'd never seen them before.

"We planted them last October when we moved in," he said. He looked towards the house again.

"Come in and have a cup of tea," his wife said. "You can't go back in like that. Will he calm down in a bit?"

"Yes," Joanne said. "He'll probably go out, or go to bed for the rest of the day. That's what he usually does."

She could tell the man was willing her not to accept the offer of tea. He was only a few inches taller than Joanne, slightly built, and obviously terrified that Steve would come round and hit him if he got involved. She hadn't expected the couple to do any more than witness Steve's violence and stop him really hurting her; this invitation was a bonus. It would give her a chance to set the scene for what was to follow. Soon. Very soon.

"I'd love a cup of tea," she said. "If you're sure?"

She sat in the neighbours' house sipping the tea, a bag of frozen peas pressed to her cheek.

"It'll be all right," she reassured the young man, whose name she'd now discovered was neither Kevin nor Keith, but Colin. "He won't come here to get me. He'll already be feeling sorry, I expect."

"Has he done this before?" Marie, the young woman, asked.

Joanne looked at her cup.

"Yes," she said. "I left him nearly two years ago now. We were separated for over a year, then we decided to give it another chance. We've been married for twenty years, you see. I told him that if he hit me again, that'd be it. Everything was fine at first, but over the last few weeks it's been…we've been arguing a lot."

Colin was looking everywhere but at her, embarrassed. He wanted to do as Steve had advised and keep his nose out, Joanne could see that. But he could hardly say so in front of his young wife, who was clearly very concerned, without appearing heartless. Joanne felt sorry for him.

"You should leave him for good," Marie said. "If Colin ever hit me, I'd divorce him." She looked at him fondly, sure that he would never touch her.

"I'm worried about him, though," Joanne said. She took the bag of peas away from her face. "The last time I left him he got really depressed and threatened to kill himself. I'm frightened that if I leave him again, he might go through with it."

Colin and Marie looked at each other uncertainly. This was beyond them, Joanne realised. They were a young middle-class couple from a good neighbourhood, who'd probably never seen any violence in their lives apart from the sanitised fights on TV.

Joanne handed the peas to Marie.

"Thanks," she said, standing up. "You've been really kind. I'd better get back though."

"Will you be all right?" Marie asked. "You don't have to go back yet, if you don't want."

"Yes, I'll be fine. Like I said, he'll probably have gone out to calm down. He'll be OK when he gets back. We'll have a talk about it and sort everything out. Best if you pretend nothing's happened next time you see Steve. He didn't mean what he said to you," she reassured Colin. "He was just in a bad temper, that's all. He'll be fine the next time you see him, I'm sure."

Marie came with her to the door.

"You know, you shouldn't stay with him if he hits you. It's not right," she said worriedly. "There are refuges and things you can go to."

"I know," Joanne replied. "I'll have to talk to him, tell him that if he does it again, I will leave. It's just…difficult."

The expression on Marie's face told her that in her eyes it wasn't difficult at all. A man hits you, you leave. If only it was as simple as that. It was impossible to explain to someone like Marie how it worked, how they hooked you in, made you dependent on them until you didn't think you could breathe without them telling you how to do it. *He has no hold over me anymore,* she reminded herself triumphantly as she walked up the path. *I've just got to make the final break now, that's all. I can do this, I can. I'll go over it now, while he's out.*

He wasn't out. He was sitting in the lounge, in the dark, waiting for her to come back.

"Did you enjoy that, telling your new friends what a bastard you're married to?" he said as she walked in the room. Joanne hadn't expected this; he was a creature of habit, and this was not how he usually behaved. She felt the triumph disappear and the fear creep in to replace it. She stayed in the doorway, wary, trying to gauge his mood. His voice was low, almost gentle, but that didn't mean anything. He adjusted his tone to suit his purposes, not his temper.

"I didn't tell them that," she said. "Like you said, it's none of their business. I just wanted to stay out of the way for a while, give you time to calm down a bit. I thought you might have gone out."

"No," he said. "I didn't go out. I sat here and thought about what you said. Do you really want a divorce?"

"No, not really," she replied carefully. "I just don't want things to be like they were before."

"It's Kate who's put you up to this, isn't it?" he said.

"No," Joanne replied. "Kate's got nothing to do with this."

He leaned across and switched on the lamp at the side of the chair.

"Don't treat me like an idiot, Jo. Do you think I don't know what she's up to? You would never have had the guts to take me to court, to leave me like you did, if it hadn't been for her pouring poison in your ear. She's always had it in for me, ever since she came on to me years ago and I told her I wasn't interested." His voice was quiet, neutral, far more intimidating than if he'd screamed and shouted. She'd seen him like this before, when had that been? A long time ago. She couldn't think, with the butterflies in her stomach and her heart pounding against her ribs. He shouldn't be here. He should have gone out, come back later, subdued.

"Steve, it isn't like that…" she began.

"So now she's trying to get you to divorce me. She'll do anything for revenge, won't she?" he continued, as though she hadn't spoken. He leaned forward in the chair. "Come here," he said softly.

Joanne remained in the doorway, poised for flight. He seemed calm, controlled, but his mouth was set in a hard line, his eyes ice-cold; his fingers clenched on the arms of the chair. Suddenly it came back to her when she had seen him this cold, only once before, it must have been ten years ago, more.

That time he had taken her home from a night out, waited until she was in bed, and had told her he fancied a snack and was nipping out for some crisps from the late shop.

Then he'd gone back to the pub, waited outside for an hour in the snow for the man who had chatted her up at the bar to come out, had followed him until he'd parted from his friends, and then had punched and kicked him senseless, taking great care to ensure that the man could not identify his assailant.

After that he had come home, dragged her out of bed, filled the bathroom sink with water and held her face under it until she'd almost lost consciousness. Then he had pulled her head out of the water, looked at her with the same ice-cold expression on his face as he wore now, and had told her, quite calmly, what he had done to her perceived lover, and what he would do to her if she ever flirted with anyone, ever again.

For days afterwards Joanne had wondered if the man was all right. She had even contemplated phoning the police anonymously. But she realised that Steve would guess it was her who'd reported him; he hadn't told anyone else, as far as she knew. She hadn't dared do it; she'd been too frightened of what he might do to her if she had.

Remembering that night now, and how convinced she had been that he was going to drown her, her blood ran cold. The hot Steve she could deal with; he would hit her once, maybe twice, then the guilt would set in. This cold Steve was a different man altogether. It had not been part of her plan to make him this angry. She had miscalculated. She ran her tongue over her lips nervously.

"Steve, I'm sorry," she said. "I don't know why I said I wanted a divorce. I didn't mean it."

His face remained impassive, his gaze pinning her to the spot. She couldn't run now, she realised. Her whole body seemed to be made of jelly; her legs would fold under her if she tried.

"I'm not going to hit you," he said calmly. "I just want to talk to you. Come here."

She took two shaky steps into the room, and he reached

out suddenly and grasped her hand, holding it gently as though it was something fragile, precious.

"I've been thinking," he began, "about the last five months. It's been good, hasn't it? I've let you do your night class, go to work, do what you want. We've been out for meals, to the theatre. I've given you everything you wanted, and I haven't complained or laid a hand on you once, have I?"

It wasn't quite like that. He had complained, with increasing frequency over the months, about having to get his own tea, about her spending too much time with other people instead of him. But now was not the time to contradict him. Her free hand lifted instinctively to her face, and he nodded slightly.

"Ah, well, yes, until today. I'm sorry about that. I shouldn't have slapped you like that, and with the neighbours watching too. You'll be fine in a day or so," he said, dismissing her bruised and swollen cheek with a smile. "But we need to get a few things straight. I've let you have your own way too much, I can see that now. I should have been a bit firmer from the start, but I wanted you back so badly I would have agreed to anything. But it's not working, is it? So here's how it's going to be from now on," he continued, his fingers gently stroking the back of her hand. "You can carry on working, for now, and you can finish this computer course of yours. But I'm going to buy you a mobile phone, and you're going to keep it with you, switched on, in case I need to contact you."

Joanne tried to take her hand from his, but his fingers tightened round it immediately, and she subsided. She was trembling, and knew he must feel it, although he gave no indication as he continued talking.

"You can carry on going to Kate's while she's away, to water her plants, seeing as you've promised. But when she comes back, the visits stop. I give you something, you give me something. I think that's only fair."

"Steve, I can't…" Joanne began.

"Yes, you can," Steve interrupted. "Because if you don't, you'll be sorry." His hand tightened round hers, just enough for it to be uncomfortable. "We need to get one more thing straight, that's all, and then we can carry on as before. Don't you ever mention divorce, or think about leaving me, ever again. Because I'll tell you now, if you do, I'll find you wherever you go, just like I did this time. But when I do, I won't beg you to come back to me. I will never, never let you put me through the hell I've been through these last two years again. If you leave me again, I'll find you and I'll kill you. You and any man you're fucking at the time. It's as simple as that. Do you understand me?"

He looked at her, his face pleasant, his eyes locking with hers. His fingers tightened again round her hand, until she felt the delicate bones grinding together, and then he slowly squeezed harder and harder until she fell to her knees at the side of his chair, screaming that she would do anything, anything, if he would only stop.

Then he released her and stood, looking down at her as she cradled her crushed hand in her lap, her face twisted with agony, tears streaming down her cheeks, her breath coming in harsh gasps.

"Good," he said pleasantly. "That's that sorted, then. I'll pick a phone up for you tomorrow on my way home from work. Right, I'm going for a shower. We can get a takeaway tonight if you want. You won't be in the mood for cooking, I shouldn't think."

She heard him go up the stairs, saw the light dim slightly as he switched the shower on. She tried to flex her fingers but even the slightest movement was unbearable. Slowly she got to her feet and went into the kitchen. She filled the washing bowl with cold water, dropped a whole tray of ice cubes in it and immersed her hand, waiting for a few minutes until the pain started to ease. Then carefully with the other hand she started tentatively to open her fingers, until she was as sure as she could be that none of the bones were broken.

Her breathing was back to normal now, her heart had

slowed and her mind was clear; she felt cold, as cold as if she had submerged her whole body in ice water, instead of just her hand.

He had done what she'd been waiting for, and more, she realised. He had made it easy for her. She reached for the kitchen roll, wiped her eyes, and gently patted her injured hand dry. Then she took some Ibuprofen for the pain, and rummaged in the drawer for the takeaway menu, coming up with two. She went to the bottom of the stairs.

"Indian or Chinese?" she shouted up, her voice calm. She *was* calm, she realised. Completely and utterly calm. It was such an immense relief to have had the decision made for her, when she'd been unable to make it herself. She would pay for the takeaway tonight, she thought. Her treat. He deserved it.

* * *

February.

When Steve came home from work he found his wife in the kitchen poring over a recipe book. A colourful array of bottles and fruit was scattered along the work surface. As he came into the room she looked up at him and smiled.

"Hi!" she said brightly.

"What are you doing?" he asked.

"I found a book on cocktails in the charity shop," she explained. "I thought we could have a cocktail evening, use up all these bottles of weird liqueurs that Dave and Evelyn bring us back when they go away. I've made some snack stuff, tapas they call it in Spain."

"Tonight?" Steve said, a puzzled look on his face.

"Well, yes, that's what I thought," Joanne replied, the smile fading. "Though if you've planned something else, I suppose the food would keep for one day." She glanced at the clock. "I could still make my class, if I leave now."

"No!" said Steve immediately, as she'd known he would. He'd agree to anything if it stopped her going to her course. "No, I didn't have anything planned. That sounds great."

He took his jacket off and hung it up, then came back. She had piled her hair up on top of her head and secured it with a clip. Her exposed neck was long and slender, and she was wearing a close-fitting lacy top that left little to the imagination. He came up behind her and slid his arm round her waist, nuzzling gently at her neck. She shivered slightly.

"What are you making?" he murmured.

"I thought we'd start with a Sea Breeze," she said, "and then I can use up the sloe gin in a Slow Comfortable Screw."

"Sounds good," he said, his hand wandering downward. "Can't we start with the Slow Comfortable Screw instead? It'll give us an appetite. You smell gorgeous, by the way."

She turned in his embrace to face him and put her palms against his chest.

"And you don't," she said lightly, smiling. "You smell of paint and turps. And sweat. Have a shower. And then you can go and get a DVD while I finish getting everything ready."

By the time he got back, she'd laid out the food on the coffee table in the lounge and had mixed the first drinks.

"What did you get?" she asked.

"They were doing two for one, so I got Desperado and Once Upon a Time in Mexico," he said. "I thought they'd go with the tapas." She watched a little nervously as he sipped his drink. "Mmm, lovely," he pronounced, looking pointedly at her.

She smiled, ignoring the insinuation, and sat on the chair. She must not let him carry her off upstairs now. Sex was not part of the plan, if she could avoid it.

"The next one's already mixed in the fridge," she said. "Drink up, and eat something. I don't want you getting drunk quickly. I've got big plans for later."

"Have you?" he said, his eyes lighting up.

"Yes, and you've got at least another six drinks to get

through first. And the film," she replied firmly. "Put it on, will you?"

They settled down to watch the first film which, she had noted from the DVD case, was one hour and forty minutes long. Add a short break between the films, say fifteen minutes, then the second was an hour and thirty-seven minutes. Plenty of time, maybe too much. She would have to play it by ear.

They got through four cocktails during the first film, and all the tapas. By the closing credits Steve's eyes were drooping a little.

"Are you all right?" Joanne asked as she swapped the DVDs over. "You look a bit tired. Did you have a hard day at work?"

Steve had been lying full length on the sofa, but now he sat up and stretched.

"No, not particularly," he said. "I do feel a bit sleepy though."

"Don't you want to watch the other film?" she asked, injecting disappointment into her voice.

"'Course I do," he said. "I want to know what happens next. Tell you what, I'll make the next drink. Moving around'll wake me up a bit. What is it?"

"It's a Blushing Piña Colada," she said. "I've already made most of it up. It's in a jug in the fridge."

She followed him into the kitchen, watching him closely. He was walking a little unsteadily and had his hand pressed to his chest.

"I thought you could handle your drink," she teased.

"I can," he said crossly. "I just feel a bit odd, that's all. A bit dizzy, as though I've got palpitations or something. It must be mixing my drinks."

"Well this one should be OK then," she said. "It's got no alcohol in it. I thought I'd give us a break, ready for the piece de resistance - Mexican Hot Chocolate. Perfect for the film. Look, you go and sit down and flick through the trailers. I've only got to pour grenadine in, and it's ready."

When she took the drinks in, he insisted on her sitting with him on the couch. She wanted to keep her distance from him; this proximity made things harder for her, but if she demurred it could cause an argument. She curled up next to him and tried to concentrate on the film. Half an hour into it she asked him to pause it while she made the hot chocolate.

It was incredibly rich and very spicy. She took a sip of his drink, as she had of all the drinks before, then added a spoonful of sugar, stirring it well before taking another sip. She had had to hurry things along a little, and hoped he wouldn't notice the slight bitterness.

She took the drinks in and handed his to him, intending to move back to the chair with hers, but he grabbed her hand and pulled her down next to him, wrapping his arm round her shoulder and pulling her into him so that her head was resting against his shoulder. He cupped one breast in his hand, squeezing it until she winced slightly.

"Hmm, that's nice," he mumbled, rubbing her nipple between his fingers, his voice slurring slightly.

"You need to drink the chocolate while it's hot," she said. She reached over and pressed the play button on the remote, and to her relief he stopped playing with her breast, although he kept his hand cupped round it. She watched as he drank the chocolate, relieved that he didn't comment on its taste.

Then she sat and watched the rest of the film, registering nothing of it. Her whole being was concentrating on the man sitting next to her. She waited until his eyes drooped and then closed, and his hand fell away from her breast, landing heavily on her lap. Then she waited some more, until the closing credits of the film ran and the DVD switched itself off.

Then, very carefully so as not to disturb him, she eased herself off the couch and went to sit on the chair. The room was dark. She would have to put the light on.

She couldn't. She couldn't see him like this. She could not remember him for the rest of her life looking vulnerable, almost boyish, as he always did when asleep. She needed to remember him with his face twisted in rage, or smiling as he crushed her hand and watched her grovel and beg him to stop.

Get a grip, she told herself sternly. *You have to put the light on. You have to be able to see what you're doing.* She got up, switched the lamp on, and then stood over him for a while, summoning up her courage. Gingerly she put her fingers on his neck, felt for the pulse. It was still there, but slow, a little fluttery.

She picked up the cups, took them into the kitchen, carefully washed and dried them, and hung them on the cuphooks. She reached into the cupboard under the sink, put on her yellow marigold gloves, then retrieved the carrier bag she had put away earlier from the back of the food cupboard. She picked up the glass Steve had drunk his Piña Colada from, careful not to smudge his fingerprints, and took it into the lounge. Going back into the kitchen she collected the half-empty bottles of vodka and tequila, and put them all on the coffee table.

Steve was still in the position she had left him in.

She sat on the floor near the couch and looked at his chest, watching for the rise and fall that would tell her if he was still breathing. She saw no movement for what seemed an age, and then suddenly he sighed deeply in his sleep, making her jump.

"Oh God," she whispered desperately. "I can't do this, I can't." She sat on the floor, her arms clasped round her knees, crying and rocking backwards and forwards.

You have no choice, she told herself. *You've already done it. You can't go back now.*

She steeled herself, then wiped away her tears and set to work, half-filling the glass with vodka. She tipped the empty blister packs of antidepressants and the bottle of sleeping tablets out of the carrier bag onto the table. Then she picked up his right arm and carefully wrapped his hand around the vodka and tequila bottles, pressing his fingers against the glass. She ensured his prints were on the blister packs and the bottle of sleeping tablets too, and then she picked up the carrier bag, which contained the capsules from which she'd tipped out the powder into his drinks, and the unused packets of antidepressants. She stood at the doorway looking round the room, making sure she hadn't forgotten anything.

She stuffed the carrier bag into her shoulder bag, which was in the hall. She couldn't pack any clothes, but she could justify grabbing her bag on the way out. She looked at her watch; five past ten. She picked up the phone and dialled Kate's number, waiting for the answerphone to kick in before replacing the receiver. She waited ten minutes, then rang again. Once again she listened to the answerphone message, then hung up.

Nearly there, she told herself, summoning the courage to do the last thing she needed to do before she left. She stood for a moment looking at her reflection in the hall mirror. Then she stepped back two paces and ran forward, smashing her forehead into the mirror with all her strength. It splintered, several shards falling on to the carpet, one gouging a piece out of the skin above her eyebrow.

She hadn't planned for that, but it didn't matter. She leaned dizzily against the wall, running the imaginary scenario through her head, basing it on several real ones from the past. Then she staggered to the stairs and sat down until her head cleared properly. The blood was pouring down her face, dripping onto her skirt and the stairs. It probably needed stitches, but there was nothing she could do about that now.

She went into the kitchen, grabbed a piece of kitchen roll, and pressing it over the wound she picked up her bag and went out, closing the door quietly behind her before running down the path and out of the street. The rubbish collection was on Tuesday and most people had already put their wheelie bins outside ready for the morning. Without breaking stride, Joanne lifted the lid of one and dropped her carrier bag into it before continuing on to the bus stop.

The bus came a couple of minutes later, and she allayed the driver's concern by trivialising the cut, telling him that it looked worse than it was; she would be fine, her sister would dress it for her. She just felt stupid, tripping over the kerb like that. It wasn't as though she'd had *that* much to drink, she said.

She was used to making excuses for cuts and bruises; she had done it for over twenty years. The driver accepted her story, even though she was trembling visibly. Shock, she said, but she was fine, the bus stopped right outside her sister's flat and she wouldn't have to walk far. He would remember her though, she was certain of that.

Once in Kate's she examined the wound properly. It was over an inch long, and deep. It would probably scar, but that was the least of her worries. She dressed it, using thin strips of micropore tape in lieu of stitches, then made herself a cup of tea, adding three spoons of sugar. Hot sweet tea was good for shock, she told herself as she sat in the lounge, sipping it and thinking. She *was* in shock; she couldn't believe she'd actually done it. She felt detached from the events of the evening somehow, as though she'd seen them on the TV, or witnessed someone else doing them.

There was only one thing left to do now. She finished her tea, then looked at her watch. Just after eleven. That meant it would be six thirty in the evening in India now. She leaned across and picked up the phone. Kate wouldn't mind her making a long-distance call. Not when she was about to give her the good news that she had left Steve, and this time was never going back.

It was the waiting that would be the hardest part now. Joanne tried to keep her mind occupied by going over her story to get it right.

Kate had accepted it without question, was delighted that Joanne had kept her promise to leave Steve if he ever hit her again. She was concerned about her injuries though, and worried that he would talk her into going back. At one point in the conversation she had offered to fly home, but Joanne had told her she was fine, she just wanted to spend a couple of days recuperating, then she would start divorce proceedings. No, she would not let him in if he called round, she promised. It was over, there was no going back now.

Of course it would be harder to talk to the authorities, she knew that. They might be suspicious; she had to get not just her story, but her reactions right. *I can do this,* she told herself firmly. She had had to lie all her life; to her father when she'd taken A levels; to everybody when Steve had hit her; to herself, trying to convince herself her marriage was not a mess; and to Amy when she'd said she wanted to go back to him. That had been the hardest lie of all. Amy hadn't spoken to her since that phone call five months ago.

Five months. How had she lived with him for that long without giving herself away? How could he have believed that she would actually want to go back to the man who had sexually abused his own daughter, and other people's daughters?

Arrogance, that was it. He was the most self-centred and self-deluding man she'd ever met. He thought there was nothing wrong in doing what he'd done, therefore there *was* nothing wrong. And the courts had justified his opinion by handing out such a light punishment. He would never have changed. She'd had no choice but to do what she'd done.

Now she had to think like him, and not just go over her version of events, but actually believe in them. She had to convince herself that they had argued, he'd hit her and she'd walked out. If she could do that, then she could convince everybody else as well. That was what Steve had done, countless times.

But first she needed to get some sleep. Now it was all over, her energy had drained away, leaving her exhausted. It could be a day, maybe more, before anyone found him. It was late; nothing would happen until at least tomorrow.

She borrowed a nightdress of Kate's and went to bed, where she tossed and turned restlessly for an hour or so before sinking into a deep, dreamless sleep.

CHAPTER SEVENTEEN

The sound of the doorbell ringing eventually roused Joanne from her slumbers. For a moment, completely disorientated, she had no idea where she was, and lay back for a minute to let her mind clear. She turned her head and peered drowsily at the clock on the bedside table. Nine thirty. Then the bell rang again, shrill and insistent, making her jump, and suddenly she remembered everything and was wide awake.

She leapt out of bed and put Kate's dressing gown on, tying the belt round her waist as she pressed the intercom button on the door.

"Hello?" she asked nervously, her heart banging. She wasn't ready for this, not yet.

"Miss Maddock?" the male voice, sounding tinny and distant, came through the speaker. Joanne closed her eyes, relief surging through her. It was not the police after all, but some salesman or colleague of Kate's. She would have the time she needed to prepare her reaction.

"No," she said. "She's away at the moment. I'm her sister. Can I give her a message?"

"Mrs Harris?" the voice came back. "It's the police. Can we come up for a moment, please?"

The relief drained away, instantly replaced by an adrenaline surge so strong she felt nauseous. She pressed the button to open the door, and then leaned against the wall, trying to collect herself. She had about thirty seconds, she knew that. They must be here about Steve. She could think of no other reason why they would know her by name. But how would they know Kate's address?

Think, she ordered herself. The address book was by the phone. She had left her mobile phone at the house, and Kate's was the first name in her contact list. That would be it. That had to be it. The only other way they would know was if Steve had told them, and that was unthinkable.

She had to move. The police would expect her to have the flat door open for them. They would expect her to be worried, wondering what was wrong. She had to get this right first time; her future depended on it. *You've been rehearsing this for months,* she told herself. *Stop panicking; you can do it.*

She took a couple of deep breaths to calm herself, then walked to the door, legs shaking, and opened it as the police stepped out of the lift. There was a man and a woman, and they both looked impossibly young to her, too young to take on the responsibility of telling a woman that her husband had committed suicide. She felt a stab of sympathy for them, and that helped her to calm down. Thinking of others was what she did well.

The woman police officer was looking at her face with concern, and Joanne lifted her hand to her eye, realising that the dressing she'd put on had come off in the night. The skin around her eyebrow felt crusty as she touched it gingerly.

"I had an argument with my husband, and he…" she started to explain. There, the first lie was out. Hesitate, then make an excuse for him, that was what she'd done for twenty years. "He has a bad temper, he's had a lot on his mind recently," she said, then stepped aside, motioning them to enter the flat.

"You should go to the hospital with that," the woman said. "It looks as though it needs stitches."

"Yes," Joanne replied automatically. She didn't want to talk about her wound. She'd had far worse than that in the past. She needed to know why they were here, now. "What's happened?" she asked as soon as they were in the hallway.

Her voice was trembling, and she hoped that they would interpret that as worry rather than guilt.

"How long have you been staying here?" the male officer asked. He seemed a little more brusque than his female companion, but neither of them looked as Joanne imagined they would if they were interviewing a murder suspect.

"Just since last night," Joanne answered. "I walked out after he…" she pointed to her face. "We'd been separated, you see, but he begged me to come back. He promised he'd be different this time. Things haven't been too bad…well, they have, but he hadn't really hurt me, not until last night. I was frightened, because the last time…" she let the words trail off, aware that she was in danger of rambling, and in rambling, slipping up. She had to keep it simple. "So I left. I got the bus here. I've got a spare key, you see, I'm looking after my sister's plants and things. Is it Mum?" she asked suddenly. "Has something happened to her?"

"No, no," the female officer said. "Your mum's fine. It was her who told us you might be here at your sister's. Why don't you come in and sit down? Constable Slater will make us a cup of tea."

Joanne led the woman into the lounge whilst Constable Slater vanished into the kitchen, clearly relieved at having avoided the distasteful task. She sat down and looked at the policewoman.

"Has your husband seemed upset or depressed about anything recently?" the officer began.

"I don't know," Joanne answered. "He doesn't talk about his problems with me much. But he's been suffering from depression for quite a while now. He's taking antidepressants. Why?"

"It seems as though he took an overdose last night. But it's okay. The postman saw him lying in the hall this morning and called the ambulance. He's in hospital. It's a bit early to say yet, but he's probably going to be all right."

"No," Joanne said, the blood draining from her face. "No, it isn't possible. He can't…" Snow blurred her vision, quickly becoming a blizzard, and there was a strange buzzing in her ears. Vaguely she sensed the policewoman jumping to her feet, then everything went black.

* * *

Joanne sat on the leather couch in the lounge, feet curled under her, pondering what to do next. She would have preferred to go to her spot on top of the hill in Aberystwyth; but that had been in her other life, a life that suddenly seemed so remote that she wondered if she had in fact dreamt it all. Anyway, it was impossible to go there – her life was here now, and what a mess she had managed to make of it.

She had sat here all night, while the amber light from the streetlamp outside was slowly replaced by the pearly grey of dawn, and was still no nearer a solution to her predicament. She hadn't planned for this. She thought she'd planned for everything, but not for this.

The police officers had been kindness itself with her once she'd recovered consciousness. She had only been out for a few seconds, the lady officer had reassured her, and it was only to be expected. She'd had such a shock.

Very true, but not for the reasons they were assuming. She had drunk the tea, then got dressed and gone to the hospital in the police car. Assuring the officers that she would be fine now, she had walked down the corridor to the ward feeling like a condemned prisoner walking to her execution.

The sister had expressed concern over her eye, advising her to go to casualty. Mr Harris was unconscious, she said, but they had pumped his stomach and he was going to be all right, once he'd slept off the effects of the tablets he'd taken. Of course he would have to see a psychiatrist as a matter of routine, but after that he should be able to come home in a couple of days.

Having no other choice, Joanne had gone in to see him. He was asleep, his hair tousled, his arm lying limply on top of the blankets. Sleeping he looked vulnerable, innocent; whenever she had watched him as he slept before, she had always felt a pang of love, and regret that it had all gone wrong. Now she was shocked by the strength of her hatred, so fierce it drove the breath from her body, and she collapsed into the chair at the side of the bed. The sister, misinterpreting, assured Joanne that he really would be fine, then tactfully drew the curtains round the bed and left her alone with her husband.

She had sat with him for a short time, watching his chest rise and fall, willing it to stop with all her heart. Looking at his hand lying limp and helpless on the blanket only reminded her of how many times she had seen it clenched and coming towards her at speed, of how he had used it to assault his daughter. She wanted to put a pillow over his head and hold it there until he stopped breathing. If she did would he wake up, fight her, call for help? She covered her face with her hands. It was pointless. She would never be rid of him. He was unstoppable.

What had he been doing lying in the hall? He must have woken up at some point in the night and managed to stagger into the hall before collapsing again. Would he have died anyway, if the postman hadn't seen him through the glass-panelled front door?

God, she thought despairingly. *All that research, all that planning, and I still couldn't do it right.*

Now, back at home, she thought about the nursing sister's reassuring words. It was very common for people to misjudge the number of tablets they needed to take to kill themselves, she had said. Obviously this was true. Joanne had misjudged badly, and when Steve woke up he would make her pay for it, of that she was sure.

The hatred she had felt at the hospital had now been replaced by blank terror. What *would* he do? If she could determine that, she could plan her next move. Would he tell the police that his wife had tried to murder him? She chewed absently on her fingernail and thought about it. No, he wouldn't do that, she was sure. He wouldn't want to give up his power over her by denouncing her. He would want to make her suffer, and he would want to *see* that suffering, which he couldn't do if she was in prison.

The most likely thing, she decided finally, was that he would tell her he knew what she'd done but that he forgave her because he loved her. He'd be able to restrict her freedom completely, hit her whenever he wanted, and would expect her to be grateful and beholden to him for the rest of her life because he hadn't turned her over to the law. Yes, that was what he would do, she was certain of it.

No.

She would not let him do that. She had seized her one chance for freedom, and it had gone wrong. But she would not let him control her life, ever again. She would wait for a day or two. He had looked terrible yesterday in the hospital, years older than normal, his skin pale and flaccid. Maybe he would still die. Hospitals made mistakes; she read about them in the papers all the time. The tablets must have been in his system all night. It was possible.

And if not, if he recovered consciousness, which, she had to admit, did seem the most likely thing, she would go to see him, let him tell her how he forgave her for what she'd done, how he loved her, and how they should just forget about it, would watch the triumph light his eyes as he thought of how he would wield his power over her for the rest of her life. Then she would go straight to the police and confess everything.

She was afraid of going to prison but nothing could be as bad as having to live beholden to him for the rest of her life. If she ran away again, he would find her; at least he couldn't touch her in prison. She could deny him that small victory.

She sat and thought a little more. A story like that would almost certainly get into the national newspapers; she would tell the police that she had found out he'd been molesting children, and that was why she'd decided to kill him. She would refuse to give any names; maybe Amy, or one of her schoolfriends that he'd assaulted would come forward. Then she would have achieved what she wanted, albeit not in the way she'd hoped for; she would be free of him, and would have made sure he couldn't hurt another child.

Her decision made, she felt better. The future didn't hold the promise she had hoped it would, but she could at least still take control of it. That had to be worth something.

* * *

Once again she walked down the corridor to the ward, and once again felt like a condemned prisoner. When she had rung the hospital this morning they had told her that it was good news. Her husband was awake and had been asking for her.

Yes, she thought, *I bet you can't wait to savour your victory, you bastard.*

At the entrance to the ward, the nurse intercepted her.

"He's much better," she said cheerily, "but he's still very drowsy, and a bit confused. So I wouldn't stay too long, and it might be better if you don't ask him why he…you know. Not until he's seen the psychiatrist."

Steve was propped up on the pillows, his eyes closed. For a moment she thought he was asleep, but then he opened his eyes, saw her, and smiled. It was a smile of genuine delight to see her, and threw her completely. It was not what she'd been expecting, not at all.

She went closer, sat down on the chair at his bedside, and when he reached for her hand she let him take it.

"How are you feeling?" she asked.

"Tired," he said. "The doctor told me I took some tablets or something. I don't remember." His forehead creased in puzzlement. "What happened?"

"Don't you know?" she asked. It wasn't possible. He was doing this to lull her into a false sense of security. Then, just when she thought she'd got away with it, he'd hit her with the fact that he'd known all along what she'd tried to do to him.

"We watched a DVD," he said hesitantly, his voice slurring with the after effects of the tablets. "And we had a few drinks. I remember that. Then I went to sleep. I don't remember anything else until I woke up in here this morning." He let go of her hand, and lifted his off the bed, pointing to her face. It seemed to take a great effort; after raising it only a few inches his arm slumped back onto the bed. "Did I do that?" he asked.

She would play his game, humour him for now. After all, it didn't matter whether she confessed to the police now, next week or next month.

"Yes," she said. "You banged my face against the mirror, and it broke."

"God, I'm sorry, darling," he said. "I must have been drunk. I don't remember any of it." Tears came into his eyes. "We were doing well, weren't we?" he said remorsefully.

Either he was the best actor on the planet, or he really didn't remember. Was it too much to hope for? For years she had listened while he told her his version of his latest assault on her, so insistently and repeatedly that she had ended up doubting her own memory of events. It was worth a try. Anything was worth a try.

"You were pretty drunk," she said, her mind working rapidly. "I went up to the bathroom and found all your antidepressants at the back of the cabinet." What was she doing going through the bathroom cabinet? She skipped over it; she would come up with something if he asked. *Keep it simple, only add in details if you have to.* "I brought them downstairs and threw them on the table, and asked you why you hadn't been taking them when you'd told me you were depressed. We had an argument and you...did this," she explained, pointing to the wound, now neatly stitched. "Then you went upstairs and I told you that was it, I was leaving, and I ran away before you could get back downstairs. I got the bus to Kate's and stayed there the night. The police came round yesterday morning and told me what you'd done. I guess you must have taken the tablets."

She watched the expressions cross his face as he absorbed what she'd told him, tried to remember any of it, and failed. She dropped her head so he couldn't see her face, hoping he would think her too ashamed to look at him.

"I know you've said you couldn't live without me if I left," she murmured. "But I didn't think you meant it. You nearly died."

"Are you going to stay at Kate's?" he asked.

She shook her head.

"No," she said. "I went home yesterday, after I'd been to see you. I don't know what to do, to be honest."

"Don't leave me," he pleaded. "I must have been drunk. I never would have hit you otherwise."

Why not? she thought. *You've hit me hundreds of times when you were stone cold sober.*

"I don't know, Steve," she said. "I'm frightened of you."

"I'll make it up to you, I promise," he said earnestly, as he had many, many times before. "I don't remember any of it. You do believe me, don't you, Jo?"

She looked at him.

"Yes," she said. "I believe you."

The relief on his face was mirrored only by the relief she felt in her heart. He really didn't remember. All she had to do now was pray that his memory didn't return when the effects of the drugs wore off completely.

* * *

Two days later Steve came home. He had had a preliminary appointment with the psychiatrist, who had said he would send a follow-up appointment through the post. For a few days he was a little sluggish, sleeping for longer than usual, but the following week he went back to work, telling his employers that he'd been off with the flu.

Joanne spent the next two weeks in a state of permanent

terror that he would come home one night and tell her that he'd remembered everything, that he'd thought the cocktails tasted strange, that he knew she'd poisoned him. But he didn't.

Instead they were going through another 'honeymoon period', as the counsellors had called the period of contrition after the latest assault. The only difference was that Steve expected her to be contrite, too; after all, if she hadn't left him he wouldn't have been driven to such a desperate act, and all because he loved her so much.

Eventually she realised that he wasn't going to remember, because what he *did* remember was in fact what had actually happened; they had watched two DVDs, had drunk several cocktails, then he had fallen asleep. The reason he accepted her alternative version of events was because he underestimated her. Never in a million years would he believe her brave enough even to lie openly to him, let alone try to kill him.

She began to relax, but instead of feeling better, she found that the fear which had filled her for the last weeks had been keeping at bay the depression; now there was a space it sneaked in to fill it, leaving her feeling permanently tired and hopeless.

She had had her chance to be rid of him forever, and had failed. Now she was stuck with him for the rest of her life. She would never have the courage to leave him again. She couldn't anyway; at least while she was with him she had a chance to stop him hurting anyone else's children.

The future stretched bleakly ahead of her; another twenty years or more of the hell that she had endured for the last twenty. Only worse, in a way, because at least at the beginning she had loved him and had believed in his promises to change. Now she hated him, and knew there was no hope. He would never change, and even if he did she could never love him again, ever. It was all she could do not to pull away in disgust when he touched her. The only thing that had kept her going through the first months of her reconciliation with him had been the belief that it would be temporary. Now that belief was gone, and despair had replaced it.

In April Kate came back from India, with a deep golden tan and a million photographs to show Joanne. Joanne didn't tell her sister of the argument she'd had with Steve to get his permission to spend another evening with her. She had promised that it would be the last one; she had to return the key, and Kate would expect her to go round and look at the holiday photos. He had agreed, but reluctantly.

They sat together on the couch, various snacks spread out on the coffee table, and went through the photos. To Joanne the scenes they showed they were unbelievably exotic; women in saris of intensely bright colours, colours that would clash hideously in cloudy England, but which somehow looked right in the sun-drenched subcontinent; the densely crowded streets of Delhi, with cars and yellow-and-black motorised rickshaws weaving carefully round the cows lying unconcerned in the middle of the road; the hordes of people washing their clothes and themselves in the waters of the sacred River Ganges at Varanasi.

"It's really polluted," Kate said. "They bathe in it hoping for blessings, but they're more likely to die of some water-borne disease. I've seen people drinking the water there while a half-burned corpse drifted past a few yards away. It's incredible. I've got a photo somewhere." She rummaged through the pile of prints, while Joanne shuddered.

"It sounds horrible," she said.

"Well, it is. It's horrible and beautiful, all at the same time. Ah, here it is." She passed it to Joanne, who scrutinised it, fascinated and horrified. "For instance, a few hours after this was taken, when it got dark, we went out on a boat. All the people were putting candles and flowers in little waxed paper boats and setting them to drift on the river. There were hundreds of them, and it looked like fairyland. It was wonderful. None of the pictures I took turned out, though."

She sat back and took a deep drink from her glass of wine. "It's the most amazing country. The photos don't do it justice."

"I suppose you have to go there to really appreciate it," Joanne said wistfully.

"I'm going back next year," Kate said. "Rob's going to take a bit of time off, and we're going to go down to the south. It's really different down there, apparently, much more tropical. Why don't you come with me?"

"What?" Joanne said, taken aback. "Don't be daft. I couldn't. Besides, Rob won't want me tagging along with you."

"It was him who suggested it, actually," Kate said. "He thought it might do you good to go somewhere completely different, and so do I."

"Did you tell him about…?" Joanne's voice trailed off.

"Yes, of course I did. He felt the same way I did, that it's a bloody shame Steve didn't make a better job of it. He can't get anything right, can he?"

Joanne wondered what Kate would say if she admitted that it was her, not Steve, who had failed. For a moment the longing to share what she'd done with someone was so powerful that she actually opened her mouth to confess. But then Kate spoke again and the moment passed.

"Still," she said. "With a bit of luck, next time he'll do better."

"What do you mean, next time?" Joanne asked.

"Rob was telling me, a lot of people who finally commit suicide have attempted it before, sometimes more than once." Kate eyed her sister sharply. "Don't tell me you wouldn't have been relieved, on some level, if he'd succeeded," she said.

Joanne looked away. She could admit that much, at least.

"Yes," she said. "I would have been relieved. But I'd have felt guilty as well."

Kate leaned forward and squeezed Joanne's arm.

"Why? It's not your fault if he decides to top himself, is it?" she said. "Well then, if it's some sort of misguided guilt that's stopping you leaving him, like you promised me you would if he hit you again, then at least come to India with me. Try and concentrate on the relief rather than the guilt. With a bit of luck he might have another go at it, and do better next time."

"I can't," Joanne said. Kate might as well have suggested she fly to the moon. It was impossible.

"Yes you can," Kate insisted. "You can do anything you want, Jo. You learnt that in Aberystwyth. Don't let that useless piece of shit make you feel guilty because he took a few pills. You're not responsible for his life; he is. Take responsibility for yours, for God's sake. You've done it once, you can do it again."

Could she? Joanne thought later that night, in bed. Steve lay beside her, snoring gently. Could she do it again, but get it right this time? It hit her now for the first time that if he *had* died, she would have got away with it. No one had suspected for even a moment that she had tried to kill him. Not even Steve. Not even Kate, who knew her better than anyone. What were the statistics for repeat suicide attempts? She would have to go back to the library, do some more research.

She turned over, putting a space between her and her husband. Maybe, just maybe, there was some hope after all. She would start tomorrow.

* * *

A month later, she knew so much about suicide she could have written a book on it. Women were far more likely to try it, but men were more likely to succeed at it. She knew that Kate was right; most people who attempt suicide don't complete it first time. She knew that nearly half of the people who attempted suicide once would try it again, usually within a year of the first attempt. If she could do it again, soon, there was a very high chance that she'd get away with it.

And that was where the problem was; she had no idea how she *could* do it again. Shaken by the realisation that he had nearly killed himself, and with no memory of it, Steve had agreed to take the new antidepressants prescribed to him by his doctor. They were much less toxic than the ones he'd been given previously, and he was only allowed a month's supply at a time. There was nothing she could get him to take without him knowing, that would guarantee his death.

She had looked up all the other common ways people used to kill themselves, and had, with thought, dismissed them all. She didn't have the strength to drown him in the bath, hang him, or hold a plastic bag over his head until he asphyxiated; she didn't have the technical knowledge to electrocute him, nor could she see any way to get him to sit in his car for a few hours with the engine running and a tube pumping the exhaust fumes into the car. Shooting yourself was the most popular method of suicide in the US, and a very successful one; but she lived in the UK, where people didn't own a gun as a matter of course.

Suzy Devine had killed herself by cutting her wrists. She had obviously researched it as well; she had drawn the razor up her forearm, not across it as you saw in hospital dramas on TV. Due to her research Joanne now knew the anatomy of the human body quite well; she knew that people often cut their own wrists or even their throats very deeply, and still didn't die; she knew that if you wanted to stab yourself in the heart you had to drive the knife up under the ribs, and even then, unless you were very accurate, you might miss all the vital organs. Even if Joanne managed to overcome her revulsion at the thought of stabbing Steve, she knew there was no way she could do it and make it look like suicide.

What else?

For a short time she contemplated pushing him off a cliff or a high building. She could suggest a weekend away, somewhere with a very high building; Paris, Blackpool. Cheddar Gorge. Dover. There were lots of likely places. She could wait until they were alone then push him off, tell the police that they had gone away together as a last ditch attempt to salvage their marriage, that she had told him it wasn't working, and on impulse he had…

It was ridiculous. What were the chances of being alone at the top of the Eiffel Tower, or even Blackpool Tower, for that matter? They probably had railings to stop people jumping off anyway. And even if she did get him to walk along a clifftop path, she would have to get him right to the edge before she had any hope at all of succeeding in pushing him off. Even if she did, there was a good chance he would grab at her and take her with him.

It wasn't possible. She'd had her chance to be free of him and live her life, and she'd blown it. When it came down to it, Joanne concluded after all her research, she had three choices left to her.

She lay awake, night after night, running these choices over and over in her mind. She couldn't leave him again; that was just running away from her responsibilities. Even if he didn't find her this time, she'd be permanently on edge, fearing that he would. And she would spend the rest of her life wondering if he was abusing someone else's daughter, and if she ever found out he had she would feel as guilty as he was for giving him the freedom to do it.

She couldn't kill him, then phone the police and confess it. In theory she could; her research had given her the methods. But even the thought of stabbing him in his sleep, the only way she could think of that would have any chance of success, made her feel sick with horror.

With hindsight, she had no idea how she'd ever got up the courage to poison him, as bloodless and easy as it had seemed to be at the time. She would never be able to stab him, not in cold blood. Maybe in the heat of an argument; but he was twice her size, and many times stronger; he could disarm her easily. In any case, customarily she was so frightened of him when he threatened her that her limbs went to jelly; she hardly had the strength to stand up, let alone kill him.

Which left only her third choice; stay with him, try to make the best of things and get through the long days as well as she could. At least then she could keep an eye on him, stop him from becoming acquainted with any other young girls.

It was the only thing she could do. She had made her bid for freedom and lost. She would just have to come to terms with it.

CHAPTER EIGHTEEN

August 2007

It was a perfect summer day, hot and sunny, the temperature edging into the low thirties. It had been like this all week, and Joanne's neighbours were taking full advantage of the glorious weather. Everyone spent as many sun-drenched hours as possible outside. Children, enjoying the long school holiday, played in inflatable paddling pools, shrieking and laughing as they sprayed each other with water. Mothers and teenage girls lay on flower-patterned sun loungers, exposing as much of their white limbs as decency allowed to the sun, attempting to achieve a Mediterranean tan in record time. The air waves hummed with the sound of competing radio stations, and in the evening the charcoal smell of burning meat inexpertly cooked on rusting barbecues pervaded everything.

Joanne had spent the morning tidying the garden, pulling up weeds and trimming the grass. She had bought some late, leggy bedding plants at the local supermarket, had planted them in the borders and was eyeing their wilting leaves and drooping flowers doubtfully when Marie spoke from directly behind her, making her jump.

"They'll probably pick up when they've been watered," she suggested.

"I hope so," Joanne said. "It's a bit late for them, though. They should have gone in in April really."

"We're having a barbecue tonight," Marie said. "I wondered if you'd like to come. It's nothing special, just a few burgers, sausages, a couple of bottles of wine, that sort of thing. My sister's up from Coventry. It'd be nice for you to meet her. You can bring Steve as well, of course," she added, as an obvious afterthought.

Joanne smiled.

"It's nice of you to ask," she replied. She searched in her head for an acceptable excuse. There was no way Steve would go to a barbecue, or let her go to one. He'd done nothing but complain about the stench from them all week, moaning about having to close all the windows just as the temperature dropped to an acceptable level.

He'd been on edge all week, come to think of it. Joanne had initially assumed it was the heat; Steve had always hated very hot weather. But over the last couple of days she'd been able to do nothing right. He was spoiling for a fight, she could sense it, and the last thing she wanted was for him to explode in front of the neighbours and hit Colin. Maybe she could say they were going to the cinema or something.

God, she was tired of making excuses; to her mother; to Kate for her increasingly rare visits; to the pleasant elderly Avon sales rep who Steve had told to piss off the week before.

"It's OK," Marie inserted into the silence before Joanne could speak. "If you're doing something else…"

"No, we're not," Joanne interrupted, surprising herself. "But Steve hates barbecues, and he's been in a really bad mood all week. I don't think it's a good idea."

Oh, that felt so good, telling the truth. Why didn't she do that all the time? Why was she still protecting him in spite of all he'd done? Years of training, that must be it. Better to make excuses than suffer the consequences if he found out she'd been telling the truth behind his back.

"Right," said Marie. She hesitated for a minute. "Look, if you want to get out of the house, for any reason," she said, "you're very welcome to come anyway. My brother-in-law's a big bloke, and he can handle himself. God, I didn't mean that the way it sounded." She blushed, and Joanne laughed.

How long was it since she'd laughed? She couldn't remember.

"It's all right," she said. "I don't want to get you involved in my problems. But I appreciate it, I really do." To her surprise her eyes filled with tears at the unexpected kindness and she had to make an excuse to go in before she burst into tears.

I'm cracking up, she thought later back in the kitchen slicing tomatoes and cucumber for the salad she was preparing for dinner. She was wound up tight like a spring, unbearably tense, awaiting the explosion. She hated it when Steve was like this, building up to an outburst. Sometimes she felt like deliberately provoking him just to get it over and done with. At least once he'd hit her it would be finished, and everything would go back to normal for a while.

But then sometimes he would calm down for no apparent reason, without having hit her. He would just suddenly bring home flowers or chocolates, apologise for his surliness, and she would feel almost dizzy with relief at the reprieve. No, it would be mad to push him over the edge when there might be no need to.

She got the chicken out of the fridge and carefully cut it up, making sure there was only white meat on the slices for Steve. What else? Lettuce, radishes, spring onions; Steve liked traditional salads, nothing exotic like rocket or couscous. She would carve the radishes into little flowers, that might make him smile. It was worth a try.

God, it was hot. All the windows were open and there still wasn't a breath of air. She moistened a paper towel under the cold tap and pressed it to the back of her neck, lifting her hair out of the way so it wouldn't get wet. Out in the front garden Colin was mowing the lawn. He caught her eye, smiled and raised his hand, and she waved back. They were a lovely couple, very well suited. It would be nice to be able to get to know them better. He certainly had a way with plants. The borders were a riot of blooms.

As she admired the garden, there was a screech of tyres and Steve's car appeared round the corner. Joanne looked in dismay at the mess in the kitchen. What was he doing home at this time? It was only three o'clock! She switched the kettle on, turned the hot tap on full, hurriedly scooped the plastic wrappings into the bin and put the dirty crockery and cutlery into the washing bowl. There would be no time to make the radishes fancy, they would have to do as they were.

She put the remains of the chicken back into the fridge, and when she looked back Steve had parked the car haphazardly, blocking half of next door's drive. There was a large dent in the front wing and she knew then that no amount of carved radishes would avert what was coming. She could see him in the front seat, talking animatedly into his mobile phone. She neither knew nor cared who he was talking to. It gave her a few more moments, that was what mattered.

She poured boiling water on to the tea leaves in the pot, stirring them frantically with a spoon. Steve hated that; he liked his tea to brew naturally. But he also liked it to be ready for him when he came in. She poured it into a cup, added milk, and then plunged her hands into the washing-up water as he opened the car door. Her thumb slid along the blade of the carving knife, and she drew in a sharp gasp of pain.

Steve got out of the car, his face like thunder, and Joanne forgot all about her thumb. Colin had switched the mower off and was saying something to Steve, no doubt about the positioning of his car.

Don't hit him, she prayed silently. He didn't need to; whatever Steve said made Colin recoil as though he *had* been hit, and then the front door crashed open and her husband appeared in the kitchen doorway.

"What happened?" she asked calmly, her heart racing. She lifted a plate out of the bowl and set it to drain. The blood welled up along the pad of her thumb and she put it back into the water. No time for that now.

"Can't you see?" he said, angrily gesturing out of the window. Colin, who had been watching, turned hastily away and switched the mower on again. "Some fucking prick ran into my car in the car park and then pissed off without owning up. I'll break his bloody neck tomorrow."

"Did you see him do it?" Joanne asked.

"Of course I didn't see him do it, you stupid cow, or he'd be in the hospital now, wouldn't he? But there's yellow paint all over the wing and there's only one person with a yellow car who parks in the same car park. I'll be waiting for him tomorrow. Fuck!" he shouted suddenly, smashing his fist into the door.

Joanne felt all her muscles tense, and forced them to relax. A cold dread settled in the pit of her stomach. She felt sick.

"Won't the insurance pay for it?" she ventured.

"That's not the fucking point, is it?" he shouted. "The point is, he didn't even have the balls to come in and admit it to me."

I'm not surprised, Joanne thought. If she were Mr Yellow Car, she'd be halfway to Scotland by now. Anything rather than face an irate Steve tomorrow morning.

"I made you a cup of tea," she said. "And I thought we'd have a salad for dinner, as it's so hot. I was going to carve the radishes…"

"What the fuck's this?" Steve interrupted. She turned round. He was looking at his tea in disgust. "It looks like gnat's piss."

"I'm sorry," she said, turning back to the washing-up. The bubbles had dispersed; she could see the thin line of blood blooming out of the cut. It must be quite deep. "I'll make you another one as soon as…"

She gasped in shock as the hot liquid hit the back of her head, drenching her hair and the back of her dress.

Here it comes, she thought. *At least he didn't throw the cup as well.*

"How many years have we been married?" he said furiously. "And you still don't know how I like my tea?"

"You were early," she pointed out, "I didn't have time to make it stronger." She put the carving knife on the drainer then started washing the spoons. "I've nearly finished this," she said. "Then I'll make you another one. Why don't you go and have a shower?" Thank God the tea hadn't been hot enough to scald her. It was dripping uncomfortably down her back.

"And *salad*?" he continued as though she hadn't spoken. "You think a salad's enough for a man who's been working all day?"

Nothing would be enough for him today, she realised. If she'd employed Gordon Ramsay to come round and personally cook him a three-course meal, it wouldn't be good enough. A sudden, unexpected rage momentarily flooded her with energy, and she wished desperately that she had a black belt in karate or could produce a gun from somewhere and watch him grovel, begging for his life. Then he'd know how it felt, the bastard.

The energy drained away as quickly as it had come, leaving her shaking. There was nothing she could do, nothing. She had tried everything in the past. Nothing worked when he was like this. Still, she would try to placate him. It was the only thing she *could* do.

"I thought…" she began.

"No, you didn't. You never think. Look at me when I'm fucking talking to you!" he roared.

She jumped violently, and turned to face him. She'd been avoiding that. Looking him in the eyes when he was in this mood was a challenge, an invitation to him to hit her. Her heart was pounding, her mouth dry. She looked at his right hand, clenching and unclenching at his side. Everything depended on whether it was open or closed when he finally raised it to her. If it was open, she would probably get away just with bruising. She braced herself. If it was closed, she would have to duck. There was no space to jump back or run.

"Steve, I…" she began, raising one hand, palm outwards.

She ducked as his fist swung towards her, but it still caught the top of her head with enough force to knock her sideways. She grabbed hold of the drainer in an attempt to stop herself falling and took it with her, plates and cutlery crashing to the quarry-tiled floor.

She pulled herself up on to her hands and knees, the kitchen spinning crazily around her, then she felt his hand grip her hair to lift her up. Her legs were boneless, and she screamed in pain as her scalp took her whole body weight. He shook her hard, once, and spat something at her that she didn't hear, and then she raised her hand instinctively, defensively and punched him as hard as she could in the chest in a vain attempt to make him let her go.

He released her so quickly that she collapsed back on to the floor, her breathing coming in hard, fast gasps. The knife clattered across the tiles. She looked in surprise from its blood-covered blade to her thumb, at the blood still welling up from the horizontal slice across the pad. She hadn't realised that she'd cut it that badly. There was no point in trying to get up again; the fear had done its job now, and her legs and arms were useless, jelly. She waited for the next blow. Maybe then he would go out and she could clean the kitchen up, dress her thumb.

Nothing happened, and after a few moments Steve made a strange inarticulate moaning noise in his throat. She looked up at him through her dripping hair. He was staring at her, his eyes wide with surprise, bright blue in the afternoon sunlight coming through the window. His mouth opened and he moaned again, then his legs folded under him and he fell to his knees beside her before toppling slowly over on to his side.

Is he having a heart attack? she wondered distantly, still dazed from the blow. There was a strange dark stain spreading across his black T-shirt. She reached out, put her hand tentatively on his chest, and when she took it away her palm was bright red. She blinked, looked at her hand again, then at the knife lying on the floor, and suddenly, in spite of the heat, she felt a chill run down her spine as she realised what had happened, what must have happened.

No, it wasn't possible. She'd dreamed about doing it, lots of times, but even the thought of it had made her feel sick. There was no way she could have done it.

She sat on the tiles and leaned back against the cupboard. She didn't remember picking the knife up. She hadn't picked the knife up. Surely she'd have remembered if she had? She'd just punched him in the chest, that was all, hoping to get him to release his grip on her hair. Even if she had somehow had the knife in her hand, she hadn't done it right, anyway. You were supposed to drive the knife up under the sternum; otherwise it was likely to be deflected by the ribs. He couldn't be dead. You had to do it just right, something like that, and even when you did, it didn't always work. The human body was incredibly resilient.

Lethargy replaced the chill, and her limbs became heavy, leaden. Dimly she registered that she must be in shock, but everything seemed unreal, dreamlike.

She looked at him again. He was lying very still now; he could have been asleep, except that his eyes were open, staring sightlessly at the fridge. It wasn't possible. He couldn't be dead, not from one little blow. He was unkillable. In a minute he would come round, and then he would be *really* angry. She should clean up the mess before he did. She sat there unmoving, her knees pulled up under her chin.

The lawnmower had stopped, but she could hear children playing in a garden nearby and the distant sound of a siren, slowly getting closer. The tea was cool now, dripping from the ends of her hair; and the cut on her thumb had started to congeal. It was quite nice really, peaceful, sitting like this. The quarry tiles were cool against her bare feet. In a minute she would get up, clear up the mess, make some more tea, stronger this time, the way he liked it. But she was so tired; she would close her eyes, just for a minute, and then she would feel well enough to tidy up.

She started awake, suddenly aware of another presence in the room, and looked up into the face of the uniformed man leaning over her. There were two other men in the room as well, crouched down over Steve. How had they all got in without her hearing them?

The man was asking her if she was hurt, and she shook her head, wincing as the pounding started. That would be from where Steve had caught her on the temple when he hit her. She'd take some paracetamol, put an ice pack on to reduce the bruising. If she brushed her hair forward, no one would notice…

The man was saying something else; she could see his lips moving but couldn't quite make out the words. His eyes were brown, kind, but wary at the same time. She closed her eyes tight for a moment, willing the pain away, then opened them again. She opened her mouth to speak, but nothing happened. She cleared her throat and tried again.

"I'm sorry," she said. "I didn't mean to hurt him. I just wanted him to let go of my hair. Is he going to be all right?"

The policeman squatted down beside her.

"Are you injured?" he asked, and she heard him properly this time.

"No," she said. "Not really. I ducked, but he knocked me over." She lifted a hand to her head. It felt sore, but not too swollen. She would be okay in a day or so. She looked around the kitchen. "What a mess," she said apologetically. "I'll have to clear it up. He likes everything tidy."

"I wouldn't worry about that now," the policeman said gently. "Do you think you can stand up?"

She wasn't sure, but with the policeman's help she managed to get to her feet. In the garden there was another policeman, talking to Colin and Marie. And at the gate there were some more people, but no one spoke to her as she got into the police car.

But then she didn't expect them to; they didn't really know her. Steve had never liked her talking to the neighbours. He didn't like her to talk to anyone. The inside of the car was hot and stuffy, but the window felt cool when she rested her cheek against it. She closed her eyes again and let the world drift away.

EPILOGUE

September 2008

Joanne had been sitting so long that the hard wood of the bench was pressing into her bottom, and she shifted a little on the seat to try to ease the discomfort. She had lost weight in the last few months, and had little or no padding to protect her from hard seats. She looked around. The park was deserted now and the burger van had gone, which was a pity. She could have done with another cup of coffee. Still, it didn't really matter. She was nearly ready to go home now. Nearly.

She stretched her arms above her head, and then examined the slender circle of her wrist poking out from the sleeve of her jacket. Her wrists had always been bony; she could circle them with her own thumb and little finger. Incredible that such a thin arm was capable of killing a huge man like Steve, with just one blow. Even now, after examining the event and those leading up to it in great detail with the police, the psychiatrist, and the solicitor Kate had engaged for her at great expense, Joanne still couldn't remember actually picking the knife up off the kitchen floor. In her mind she would probably always remember punching him only with her clenched fist, not with a knife.

Of course the evidence and common sense told her that she had; no one her size could fell a man of Steve's build and strength with one feeble blow to the chest. Then there was the blood, of course. And the fact that Colin, an honest man if ever there was one, had testified in court to having seen the sun glint off the blade in her hand seconds before she drove it cleanly between her husband's ribs and straight into his heart. Thankfully he had also seen Steve hit her beforehand, and had heard her scream of pain as he lifted her from the floor by her hair.

It was Marie who had phoned the police and the ambulance. She had thanked them for that, but thought it would be nice, now that it was all over and no one could accuse her of trying to influence witnesses, to buy them something, flowers, an excellent bottle of wine, a garden centre gift token, perhaps.

She had so many people to thank. Kate, who had been perfect; there was no gift Joanne could ever buy to repay her sister for her emotional and practical support. She could not have survived the past months without her. And the police for another, who in spite of Joanne's misgivings and previous negative experiences with them, had been courteous and sympathetic.

Of course they'd had no reason to be otherwise. They'd allowed her her one phone call after taking her to the station, and in spite of Kate urging her to say nothing until the solicitor arrived, Joanne had put the phone down and immediately told the interviewing officer that she intended to plead guilty to killing her husband. She had made things easy for them in many ways.

At that point she really hadn't cared what happened to her. It wasn't important whether she spent the rest of her life in prison or not; what was important was that Steve would never be able to hurt her, Amy, or any other female, ever again. Everything else was secondary to that.

Of course once the solicitor, Mr Jarvis arrived, a brisk efficient man in a crisp grey suit, with matching grey eyes and a warm smile that belied his cold proficient exterior, the legal machine had started to move, sweeping Joanne along on its conveyor belt of hearings, meetings with professionals, interviews and assessments.

On Mr Jarvis's recommendation, she pleaded guilty to manslaughter on the basis of provocation. To her surprise she was given bail, and was allowed to stay at Kate's while waiting for her court date.

Kate had rung Amy to tell her what had happened, and Joanne had been heartened to hear that, while expressing no emotion about the death of her father, Amy had at least asked how her mother was. Four weeks ago Amy had telephoned Kate out of the blue, to wish Joanne good luck at the pre-sentencing hearing. Kate had asked Amy if she wanted to speak to her mother, who was sitting in the chair opposite her sister, and Amy had said she was not ready to speak to Joanne yet.

Yet. What a world of hope there was in that one word. Joanne had laid awake night after night, running through imaginary conversations with her daughter, trying out different ways to make Amy understand that her return to Steve had not been a betrayal, but a way of trying to take responsibility for her own part in his abuse of their child. She had half-decided to tell Amy that she had reconciled with him only because she'd intended to kill him, but that she hadn't had the courage to carry it through. But perhaps it would be better if, no, when, Amy rang, to play it by ear, see how things went before deciding how much to reveal.

One thing was certain though; she would never tell anyone of her previous, failed attempt to kill Steve by overdose. That was her secret, and she alone would carry the burden of it to her death. The more time passed, the easier it became not to tell people, and the less she thought about it.

Eventually, she realised, all of this would fade, become part of her distant memories, her 'previous life', rather than her present one, as it was now. She would remember sitting on the park bench now as the time when she had begun to put the past behind her, had started to move on.

She would wait a few months, until everything had died down, then she would put the house on the market, move somewhere where no one knew her, where she could start afresh, with the added bonus that her heart wouldn't start racing every time she saw a well-built man with blond hair.

She would keep in contact with a few people from her old life; Kate of course, Colin and Marie. And Mike, who had called round to Kate's to see her and had offered to testify to Steve's possessiveness, extreme jealousy and violent nature if she wanted him to. Joanne had been touched by that, even though Mike had dismissed his offer as nothing, saying he was only doing it so that his mother wouldn't invite him to any more family get-togethers. She knew the real reason why he was offering, and though she had no romantic interest in him, still he was a good friend, and she had only too few of those. Yes, she would keep the contact with Mike.

She stood up, put her hands in her pockets and started to walk to the gate, picking up speed as she went. The brisk walk home would do her good. She'd got chilled, sitting still for so long; but the thinking had helped, given her a sense of proportion. She was ready to move on, pick up the threads and build a new life for herself. She knew she could do it. That was one of the things Aberystwyth had given her.

The other thing Aberystwyth had given her was waiting at the gate. He smiled as she approached and she stopped and looked up at him.

"I thought you'd changed your mind," she said.

"No, there was a pile up on the M6," Andy explained. "I didn't get there till lunchtime, and it was all over by then. I rang Kate, and she told me you'd got probation. Congratulations. I'm sorry I wasn't at the court to hear it. I really wanted to be." His voice was truly regretful.

"Did Kate tell you I was here as well?" Joanne asked.

"Yes, but she also told me you wanted to be alone for a while. So I went off to a café and had something to eat before I came down."

Joanne looked at the sun, now low in the sky. She had been here much longer than it would take to have something to eat.

"How long have you been here?" she asked.

He blushed. He always hated that, that he blushed so easily. It was the legacy of fair skin and red hair. She found it endearing. Whatever his feelings, they were always on his face, easily readable. He would never be able to lie while looking as innocent as a new-born child, or smile pleasantly while he crushed her hand to pulp.

"A couple of hours," he admitted. "You looked preoccupied. I didn't want to disturb you."

"I was," she said. "Thank you."

He shrugged.

"Do you want a lift home?" he asked. "Or would you rather walk?"

Whatever she chose, he would not try to persuade her otherwise. It was that that made her opt for the lift instead of walking as she'd intended.

Instead of parking outside her house as she'd expected, he stopped a bit further down the street and peered through the windscreen.

"It looks clear," he said. "Do you want me to go and check to see if there are any reporters hanging around? They might be waiting round the side of the house, or the back."

"No, it's all right," she said. "I can handle it if they are."

She could, she realised. She could handle anything now, anything at all. She didn't need a man any more. She had never really needed one, but Steve had never given her the space to realise that. "Are you staying in Manchester overnight?" she asked.

"No," he said. "I'd rather get straight back to Birmingham. I've got an early start tomorrow. The gym's opening next Friday and there's loads to do yet. And I think you need some more time alone, to decide what you want to do next. I'll give you a ring in a couple of days, to see how you are. Would that be okay?"

"Yes," she said. "That would be lovely."

He drove up to the gate, and she got out of the car and closed the door. She started to walk away, then turned back and knocked on the window. He wound it down.

"I know what I want to do next," she said. "I want to let things settle down for a bit, and then start again, where we left off. Do you think we could do that?"

He smiled, and his whole face lit up with sheer delight.

"Yes," he said. "I think we could do that."

She stood at the gate and watched until his car had gone from sight. Then she stood for a little longer, listening as he stopped at the junction, then revved again out on to the main road, merging into the hum of all the other traffic.

Then she walked up the path and into the house. There seemed to be no reporters. Perhaps they would forget her quicker than she'd expected. Perhaps they already had.

Birmingham. Would that be a good place to make a new start? She would have to go and have a look round. Next Friday might be good, if her probation conditions allowed it. She would have to check. If so, she would just turn up. It would be a nice surprise for him. It was relaxing to know he would put no pressure on her to do anything she didn't want to do. He wanted her, as she was beginning to realise she wanted him. But they didn't feel they needed each other to survive, and that made all the difference.

Need was destructive; need brought dependency, then restriction, and tyranny. What had the statistics said? She had looked them up on the net one night at Kate's. Twenty-five per cent of women had suffered abuse at the hands of their male partners at some time. Until now she had seen that as an impossibly bleak figure. One in four women was hiding bruises, constantly walking on eggshells for fear of saying the wrong thing.

Now she saw it differently. Three out of four women did *not* suffer abuse. They lived alone successfully, or as equals with their partners. Those women were confident, independent, didn't need a man; but if they wanted one, they could find one. A caring one, one who respected their opinions, encouraged their talents. Seventy-five percent. The vast majority.

She had lived the last twenty years in the minority, believing that was all there was. Now it was time to move on. It was going to be good to be part of the seventy-five percent, at last. Very good indeed.

ABOUT THE AUTHOR

Julia has been a voracious reader since childhood, using books to escape the miseries of a turbulent adolescence. After leaving university with a degree in English Language and Literature, she spent her twenties trying to be a sensible and responsible person, even going so far as to work for the Civil Service. The book escape came in very useful there too.

And then she gave up trying to conform and resolved to spend the rest of her life living as she wanted to, not as others would like her to. She has since had a variety of jobs, including telesales, teaching and gilding and is currently a transcriber, copy editor and proofreader. In her spare time she is still a voracious reader, and enjoys keeping fit and travelling the world. Life hasn't always been good, but it has rarely been boring. She lives in rural Wales with her cat Constantine, and her wonderful partner sensibly lives four miles away in the next village.

Rather than just escape into other people's books, she decided to create some of her own, in the hopes that people would enjoy reading them as much as she does writing them. Following the success of her first books, The Jacobite Chronicles, a series of historical books about the Jacobite Rebellion of 1745 in Great Britain, she has decided to branch out into contemporary fiction for a short while, and hopes people will enjoy her modern novels too.

Follow her on;

Website
www.juliabrannan.com

Facebook
www.facebook.com/pages/Julia-Brannan/727743920650760

Twitter
https://twitter.com/BrannanJulia

Pinterest
http:www.pinterest.com/juliabrannan

Made in United States
Troutdale, OR
03/29/2024